A Mistake of Consequence

TERRI EVERT KARSTEN

abbott press

Abbott Press books may be ordered through booksellers or by contacting:

Abbott Press
1663 Liberty Drive
Bloomington, IN 47403
www.abbottpress.com
Phone: 1-866-697-5310

Because of the dynamic nature of the Internet, any web addresses or links contained in this book may have changed since publication and may no longer be valid. The views expressed in this work are solely those of the author and do not necessarily reflect the views of the publisher, and the publisher hereby disclaims any responsibility for them.

This novel is a work of fiction. Characters, incidents, and locations are products of the author's imagination or are used to create a fictitious story and should not be construed as real.

ISBN: 978-1-4582-1825-4 (sc)
ISBN: 978-1-4582-1827-8 (hc)
ISBN: 978-1-4582-1826-1 (e)

Library of Congress Control Number: 2014920551

Printed in the United States of America.

Abbott Press rev. date: 2/10/2015

For all the strong women in my life—my wonderful sisters and nearly sisters, all sorts of fantastic daughters, and of course, Mom.

Special Thanks to Chris for her drawing of a luckenbooth brooch and to Lisa for proof-reading the entire manuscript. Any errors which remain are my own.

Part I

Freight

Edinburgh, March 1754

CHAPTER I

My first mistake was throwing the wine in his face.

The crystal glass shattered against the hearth. The gentleman kneeling in front of me flinched, his wine-spattered face frozen in astonishment. Shocked silence filled the drawing room, a silence so profound I could hear the hiss of the candle on the table. A log crackled and spat in the fireplace. Then everyone spoke at once.

Grandfather was the loudest. He strode across the room and bellowed, "You will apologize to my guest this instant!" Towering over me, with a look as fierce as a Highland warrior, Grandfather meant to frighten me into obedience, but I knew the picture false. Even when Bonnie Prince Charlie's troops had taken Edinburgh nine years ago, Grandfather had stayed well clear of the fighting on either side.

"I will not!" I braced my hands on my hips, my chin thrust forward. "I'm not the one who invited him here."

Mam's hands, a-flutter with lace cuffs, flew up to cover her mouth. My sister Elspeth, standing behind Grandfather, shook her head at me, whether in dismay or in warning, I could not tell.

"In this house, ye will do as I say," Grandfather shouted.

"Aye, as long as you say what's right and reasonable." I was trying not to shout at him, but I had to raise my voice to make him hear me. "I'll not apologize to anyone insulting me."

The gentleman still knelt at my feet, his mouth forming an O as round as his pale eyes and bald head. Beads of red wine rolled down the end of his nose and dropped onto the black velvet of his frock coat where they left damp, shiny spots. He drew a linen handkerchief from his waistcoat pocket and dabbed his face. "I meant no insult," he began.

"Insult?" Grandfather interrupted him. "Are ye daft, girl? He meant to marry ye, though God knows why, shrew that ye are."

Marry me? Preposterous! I didn't even know his name. Mam, Elspeth, Grandfather, and even the gentleman all blathered some nonsense. I spun on my heel and ran.

"Wait, Callie," Mam called after me. "Ye're making a mistake!"

I snatched my shawl from the peg in the hallway and pushed outside. The door slammed behind me, cutting off Grandfather's imperious command to return at once.

The city glowered under a murky sky. Grandfather's house stood near the citadel in Leith, a few miles north of Edinburgh, near the harbor and his shipping interests. Now, as evening fell, a fine mist swirled up from the firth and settled on house and lane, chilling the air. Dampness made the cobblestones under my feet slick. As I paused, the front door flew open and Elspeth hurried toward me.

Grandfather threw open the window sash and thrust his head out. "Ye heathen! Have ye no sense? Ye've got the manners of a barbarian."

Mam joined him at the window, her shrill voice carrying down the street. "Ye will never find a gentleman to marry, do ye not learn to mind your temper."

I clutched my shawl and stormed away, ignoring the wet seeping through the thin soles of my drawing-room slippers. The problem was not my temper, but Grandfather's endless stream of pitiful suitors.

"Go on with ye then, if ye'll no see any sense. Ye're no granddaughter of mine!" Grandfather yelled.

Elspeth caught up to me and grabbed my arm. "Slow down, Callie," she panted. "He's only trying to help. You've got to marry someone. You're almost twenty!"

I snatched my shawl free of her grasp. "I don't have to marry some stranger *he* brings home." It wasn't that I objected to marriage. Nearly all my friends had long since married, and most seemed happy enough. I didn't know what exactly I was waiting for, just not someone Grandfather picked.

"Slow down, Callie," Elspeth repeated. I ignored her, and she dropped back. "Don't be so stubborn," she called.

My anger carried me past the shuttered shops on Dock Street, the pale glow of candlelight spilling through their sashes into the gathering dusk. Dock Street led to the Abbot Ballantyne's Bridge. The steeple of the parish church with its windows covered with latticed wood rose high above the square, stone buildings flanking the narrow street. During the day, busy servants and ladies shopping jostled elbows with burly sailors and dawdling apprentices, as cart drivers pushed through the crowd, holding their horses to a slow walk. Tonight, however, most folk had gone home to their suppers, leaving the street nearly deserted. A single carriage clattered by. I ducked into the shadow of a doorway. Had Grandfather sent the footman after me? The last time I'd run off was when Grandfather swore I would disgrace him if I didn't dance with a fat man old enough to be my father. The footman had dragged me back, but it did no good. The gentleman declined to dance with me when I returned.

Now the carriage disappeared around a corner, and the clop of the horse's hooves was muffled in the gloom. I crossed the stone bridge, passing the tollbooth. The toll man dozed at his post and did not waken at the soft pad of my slippered feet. I walked along the river toward the harbor. If Grandfather did send the footman, he would expect me to go straight on to Leith Walk and turn toward Edinburgh. Most of our friends lived that direction.

A light drizzle started, and the breeze spattered the droplets into my face, but neither dampened my anger. Grandfather thought my marriage nothing more than a business proposition. The fellow who had proposed tonight had never even met me before. How could he think he wanted to marry me? Surely after this introduction, he would never want to see me again. But Grandfather would undoubtedly bring another hopeful home tomorrow, and Mam and Elspeth would keep fussing at me to choose someone from the parade of potential candidates.

I was so upset that I paid little attention to where my feet carried me. The sharp tang of briny air gradually replaced the musty smell of cramped houses. Cobblestone streets gave way to wooden planks, and I walked right out onto the pier.

The night had darkened. Black lumps of what I took to be cargo dotted the wharves. Most of the ships were shuttered as tight as the shops had been, but near me, a long three-masted beauty of a ship had more than its share of activity on the pier near its mooring. A crowd of people gathered near the gangplank. Too bad I had not grabbed my heavy woolen cloak rather than a flimsy shawl. The cloak would have been warmer and far less noticeable. The lace trimming my bodice drooped in a sodden mass, wet from the drizzle, but bedraggled or not, it was still lace and not at all what a sailor's wife might wear.

As I hesitated, I realized this group was not just sailors but mixed company of all types, mostly men. A few children scampered around the edges of the crowd, playing tag. Perhaps it was a leave-taking, or maybe a funeral, though I couldn't imagine why anyone would hold a funeral on the pier. The women, wearing work-worn linen and woolen garments, looked tired and scared. Some were crying; others crossed themselves in prayer. Most of the men wore rough workmen's clothing but a few had frockcoats that marked them as merchants. No one dressed in the high fashion of those gentlemen frequenting Grandfather's dinners and from whom I was supposed to take my pick for marriage.

The thought of that endless stream of suitors renewed my anger. I would not be bartered off to the highest bidder like a horse from one of Grandfather's estates.

The stamp of my foot, or perhaps just my presence, alerted an older man standing among a cluster of young women near my own age. He stared at me a moment, then separated from them and hurried toward me, flapping his hands and beckoning. With his white wig askew, his dark coat stretched tight across a round belly, and his striped stockings revealing short, skinny legs, he resembled an agitated chicken. I stepped back, stifling an urge to laugh. I half expected him to cluck at me.

"Come, come, Miss MacLaughlin," he said in a clipped English accent, speaking before he was even near me. "You are late and keeping the others waiting. I thought I made it clear what time to be here and that dawdlers would surely be left behind."

"I beg your pardon, sir. There is some mistake. I am not Miss MacLaughlin and I have no appointment." I backed away from his flapping hands.

At the same time, two other men emerged from the shadows of the waiting cargo. These men were much rougher, the kind Mam warned me about. I sucked in sharply as they slid to either side of me. I turned to run, but they grabbed my arms, their fingers digging in painfully.

"Let go of me!" I twisted, trying to pull free. "Help! Someone!"

The chicken man nodded, and the scoundrel on my right jabbed me hard in the ribs. I sagged and gasped for air, just as the other fellow hit me in the jaw. Pain blackened my vision and turned my legs to jelly. The man on my left caught me neatly and scooped me up like a child. The other tore away the lace at my bodice with a swift jerk.

"Taken a bit faint, sir," he called out, presumably to the chicken man. It had all happened so fast no one on the dock even noticed.

I struggled, but none of my limbs quite worked. The dark, scruffy face of the man carrying me looked fuzzy through the watery haze of my tears. Even my voice refused to obey. Had the blow broken my jaw?

The gangplank swayed underneath us as the man carried me. Fighting dizziness, I tried to escape. Then, as suddenly as he had picked me up, he dropped me. I managed a squawk before someone caught me and pulled me down into the darkness made thick with the stench of bilge water and mildew. One set of grimy hands after another shoved me forward, away from the hatchway. Still dazed, I had a brief impression of dozens of faces blurred in the gloom. I was deposited on a plank of wood. I lay there, my head throbbing.

More humans were crammed together in this narrow space than I could imagine. I gagged on the odor of sweat and unwashed bodies. Grandfather had bellowed at me for years, but no one had ever hit me. The shock of the blow as much as the pain left me speechless. The calls and curses of the crowd blurred into an indecipherable roar, and the formless, jerking shapes around me were too fuzzy to be real. Or perhaps I was the one no longer real.

I covered my face with my hands and moaned. But the ache in my jaw was far too insistent for this to be a dream. Unbelievable as it was, I had been dumped in the passenger hold of the ship I had seen moored, and I was stuck here along with a good many other people.

That thought set me reeling again. For all the years I had spent in the harbor town of Leith, within the sight and smell of the water, for all the times I had escaped my tutors and my maids to sit on quays and watch the great tall ships, I had never set foot on board one, not even a small schooner. Grandfather had said my desire to feel a ship beneath my feet was only romantic twaddle brought on by reading foolish novels like

Robinson Crusoe. Mam merely said 'twas unladylike, and that was that. It had been rare in my life for me to agree with either Mam or Grandfather, but at this moment, I would have sworn they were right.

Still shaky, I worked my way back toward the lighter grayness that marked the hatch. But more people crowded down into the dank hold, jostling me away from that opening. I had to duck to avoid hitting my head on the low crossbeams. I jabbed my elbows into backsides and ribs, shouting as I did so. But the general uproar drowned out my voice. One lusty woman shoved back at me, her elbow hitting me squarely in the ribs and her ample hips knocking me into another bunk. The crowd was so thick it seemed a tangle of disconnected arms and legs and bundles writhing with a dizzying energy. Someone stepped on my hand as he clambered into a berth above me, and a rough burlap sack filled with hard and smelly onions banged into my head. I clutched the rough wood to keep from falling.

By the time the dizziness passed, the congestion had thinned out, not because there were any fewer people, but because most had settled into their places. A few had hung punched tin candle lanterns from the overhead beams. Swaying pinpricks of light cast a pox-like pallor on the grim faces surrounding me.

The narrow aisle between the rows of bunks was nearly empty for the moment. I pushed my way back toward the ladder, grabbing the rough wood frames on either side of the aisle for balance. No one stopped me, but no one moved aside either. Just as I reached for the first rung, someone lowered a water barrel down, missing me by inches. I fell back to make room for the water and the burly workers who manhandled it through the opening and into position behind the ladder. I started up a second time, but two empty buckets and a lantern followed the barrel. Finally, the way was clear. I could see a square of dim sky through the opening above me.

Grasping the sides of the ladder, I pulled myself upwards. No sooner had I set my foot on the bottom rung, when the heavy hatch cover overhead was dropped into place with a thud. The shock of it knocked me backward. The hem of my gown caught on a ragged splinter and ripped as my back hit the floor with enough force to knock the wind out of me.

For a moment everything stopped, but the silence following my fall was so brief I wondered if I had imagined it. In the shifting lantern light, the ordinary wooden ladder looked like a scarecrow from the other world, waving spindly arms as if to ward me off. With a shriek, I clawed up it, shoving my shoulder against the hold door.

"Help me!" I screamed. "Let me out."

No one moved to help me. No one even paused. The rat-like scurrying continued as if I were both inaudible and invisible.

I pounded on the thick wood, but there was no response, above or below. My cries of alarm grew more shrill. I had to get out. I was suffocating. My hands were battered and bleeding, but I ignored the pain and kept pounding. This couldn't be happening.

I felt a firm grip around my waist and heard a low voice not far from my ear.

"Come down, lass. The hold is shut up tight. With the night and the storm coming on, ye willna' be wanting it opened now, will ye?"

Shadows hid his features, but the voice on the ladder below was a man's, with a Highland lilt to it. He pulled me downward with such gentle insistence that I nearly gave in.

"I do want it opened." I tried to shake him off. "Please!" I took a deep breath, trying hard to steady my voice. I might be locked in this horrible place all night. "Please," I repeated as calmly as I could. "There's been a mistake. I don't belong here."

He chuckled softly, a pleasant, comforting sound. Maybe I had found someone to help me at last. Then his words took away the reassurance of his laughter. "Ye are likely right, lass, but there's no help for it tonight. We're shut tight now until morning. The sailors willna' open it, even were someone to die, for they're that busy up top."

My tenuous calm vanished, and I shrieked. "No!" Anger and fear gave me strength. I kicked out to dislodge him. I didn't have much leverage in the cramped quarters, but my heel hit his belly. He grunted and let go. I pushed upwards, trying in vain to shove the hatch cover open with my shoulder. "Help!" I shouted again.

His boots scraped on the rungs as he came after me. I flailed wildly in the darkness to ward him off. Then his strong arm wrapped itself firmly around my waist and hauled me down.

I screamed and kicked, but I might as well have been a naughty child held by the nurse for all the good it did. He dragged me back the length of the hold and plopped me unceremoniously on a bare plank board. I struggled to sit up, but his hands pushed down on my shoulders and held me still.

"Lay still, lass, and bide here. There's no use raving against the night. This hold willna' be opened before morning, and ye had best resign yourself it."

His breath tickled my ear, but his words renewed my terror. I couldn't face a night shut up in this coffin for the living. I couldn't think what to do. Nothing, not my education at the hands of some of the finest tutors in Edinburgh, nor years of scoldings from Mam and Grandfather, none of it had prepared me to suffer a night in the dark hold of a ship with a mass of heartless strangers. "I can't stay. They'll be looking for me." My voice wavered.

"Ye can. Ye will. For surely if ye rise off this bunk I shall tie ye to it." His voice was still low, but not so soft. It was as hard as his arms holding me flat against the plank, demanding compliance.

Hot tears of anger wet my cheeks. I couldn't get away, but clearly he meant no harm. He went on whispering, the rough stubble of his chin scratching the curve of my neck. "Hush, lass. It's no so bad as ye think. Ye will be fine in the morning. Ye are frightening the others. They've troubles enough of their own."

"I'm not frightened," I lied. "I only need to get out."

"But ye will bide till morning?"

Perhaps he was right. Surely everything would make more sense in daylight. Not trusting myself to speak, I nodded. There was no choice, really. While his voice was soft and persuasive, I had no doubt he would carry out his threat to lash me to the bunk if I did not agree.

"All right then." He let go of me. The sudden release left me nearly as breathless as before. I raised one hand to clutch at him, but let it fall. He backed away, melting into the dimness and mingling with the other shadowy strangers surrounding me. I lay still, willing myself to wake from what had to be a nightmare.

One by one the others blew out the lamps, and the darkness closed in on me like a suffocating cloak.

CHAPTER 2

I finally slipped into a deep slumber just before dawn.

That was my second mistake. Some mistakes are minor, forgotten the next day. Others are calamitous, disrupting the whole pattern of life. Mine were of the second sort.

When I finally awakened, a good many of the people crowding the hold the night before were gone. The hatch stood wide-open and bright sunlight spilled through the opening, erasing all signs of last night's rain.

I sat up and banged my head on the wood frame above me, having forgotten how closely the bunks fit together. The painful bruise added to the ache in my jaw, but I tried to ignore both as I stumbled toward the ladder. The floor made of narrow planks laid across the ribs above the cargo hold swayed beneath me. The pungent smell of tar mingled with the odors of old fish and strong onions. My stomach churned. I pressed onward. I had to get off this wretched ship.

I climbed the ladder and stepped out onto the main deck just as the ship rolled sideways. My belly lurched with it, and I clutched the hatch door. The ship groaned beneath my feet like a beast. I couldn't walk without hanging on to something. Bracing myself against the large mast midship, I looked about for someone to assist me. People stood in clumps about the deck. Several hung over the sides, staring into the deep water.

Water, I realized. Not docks, not cobbled streets winding up the hills above the harbor, but empty water. The shock hit me as powerfully as the blow to my jaw the night before. Open sea surrounded us. Gulls wheeled and called, their cries fading away in the vast, empty sky. In every direction, gray, undulating waves rose and fell with a sickening irregularity.

The sight of so much water was my undoing. As the ship heaved upwards with the wave, my stomach heaved on its own. I stumbled to the railing and leaned over just in time.

Emptying my stomach should have helped, but it did not. Long past emptiness, my gut knotted and twisted like a rag being wrung dry. Finally, spent and dripping with sweat, I sagged against the side of the ship. A brisk wind cut right through my thin dress. I had left my shawl on the bunk. None of the milling people paid the slightest attention to me. Many, looking as miserable as I felt, bent over the railings. I crouched against the bulkhead and tried to order my thoughts. Sleeping, I had missed the unmistakable sounds of anchors weighed and sails hoisted.

Perhaps I was still asleep. Any minute, I would wake up in my own chamber with a marvelous story to tell Elspeth. But I knew better. No dream let me feel the splintery wood decking through my skirt, or taste the bile as I retched.

I groaned. I needed to find the captain and demand that we return to port immediately. Grandfather would be furious. Even now, I couldn't really believe I'd been kidnapped. Why me? Certainly Grandfather had enough money to pay a ransom, but how could anyone demand a ransom from the middle of the ocean? It made no sense.

Yes, finding the captain was the proper thing to do, but the thought of rising to my feet on that wallowing, tumbling deck made my empty stomach convulse ominously. I closed my eyes.

I'm not sure how long I sat there, knees drawn up inside my skirt, too miserable to move. Exhausted, I dozed. I was startled awake by a calm, low voice. I immediately recognized the soft, lilting Highland burr from the night before. My eyes flew open, but I had trouble focusing. My first impression was that of an African lion, like those in Grandfather's engravings. The head in front of me was wreathed in a mass of coppery hair, resembling a tangled mane of curled cedar shavings. Behind him, a tall mast swayed toward me. I shut my eyes again and spoke without looking. "Please sir, I must find the captain. There has been a terrible mistake."

There was no answer. Perhaps I had dreamed the young man. I opened one eye. He was regarding me silently. By squinting, I could keep him in focus. His eyes caught my attention. They were tawny-gold, flecked with black. He wore a simple linen shirt of fine material, open at the neck, and rough britches like those worn by Randolph, our stableman.

Such a fine shirt with such rough pants seemed incongruous. I opened the other eye. Nothing changed, except he seemed to sway back and forth like a drunken man.

I pulled myself up by the rail. The deck pitched and wallowed underneath me like a cork bobbing on the pond, and my gorge rose. I gagged and leaned over the side again.

"Ye would have done better to stay put." His voice was sympathetic, but amused.

I wanted to give him my most withering look, the kind I used to discourage the suitors Grandfather brought home, but I could barely manage standing. "I must get back to Scotland."

The young man ran his fingers through his curls and frowned. "Well now, with the wind favorable and brisk as it is, we canna' turn back, lass. Why did ye get on board if ye only want to go back? Is it a change of heart from the seasickness?"

I ignored his questions. I couldn't begin to explain. The fight at home, the kidnapping, the shock of finding myself alone and at sea- it was all too confusing. If only the deck would not stagger about so!

"Ye ought to take yourself back below and lie down. Give it a few days, and the seasickness will surely pass. Let me help ye." He took my elbow.

I tried to think. Convincing the captain to turn the ship around might prove difficult. I had an uncomfortable feeling he would not consider my predicament more important than his own business. I might be stuck aboard for several days until we arrived at port and I could find a way to travel home, not an easy prospect considering I had come away with neither purse nor pocket. Grandfather would surely pay whatever the voyage cost, but getting a message brought another set of challenges. Without coin, how could I secure a messenger?

Suddenly it occurred to me I had no idea of our destination. I squinted up to see which way we were going, but I had never been very good with directions. With the sun behind us didn't that mean we were going west? It seemed unlikely. "Where are we bound? Calais?"

At this he laughed out loud. "Ye really have been caught in some dreadful mix-up, lass. Did ye not know we're bound to America? Philadelphia will be our next stop."

"America?" I stared at him. "You can't be serious. That's across the whole ocean."

"Aye, 'tis." His tawny eyes clouded with a faint worry.

"I cannot go to America," I wailed. "I haven't even packed a dress."

"Unless ye plan to swim back to Scotland, there's nowhere else for ye to go." He took a firmer hold of my elbow, as if he feared I might leap overboard.

My knees buckled. Mam always said my temper would get me nowhere. She was wrong. It had gotten me on a ship heading towards the wilds of America.

CHAPTER 3

The next few days blurred together. After the young man steered me down the ladder to the hold, he turned me over to the woman in the berth across from mine, the one who had spent half the night crying. She helped me put a straw tick on the bare planks of my bunk and showed me a bucket nearby, for anyone who needed it. There were many of us. The hold stank from vomit, and the air turned putrid since the hatch was shut each night. The ship plowed westward through the waves, and I stayed below, sicker than I'd ever been.

Grandfather always said nothing could keep me down for long, and in that at least, he was right. I was miserable for several days, but one morning I awoke feeling ravenous. Daylight spilled through the open hatch, so I took up my shawl and ventured on deck for the second time.

The air was bracing, fresh and clean, a welcome relief from the stench below. I filled my lungs. I might survive after all.

But walking the rolling deck was still difficult. I stumbled toward a small crowd gathered around the center mast.

No one paid me any more attention than a stray dog. I was wearing one of my oldest gowns. I had chosen it quite deliberately when Grandfather announced there would be a suitor at dinner, thinking to dissuade the caller from the outset. I'd torn the gown on the ladder that first night and slept in it for days after. I had no comb for my hair and no rag to wash my face. Little wonder they thought me of no more consequence than a beggar.

Over the tang of tar and salt air, I could smell food - bread perhaps, or porridge. My stomach growled. Obviously I couldn't wait politely for someone to feed me. I tapped the shoulder of a fellow nearby. "Is that bread up there?"

"Aye, Miss," he grunted without turning.

I squeezed past him and snatched a share of the hardtack and salted herring being passed out. Mam might insist on politeness, but I was starving.

As I gnawed on the hardtack, I considered what to do next. Dozens of people milled about among various barrels and crates lashed to each other and secured on deck. Everyone wore the same dingy woolens, but I had no trouble telling the sailors from the passengers. The sailors moved with purpose, striding as easily as a lady crosses her own drawing room. The passengers lurched into each other and wobbled about like pigeons scavenging in the town square. The ship itself was of middling size, neither as small as the barks that plied the firth near shore, nor among the largest of the oceangoing brigs. At either end a deck rose above the ship's broad belly, and three masts carried yards of canvas. A brisk wind filled the sails and drove us forward.

At one end of the ship stood a big wheel manned by a rough-looking fellow with rolled-up shirtsleeves. Wild, greasy hair blew across a face bristling with thick, coarse whiskers. A fierce scowl made it plain he was not inclined to talk. No matter. I stumbled toward him.

"Good day, sir." I was going to attempt a curtsey, but it took a great effort just to stay upright. "Are you the captain?"

"Who me? Not likely. Captain's in his cabin on the foredeck."

"Thank you." I turned to go. Then I turned back. "Where is the foredeck?"

"I wouldn't bother him just now, if I were you, Missy," he said. "He doesn't talk to … passengers."

Clearly he intended a different word to describe me. "He most certainly will talk to me," I insisted. "Just point me in the right direction."

The sailor laughed rudely. "Hey, Davy," he called out. "This gal thinks she's going to talk to the captain."

Davy turned out to be the young man with the cedar curls. He had been lounging on a pile of rope, whittling something. At the sailor's words, he rose nimbly to his feet. "Ah, the young lass with the mistake. Feeling better, are ye?" He winked at the sailor by the wheel. "I'll show ye to the captain's cabin." He strode toward a doorway not far from the wheel.

I hesitated. Was he really leading me to the captain? His lighthearted grin did not inspire trust, but my options were limited. I stumbled along behind, staggering from one railing to the next like a drunken schoolboy. I couldn't understand it. My legs worked in the normal way, but the deck of the ship never seemed to be where I set my foot.

Davy waved his hand at one of the cabins overlooking the main deck. "Here ye are, lass. I'd warn ye not to disturb the captain just now with tales of going back, but ye will not likely listen to me. Ye might do best to find it out yourself." He leaned against a railing to watch.

I would have preferred not to have an audience, but I wouldn't let that dissuade me. I meant to get back to Scotland, no matter what it took. I knocked.

My intention was to present my case rationally, since men listen to reason instead of their hearts. I intended to promise the captain reimbursement from Grandfather and payment for his trouble. I felt sure he would help me.

It didn't happen that way at all. I hadn't counted on the cursed pitching of the ship. Just as the captain opened his door, I lost my footing and fell into his arms.

He shoved me roughly aside. I fell to one knee and grabbed for something to catch myself. Unfortunately, I caught the cloth on his table. Instead of helping me balance, the whole cloth along with the remains of the captain's dinner crashed down around me.

The captain swore, "What in the name of creation is this?"

His language was certainly more colorful than Grandfather's, but his blustering was the same, so he didn't frighten me. Mam says one should always be ladylike, but that is difficult to do while sprawled on the floor of a rocking ship, surrounded by overturned dishes, and faced with a furious sea captain. I raised my voice to be heard over his shouting. "You must take me back to Scotland this instant." I stood up, keeping the table between us while I waited until he ran out of things to shout.

I tried again. "I must return at once."

This loosened his tongue and I was forced to wait once more until he ran out of breath.

"There has been a terrible mistake," I said as soon as there was another break. "I'm not supposed to be here."

He seemed to have finally heard me, for at this he stopped and looked at me keenly.

"Are you telling me you are a stowaway?" he asked, his voice suddenly calm.

"Of course not! I'm the granddaughter of Lochbar McIntyre. It's all a mistake."

The captain strode to the door. "Shakleton!" he shouted.

The little man who resembled a stuffed chicken elbowed his way through the crowd that had gathered at the railing and entered the cabin.

"What seems to be the trouble, Captain?" he said. He pulled out a blue silk handkerchief from his waistcoat pocket to mop at the sweat on his forehead.

"This gal says she doesn't belong here. Are you trying to pass off a stowaway?"

"Not at all," Mr. Shakleton said, his voice firmer. "That is Sally MacLaughlin. Her papers are all in order."

"I am not Sally MacLaughlin," I protested vehemently. But no one seemed to hear me.

"Show me the papers," the captain demanded.

Mr. Shakleton hurried away.

The captain and I glared at each other. "I'm not Sally MacLaughlin."

The captain did not deign to answer. He tapped his foot impatiently.

Mr. Shakleton soon returned with a bundle of papers. He set them on the table and untied the string. He shuffled through several loose leaves before extracting one. "Here we are."

'Terms of Indenture' was written on the top with a fine, black ink.

"Sally MacLaughlin," the captain read, peering at the paper, then at me. "Is that your mark?" he pointed to an X on the bottom of the page.

I moved to read the page, but he snatched it away.

"Is that your mark?" he demanded again.

"Of course not! I know how to write! I have no idea who this Sally MacLaughlin is, but I am not she. I am Caroline Beaton, granddaughter of Lochbar McIntyre."

The captain looked at me, then at Mr. Shakleton and back to me. Then he laughed, a short rude bark. "Ha. So you say." He grabbed my skirt and fingered it before I could snatch it away. "Clothes finer than the filth would show," the captain went on. "A voice showing some education. My guess is a lady's maid, got uppity and took off, wouldn't you say, Shakleton? Maybe a thief as well as a runaway? Now she's thought better of it, changed her mind."

Mr. Shakleton mopped at his forehead again, his mouth working toward some sort of answer but the captain waved him off. "It's no matter. This page," he jabbed a stubby finger at it, "says you're Sally MacLaughlin, and you've set your mark here for service in the colonies to pay your passage." He looked up from the paper and glared. His lips pulled back in an angry sneer, revealing crooked, broken teeth. "If you're not Sally MacLaughlin, then you are a stowaway, and I'll have you clapped in irons for the rest of the journey. Which is it to be, Missy?"

I opened my mouth, then closed it. I had no proof of who I was.

"Well?" His black eyes glittered in triumph.

"It's all a mistake," I said, but the fire was gone. I may be stubborn but I know when I am beaten, at least for the moment.

"So it's Sally."

I nodded, unable to trust my voice.

"All right then, Sally. Get yourself back to the lower deck with the rest of the blasted freights and stay there. If I see you again, I'll clap you in irons even if you aren't a stowaway."

"Wait." I braced myself against the table. "At least provide me with a cabin. The hold is noxious . . . " My voice trailed off under his unwavering glare.

The captain shoved me out the door. "Sailor!" he shouted to the crowd outside. "Get in here and clean up this mess."

Mr. Shakleton followed me out and gripped my arm just above the elbow. "I would be careful if I were you, Miss MacLaughlin," he hissed at me, with a voice like a snake. "It is illegal to impersonate another person to worm your way aboard for a free trip across the ocean."

I jerked away from him. "I never impersonated anyone. Why in God's name would I? I don't want to go across the ocean. I want to go home."

"So it's my word against yours, Miss MacLaughlin, is that it?" He deliberately let his eyes scan the length of me, taking in my bedraggled dress and hair, torn slippers and grimy face. He hooked his thumbs in the lapels of his frock coat. "Who do you think they'll believe, Miss MacLaughlin?"

"You had them drag me aboard!"

"Me?" He affected a look of bland innocence. "I'm a simple businessman."

I scowled, appalled at his presumption. But he was right. No one would take my word against his without some proof.

"I thought you'd see it my way. So I don't imagine you'll be squawking to any of the authorities when we reach our destination either. It would be most unpleasant for you to find yourself in jail, wouldn't it?"

There had to be something I could do to free myself of this oily man, but I couldn't think what.

"I trust I've made myself clear." He waited until I nodded. Then he took out a pocket handkerchief and fastidiously wiped off his fingers before leaving me.

I was used to getting my way. Sometimes it took a while, but in the end, I got what I wanted. How could I argue if I wasn't even allowed to talk?

Overhead, the great white sails swelled in the wind; the ropes creaked and slapped against the mast. But there was no comfort here such as I'd felt on Leith's dock. Around me, the crewmen hauled on lines and shifted rigging in an endless bustle of activity as meaningless to me as the parading of ants. Not a one of them cared the least bit what happened to me. Two sailors had dragged me aboard with nothing more than a nod from Mr. Shakleton. The passengers, or 'freights' as the captain had called them, gathered in small clumps on the main deck. They were a forlorn-looking lot, resembling a flock of dirty sheep as they shuffled out of the way of the sailors working, bleating a little if someone got too close. There would be no help from that quarter either.

I stared out at the dark water for a long time, not trusting my legs to carry me on the rolling deck, nor my voice to speak without sobbing. It didn't matter. No one would listen. Never before had I felt quite so alone.

Eventually, a young woman approached me. "I am sorry for your trouble." She patted my arm.

"Thank you."

She went on as if I hadn't spoken. "Only I'm thinking, 'tis better ye to have the trouble than our Sally."

Her words startled me out of my reverie. "Whatever do you mean?"

I turned to inspect her. She had a fair, round face and would have been pretty if not for the pock marks and freckles liberally scattered in equal parts across her cheeks and nose. Her gray eyes twinkled, as if she were hiding some laughter and could only just keep from letting it out.

"It's only . . . well, it seems ye have the strength to get out of it. I watched ye with the captain just now."

Her impertinence made me angry. I grabbed her shoulders and faced her squarely. "I want an explanation, not another riddle. Who are you and who in heaven's name is this Sally?"

"I'm Peg," she said, unperturbed by my grip. "Peg Willet. It's Sally MacLaughlin they've taken ye for. She signed the papers for the crossing, only she thought better of it and decided not to come. We thought they would just leave without her, but Mr. Shakleton was fair fashed. Twenty girls he'd promised the captain, as freight. I thought they might go after her. And then ye happened along . . . " She winked at me, as if I should share in the joke, switching me for Sally and saving the wretched girl from this trip.

"You know her?"

"Oh, aye. She lives in the same lane as me. We signed on together and . . ."

"You knew her," I repeated. "You knew I wasn't Sally. You let them take me even though you knew." My fingers dug into her shoulders. "Why?"

She winced. "Well, it seemed the will of God, ye coming along just as ye did." She shrugged, her apologetic smile revealing a chipped tooth. "And ye seem bonny enough. I thought ye could survive the trip. Sally couldn't. She hasn't much strength."

I glared at her. "Didn't it occur to you I might not want to go?"

Her grin widened. "Well, I did have the idea, ye ken, with ye kicking and screaming and carrying on like a piglet with the butcher on his tail."

I wanted to kick her. I would show her carrying on! "You're no better than that Mr. Shakleton!" I shook her hard enough to rattle her teeth.

She pulled out of my grasp with more strength than I imagined, and for the first time, the smile left her face. "I've said I'm sorry for your trouble. I have no wish to see ye hurt, nor to take any part in hurting ye." Without the twinkle in them, her eyes were a flat, dull gray, like a light had gone out. She rubbed a hand across her brow, tucking a stray wisp back under her mobcap. "But if ye think I could have done ought to stop Mr. Shakleton, or those sailors . . . well, ye have a mighty strong faith in me, more than I can match." She shook her head, and a wry smile brought the twinkle back to her eyes. "Do ye really think my bit of a scream added to yours would open that hatch?"

She was right, but I wasn't ready to give up being angry. "You could have done something."

She laughed lightly and tucked my arm into hers. "Come along." She patted my hand. "Let's find a place to sit out of the wind."

There is no sense moping about bad fortune. This ship was going to Philadelphia with me aboard, whether I wanted it to or not. I squared my shoulders and looked around to take stock of the situation.

There was little to cheer me. The ship, which seemed so large at the pier, was like a speck upon the vastness of the ocean. But, as Peg told me, this bobbing tub carried nearly two hundred passengers, along with two dozen crew members, several crates of chickens, a pair of young pigs, and a cargo hold filled with barrels and crates with goods for the Americas.

"There's a goodly number of rats too," Peg added. "I heard them squeaking in the night."

The deck in the middle of the ship was crowded with passengers walking about or idling away the time with cards or dice. The chicken crates took up one corner of the deck, and a large water barrel with a constant guard stood by the center mast. Amidst this commotion barefoot sailors with their long hair plaited and coated in tar worked constantly, coiling ropes, polishing brass, scrubbing the deck, or retying lines. Peg and I sat near the chicken crates until we got cold and Peg led the way below.

The hold or 'between decks', where the passengers spent most of their time, had been dark, cramped and unbelievably noxious from the first. After several days at sea with a cargo of seasick greenhorns, the situation had not improved.

The piss and slop buckets, cleverly designed with a wide bottom and a narrower top, did not tip easily. Some people had taken on the chores of emptying them, but not often enough to keep the ship's surge from causing spills.

Peg held her kerchief over her face with one hand and used the other to steady herself along the plank floorboards. I followed her as far as my own bunk. Hers was further forward. She mumbled something about tomorrow, then disappeared into the gloom. I sat down. The smell was so bad I tried to hold my breath, but I couldn't hold it long. Then I had to suck in great lungfuls of the putrid air. I tried short, shallow breaths, but that didn't lessen the stench.

"Just don't think about it," the woman from across the aisle said, after I had tried several different breathing patterns. "After a while, ye won't notice it anymore."

"Really? How long does it take?"

She wrinkled up her nose. "Well now, I'm not so sure, since I haven't come that far myself quite yet. My name is Mary Rawles. It looks like we'll be neighbors."

"I'm Cal. . . ." I started, then stopped. If Mr. Shakleton was right, I faced jail and legal action as a stowaway. Would it be best to use Sally's name or my own? In the end, I decided I didn't care. "I'm Callie Beaton, though some call me Sally MacLaughlin."

"Pleased, I'm sure." She accepted my double name without a flicker. "My husband is William Rawles. He's cramped up with the sickness just now."

I recognized Mrs. Rawles as the woman who had helped me. Though she did not seem to be suffering from seasickness herself, she looked done in. She had two children, both fussing for attention, and her husband lay on the berth, moaning. At that moment, he leaned over the edge of the bunk and retched into a bucket placed near his bunk. The nauseating smell of vomit almost turned my stomach again.

With a sigh, Mary set the baby in the little girl's lap. "Mind your brother, Leah." As she reached for the bucket, both children set up wailing.

I stepped over to her bunk. "I'll mind the bairns."

She hesitated. "We don't ask any favors. They'll do."

"It's not a favor." I picked up the baby, put him up to my shoulder and patted him soothingly. "I never thanked you for your help. You emptied the bucket for me, didn't you? I expect minding your bairns will be more pleasant."

"Well, aye." A smile flickered across her face and was gone nearly before I saw it.

"Ye would never guess a wee slip of a girl like yourself could puke so much. I'll be back directly." She grabbed the bucket and started up the ladder.

By the time she returned, six year old Leah sat by my side making shadow puppets with me. The baby, "wee Rabbie," as Leah named him, was only too happy to have his mam back. She set the bucket on the floor planks. It had been emptied, but not rinsed, and I realized that without a very long rope there was no way to reach the seawater. No wonder the hold continued to smell. I slipped back to my own berth, and Leah scooted across the aisle to sit with me.

"Come back here to me, ye wee imp," Mary said sharply. "It's not our place there."

"She's not hurting anything. There's a good deal more room, with only me to fill it up."

Mary smiled her quick smile again. "Sure, there's not all that much of yourself. either. All right, Leah. But send her back directly if she bothers ye." She bent to nurse Rabbie.

"Oh, Leah is a quiet lass, just like a church mouse. Here Leah, do you see this church?" I twined my fingers together to show her a church with the people inside, and then I taught her the clapping game Elspeth and I had played when small. Leah caught on to the rhythm quickly. We went faster and faster, until our flying hands missed and she tumbled forward into my lap. We both laughed, the first real laughter I had heard in days.

Mary raised one dark eyebrow. "If all the church mice were as quiet as this one, we'd never hear the sermon for the racket."

Leah and I started clapping again. With big, serious eyes, and fine blond hair, she looked as fragile as a fairy child from another world. I remembered the old nurse who told me endless tales of the fairy folk, a cold lot full mischief and magic. Elspeth and I had looked for fairies in the garden, but only in the daylight. What would Elspeth think if she saw me now, playing in the gloom with this pale child?

I shook my head to clear away such musings. Thoughts of home could only remind me of my misery. I turned my attention back to Leah and the clapping game. "How do you like the fine big ship we're on?"

My sarcasm was lost on the child. She shook her head so hard she lost the rhythm. "I do not like it at all. It's dirty and smelly and we had to leave Tom Dhu with Gran."

"Tom Dhu?"

Leah nodded. "Aye, our cat. Mam doesn't like it either. It's only Da who likes it here." She leaned over to whisper in my ear. "It's because of the rats."

"The rats?"

The girl nodded solemnly. "Aye, Da hates them. He's always going on and on about it."

I raised an eyebrow in Mary's direction. "Rats?"

Mary sighed. "Not rats, rents. The rents were too high and the last crop was bad. Too much rain."

"He's very sick," I observed. "Was I that color?"

"Serves him right." Mary's voice was bitter. "He's the one as wanted to come away."

"Why?" I couldn't think of any reason to voluntarily cross the ocean to some unknown wilderness.

She shrugged. "We'd no place to go. Will heard there's land in the colonies. Good land, for farming. Once our service is over, we can start fresh."

"It sounds a good enough plan," I said dubiously.

"It's his plan." She scowled at her husband. "A few years of service and then a farm of our own with no rent to pay."

"Service? I don't understand."

"To pay for our passage, we'll bind ourselves out for service in the colonies, working for whoever buys our indenture from Mr. Shakleton."

"For how long?" I had heard of indentures, but thought the arrangement more like an apprenticeship. This sounded like hard labor without the benefit of learning a trade.

"Seven years each for me and Will. Another five apiece for the bairns if we work it off for them, as they're neither one old enough to work yet. But they're both small and won't eat over much."

"Twelve years before you can start on your own?" I was horrified.

"Aye, if we're lucky. Will says it's better than starving with no work to be had."

"And you? What do you think?"

"I'd sooner be dirt poor and begging on my Mam's hearth than aboard this ship, so help me God." Mary crossed herself. "As it is, I'll not likely see Mam or Da again." She stroked the baby's hair, her voice catching.

"There's letters," I said, searching for something to comfort her.

This time her smile was tilted, as if only one side of her face could manage it. "Aye, no doubt. But as none of us can read, I misdoubt letters will be of much use to us."

"Oh." I felt humbled. Suddenly I saw my own future was not so bad. I would be going back to Scotland after all.

Mary reached across the narrow aisle between us and lay a hand on my knee. "It's all right now," she said. "I've done my crying. It's time to look forward. Ye have been a comfort to me for listening. I know ye have your own troubles . . . Callie."

I smiled gratefully at her use of my own name. If she could keep up a good face, surely so could I.

Gradually the people around us settled in for the night, spreading out blankets or bunching up clothing to serve as pillows. I offered to keep Leah with me so Mary, her husband and the baby would have more room. There were several empty bunks, including the one above the Rawles, since some of the men preferred the open air on deck to the cramped hold, but Mary didn't want Leah to sleep in a bunk alone.

Curled beside me, the child went to sleep right away, but I found it hard to get comfortable. The straw mattress crackled whenever I shifted positions, and prickly bits poked me through the ticking. When I finally drifted off, it was quite late. I didn't waken the next morning until well after the hatch was first opened. I was just stretching my arms, stiff from holding Leah close all night, when Davy McRae swung down the ladder.

He tipped his head in my direction, then turned to Mary and said, "Mistress Rawles, they are dishing out pease porridge. It's not so good, but it's hot, and I've heard them say we'll not have hot food again for two days or so."

"Thank you, Mr. McRae." Mary looked toward the ladder and then back at her husband. I couldn't tell if he slept or not. He moaned without stopping, a constant, low misery in the background of all else. His eyes were closed shut. Just listening to him made my own stomach flop rebelliously again.

"Dinna' worry about him," Davy McRae said. "He'll not want anything just yet. I'll give him some water, should he wake enough for it."

Mary turned around and dug out a pair of bowls from her bundle. "All right then. I'd best see to the rest of us. Come along, Leah."

I settled back against the ship's bulkheads, hoping the growling in my stomach wouldn't betray my hunger. I had no bowl or spoon or anything else with which to eat. I would have to wait for salt tack and herring again, since they could hardly dish out porridge into my bare hands.

"Ye had best go too, lass," Davy told me. "There's none to bring it down to ye."

"I'm not expecting any such thing," I said hotly.

"Well, then why don't ye go and eat? Mind, if ye were to tell me ye already found all ye can manage and were fair full, I'd have to call ye a liar, lady or no."

I laughed in spite of myself. "I would never try to fool you with such a story."

Mary had the children in hand. "Come and eat with us, Callie."

I shrugged. "I came away with naught but the clothes on my back."

"Is that it? That's no bother. I'll feed Leah out of my own bowl, and ye can use Will's, as he's too sick for the use of it just now."

Grateful, I followed.

Davy was right. The porridge, made of peas and salt meat of indeterminate origin, tasted vile. It was still so salty that it made me crazy with a thirst I couldn't hope to quench with the small ration of water that came with the meal. The only thing that hid the taste was chewing on the hard, flavorless ship biscuit. Still, it was food, hot food, and it stayed in my stomach.

CHAPTER 4

After several days of wet, grey mist, the weather brightened. Leaving Mr. Rawles still moaning in his bunk, Peg, Mary and I headed up on deck with the children for some fresh air before night fell. A salty breeze blew away the last tendrils of fog as the sun slid toward the horizon and colored the sky with a brilliant display of orange and vermillion.

"It'll be fine tomorrow," Davy McRae said by way of greeting, as he came close and squatted beside the pile of ropes where we had settled. Though damp, the ropes offered a seat somewhat sheltered from the cold gusts.

Peg smiled coyly at Davy, blinking her long, pale lashes. "How do ye know that?"

He shrugged. "It's just a saying seafarers have. 'Red sky at night, sailor's delight.' Surely ye have never seen a sky any redder than that one." He pointed off toward the sunset.

"Is it red right down to the water?" Leah was too short to see over the railing.

"Aye, 'tis. Come here, lass, and I'll show ye." He swung her up to his shoulder and leaned against the rail.

Mary gasped and half rose.

"No need to worry, Mrs. Rawles." Davy's voice was easy. "I'll never let her fall."

To ease Mary's mind, I stood up near the railing too, one hand resting on Leah's ankle. Alongside the ship, a pod of great fish leaped across the blue-gray swells.

"Look! They're playing tag," Leah said. "Are they folk or fish?"

Davy nodded. "Ye're right to ask. There's folk in the sea and many is the sailor who scoffed to his sorrow. Have ye never heard of the selkies—the seal folk?"

Wide-eyed, Leah shook her head.

Davy swung her down to the rope pile and stretched out on the deck nearby. "There's a story ye need to hear, seeing as ye are traveling their road."

I had heard tales of the selkies all my life. First from our nurse in the Highlands where she spoke in hushed tones with a wary eye on the door and then in Edinburgh, where folk told the same tales, but always with a smile and a wink. Davy's story told of a man enchanted and a woman trapped by his greed. For when a selkie maid dances on the shore, she leaves her skin and any man seeing her can't help but fall in love. If he can steal her skin, he can keep her. But even if she lives as his wife for twenty years, the selkie maid never forgets her home in the sea. And when she finds her skin, as she must do, she will escape and leave all on land behind.

Davy whittled as he spoke, the shavings falling as softly as his words. At the end of the story he handed a tiny carved seal to Leah.

"He should never have taken her skin," Leah said. "It wasn't his."

"No, it wasn't, and well he knew it. But that's the terrible thing about selkie lassies. One look and a man can't help wanting." Davy's words faded, leaving a long silence.

Peg spoke first. "I'd give up any home I ever had, did ever a man love me like that."

Mary drew her children close. "'Tis a hard choice," she sighed. "Between the man ye love and swore to follow, and the home that calls ye back."

"Enough of that," I said, overwhelmed by the melancholy. I was no selkie lass longing for home, and I had no lover to call me away. I was here aboard this ship because of my own mistake. No magic, no love, just foolishness. "Give us a tune, Davy."

He sheathed the knife and drew a small fife from his shirt. His lively jig set our hands to clapping. The sun sank below the horizon, and the moon rose high above us. A few scudding clouds swept across the dim sky and a fresh breeze snapped the sails.

"Look how late it's gotten." Mary whisked up the children and hustled them toward the hatch. "The night air will bring on a fever sure as anything. With their father so low, I'm sure I don't need a sick child."

I hated returning to the stuffy, malodorous hold. But with the sun gone and the wind picking up, prickly goose bumps rose on my arms. I would have to go below or freeze. And Peg dawdled near Davy with a hungry look in her eyes. It would be a kindness to leave the two of them alone. I rose to follow Mary.

"Surely ye are not afraid of the night air," Davy said, standing when I did. "Or is it the goblins and ghosties? I thought ye weren't afraid of anything after ye went after the captain."

Peg hooked her arm through Davy's. "Sure, she's not afraid of any man."

I pulled my thin shawl tighter. "I'm not afraid. I just can't feel my toes for the cold." I tried to make light of it, but my teeth chattered. The ship rolled, and I stumbled.

Davy broke free of Peg and leaped forward to catch me. He kept me from falling but knocked Peg into the railing. "Gracious, lass, ye really are cold," he said, apparently oblivious to Peg. He stared at me, concern darkening his eyes.

Peg laughed wryly. "Perhaps I'd best be the one going in now."

I pulled away. "No, Peg, it's all right," I said, confused. Was it only concern I'd seen in Davy's eyes? Even more confusing was my own reaction. I could forget the cold and the ship and the whole great ocean, caught up in his gaze.

No. I had no business thinking such nonsense or coming between Peg and the man she so clearly desired. Without another word, I left them.

Below decks, I held Leah in my arms and curled around her on the scratchy, straw-tick mattress, her small body warming me a bit. Mary had no extra blanket, but Leah had on a woolen dress and a shawl big enough to wrap herself up in, so she didn't suffer as I did. She relaxed in my arms and soon slept.

I lay wide awake, thinking of Davy's unsettling words. "Not afraid of anything." But I was afraid. Not of goblins in the dark or blustering men, but of what would come next. What would I find in the new land, half a world away from my own? Davy McRae had a silken voice and a way with words, but his stories reminded me just how alone I really was.

I woke the next morning from a dream in which I lay warm and cozy under the quilt in my own bed. It was a delicious dream, one I was loath to let slip away. The familiar creak and groan of the planking and the slap of waves against the hull made pleasant music. It took a moment for me to realize the warmth I felt was not part of a dream, but real.

I opened my eyes. A thick length of heavy woolen cloth covered me like a blanket. The edges were rough cut and unfinished, but it reached from my chin to my toes.

I sat up. "Mary! Will you look here?"

"What is it?" She sat up in alarm. "Have ye been bitten by a rat?"

Startled awake, wee Rabbie started wailing, and Leah, curled tight against me, cried out. Will moaned. "Can ye no keep the children quiet, Mary?"

Davy leaned over the edge of his bunk above hers, his hair as tousled as a haystack.

I looked around at all the sleepy faces. I hadn't meant to wake the lot of them. "I am sorry. It's nothing."

Mary picked up Rabbie and patted him against her shoulder. Satisfied that Leah was unharmed, she allowed herself a flicker of a smile.

"Are ye telling me, Callie, ye woke us all from a sound sleep for nothing? It doesn't seem very neighborly."

"Well, it's not nothing. It's just . . . look at this blanket."

Rabbie had settled so Mary leaned over and felt the covering. "It's lovely wool," she said dryly. "Taken to pilfering, have ye?"

"No! It came in the night. There wasn't any blanket when we went to sleep."

Leah's eyes were as round as saucers. "It's from the fairy folk," she whispered. "Maybe it's a selkie skin."

"That's enough nonsense!" Mary lay Rabbie down on the bunk to change his clout.

But Leah would not give up. "Like the ones in the story Mr. McRae was telling us."

I looked up to Davy. "You tell her that's just a story."

Davy lay back on his bunk. "How can I tell the lass to scoff at a fairy gift?"

"You don't believe all that, do you?" He looked so smug I was sure he knew more about the blanket than he was saying.

"'Tis from the fairies," Leah insisted. "Ye must leave them a gift in return."

"Hush, Leah," Mary interrupted. "We'll have no more talk of the fairies. As long as we're awake, we'd best get ready for the day. Callie, will ye help me brush Leah's hair while I tend to the baby?" She nodded at the comb in her basket.

I picked up the comb. Who could have given me such a gift in the night? Not Mary or Peg. Neither had any extra blankets. Davy McRae? I knew almost nothing about him. He spent more nights away from his bunk than in it, but he was the only other person aboard this ship with a word of kindness for me. He must have given it to me. Yet why help me and never say a word? I meant to find a way to thank him.

Leah's hair, wispy as down, was tangled from sleeping. She sat quiet as a cat asleep on the hearth, eyes closed, almost purring as I brushed. I thought of Mam. I had never sat still for her when she jerked the comb through my tangles. I'd been too eager to be done to mind Mam's scolding that it wouldn't hurt if I didn't fight it.

When I finished, Mary took the comb. "Do ye sit here," she instructed. "I'll do yours."

My hair was more snarled than Leah's. The comb caught and pulled no matter how gently Mary tugged, but it felt heavenly, as if I were a wee lass again. I closed my eyes, remembering the smell of hot oat porridge and the squeak of the rocker in the corner. Mary combed it smooth, then plaited it tightly against my head. "It'll never stay," I said, patting it. "But it feels grand. Let me do yours."

Peg joined us just as I finished Mary's hair. "Your turn," I told her. "I'm playing lady's maid this morning."

Peg laughed. "Me a lady? That's a treat not likely to happen again in my lifetime."

Davy swung down from his bunk. I had forgotten he was still there. "It's a lucky man that can bid good morning to four lovely ladies all at once." He bowed, stretching a well-shaped gartered leg in front of him.

Leah dived under my new blanket, and Mary ducked her head to hide her blush. Bold Peg giggled, and offered him her hand.

He kissed it like a gentleman, then he swung himself up the ladder and out onto the deck.

Later that day, in the long hours on deck, a scheme came to me. I was being held as a passenger because of a mark upon a paper. If somehow that paper disappeared, then Sally MacLaughlin would cease to exist. If I could destroy it, all I would have to do was survive the voyage, leave the ship without attracting any notice, and find a kindly captain to sail me back to Scotland. I was a bit vague in the execution of the last part, but I could sort that out when the time came. First, I had to get that paper. I would also have to keep away from Mr. Shakleton as much as possible. He might not remember my face from the pier, but after the debacle in front of the captain, he would not forget me altogether.

I began watching Mr. Shakleton surreptitiously, perched on a wooden feed box near the crated chickens kept for the officer's meals. There was a pattern in the lives of the better folk. The captain, officers, and gentlemen gathered each evening for a meal, followed by a few games of whist in the captain's quarters, the only place aboard large enough to hold them all. Unlike the lot of us, they ate hot food daily prepared by the ship's cook in the galley.

From my perch, I could see two doors on the stern deck. One led to the captain's cabin. The other probably led to the cabins set aside for officers and the better paying passengers. The first mate and the other officers, along with Mr. Shakleton and two gentlemen I didn't know, came out that door in the morning and returned in the evening. Mr. Shakleton spent most of his time in his own cabin, emerging mid-morning to take the air on the stern decks and again in the evening to cross over to the captain's cabin. While his morning walk was usually short, in the evening he was usually out for an hour or more. There were several cabins down that hallway, but I couldn't discover which was Mr. Shakleton's. I would need time to search.

I decided to ask Mary and Peg for help. We three huddled together in my berth while Mr. Rawles and Rabbie slept, and Leah busied herself with a knob of charcoal I'd found for her. I was teaching her most of the letters, but she took most delight in writing her own name.

"Are ye daft?" Peg said when she heard my plan. "We can't go waltzing into the gentlemen's cabins. Do ye no remember what the captain said to ye?"

"Hush! Keep your voice down!" Of course I remembered. I looked about anxiously. Privacy in the hold was impossible, but no one was paying us any attention.

"Ye do owe her something, Peg." Surprisingly, Mary spoke in my support. "Seeing as how ye never told anyone ye knew she wasn't poor Sally."

"That may be." Peg gave in. "But I'm not getting myself in irons for your sake, Callie Beaton. So don't be counting on me."

"You won't end up in irons. I only mean for you to keep a watcheye out and warn me."

I explained that while the gentlemen were at dinner, I would need a lookout. I told Peg that if she waited by the chicken coops, she would have a clear view of the captain's cabin and could whistle if anyone left dinner early. The gentlemen always took at least an hour, but sometimes the cook or his boy went back to the galley to fetch something. With Peg there to warn me, I would have time to hide.

"You do know how to whistle?" I asked Peg.

For answer, she put her fingers to her lips and let out a shrill two-note blast.

An old man called out, "Stop that. Do ye no ken whistling on a ship will bring up a gale?"

"My Lord!" Peg's hands flew up to cover her mouth. "Oh Mary, have I doomed us?"

"It's only a superstition," I said impatiently.

Peg did not look like she believed me.

We put our plan into action the very next evening. Peg nervously installed herself atop the chicken coops. With a quick look around, I scurried up the aft ladder and ducked into the narrow passageway giving me access to the cabins. Since Mr. Shakleton was neither the first nor the last of the gentlemen to emerge each morning, I guessed his cabin was in the middle. It wasn't much to go on, but it was all I had for a plan.

The hallway was dark. It took a minute for my eyes to adjust. I could make out six doors, three on a side. I tried the middle one on the left.

The door opened easily into a small room with two bunks, one atop the other. A crumpled blue waistcoat lay on the bottom bunk and a Bible sat open on the table. Since it was unlikely Mr. Shakleton would be reading a Bible or rooming with a man who did, I pulled the door closed and tried the one opposite. This door opened as easily as the first. It was similarly furnished with two bunks, only these were fitted tightly into the curved hull. A small table with its oversized linen cover draped to the floor filled the middle of the room and an unlit lantern sat upon it. Opposite the bunks beside the door stood a built in chest of drawers with a washbasin and pitcher next to a razor and a neatly folded towel. There were no books or clothes lying about the room and no clues as to the occupants.

Light spilled through the small porthole set above the bunks. I began opening the drawers in the chest. In the third drawer down, I came across a sheaf of papers bound up with a piece of black string. I recognized it as the bundle Mr. Shakleton had brought to the captain's cabin.

I tugged at the string. Suddenly, the ship rocked hard. The door banged shut behind me, and a tremendous clatter erupted outside, followed by the wild squawking of chickens. Startled, I dropped the roll of papers. As I bent to pick it up, I heard voices on the other side of the door. Abandoning the papers, I ducked under the table. No sooner was I out of sight than the door burst open and two men entered. I crouched under the table and tried to still my breath. I could see only the toes of two sets of black boots. I recognized the high reedy voice of Mr. Shakleton immediately. He was discussing the price of woolens, when the second man spoke.

"And what of your own freight, Mr. Shakleton?" An odd emphasis on the word 'freight' revealed the speaker's disapproval.

My jaw dropped and I shoved my fist in my mouth to keep from giving myself away. What was Davy McRae doing here? He circled the table and scooped up the sheaf of papers I had dropped and set it on the table above me. Maybe I would be lucky, and he would decide they had fallen.

Mr. Shakleton's cackling laughter grated unpleasantly in my ears. "Now Mr. McRae, there's no reason to take that tone. They've come of their own choice, you know."

I missed Davy's answer, for at that moment his boot trod heavily on my toes, and I bit down on my knuckle hard enough to bring tears to my eyes.

My mind raced through a number of wild explanations for being underneath Mr. Shakleton's table, none of which was even remotely believable. Surely, any minute, Davy would realize he was standing on a foot and haul me ignominiously out of my hiding place. But Davy went on talking as if nothing were amiss.

". . . the bills of lading for Father? He would want me to check."

"Yes, yes of course." Mr. Shakleton seemed impatient. "But you'll have to wait. They are in my partner's keeping. No sense carrying them back and forth across the Atlantic."

Mr. Shakleton opened a cupboard, while Davy remained where he was, standing next to the only chair, his boot firmly planted on my foot. Perhaps he hadn't noticed me. His boots were thick enough. Perhaps he couldn't tell what he stood upon.

The two of them went on about freights, prices, and records. How could I get away? Even if Davy said nothing, what could I do about Mr. Shakleton? I had only seen him leave his cabin twice after dinner. Why come back so early today of all days? And what on earth had happened to Peg? I was absolutely certain there had been no whistle.

The men stopped talking for a moment. I heard the sound of a stopper being pulled from a bottle, followed by gurgling of liquid. They clinked glasses.

Would I be stuck in this ridiculous position all night? My legs were cramping already.

"Ye'll want to see the lot, no doubt. Come on then, and I'll show ye." Davy set his glass down on the table.

"Now?" Mr. Shakleton was obviously reluctant.

I crossed my fingers. This might be my chance.

"Why not? It'll only take a minute."

"I suppose it must be done." Mr. Shakleton moved toward the door, his boot tops visible again under the crack between the tablecloth and floorboards.

There was some shuffling of papers, then the two men left. I scrambled out from under the table, but hesitated before following them into the corridor. Davy had said it would only take a minute, but I had to give them time to clear the hall. I looked back at the table, but the papers were gone. Had Mr. Shakleton put it away after Davy had picked it up? Or had he taken it? I tried the third drawer again, but now it was locked.

I had no more time. I peeked out. No one was in sight, so I hurried back to the hold.

Peg was crying. "Oh, Callie!" She fell on me, hugging me and shaking me in turns. "I thought ye had been killed for sure."

"No one gets killed for hiding in someone's room." I patted her hand, meaning to calm her, but I was still shaking from my narrow escape.

"They do hang ye for thievery," Peg cried. "Why didn't ye come out?"

"Why didn't you whistle?" I demanded.

"I wanted to, Callie. But ye heard the man. A whistle on board a ship brings on a storm for sure. I was that scairt, when I saw Mr. Shakleton and Mr. McRae going in, my mouth went dry and I couldn't make a sound. I tried to warn ye anyway."

"How?"

Peg's eyes opened wide in astonishment. "Did ye no hear the clatter? I knocked the whole chicken coop over."

"You didn't!"

Peg smiled, her impish grin erasing her tears. "That I did. Then I offered to help Henry catch the chickens."

"Henry?"

"You know. The big, slow fellow guarding the water barrel. He's fair put out with me. I may just have to let him kiss me a time or two, to get back in his good graces." Peg puckered her lips and smooched the air.

"Enough nonsense, Peg," Mary said. "Did ye get your paper, Callie?"

"No." My laughter died away.

"Ah weel." She shrugged. "I doubt it would help much in any event. Ye are still aboard the ship, paper or no, and ye canna' head back to Scotland before we get to Philadelphia, whether ye be Callie Beaton or Sally MacLaughlin."

True enough, but if there was no paper, they couldn't claim I'd made my mark on it, and then I could make my case for being taken against my will. Still, no use fussing about it. I hadn't got the paper, and I didn't think Peg would help me try again.

"I don't see why ye want to go back in any case," Peg said, "since ye dinna" want your grandfather managing your suitors."

"Of course, I want to go back," I stopped. Peg was right that I didn't want Grandfather finding me a husband. Mam and Elspeth loved me as I loved them, but they wouldn't miss the wrangling I brought. The house would be a good deal quieter without me.

I shook my head. Trouble or no, all of them, even Grandfather, would worry. I couldn't leave my family in such uncertainty. I had to go back.

I helped Mary get the little ones to bed; then Peg and I brushed and braided each other's hair, while Mary tended to Will. Finally I settled in my bunk with Leah, but I couldn't sleep. Davy McRae was doing business with that slimy toad, Mr. Shakleton. I had thought Davy a good, kind man. Now I didn't know what to think. Had he seen me? He'd been first into the room, before the tablecloth stopped quivering. He must have known I was there. Had he lured Mr. Shakleton away to help me? But if he was working with Mr. Shakleton, why keep my presence a secret? I went round and round with it, but couldn't find an answer.

CHAPTER 5

With the weather so fine, the hatch door remained open even at night for a little air. Those near the door endured the cold, but those who slept further away nearly suffocated. I slept opposite the Rawles', about midway between the two ends; leaving my bunk both cold and airless. As evening came, I dawdled, putting off going below. Mary clucked at me like a mother hen with a wayward chick, but she needed to get back to Will and settle the children. I waved her away and walked alongside the railing, enjoying the quiet.

Now that I could manage walking about, I liked the ship. Not the dark, smelly hold of course, but on deck where the white sails fluttered and the music of the seas slapped a rhythm against the wood planking. Out here in the wind and the dark, I felt an unfamiliar freedom. It didn't make sense. I had been taken against my will and could no more leave this ship than I could walk on water. And yet—here no one told me what to do or how to do it.

A stiff breeze swirled down from the billowing sails and blew the stray ends of my hair into my eyes. I pulled the blanket I wore as a cloak tighter. It was getting late. Except for a few men playing cards, the deck was empty. I turned to go below and saw a pile of coiled ropes stored close to the crew quarters' hatchway. The ropes would be sheltered, out of the wind.

It took only a moment to decide and not much longer to settle myself under the ladder. The ropes made a damp, lumpy mattress, but at least I could breathe. Perhaps I could stay out here all night. Others had.

I lay still, listening to the boards creak as they rose and fell with the waves. The wind slapped ropes and stays against masts and spars. Occasionally, one of the crew passed by and I could hear steps on the ladder or voices in conversation. I fell asleep, imagining myself a small bird curled in a nest.

Quite suddenly, I jerked awake as a heavy weight, like a sack of flour, fell on me. Sleep-befuddled and with the wind knocked out of me, I gasped for breath. The weight, which smelled of man's sweat and tar, moved.

"Here, what's this?" a gruff voice asked. A large hairy hand groped across my chest.

Still gasping for air, I tried to wriggle out from under him. The hand on my bosom fumbled at the laces of my bodice. I kicked and beat at him with my fists, but it was like hitting a wooden post.

"Hey, what you got there?" a second voice asked.

Hairy Hands straddled me, pinning both my arms over my head. "Either I'm dreaming, Ned, or I've got me a selkie lass come to warm my bed tonight."

His breath huffed hot in my ear. Rough, chapped lips and scratchy beard stubble scraped across my cheek. I twisted my head as far away from him as I could.

I tried to cry out, but with his full weight on my chest, I could barely breathe, let alone talk. His breathe stank of rum. He was too drunk to manage much of anything, but he was strong. I couldn't break loose.

"Your selkie needs taming," Ned said. "I'll hold her for you, if you share after."

A third voice chimed in. "What's up here, lads?"

I thrashed wildly, but to no avail.

"It's a selkie," Ned told the third man blandly. "You'll have to wait your turn."

The latest man had a lantern with him, its glow framing my attacker's head. Hairy Hands tried to push my skirt up, but it was underneath him. He pulled back and fumbled at his own britches. The shifting of his weight eased some pressure on my chest and I finally sucked in enough air to scream.

The wind blew the sound away.

"That's no selkie. It's one of the girls from between decks." The third man spoke again and I recognized the voice of Davy McRae. What was he doing here?

"It makes no never mind," Ned said. "She was waiting here for us."

"Oh, ye are wrong there, laddie," Davy went on conversationally. "It makes some difference to her, of course, and Mr. Shakleton, the factor, will take it a bit hard do ye soil his goods. Ye will have to let her go."

"You can't mean it, man! She was here waiting for us."

"Mayhap, but she's no very pleased with what she found." Davy's voice was as calm as if they were discussing the worth of a horse at market. Furious, I fought to kick myself loose and sucked in my breath to scream again.

Hairy Hands was having none of Davy's talk either. His left hand squeezed my wrists together and his right pulled open his britches.

Davy was through talking as well. He planted a booted foot on Hairy Hand's rump and shoved. Caught off balance, Hairy Hands loosened his grip on my wrists. That was all I needed to get one hand free. I clawed for his eyes and raked my fingers down his cheek.

"Damn! She's got selkie claws right enough." Hairy Hands drew back. I squirmed out from under him and scrambled to my feet. I snatched the blanket and ran for the hold, ignoring the angry howls of both Ned and Hairy Hands yelling at Davy.

I didn't stop to hear what followed. Stuffy or not, I would sleep below deck.

In the morning, I kept a wary eye out for a sailor with a scratched cheek and avoided Davy altogether. My debts to Mr. McRae were mounting. I hadn't yet found a way to thank him for the blanket. I couldn't thank him for saving my skin in Mr. Shakleton's quarters, and now he'd rescued me again. I was more embarrassed than frightened. It was only drink that befuddled the sailors and made them come after me. Still, I didn't want to talk about it. Luckily, I didn't see the sailor I wounded or Davy for several days.

In that time the weather held fine, chilly but dry, and I spent as much daylight as I could out of the hold. Late one afternoon, Peg and I sat in the shelter of the mast with the children. Mary, glad of a few minutes' respite, was bringing supper down to Will. He had grown stronger in the last two days and seemed to have finally gotten over the seasickness. Peg held wee Rabbie on her lap, playing peek-a-boo, while Leah and I played

Cat's Cradle. The little girl's stubby fingers patiently twisted the string into each new pattern, over and over again.

Suddenly, Peg jabbed her elbow into me.

I dropped the string as I slipped it off Leah's fingers. "What is it?" I was annoyed. Peg's greatest skill, I'd learned, was gossiping.

Peg jerked her chin toward the hatch to crew quarters. Several off-duty sailors lounged about the ladders going up to the fore deck. A pair played checkers and a third one whittled. Three or four others watched the checker players. Donal and Malcolm Grant, the two brothers in the upper bunk just past the Rawles', leaned against a crate. Davy McRae sat near enough to see the game, but far enough away to be by himself for all that. He ran his fingers through his tangled hair.

"I don't see anything out of the ordinary." I stretched out the string and wound it back on Leah's fingers.

"No? Do ye not see that Davy McRae? He's up to no good, that one."

"He's only watching the game like the others."

"Just ye watch him now."

Davy laughed just then, rose, and clapped one the sailors on the back. Still laughing, he swung down the ladder into the hold.

I cocked my head and lifted an eyebrow at Peg. "What's to fret about?"

"Are ye blind?" She shook her head with some impatience. "Why is Davy McRae going into the crew's hold? Answer me that, if ye can."

"Och, Peg, you'll see a mystery in a pot of porridge. He's only collecting on a gambling debt or the like. There's no great harm in that."

Peg set her chin stubbornly. "I've got a pair of eyes in my head, unlike some I could name. It's not every one as has the free run of the crew's quarters. Ye wouldn't see either one of us anywhere near there, now would ye?"

I ducked my head to hide my sudden alarm. I had not told Peg about the incident with the sailors. I had no idea if Davy had even recognized me.

"Mark my words," Peg went on, apparently too caught up in her warnings to notice my discomfort. "That man is hiding something. I'll lay odds on it."

Davy came back out of the hold, tucking a small bundle into his shirt as he settled back down beside the men playing checkers.

Peg nudged me in the ribs again. "Don't stare at him so." She winked conspiratorially. "He'll think ye have noticed how very handsome he is."

My cheeks burned. Davy McRae was very handsome indeed. His hair was just shy of the red-gold you could find in firelight, and his eyes glinted with amber light. He had the easy grace of a cat ready to spring. I couldn't deny the man intrigued me.

Peg laughed. "So ye have noticed. Well, ye needn't worry. We've all set our sights on him, but he's not seen anything in the whole lot of us."

I wasn't sure if she meant this as comfort or was still teasing. Either way, I didn't care for it. "I'm not looking at him," I told her. "I just want to get home."

"Mayhap he's the one to help ye. He's up to something, he is. I know mischief when I see it. Shall I ask him for ye?"

"Peg, you're impossible! I'm not interested in that man or anyone else."

"Don't get yourself nettled." She patted my arm. "I was only asking. If ye have not set your cap on him, then he's fair game. Though it seems he has an eye for ye."

"I thought you said he was up to something,'" I reminded her.

"Still worth catching." Peg winked.

Wee Rabbie started wailing and rooting in Peg's bosom. She shoved him at me. "Take him back down to his Mam. I'll take Leah for a bit of a walk. Maybe Mr. McRae will have another story for us."

Peg's love of drama outweighed her common sense, so I meant to ignore her. But in the next few days, I noted something odd about Davy McRae. Not so much in his manners—no faulting him there. He had an easy grin, and his eyes sparkled as if he found the whole world amusing. But he alone seemed perfectly comfortable in any part of the ship, with crew, officers, or passengers.

Most people on board knew their places. The passengers slept in the between decks hold or walked about on the middle deck. Not all of the passengers were 'freights', or indentured, like Peg and the Rawles. Nearly a third of those in the hold had bought their passage free and clear, but little distinguished them from the rest of us. Certainly, no one from the hold ventured near the quarters of officers or crew.

That group scrambled about all decks as they worked, climbing masts, scrubbing, and hauling on ropes and pulleys. Woe to the unlucky passenger who got in their way. No sailor had any qualms about shoving an errant passenger back. But they seldom, if ever, ventured into the passenger's quarters. Not that I blamed them. I would as soon stay away from there myself. But they didn't mix. Except for an occasional "watch yourself there" sort of warning, they rarely even spoke to us. The captain and the other officers walked the length of the ship to inspect and give orders, but never to talk to passengers. Mr. Shakleton and the other gentlemen kept to themselves in their cabins.

Only Davy might turn up anywhere. He played at cards and dice with the sailors and shared their rum, but he often slept in the hold and usually took his meals with the rest of us. Twice I saw him coming out of an officer's cabin, and another time he and Mr. Shakleton leaned against the rail outside the captain's cabin, deep in conversation. Davy didn't really belong anywhere, yet he fit in everywhere. Just what business did he have with Mr. Shakleton?

CHAPTER 6

One day, dark clouds piled up against each other shortly after noon, turning the sky a mottled grey. "Storm coming," the crew muttered as they ordered us below and closed the hatch. Without lanterns, food, or escape, we waited in the pitch-black hold like sheep in a pen.

The weather worsened, and the wind screamed overhead and slammed ropes against mast and spar. The hold buzzed with the murmured prayers of nearly two hundred people begging God for salvation as the ship rocked back and forth like a bauble brandished by a giant sea monster. Suddenly, the ship heeled sideways, flinging me and dozens of others to the filthy floor. Women screamed and children shrieked. The sound of prayer mingled with the moans and retching from the souls packed between decks like herring. Another wave crashed over us, and I thought sure the ship would break apart. Nothing could stand that much battering.

I did not want to die sprawled on the floor. I clawed my way back up, grabbing at the wooden planks and rails. My hands found Mary.

"Help me, Callie," she screamed in my ear. "I canna' hold the three of them."

Will retched unceasingly, dry heaves from an empty stomach. "Never mind about me, Mary," he gasped. "Mind the bairns."

Leah and Rabbie's panic-stricken wails echoed the cries around us. I pulled Leah close and wedged her between the ship's bulkhead and me. Then I took the baby in my arms, bracing my legs against the upright posts. Mary held onto her husband and Peg held on to me.

"Where's Davy?" I shouted to Peg. "We could use his help here."

"I haven't seen him. Oh Lord, help us!" The ship slid sideways and then tumbled forward, as like a loose rock rolling down a mountain. "He'll be washed overboard."

My grip on the baby tightened. Nothing could be left on deck. "God," I begged, "let us be swallowed by a whale and die. Better that than this living entombment." The black air enveloped me like a shroud. I could taste fear like bile in the back of my throat.

God did not answer me, and the nightmare went on. Mary, Peg and I clung to each other, the children, and Will. Rabbie and Leah grew too weak to cry. We prayed until our voices were hoarse croaks, and still the gale raged on.

It lasted two days. I dozed in fits and starts, jerked awake each time the ship slammed into the trough of a wave. Finally, the winds died, and I slept deeply.

I was awakened, not by the wild yawing of the ship, but by bright sunlight piercing the hold as the sailors opened the hatch.

"Mary, wake up." I leaned over and shook her gently. "The storm is over. We're alive."

"God be praised." Mary opened her eyes. "God be praised."

God be praised indeed. After the storm, Mary and I took stock. Peg and the bairns were fine, though a bit green and queer looking, and Davy had not been swept overboard. He had weathered the storm on deck with the crew. But not everyone came through the storm so well. Will Rawles, who still suffered from seasickness in calm weather, looked like a ghost. Even more sobering, three children, tossed about by the storm and too weak to fight it, had died, along with a woman I didn't know. I joined the throng on deck to pray for their souls in eternity. Without ceremony, without even a shroud, for no one had blanket or cloak to spare, the four bodies were thrown overboard. There was no sound as they sank beneath the now placid sea.

I turned away, shuddering. Never again, I vowed, would I ride out a storm in that wretched hold.

There was a great deal to do in the aftermath of the storm, mostly cleaning. This was difficult because even with sea surrounding us, we had no water to spare for washing. We dipped the hems of our skirts in the puddled rainwater and shared the tiny bar of soap Mary had brought. We had no tub, dry rag or towel. I didn't even have a change of clothes. I did my best to sponge off my dress and wear it wet until the sun and the breeze dried it.

"I'm worried about Will," Mary confessed as we worked on deck near the hatch the day after the storm. "Nearly everyone else is over the seasickness, but my man canna' even get out of the bunk without another fit. I've never seen him so weak."

Peg swished the last of wee Rabbie's clouts in a half-bucket of seawater. The seawater gave the baby a terrible rash, but there was naught to do about it. "It's always women who are stronger," she said without looking up. "The men boast and bluster, but at the first touch of fever, they turn helpless as babes. Women bear the brunt and carry on."

"Ye are right enough there." Mary smiled briefly, erasing the deep lines of worry creasing her brow.

"Does he have a fever?" I asked. I took the clout from Peg and wrung it out.

"No," Mary was thoughtful. "He's cold and clammy, but there's no fever."

"Good," Peg said. "No one ever died of seasickness."

"Perhaps not," Mary said. "Still, the air in the hold is so bad. Don't they say putrefaction can cause a man to sicken?"

Peg and I kept the children on deck while Mary tried again to get her husband to drink a few sips of clear water. He had eaten almost nothing since leaving Scotland. His hollow cheeks and dull eyes made him look cadaverous in the dim light of the hold.

Mr. Rawles was not the only one suffering so. Though most of the passengers had gotten over the seasickness, several women and a few children had started coughing. Day and night the wracking sound kept me awake.

That evening I lingered on deck after Peg took the children down to Mary. The ship with its cargo of the sick and dying was a coffin floating toward a watery grave. Leaning against the railing, I stared into the water surrounding me like the gaping maw of a sea monster, ready to swallow me whole. What difference did it make to anyone if I stayed afloat or sank beneath the waves? The fathomless sea roiled past the ship's planking in never-ending undulations of foamy water. I felt alone in all the universe.

I didn't hear the man's approach until a board creaked. I whirled, remembering the drunken sailor, and spun right into Davy McRae.

He must have been as startled as I was, for his arms caught me to keep us both upright. When he realized who I was, his arms loosened but did not let go. "Steady there, lass, else ye will be over the side and into the depths before ye know it."

I shivered.

Davy's arm tightened around me. "Ye ought not be out here in the cold. It's no verra safe up here for a lass after dark."

"Is any place aboard this wretched ship safe?" I shook my head. "I can't breathe below decks. Besides, I'm not afraid of your story demons." I knew I should pull free, but his eyes kept me. "Peg's gone in for the night," I said, without moving away.

"And ye have not." Davy did not move either. "Ye ought to fear the human devils here about."

"Oh, aye, there's human devils sure enough, but what more can they do? I'm all alone and . . .. " My voice caught and I stopped, unable to go on without crying.

Davy said nothing for a time. He pulled me even closer and stroked my arm, then let his fingers trail across my neck under my hair.

One part of me scolded. Why was I listening to this beguiling human devil? Peg had set her cap on Davy McRae. But the desire to stay in his arms drowned my scoldings. I held my breath, my skin warmed by the touch of his fingers.

He brushed the hair back from my cheek. "Look up, Callie."

I did. The sky, a deep velvet with a million pinpricks of stars stretched from black ocean to the farthest spheres with naught to break it.

"Ye may feel ye are an insignificant speck, but are those not the same stars as shine above Scotland? We're all specks, Callie, no matter where we are, and there are those who would notice when even one speck is lost."

He was right, of course. There were Peg and Mary close to hand, and Mam and Elspeth and Grandfather so far away. And Davy, though he had no reason to do so. I straightened. I spoke no word, but he must have sensed the change in me, for he loosened his hold.

"Ah, Callie," he said, his hand still lingering on my arm. "Ye claim ye are no selkie, but ye may as well be for the charm ye have set on me. Are ye sure ye have no fairy blood at all?"

The spell was broken. I pulled free of his touch, then wrapped my arms tightly around myself. "It seems to me you've done the charming here tonight. Do you talk so to every lass you happen upon?"

His teeth glistened in the starlight as he smiled. "Nae. Only those with a selkie's soft brown hair and a selkie's longing for home."

Home. Yes, I did long for home, but I hadn't been thinking of it, not really. I'd only been feeling sorry for myself. I took a step toward the hold, then turned. "Thank you."

"For what, lass? I've done little enough to ease ye."

He had reminded me I had a place to go and a plan to get there. "For the blanket."

"Ye guessed that, did ye?" He smiled. "I could hardly stand by while ye shivered yourself to death, now could I?"' Then he took my hand and kissed it, his lips soft as a feather's touch upon me. "Good night, Callie."

I went below, warmer than I'd been in weeks. I would get home, somehow. I lay on the bunk and put my hand to my cheek. The place where Davy's lips had brushed my skin stayed warmest of all.

CHAPTER 7

After the storm, Will Rawles fell sick again. Despite Mary's attentions, her husband did not improve. His breath was shallow and fast, and he ate little.

"However can a body be seasick so long?" I asked. Mary handed me wee Rabbie as she prepared to empty the bucket once again. "What is it? Near four weeks now?"

"It's not seasickness any more. I'm sure I don't know what to do." The shadowy light made deep crags of the worry lines in Mary's face. "He's purged himself clean more times than I can count. There's naught left in him." We could both see he was wasting away.

"He needs a doctor." But I knew as well as Mary there was none to help us.

Mary left with the bucket. Crooning softly to Rabbie, I sat across from Mr. Rawles. Even in the dim light he looked ghastly. His eyes were sunken and his lips had taken on a bluish cast.

Impulsively, I put my hand on his. It was cold and clammy, more like a fish than a human hand. Startled, I jerked back.

"Oh, Mary," he moaned, his voice whispery soft through cracked lips.

I put my hand back, clammy or no. "Hush, now. Mary will be right back."

"I'm so sorry, Mary. I never meant to leave ye alone."

"Hush. You'll be right as rain in a day or two." He didn't seem to hear, but rocked his head back and forth, eyes open but unfocused. Was he already seeing the ghosts he would soon join?

Leah peered at him over my shoulder. "Da is very sick. We mustn't bother him," she recited, then turned her pale eyes on me. "When will he get better? Mam says soon, but it's been days and days."

"Leah." I spoke softly. "Run now. Call your Mam as quick as you can."

No sooner had she left, than Will squeezed my hand. "Promise me!" His voice was barely audible, but it was clear. His eyes focused on me.

"Save your strength." If only Mary would hurry.

"Promise ye will care for her. I can't leave her alone."

"Mary's fine. You need not worry for her sake."

"Promise . . . " He tried to rise, his breath ragged.

Gently, I pushed him back down. "I promise."

"She's not so strong . . . " His voice trailed off.

Mary rushed in, dropping the bucket with a clatter. "What is it?"

"He's asking for you, Mary. I'll mind the bairns."

She bent over her husband. "I'm here, Will. I'm here now."

I took both children to bed with me that night, while Mary wrapped her arms around her husband, trying to warm him.

Her cry woke me before dawn. "No . . . no," her voice rose to a keening wail. "No!" The word stretched out as if his death pulled her so thin she would snap. *No . . .* A word of power uttered helplessly by a woman without power, alone now in a dark, smelly hold, in the middle of the ocean, a world away from any hearth or home she'd ever known. *No . . .* A useless, flimsy shield against the awful pain of loneliness.

I thought of my promise. How could I possibly help? Powerless myself, what comfort could I give? I wrapped my arms around her.

We stayed that way until dawn. Peg took the children up on deck, and Mary and I cleaned him up as best we could.

"What will we do for a shroud?" Mary wailed. "I can't send him cold into that dark empty grave."

"Use this." I tugged at the privacy blanket Will hung by their bunk weeks ago when he set out across the world so full of hope. I helped her wrap him, and Davy carried him on deck.

There was no minister. Mary hugged the stiff bundle that had been her husband. "I can't do it. I can't just throw him in the sea."

"Can you do something?" I asked Davy. His voice had soothed us so many nights.

He looked at me, then touched Mary's shoulder. "I'm not much for a holy man," he said, "but I'll say a few words, an' it be some comfort to ye."

"Please." Mary stood up, trying to compose herself.

Davy closed his eyes as if searching inside himself. Then he looked over the small knot of people gathered at the ship's railing. His eyes found Mary's. "Unto your hand, Lord, we commend the soul of Will Rawles, husband and father." Davy's words mingled with the slap of the sea against the ship and the whisper of wind against the sails, weaving a bit of comfort. "We pray that ye bring his soul to ye in the glory of Heaven and protect his widow and bairns left here on earth."

Mary, Peg, Davy, and I said the Lord's Prayer. Then Davy played a tune on his fife.

The crew lifted the body to throw him overboard. "Wait!" Mary clutched at the corpse.

"'Tis no use putting it off." Davy pulled her back.

She shook him off. "Just a bit. I'll no be long." She turned back the shroud and kissed her husband. I shuddered to think how the cold lips of a dead man would feel. But Mary dried her eyes, took wee Rabbie from me, and held Leah by the hand. "Say goodbye to your Da," she said. Then she stood straight and silent as they slid the corpse of Will Rawles into the sea. The body hit the water with a splash and sank from sight.

After that, Peg moved her bundle from the bunk she shared with three others to join us. "It's closer to the air," she explained, but I knew it was for Mary.

I helped by amusing Leah whenever I could. We played cat's cradle and practiced the alphabet. I kept an eye on the sky, praying the weather would hold. But late one afternoon, the sky took on an ominous greenish cast.

"Get the freights below," the captain shouted, "and shut the hatch."

The passengers were already pushing toward the hold. I took Rabbie while Mary held Leah. A spatter of rain washed my face, and a tremor swept the crowd jostling me in their hurry to escape. Peg linked her arm in mine, her eyes bright with fear. My throat tightened. But my fear was not the same as theirs. It wasn't the storm that frightened me, but the hold, a dark coffin, with my own living corpse locked inside. The mob swayed forward, carrying me along.

I shoved the baby into Peg's arms. "Go on," I told her. "I'll be right along."

"There's no time," Peg shouted over the wind. "They'll shut up the hold."

"I need some air. I'll be along in a minute." Already the inexorable press of the others separated us. "Stay with Mary," I shouted. "Don't worry about me."

"Ye are daft," she said, but with the babe in her arms and people pushing between us, there was no space to argue.

I eased my way to the edge of the throng. There I drew a deep breath. Raw air filled my lungs. I meant only to breathe deeply before entering the stifling hold, but once free of the crowd, I knew I couldn't go below. I would die. Every sense that I possessed screamed at me to stay out of the vault. I didn't care if I was washed away. Anything was better than that cramped and suffocating darkness.

I pulled my blanket like a cloak around my shoulders. The squalls were coming faster now, pelting water across the deck. I stood out of sight in the shadow of the ladders to the upper decks and watched. As the last passengers descended, two crew members lifted the hatch cover. I had a moment, no more, to join the flock below, to claim my place among them.

I did not move.

The sailors heaved the hatch cover into place and secured it, then hurried to help their mates with the rigging. It was too late.

But I could not just stand there. The ship rocked from one side to the other. A wave crashed over the railing, and I tasted the salt-water. I wasn't far from the ropes I had tried before. I paused, remembering. Where were Hairy Hands and his friend now? But I hesitated only a moment. Only a terror as great as mine would make anyone choose such a bed this night. I scrambled across the deck, settled myself amid the ropes and braced against the storm.

Black, roiling clouds filled the sky. The wind intensified, roaring past the groaning masts and tearing at the sails, which had been furled and lashed tight against the spars. Huge waves slammed the ship. One after another crashed over the deck, drenching me. The cold set my teeth chattering. The ship heaved, and the pile of rope, with me in it, slid sideways. I grabbed for the ladder and hauled myself back.

Clearly, I had made a mistake. The wind slapped me with more fresh air than I could suck in and nearly tore me from my precarious shelter. The ship bucked against the waves, intent on dislodging me. I stared through the lashing rain at the hatchway where Peg, Mary, and the others lay in safety—miserable safety, but safety nonetheless.

Such thoughts were useless. I could only hold on and wait out the storm. I looped both arms around the ladder. The previous storm had lasted two days. It seemed unlikely I could last that long.

Between flashes of lightning I could see men hauling themselves along the railing, coiling ropes, reefing sails, and shouting. The swirl of activity made little sense as I concentrated on hanging on. My arms went to sleep, and I closed my eyes.

Suddenly, a heavy boot trod on my fingers. I squealed as much in surprise as pain.

The roaring wind drowned my shout, but a moment later a face appeared between the rungs of the ladder. "What in the name of God are ye doing out here? Ye are soaked to the skin, and it's a wonder ye havena' been washed away." Davy stared at me, his own curls darkened by the rain and plastered to his head.

My teeth were chattering too hard to answer.

He reached for me. "Come to me, lass. I'll see ye safe." He pried my stiffened fingers off the rough wood.

"Where are we to go?" I shouted. My arms tingled as the blood rushed back into them.

"Just come along," he shouted back. "I'll show ye."

He pulled me to my feet, and I stumbled forward. With one arm around my waist, and his free arm grasping one rung and then the next, Davy hauled me up the short ladder to the foredeck. My feet were as clumsy as blocks of wood, and my fingers only tingled. We made our way along the rail. Rain pelted my face, hard as small stones, and soggy tendrils of hair stung my eyes. A flash of lightning crackled across the clouds, silhouetting the dark shapes of the sailors heaving on lines and tying down ropes as if in a still life. A dozen steps took us near the bow where a smaller boat was tied down under a tarp. Beyond this lifeboat, the ship's bowsprit aimed toward the sky like a lance point as the ship climbed a huge wave. Then abruptly we dropped as if the bottom had fallen out. The ship plummeted into the slough between the waves. I fell to my knees. The next wave crashed over us, sweeping the deck clean of every scrap of clutter, carrying the chicken coop with it. Without Davy holding me tight, I would have been swept clear myself.

Davy loosened a corner of the tarp over the boat and hoisted me inside. He climbed in after me, and he tied the tarpaulin down again around us.

As suddenly as if chopped off by a cleaver, the cold rain ceased to beat upon us. I could hear it still, pounding on the oiled canvas tarp overhead, but now there was a barrier, thin though it may be, between me and the furious maelstrom.

"Did ye think ye were a selkie, to walk out on the water?" His anger startled me. "What kind of fool idea made ye stay on deck when the captain ordered all below?"

"You didn't go below." I was indignant. He could hardly accuse me of being a fool for doing the same as he did. "Nor did you the last storm."

"Did ye never think, lass, there's a wee bit of difference between the two of us?" His voice was thick with sarcasm. "I, for one, know the working of a ship and could help out the crew in a time like this. Yourself, on the other hand, ye canna' tell a sheet from a halyard and haven't even the sense to come out of the rain. What could ye do save get in the way?"

"I never got in anyone's way! No one even knew I was there until you came along."

"And no one would have seen ye washed overboard either. Just how long did ye think ye could hold fast to that ladder?"

I didn't answer. Outside, the rain pounded, and the wind howled. The small boat seemed a fragile bubble against such a force. I couldn't stop shivering.

"Not afraid are ye?" Davy took my hand, his anger gone.

"No," I lied. This ship seemed as frail as the insubstantial leaf and stick boats Elspeth and I set sail on the loch. Over and over we'd tried to make the boats stronger, but they always sank, tipped over by a wave. I couldn't help but think I was on such a boat now, with the same doom upon me. "I'm just cold." My teeth chattered as if to give the lie truth. I drew my knees up to my chest. I was soaked through and the wool cloak felt no warmer than gossamer.

"I'm sorry to berate ye so. Ye had no way of knowing what a storm like this can do." He shifted to give me more room. "Ye had best take off your wet things."

"What?" I squeaked. "I can't do that with you not six inches away."

"I'll not hurt ye. I give ye my word." He paused, then continued wryly, "And it's too dark to see ye in any case. Just take off your skirts and such and keep the cloak around ye. It's wet too, but the wool will warm ye better on its own."

He was right about the wool of course. Still, Mam's voice echoed in my head, reminding me over and over to never trust a man.

I shivered violently. Mam wasn't here, and it didn't matter if I could trust him or not. If I didn't do something, the cold would shake my bones loose from their joints. I tried to unclench my hands, but my fingers shook too much to untie the laces of my bodice.

"I . . . I canna' loosen them," I said after a moment.

"Let me help."

I sat very still, hardly breathing as Davy's fingers tugged at the wet, knotted laces. Davy's touch was firm, with the sureness of one used to such a task and the patience to see it done. His fingers trailed the line of my collarbone and brushed against my chest. Their warmth set a fire going in the pit of my belly. As he pulled off my bodice, the warmth spread upward, melting the ice coursing though my veins. Wordlessly, he helped me strip my wet shift over my head. I closed my eyes. If Davy McRae had the same idea now as Hairy Hands, there was naught I could, or would, do to stop him.

But he kept his word. I wrapped my bare body in the wet cloak, then lay against the ribs of the small boat. Davy took off his shirt, then pressed close, wrapping me tight in his arms to lend me the heat of his body.

For several minutes, we lay side by side, silent save for the muted roar of the wind. I stopped shivering as his breath warmed my ear, and his arms circled me and held me safe. The storm seemed very far away.

"Warmer, lass?"

The ship lurched sideways across the waves. Startled, I gasped and slid against a wooden support for one of the ship's benches.

Davy tightened his grip. He tucked the blanket more firmly under my chin. "Hush, lass. We're safe enough here for now. We've time for a story, aye? I'll tell you one. 'Tis not my first time crossing the ocean."

"Oh?"

"I was verra young my first voyage, not much above eight years. I wasn't a very good child, ye ken, with a great deal too much sass and not enough sense. It seemed everything I thought up to do one or the other of my parents took exception to. My father was no very pleased with my behavior in general. He still isn't, but that's another story."

I couldn't see his face, of course, with my back to him and the darkness around us, but I could imagine the wry smile accompanying that remark.

"When my father could not bear it any longer, he sent me away to my mother's brother in France. The ship was somewhat smaller than this bark, but steady enough and a real beauty. The minute I saw it, I was smitten. That ship, sleek on the water, called to me. It was late in the season though, and the weather turned rough the first day out. My stomach went queer. Ye will know what I mean about that."

I shuddered, remembering the wrenching seasickness of the first few days.

Davy shifted, pillowing his head on his arm. "The first night out, the wind screamed and bashed the ship, and the waves crashed against us. I was sure I would die, and I began crying. My bunkmate was a gray haired old codger. He'd been round the world more times than he could count, and he'd lost three fingers and an ear along the way. He jerked me up, shook me by the shoulder, and told me there was no sense in whimpering.

"'But . . . but . . . what if the ship sinks?' I asked him.

"'Do ye want to go to your Maker a sniveling babe or a man? Buck up, me lad. We're no going to die right now, but if I am wrong, and we do go down, all the tears in the world will no prevent it. Come along.' He dragged me on deck to face the wind with the spray washing over me.

"Shout it down, lad," he yelled in my ear. "Show what you're made of."

"And so I did. As I yelled and screamed at the wind, I forgot to be afraid. It's no very sensible." Davy shrugged. "But I would sooner take the storm head-on than any other way."

I imagined him there as a little boy, blown away if not for the old sailor beside him, a lad barely tall enough to see over the railing, eyes squinted against the wind, hair whipped back and a grin stretched across his face. Then I thought of him now, taller, standing against the wind on his own, the same wide open smile daring the world to show him what life had to offer.

"Still cold, lass?"

I shook my head. I was no longer cold with him so close, and though the storm still raged, my fear was gone too. "Just tired." The shivering had left me weak and exhausted.

"Lay your head a bit then. Morning will be here before ye know it."

CHAPTER 8

When I awoke, Davy was gone, and the drumming rain on the tarp over the lifeboat was gone as well. I wriggled into my wet gown and crawled from my shelter. The sun warmed the sodden deck with a steamy haze. I hurried to the middle deck, where the between-decks folk were just emerging. Peg, Mary, and the children were more joyful to see me than I imagined possible.

"I thought sure ye had washed away," Mary said.

"Maybe she's more selkie than not," Peg teased. "Did ye swim along the ship then, Callie? I thought sure ye would turn and swim the other way."

Leah tugged at my hand. "Are ye really a selkie? Like Mr. McRae was saying?" Her eyes shone with excitement.

"Nonsense. I'm no more selkie than you." I glared at Peg. "Some folks just run on and on and don't know what's good for them."

"Oho, and who's talking now about what's good for ye?" Peg put her hands on her hips like a scolding goodwife. "Staying out in the rain and thunder like ye were fish, not flesh."

I laughed with her, but my smile was forced. Peg was eager to tease me, but what would she say if she knew where, and with whom, I'd spent the storm? Even good-humored Peg would likely object to the man she meant to catch spending the night with me.

I didn't see Davy all day or the next, which was just as well. I wanted to thank him, but even thinking of his arms around me made my throat tighten. Finally, I realized it was best not to say anything. No one need ever know what had passed between us. He had saved my life. Surely my confused feelings were no more than profound gratitude. It was best to leave all thoughts of Davy McRae to Peg or some other willing lass. After all, he was going to work in the colonies and I was going back to Scotland.

Shipboard life returned to its dreary routine. Fair weather followed the storm. The sails luffed half empty in the meager breeze. Mary wrapped herself in a blanket of sorrow. Even Peg's ready smile was locked away, a sigh more likely to pass her lips than a laugh. The dark water sliding past the ship seemed the same water as the day before and the day before that. I paced the decks, but no amount of fretting moved us any faster.

Tension on board grew as the ship slowed. The sailors muttered about short rations and the guard on the water barrel was doubled. The captain's mood darkened. At least once a day he stormed out on deck to bark terse orders at the men and scowl at the freights.

"It's because he's lost his eggs for breakfast," Peg declared, watching him. "I know a hungry man when I see one." We sat near the center mast, Leah and I playing cat's cradle, Mary rocking the baby, and Peg, as usual, watching the sailors.

"He's hardly hungry," I protested with a hand on my own empty belly. "Sure the chickens are gone, but he still has his cook and three meals a day. We're the ones with something to complain of." Pease porridge every third or fourth day, and weevily biscuit between times did little to keep hunger at bay.

"He's out of temper because we're moving too slowly," Mary said. Then she sighed. "I can't say as I'm enjoying myself, and I know ye are anxious to see Philadelphia and turn around home again, Callie, but I'm no very keen to see this journey's end."

"Ach, Mary," Peg said. "Maybe it won't be so bad."

Mary gave her a wan smile. "Perhaps. Never mind me."

The afternoon gave way to evening. Mary and Peg took the children to their bunks before night fell, but I dawdled by the railing since I knew the hatch would stay open in such fair weather. It was tempting to spend the night on deck as several of the men did. But I gave up the plan with a sigh. Lucky as I'd been so far, I couldn't expect Davy McRae to turn up and rescue me if I ran into trouble again. Still I didn't go below until a myriad of stars dotted the sky.

By the time I went down, most folk had settled for the night. I moved slowly, feeling my way along the planks to my own berth. Leah was already wrapped in her cloak, fast asleep. I eased onto the straw tick without disturbing her.

I closed my eyes, but sleep did not come. An untuned concerto rising from the ragged breathing of so many souls wrapped in dreams buffeted my ears. I turned from side to side, trying to find a comfortable position, to no avail.

After awhile, some of the men came below. They spoke quietly as they passed my bunk, but made no real effort to soften their heavy footsteps rattling the plank walkway. Soon their snores joined the disharmonious medley. Not long after that another pair came down the ladder. So it went for an hour or so, until all who planned on sleeping in the relative comfort of their berths had come below, and those few who preferred the open air had found places on deck. Still I lay awake, rocked by the swaying of the ship.

Maybe an hour after the last of the passengers came below, I heard a new sound, a slow creak. Curious, I strained my ears, until the sound came again. It was not the hurried scrabbling of rats, or the solid thud of a man walking, but a slow sound, as a single foot upon a stair step. Someone was coming down the ladder, but so slowly, so quietly, as to remain unheard by the sleepers nearby. My heart thumped, irrationally alarmed. Why would anyone sneak into the open hold? I sat halfway up. The straw in my mattress rustled. The creaking stopped.

The darkness made it impossible to see anything beyond a shadow blocking the hatchway. The figure was clearly a man, not a monster. I lay back down. No need for fear. Had I gone so far from home I couldn't imagine a gentleman among the passengers, someone who only wanted to avoid disturbing his fellows' sleep?

After a minute, the figure continued his slow progress down the ladder and along the walkway. He took a step forward, then paused. His movements were too careful to wake anyone, but the measured pace irritated beyond belief. I wanted to scream, but I forbore. The man was only trying to be polite.

The steps stopped right beside me with a pause much longer than previous ones. Involuntarily, my eyes flew open. What was he waiting for? Just then he took two quick steps, carrying him beyond my berth to the next set of bunks. There he climbed to the top bed and joined the sleeper there.

A scuffling arose. For a moment, the two thrashed about. Then one of them coughed, and both were silent again. I smiled. His efforts to be quiet came to naught if he woke his companion so roughly. I could picture the two brothers who slept in that berth, Donal, a youth of sixteen or so, and Malcolm, in his twenties. I had seen them on deck often enough, playing cards or watching the game. Their parents, the Grants, slept in the berth below. Knowing it was one of the two, probably Malcolm, who came creeping in so late, put my mind at ease. Of course he would want to avoid waking his parents.

Not long after that I fell asleep, only to be wakened by a scream.

In the morning light spilling through the hatchway, Mrs. Grant stood on the edge of the lower berth. "My boy, my boy," she cried.

Her husband put his arm around her, his chest heaving with sobs he wouldn't release.

"What's happened?" I looked to Peg sitting beside Mary on the bunk opposite mine.

"Donal's dead," she said.

"Dead? I didn't know he had even been sick."

Peg shook her head. "He's been stabbed. Someone's just gone above to tell his brother."

"What?" I sat up straight. "Weren't they both in bed?"

Just then Malcolm came crashing down the ladder. "Donal? Where's my brother? What's happened?" His wail joined his mother's cries.

It couldn't have been Malcolm sneaking in last night. Seeing him now reminded me just how big and clumsy he was, like a bear, with overgrown arms and legs. I closed my eyes, recalling the shadow. A small, quiet man. I had only thought it was one of the Grant boys because of the bunk. But why kill Donal, a boy with a shy smile and not an enemy in the world?

The captain sent a mate to question those of us sleeping nearby, and I told of the figure I had seen creeping in the night.

"Why didn't you call out?" the mate demanded. His eyes narrowed in suspicion.

"How was I to know what was happening? Besides, yelling for help has never done me much good," I answered, remembering the racket I made my first night in the hold.

"Well you might have prevented murder, had you screamed like any reasonable female might have done."

The inquiry didn't take long. No one else had seen or heard anything. The mate questioned Malcolm, who swore he'd spent the entire night on deck and had a half dozen witnesses to back him.

"You could have slipped away, quiet like, when the others were sleeping," the mate suggested.

Malcolm reddened. "We didn't spend the time sleeping, sir. We had cards . . ."

Mr. Grant put his arm around his son and stared at the mate. "What cause could my son possibly have to kill his brother?" His voice was hard as steel. "You're no good to us trying to find the murderer in that direction."

The mate shrugged. "I'm not likely to find the murderer in any case." He turned his back on the forlorn Grant family and pushed past me to the ladder.

"Wait!" Another man caught the mate's arm. "If there's a murderer on the loose, you've got to protect us."

"If the freights want to go about stabbing each other in the night, there's not much I can do about it." The mate shook him off like a man flicking aside a fly. "So long as there are enough left of you to pay the passage, do as you like down here."

"But what are we to do?" the man insisted.

"Set a guard if you want," the mate said over his shoulder as he climbed the ladder.

After the mate finished his cursory investigation, I thought of Davy McRae. He had not been in his bunk, nor come down to see what the commotion was all about. And wasn't Davy a quiet man, who could move about the ship as he pleased?

I shook my head to drive away such ridiculous suspicions. I could not believe the man who had held me so gently in the storm could murder a boy.

Peg, Mary, and I helped the Grants prepare their son for burial at sea. We couldn't wash the body, but only wrap him in his sleeping blanket. Tension filled the hold. First one and then another's glance shifted toward Malcolm and then quickly slid away. I bent over Rabbie, as Mary stitched the blanket into a shroud.

"We ought to set up a watch," one man insisted. No one answered him. The grim, closed faces of the poor people who had slept and eaten together for six weeks now regarded each other suspiciously. How do you set a watch when the guard may be the murderer?

As with the other burials at sea, they pushed Donal into the ocean with little ceremony. Nearly everyone from below decks attended, but that seemed of little comfort to Mrs. Grant. She leaned against her husband, with Malcolm on her other side, three small bricks, trying to build a wall against a world determined to crush them.

No sooner was Donal in the water than Mr. Shakleton approached the Grants. He cleared his throat and spoke without apology. "The price of his passage will be added to your indenture."

"Why you cold-hearted, miserable excuse of a man." I spoke without thinking. "They've just lost their son."

"Hush, Callie." Mary pulled at my arm. "He's only telling the truth. It's in the papers."

"You!" Mr. Shakleton said, clearly recognizing me. "You did nothing to stop the murder. Doesn't that make you responsible? Maybe the cost should go on your indenture as well."

"My indenture? My indenture is a sham!" I started toward him, bent on clawing the smirk off his face, but Peg swung me around, and Mary stepped between us.

"Pay her no mind, sir," Peg said over her shoulder, as she dragged me away. "She's gone a bit batty with the shock of it all."

"What were ye thinking?" Peg said when she'd got me safe to the other side of the ship. "Did ye forget the man can have ye thrown in irons?"

Mary, a step behind, joined us at the railing and patted my arm. "Take a deep breath, Callie, and calm yourself. It'll do no good for the Grants or yourself, if ye start a ruckus now."

"Is it my fault?" I looked into the worried faces of the two closest friends I'd ever had. "I should have said something, stopped him somehow."

"Ye did nothing wrong," Mary insisted. "How were ye to know it werena' Malcolm?"

"Though I do wonder ye weren't more frightened," Peg added. "I'd have screamed for sure."

All day the talk was about Donal, and who might have killed him. Hushed conversations, in groups of two or three, with dark looks and lips closed tight should anyone come close. Again and again I heard Malcolm's name in the conversation, with some nodding and others shaking their heads. Someone thought to ask who had stayed out on deck. The question passed from group to group. Who had been absent from the hold when everyone went to sleep? And always the whisper, why Donal?

As they speculated, I thought back. The dark figure, the slow steps, the hesitation in the aisle beside me, the scrabbling in the bunk, and then the cough, cut off as the knife slit the poor boy's throat. And I had lain there, smiling, thinking it only a young man come late to bed.

Late in the afternoon, not long after Mary had gone below with Leah and Rabbie for a rest, the wind freshened. I could feel it in the way the ship glided through the water, like a horse straining at the bit. Sailors left off their endless deck scrubbing and polishing and scrambled about the rigging, fixing ropes and resetting sails. Peg stood with me at the railing watching.

"Is it a storm coming?" she asked anxiously. "I dinna' think I can stand another."

I studied the men working, though I had no understanding of why they did anything. Each seemed to know exactly how far to climb and what rope to knot or loosen and where to hold on for support. "One hand for the ship and one for yourself," Davy had said once, the first thing a sailor learned before he scrambled up the ratlines topside. The men worked hard, but without hurry. I scanned the horizon. To all sides the sky was clear, the ocean an undulating vastness before us, heaving and dipping like a pot of soup on the verge of boiling.

"I don't think so." I saw none of the frantic scrambling there had been with the last storm and the waves curled alongside the ship instead of crashing against us.

"Thank heaven for that." Peg ran her fingers through her tangled hair. "What I wouldn't give for a bit of a wash.'" She sighed. "I'll just have to do with combing it out again. Come on down, Callie. Mary will lend us her comb."

I shook my head. "Not just yet." I hated going below even a moment before I had to. "Look there." I pointed to the forward rigging. "Isn't that Davy McRae?"

"It's no use watching them now," Peg teased. "They're too far away for a good gander and too busy to give ye half an eye."

"Peg! What are you going on about?"

Peg shrugged impishly. "And why not? There's another lad or two among the sailors well worth the looking, including your Davy McRae."

"He's not mine, and I'm not looking."

"Verra sensible of ye." Peg nodded, still grinning. "I gave it up meself. That Davy McRae . . . he's an odd one, he is. I've not figured him out. And when I saw he had eyes for none but ye . . . well, best save the shopping for the colonies, that's what I've decided. I've no wish to be a sailor's wife with him off to sea all the time."

"Oh, Peg, I never meant . . . " I blushed, thinking about the storm. But she couldn't know. "Look, Peg. I'm not doing any shopping here or in Philadelphia. Have you forgotten I'm going back to Scotland?"

"Suit yourself." Peg waved my words away. "It's no matter to me, Callie. There's enough fish in the ocean, I'll not chase the one that's blind to me. Come on below now. Your hair needs brushing. Ye may not be looking for a man, but just in case ye change your mind, ye will want to keep it fine." She took my arm to pull me along.

I shook free. "Leave me alone, Peg. I'll be down in a bit." I didn't need her fussing over me like a nursemaid.

Peg left, and I went back to watching the sailors. Was she right that Davy McRae had been looking at me? Peg kept her eyes on such things, but she had a vivid imagination. Likely she had let it run away with her. I hadn't even spoken with Davy since the storm. He had been avoiding me, not courting me.

Peg was right about one thing. The sailors were too far away to see clearly, but I did enjoy watching them work. The smooth, well oiled process seemed like a dance in a theater, with the rigging the stage and the sailors the dancers. As I watched many of the men swung down out of the rigging, but the man I thought was Davy and another one were still high in the forward ratlines. It was Davy, for sure. His cap had blown off, and his hair blew back in the breeze. No one else on board had hair the color of brushed gold tinged in firelight.

The two men worked near each other, with no one else close to hand. Then I saw Davy was not working with the other man. They were struggling. Suddenly, Davy slipped and plunged toward the deck. I sucked in my breath. He spun once and then caught hold of the rigging.

I let my breath back out, but he was still not secure. Slowly, he righted himself and inched across the ropes toward a lower yardarm. The second man scrambled down the rigging toward Davy. He was a scruffy fellow, the one I'd seen lounging outside the captain's cabin when I had confronted him and Mr. Shakleton. He had black stubble on his face and mean, narrow eyes. He seemed bent on reaching Davy. The two men shouted toward each other, but the wind blew their words away from me.

Still high above my head, the scene suggested a puppet show with tiny marionettes. Only they weren't engaged in a puppet play, but a deadly struggle a hundred feet overhead.

Davy pulled himself to his feet before Scruffy got to him and balanced on the boom, hanging onto the thick ropes. Scruffy reached out to grab Davy. For a moment the two seemed frozen, then Scruffy overbalanced. Both men fell to their knees on the boom and teetered there. Davy locked his arm around the beam and Scruffy plunged head first off it. His scream pierced the wind, reaching my ears just as the man was abruptly swallowed by the ocean.

Davy scrambled to safety and shouted, "Man overboard," continuously as he descended to the deck. Hands rushed to the railing where Davy pointed, but I had seen the man's body smack the water and plunge deep. No one could have survived the fall. I turned away shaken, not just because I'd watched a man die, but because of how he had died. Just as Scruffy reached out, Davy grabbed his hand and jerked. Self-defense wasn't murder, of course. Davy had no choice. But why had they been fighting? Clearly Davy McRae was not the simple storyteller he seemed.

Death aboard ship was hardly surprising, but two such violent deaths in one day left me shaken. No one else had seen the struggle and it was quickly apparent that the crew assumed it was an accident. A boy was sent up top to scan the water for signs of the man, and a dozen crewmembers lined the railings to search. The captain gave no order to turn back, or even reef the sails and slow down. I shuddered at the thought of the drowned man, abandoned to his fate. And once I had expected the captain to turn around for me! When it was apparent they would not find the body, I went below to join Mary and Peg and the children.

"They hardly even tried to find him," I complained after describing what happened.

"And why should they?" Peg said reasonably. "Sure if he's dead, they'd just slide him back in again." She patted the bunk beside her. "Sit a minute, Callie. I'll comb your hair."

Mary leaned against the bulkhead, nursing wee Rabbie. "There's nothing ye can do about it," she said without opening her eyes. "Dinna' waste your time fretting."

I looked from one to the other: Peg, too excited about her own plans to worry about a stranger's death, and Mary, too practical and too weary to worry about a man already dead. In the berth past ours, the Grant family lay silent now, after a day of spilling all their tears. Beyond them moaned a whole cargo of folk so wrapped in their own miseries and fear they couldn't find space to care about one more death. I sat on the plank, my back to Peg. I let down my hair without saying any more. They had trouble enough of their own.

The last bit of daylight was fading when Davy came down the ladder to join us. He brought our rations and handed out biscuit to Mary and the children first.

"It's Mr. McRae!" Leah scooted off the bunk to greet him. Then she turned shy, put her hands behind her back and looked down at the plank walkway. "Where have ye been?"

"Leah," Mary said sharply. "That's no polite question to be worritin' Mr. McRae about."

Davy put his arm around Leah. "Sure, Mrs. Rawles, it's no bother." He passed a ship biscuit to each of us and pulled Leah onto his lap. "I've been helping the sailors, ye know, but it's no matter now. I'm back."

"Why?" Leah asked.

"Hush," Mary scolded. "Don't be impertinent."

Davy waved away her objection and jiggled the little girl on his lap. "Ye are sure ye won't be frightened?"

Leah shook her head.

Davy spoke in a stage whisper, sending shivers up my spine. "I couldn't leave all these women alone in here with the nuckelavee."

"What's that?" Leah asked.

"Ye have never heard of a nuckelavee?" In the dim light of the lantern

I saw Davy's eyebrows raised in mock surprise. "Well, I'll tell ye. It's a fearsome creature with a huge head and a great tusked mouth like a pig. He's always hungry for human flesh."

Leah sucked in her breath.

"He lives in the sea, but he's not like the selkies. He's got no skin at all, just muscles and yellow veins. He's very strong, and his breath is poison."

Peg's hand, pulling the comb through my hair, stopped. "Is that what killed poor Donal?"

"Could be," Davy said. "Though I think the nuckelavee missed his mark with that one."

"That's ridiculous." I took the comb from Peg and finished the stroke myself. "It's just a story, Peg."

"We've missed your stories, Mr. McRae," Mary said. "Come here now, Leah, and hold your brother while I eat."

We were all silent while she settled the baby in Leah's lap. Davy climbed onto his bunk above Mary and stretched out.

Leah's clear voice broke the silence. "With so many monsters about, Mr. McRae, however could ye stay away so long?"

"Ah well." Davy's disembodied voice floated down to us. "With such a monster after me, I thought it best to avoid the crowded hold. It's hard to watch my back in the dark down here."

Peg laughed, as if he were telling another story, but my mind raced. That explained the struggle on the boom. And what of Donal Grant? The nuckelavee had missed his mark, Davy said. Did he mean the murderer had been after him? I remembered the figure's hesitation. Davy slept in the bunk above Mary, opposite mine. Perhaps the murderer had killed the wrong man.

"Is someone really trying to kill ye, Mr. McRae?" Mary said sharply. "'Tis no joking matter."

"Ye are right, sure enough." Davy leaned out of his berth to look at her. "And I'll ask your pardon, Mrs. Rawles, for making light of it."

"Can ye no go to the captain and tell him you're in danger?" Mary continued.

"That might be a bit awkward as the man that wants me dead is a particular friend of the captain." Davy looked across at me and winked. "Ye'll remember the captain has a wee temper on him. He would likely not thank me for saying his friend is attempting murder."

"Someone's still after you?" My voice was sharp with worry. "I thought . . . " I stopped, not wanting to talk about what I'd seen. "Do you know who it is?"

"Oh aye," Davy answered my question evenly. "Our good Mr. Shakleton, who hoodwinked ye."

"Mr. Shakleton?" Peg said. "But ye work with him. At least, Callie says so."

"My father works with him," he corrected Peg with the first hint of anger I'd ever heard in his voice. "He's no need of me, nor I of him."

"It wasn't Mr. Shakleton here in the hold last night." I could have added it wasn't Mr. Shakleton on the boom either. Was Davy here to protect us, or because he no longer need worry?

Davy turned to stare at me intently, his amber eyes piercing all the barriers I put up. I sank into his gaze, ready to believe anything he said. Then he nodded so slightly I wondered if I had imagined it, and his careless smile returned.

"Our Mr. Shakleton had no wish to dirty his own hands. No, the man has deep pockets and there's more than one fellow aboard this ship will do a job for gold or silver, without worrying what the job is." He lay back on the bunk, the straw rustling beneath him. "But there's better stories to tell." His voice floated down from the darkness. "Have ye heard the story of Janet and how she saved Tam Lin from the fairy queen?"

Three days later, Peg's grey eyes glittered with excitement as she joined me at the railing. "Have ye heard what they're saying?"

I didn't turn round. I had slept little following poor Donal's murder. Restless shifting and turning in the night proved I was not the only one concerned with keeping watch. But knowing others kept their own vigils did not lesson my worries nor my suspicions of Davy McRae. Unexpectedly he continued to spend nights in the bunk above Mary's, though I couldn't say if he slept or not. In any case, I was too tired to muster enthusiasm for Peg's latest tidbit of gossip.

"Callie, are ye listening?" Peg grabbed my arm. "We're nearly there. They're saying we'll be in Philadelphia tomorrow. Dry land, Callie. Can ye believe it?"

I scanned the horizon, stretching flat and hazy beyond the bow of the ship, where an empty, undulating ocean met an empty, endless sky. It was hard to believe we were nearing the end of the long journey away from home. "Is it true?" I asked. Was it possible that tomorrow, finally, I would find someone with both the sense and the authority to help me go home?

"Aye, 'tis true enough; tomorrow or the day after." Davy came up behind us, his step as silent as the fairy folk in his tales.

"Good lord," Peg gasped, putting a hand to her throat. "Ye have scared the daylights out of me, sneaking up like that."

Equally startled, I turned to face him. His tawny eyes were shadowed, unreadable.

"Your pardon." He bowed without smiling. "Have ye thought what ye will do on the morrow when we dock, Sally MacLaughlin?"

The question and the name we both knew as false caught me unprepared. Leave it to Davy McRae to bring up the uncomfortable subject.

"Not that ye need my advice of course, but I suggest ye wait to make your plight known until ye have been hired out."

Mr. Shakleton had threatened to have me thrown in jail, but surely there were laws in this colony. Or did his power extend so far? What did Davy know that I didn't?

I looked past Davy to a pair of gulls circling in the distance, white specks against a pale blue sky. How I longed for the freedom they had.

"As I see it," Davy went on, "ye have only two options. Ye can wait until your indenture is bought by some merchant, tell him of your troubles, and pray he'll see fit to help ye." He turned to face me. "The other is to come away with me, and see what chance will bring."

"Come away with you?" I repeated, confused. What preposterous scheme was this?

"I ken both choices are a mite chancy, but ye have no knowledge of your future master, and ye do know me, at least a bit."

"This is no joking matter," I sputtered. "How can you help me home?"

"Wait, Callie." Peg took my arm. "He's not joking. He's offering to buy your indenture. Aren't ye, Mr. McRae?" She flicked a look in his direction, but raced on before he could answer. "It's a perfect solution, Callie. Do ye not see? 'Twill solve everything."

"Buy me? Is that what you mean?" I choked with outrage. "How dare you? You know I've signed no indenture papers." I spun away.

He blocked my escape. "That's not exactly what I had in mind." A half smile crinkled the corner of his mouth. "Ye are worth far more than I can pay. But I am proposing to help."

Proposing, was it? His proposal was remarkably lacking in detail. "You expect me to run away and hide from the law until you figure out some way to help me?"

"Did none of those gentlemen ye spoke of tell ye how pretty ye are, lass? Better to hide from the law with me than to have to hide from your new master."

"What?" Peg had hinted at the same thing. My cheeks burned as I understood his implication. How dare he suggest such a thing! Words failed me. I raised my hand to slap him.

He caught it in mid swing.

Blindly furious, I swung with my left hand.

He caught that one too and held it, his long, calloused fingers encircling both wrists. "I'm no suitor in your grandfather's parlor, lass," he said.

I struggled to twist free of his grip.

"I'll not stand idly by while ye have your wee tantrum at my expense. If ye don't want my help, ye have only to say so, and I'll leave ye be."

"I don't want your help," I said through clenched teeth.

"Ahh." Davy let go so suddenly I would have fallen, had he not caught me again to steady me. "Ye dinna' want it, do ye say?"

I jerked free. This time he let go without a word. I stumbled toward the hold, rubbing my sore wrists.

"Wait, Callie. Ye are making a mistake," Peg trotted after me.

That's just what Mam had said when I left Grandfather's house. I faltered, then squared my shoulders and went on. I had run off from Grandfather's house in a temper. Running off with Davy McRae would be just as foolish. I wasn't going to make the same mistake again.

Below decks, Mary was nursing Rabbie. She clucked unsympathetically when I told her. "Ye have only yourself to blame. He'd never have hurt your poor wrists if ye hadn't gone to hit him first." She closed her eyes and prayed silently, mouthing the words in fierce determination.

Leah scooted up beside me right away, chattering away, totally oblivious to my problems. "Mam says we'll get off the ship tomorrow," she chirped. "And I'm to wear my good dress, what's been waiting in the trunk for me."

"Not now, Leah," I said, but Leah's brightness stopped me. I looked from the child's open smile to her mother's haunted face and suddenly realized why Mary saw fit to pray so hard the day before we docked. Leah was awfully young to be sold away as a servant, but there were four passages to pay for and only Mary able to give a full day's work. I pulled Leah close and hugged her hard, my anger at Davy forgotten. I would find a way home once we docked and my problems would be solved. But Leah's were only starting.

We ate a cold supper of hard bread and sour water on deck. By evening a shadowy smudge darkened the horizon. Gradually it grew to a dark smear, dividing sea and sky with the promise of land. The breeze from the shore hinted of trees. Men crowded the railings, and women stood in clumps, looking forward, toward the setting sun, where all our futures lay.

Before the orange twilight disappeared, one of the mates shooed everyone down. "Captain's orders. Can't have anyone jumping ship to cheat the factor of payment for passage."

"If I could swim," I protested, "I would have leapt into the sea the first day out!"

"No exceptions." The sailor shrugged.

Not far away, Davy sat on an empty crate with a few other men who had paid their own passage. He had his fife to his lips, playing snatches of tunes I didn't know. He hesitated as the sailor hustled me along. I'm sure he saw me, but after a pause, he went on playing.

The last night I spent in the hold was as dark and sleepless as the first, filled with the sounds of ship, familiar by now; the creaking boards, the slap of wet rope against the mast, the scurrying of rats in the darkness. One by one the others drifted into sleep. The dry, broken straw in the mattress Mary had stuffed for me weeks earlier pricked through the worn ticking. The hours dragged on and on. From time to time a child cried in his sleep, and the deep voice of his father whispered some comfort.

With none to whisper comfort in my ear, I lay wrapped in my own jumbled thoughts. As the night wore on, my confidence that all would be well slipped away, along with my anger at Davy. I replayed the exchange over and over. Maybe he hadn't meant to mock me and truly knew a way to help. I should have listened to him. I sighed. I couldn't change what I'd said, but I could apologize in the morning.

Still, I couldn't sleep. It was long past midnight when an unfamiliar sound caught my attention. A muffled bump, followed by a scraping sound, repeated at intervals, as if boxes or crates were being shifted. The ship rocked gently in the water, with the sails reefed and fluttering in an errant breeze. There was no storm to shift the cargo. Yet the more I strained my ears, the more it made me think of something being unloaded.

Who would think to unload cargo in the dark before we docked? The bumping and scraping went on for over an hour, ebbing at times, but never growing louder than the stealthy shifting sounds I first heard. Finally, the noise stopped altogether, leaving me wondering if I had dreamed it.

Part 2

Necessary Fiction

Philadelphia, May 1754

CHAPTER 9

I did not intend to sleep through our arrival as I had slept through our departure, so I did not sleep at all. Come morning, my eyes felt as if they had weights attached to them, and my head ached from exhaustion. I watched the light leaking through the hatchway grow from the shadows of dawn to the warm glow of morning. By the time the sailors lifted the cover, I was ready to go.

Climbing out of the hold, I smelled land even before I saw it. A gusty breeze off the shore blew away all trace of tangy salt air, bringing ripe whiffs of human habitation. I paused to close my eyes and breathe in the rich green smell of rampant vegetation mingled with the brackish odor of river water. My heart thumped with the anticipation of help near at hand.

"Go on with ye," Peg urged from the ladder behind me. "Can ye see the land?"

I stepped on deck and looked shoreward. Then looked again! Philadelphia was not the backward, savage village in the wilderness I had imagined. It was a metropolis that rivaled Edinburgh. The city sprawled along the flat plain, gently sloping upward along the west bank of the broad, smooth Delaware River. Overhead, throngs of squealing gulls circled and dove for fish and scraps. Dozens of ships of every shape and size plied the harbor. Great three-masted, square rigged, oceangoing brigs like ours plowed doggedly forward, while sleek single-masted sloops, sails bellied full, zigzagged between them like swallows in the wind. In blunt-bowed, flat-bottomed scows, seamen with thick, sun-darkened arms slapped oars against the rippling water as they crisscrossed from bank to bank, hauling men, horses, and goods.

One of these rowboats, manned by six of the blackest men I had ever seen, scraped up along side of us. With a practiced efficiency two of the men nearest our ship took hold of a couple thick towropes hanging from the railing, while the three oarsmen on the opposite side of the skiff feathered their oars and held them ready. A frock-coated gentleman stood in the bow. "Ahoy," he called to our captain. "Do you need a pilot?"

"Is that you, Jack?" the captain called down. "What are you charging these days, you scurvy-eyed thief?"

I paid little heed to the following quick exchange and the ensuing flurry of activity as ropes were thrown and made fast, and sails furled one by one. The mates bellowed at the sailors, who scrambled along the rigging, lowering sails and tying off the lines, but I looked toward shore where dozens of ships lay at anchor. Numerous wharves jutted into the water, and beyond the wharves rose the city with a myriad of buildings in row upon row, stretching further than I could see. Some of these buildings, especially those near the water, were simple one- and two-story wooden structures, but most of the edifices rose three and four stories high and were built of red brick. Above them all, four slender spires pierced the clear blue sky, reaching toward the heavens as if the inhabitants would declare their intention to touch the Almighty. My spirits rose. Here was burgeoning civilization, a place I could reasonably expect help.

With the pilot guiding, the captain eased our ship up to a dock. A pair of deck hands swarmed over the rail, trailing heavy ropes, which they looped around massive posts to hold the ship fast. Without delay, the crew slammed the gangplank down on the dock and lines of men began the arduous task of hauling out stores. One row of heavily laden men carried the goods to the dock and a return row filed back empty-handed onto the ship to get the next load.

There were many things I expected when we reached the colonies: a hot bath, a decent meal, a change of clothes. Most of all I expected something to happen. In all respects, I was disappointed. For a good deal of time, not much of anything happened. The passengers who had places arranged and passage paid for, disembarked. The rest of us - the freights - gathered together in the middle of the main deck. The men and boys over eighteen were taken off to the city hall, to swear allegiance, while the women scrambled to gather their things, calling sharply to the children to keep close.

I gathered my own meager belongings. My feet were bare, my slippers having fallen to rags several weeks earlier. I had only the dress on my back, thin and bleached nearly colorless by the sun, my shawl, and the blanket from Davy. I ought to return that, I decided, remembering my vow to apologize for my temper. We could part without yesterday's harsh feelings. I looked around. The deck was crowded with sailors and passengers, but nowhere could I see his cedar gold hair. I realized I hadn't seen him all morning.

"Where's Davy?" I asked Peg.

She stood at rail, her bundle at her feet, her smile lighting the freckled face. She had put on a clean dress and combed her hair with Mary's comb. "He'll have gone ashore with paid passengers, will he not? Did he no say goodbye to ye?" Her face clouded over a moment in worry, but then she smiled again. "It's no matter, as the two of ye couldn't quite see eye to eye."

I didn't tell her there had been no quarrels under the tarp during the storm, only the warmth of his breath on my cheek. I tried to shake off my regrets. I could hardly blame him for being too angry with me to want to say goodbye. I folded up the blanket with my shawl inside and went to borrow the comb from Mary.

Then we waited. We had been near six weeks at sea, I counted, so it couldn't be past the beginning of May. But the sun overhead quickly grew as hot as midsummer in Edinburgh. The patch of shade cast by the afterdeck midship grew smaller. After an hour or so, the men returned. We went on waiting. The excitement of the morning evaporated, leaving a silent, restless crowd. Children whined, and women hushed them. Men wiped their sweaty brows with their shirtsleeves. After enduring weeks of cold Atlantic wind, none of us were ready for the heat of the sheltered harbor.

Finally, near noon, Mr. Shakleton, wearing a crisp, clean frock coat and a powdered wig, approached the group in mincing steps, strutting like a rooster in a chicken yard, as fine as any barrister on High Street. He had a cabin to wash in and clean clothes to freshen up. No such luck for the rest of us. I would have settled for a pail of fresh water, though I'm not sure if I would have drunk it or poured it over my head to cool off first. Unfortunately I was not given the opportunity for either.

Mr. Shakleton cleared his throat to get everyone's attention, then spoke in his nasal voice. "Prospective employers will be arriving within the hour. They will inspect you, discuss the terms of your indenture, and purchase your papers from me. If you have any questions, I shall be stationed there." He pointed to a makeshift desk he'd had set up in the shade of the fore deck, a bare plank stretched across a couple of barrels. He perched on his stool behind the desk, patting his brow with a large handkerchief.

I took a step toward him. I had a lot of questions, first and most important, how dare he sell me into some service? But the captain was still on board. I thought uncomfortably of the irons or jail cell awaiting a stowaway, and so I kept silent. I would wait, as Davy suggested, and tell the purchaser of my indenture about the terrible mistake. I would promise that Grandfather would clear up the whole matter as soon as a letter could be sent home. I only needed patience, and hadn't I been practicing patience for weeks now?

Peg jostled my elbow. "Pinch your cheeks a bit, Callie," she said, doing the same to her own. "Ye will want to look fresh and strong and healthy for any handsome gentleman who casts his eye on ye."

"I'll do no such thing!" I objected.

Peg coyly tucked a curl under her cap. "Better service to a handsome gent than some old biddy who'll stick ye all day long in a hot kitchen."

Mary, meanwhile, was arguing with the first pair of gentlemen to board the ship. She never raised her voice, but from the tight hold she kept on Leah and the fierce look in her eyes, I knew she was making some sort of demand. As I moved closer to eavesdrop, the gentlemen frowned at each other, shrugged, and walked away.

"What was that all about?" I asked Mary.

"They wanted me alone and offered to find a different place for the two bairns." Her voice trembled. "Oh Callie, I don't know what I'll do if they take my children from me." She pressed her knuckles to her lips to hold back her sob.

"Hush, Mary." I patted her arm. "You've held your own so far. No one can take the bairns away."

"Aye, they can, if there's none to buy the three of us. Mr. Shakleton can dispose of us as he sees fit."

"Surely not," I protested, but there was no conviction in my words. Mr. Shakleton would have no qualms at separating them.

I meant to stay close to Mary, offering what little support I could, but the hours dragged on. All afternoon, men alone or in pairs came aboard the ship, chatted with Mr. Shakleton for a time, looked us over and either took one of us away or left alone. Most dressed plainly, as merchants, with cheap, powdered wigs moistened by sweat.

Late in the afternoon, Peg left with a grin and a wave. She followed a middle-aged man. His hair, pulled back and tied at the nape of his neck, was unpowdered. He looked pleasant enough, but I wondered how she could be so sanguine, knowing nothing about him.

The dull hours wore on, and I daydreamed. Suddenly a shadow blocked the sun. A tall man, lean and angular like a crane, loomed over me. He had a long face, made longer by his sloping forehead and narrow chin thrust forward like a beak.

"Sally MacLaughlin." He took off his hat and then his wig, not as a gesture of politeness, but to mop at the sweat dripping off his forehead. He revealed a head as bald and sloping as an egg. "I am Samuel Asher. I have purchased your indenture and will have your service for the next seven years." His mouth was a slash across the face, wide with thin lips. The narrow line of his eyebrows curved downward toward a sharp nose, and small black eyes glittered below, measuring me.

I crossed my arms across my chest. I had wrapped my shawl up in Davy's blanket, but now I wished I had kept it on in spite of the heat. His lips curved upward slightly, as if attempting a smile, but not quite achieving it.

"Sir," I began with a curtsey as smooth as I could manage barefoot on the rough ship's decking. "There has been a mistake."

"Is that so?" He did not raise his voice, but I felt more threat from him than from all the blustering, angry men I had known. I shivered in the sudden chill, and held my tongue. This was not the moment to demand I be allowed to write a letter to Grandfather.

Mr. Asher turned away abruptly, and a second man took my elbow. He had the same angular build as the first, but was unlike him in every other way. This man's skin glowed with a healthy redness instead of the jaundiced yellow the older man had, and his chin, though pointed, was not thrust forward. Dark curls softened the planes of his face.

"Ethan." The older man spoke sharply over his shoulder. "Take our Sally to the house and give her to Mistress Asher. Don't dawdle."

"Come along, Sally. My father will settle with Mr. Shakleton." A handsome man, about thirty, Ethan looked to be a gentleman.

He was the one to help me, I decided. I turned to take my leave of Mary but found I had nothing left to say, no words of advice or comfort to offer. I hugged her hard.

"God go with ye," she said, swiping at the tears filling her eyes.

"And with you," I replied in a voice thick with feeling. I pulled Leah toward me and hugged her tightly. Then I straightened my shoulders and followed Ethan down the gangplank. I did not look back.

"Sir," I began as soon as we stepped onto the dock, but he was already talking.

"You must be tired after such a journey. We've a wagon just at the end of the pier. It's not far." He offered me his arm to steady myself as my legs wobbled on the unfamiliar dry land.

"You've no idea," I said fervently.

He put a hand on the small of my back, and I stiffened. Gentleman or no, I saw no reason to permit such familiarity. I turned to berate him.

His wide, guileless smile radiated warmth and welcome. His eyes shone with innocent candor.

"I'm not Sally MacLaughlin," I said instead of the rebuke I had intended. "It's all been a terrible mistake."

"Oh?" He lowered his eyebrows in a perfect imitation of his father, but the effect on him was comical, not sinister. "Come along out of this crowd and tell me about it." He guided me firmly through the mass of sailors and dock men crowding the pier to a busy thoroughfare running along the shore. There, as promised, stood a wagon filled with crates and hitched to a sleek brown mare. Ethan helped me into it, then climbed up beside me on the seat and taking up the reins, clucked to the horse. "Now, tell me what's happened." He listened without interrupting as I explained my hasty and unplanned departure from Leith.

As I spoke, the horse carried us up the dusty street, congested with wagons, carts, and horses. Pedestrians jostled each other along flagstone walks running along either side of the wide, unpaved streets. Swarms of flies buzzed around piles of trash dumped at street corners and alleyways

Ethan shook his head in dismay as my story unfolded. He guided the mare onto a quieter street without sidewalks. No more than a half dozen pedestrians stepped between a few carriages and wagons along the beaten earth.

When I had finished, Ethan rested a reassuring hand on my knee. "I think it best we not tell Father." He held up his hand to stop my protest. "Leave it to me. You saw the man. He has a terrible temper when he believes he's about to be cheated, and he's dull as a doorpost about listening to reason. I'll fetch paper and pen for you tonight, and we'll have a letter to your grandfather by the morrow. Then it's only a matter of sending it across the ocean and waiting for the reply."

"And how long will that take?" I asked in a small voice. It meant months to cross the ocean and return. What would I do in the meantime?

"No need to worry." He squeezed my knee in comfort. "You have a place to stay with us, and I'm sure we'll be hearing from your grandfather as soon as possible."

I slumped, discouraged. It would be weeks before I could go home.

But my protector had thought of that too. "We'll go on as if you were indeed Sally MacLaughlin, for you see . . . " There was a slight hesitation as if he were searching for the right word. "Mistress Asher will be even less helpful than Father."

Mistress Asher? Not Mother?

In less than ten minutes, we crossed a stone bridge over a creek, then turned again and went on another hundred yards along the dirt road. Ethan drove the wagon past two square Georgian style homes to the third, a three-story brick house with white wood trim on the windows and doors. Ethan took us around back to the stable. A small yard, mostly given over to a neglected kitchen garden, sloped downward to a line of trees at the far edge. In one corner near the trees stood a shed I took to be the necessary. We stopped by the stable door.

Ethan held the reins in one hand and took my hand in his other. "You look to be a strong girl," he said quietly. "Can you manage the part of a servant while we sort this out? Father will surely see reason best when the payment is in his hands."

I did not want to be Sally any longer. I did not want to be anyone's servant. I did not want to wait. A wave of loneliness washed over me. I missed Peg and Mary and even Davy. They had been strangers only a few weeks before, and even though none had been able to help me back home, each had befriended me and offered some comfort. But not real help. Ethan offered something more tangible. For the first time since I'd left home, here was a man who said he knew a way to get me back. All he asked in return for his promise was a little more patience. I sighed. Patience did not come easily to me. "Yes, I suppose I can play the part," I said.

Ethan rewarded me with another of those wide, warm smiles and patted my hand. "Good girl." He jumped down and tied the horse to a hitching post. Then he took my small bundle and offered me a hand down. I stumbled, still not used to land, and he put his arm around me. "Steady."

I took a deep breath, then took up my bundle and followed him in the back door. This opened into a dark hallway bisecting the house, leading to the front door and the foot of a stairway. We didn't go that way, however, but turned and went through a doorway on the right into the kitchen, which was stiflingly hot. Two young women near my own age stood before a long wood table, rolling out lumps of dough. Both were covered in flour and wore long white aprons and mob caps, but there the resemblance ended, for one was short, with a round face and white skin as pasty looking as the dough she worked, and the other had dark hair and a long, slender face. Ethan paid no attention to either of the girls, but pushed me in front of the third woman, older and obviously the mistress of the house, even though the sleeves of her dress were rolled up past the elbow and she sat shelling beans. She was a heavy woman, her ample girth dwarfing the stool on which she sat. Sweat darkened patches of her dress and beaded her lip.

"This is Sally." Ethan kissed the woman on the cheek. "She's to replace Cora."

I didn't like the idea of replacing anyone. I turned to protest, but Ethan was already striding away.

With a little yelp, I started after him, but stopped myself. I had agreed to try Ethan's idea. I could hardly count it honest if I gave it up before starting.

I turned back to the large woman. She raised an eyebrow at my reaction to Ethan's departure.

"Sally, is it?" she said, almost humming. "And was it Mr. Asher or young Ethan who picked you out?"

The dark, slender girl giggled at this, but the doughy one blushed even redder than the heat of the kitchen had made her.

Mistress Asher smiled too, displaying blackened, crooked teeth. She waggled her paring knife at me. "I'll just warn you once, Sally. You best not take over where Cora left off."

With this ominous, if rather vague, warning, she set me to work in the kitchen chopping cabbages for the soup. Young Ethan, as they had called him may have had it in mind for me to rest awhile, but he had not told Mistress Asher his idea and she shared no such plans.

If I thought my arrival in Philadelphia would bring a change in my situation for the better, I did not keep up the delusion for long. The darker, slender girl, Lydia, handed me her rolling pin and left the kitchen. I took over her job along with the plump, fair-haired girl, whose name, I learned, was Chloe. We filled a half dozen pies with minced meat and dried apples. Then Mistress Asher sent me out to bring in more wood for the fire and sent Chloe upstairs to take care of the boys. The boys, it seemed, were a pair of toddlers, who had been napping when I arrived. With Mistress Asher's constant instructions, I chopped onions, managed the fire, and stirred the pot simmering over it. Supper was a hot, thick porridge, but it seemed my part was to serve while the family ate and only later when all were through was I allowed a bowlful. Late that evening Chloe came through the kitchen with a baby boy on each hip, looking for a bedtime sweet.

I stopped her before she could rush out again. "Is there any place I can clean up?"

She stared at me for a moment, looking as surprised as if the cat had just spoken. "You want to wash, is that it?"

"Yes, please. I've been on that awful ship for weeks."

"There's a basin and a rag in the corner there. You're welcome to dip some water from the well in the yard. Mama's likely told you to bring in a bucketful for the morning in any case."

Mistress Asher had not told me that, but I took up Chloe's suggestion. When night fell, it turned out my bed was to be the floor of the kitchen. At least with the embers of the fire still glowing and the heat of the day trapped in the kitchen, I wasn't cold. Still I wrapped myself up in the blanket from Davy. The thick wool softened the hard floorboards a bit.

It seemed I had no sooner closed my eyes than I felt the hard toe of a boot in the small of my back

"What bundle of lazy bones do we have here?" Mistress Asher scolded. "You should have been up an hour ago, getting the fire going and the porridge started. The master does not like to wait on his breakfast."

I sat up and rubbed my eyes, groggy with sleep. The windows were still shuttered but I saw sunlight through the cracks along the edges.

"What is going on here? Where is my breakfast, Wife?" Mr. Asher demanded, his crane-like frame filling the doorway. He scowled. "It's near 8:00 and the dining room is dark and empty."

Mistress Asher shrugged and threw up her hands. "It's no good asking for it now. This girl you've bought hasn't a lick of sense or an ounce of work in her."

She spoke with her back to him busily stirring up the fire to make up for my laziness, and her tone was complaining. But I could see her face. A delighted gleam flashed in her eyes, and a nasty smile cut across her face. In spite of her blackened teeth she had once been very pretty. Clearly she was much younger than her husband.

There had been no time to get dressed. Having slept in my shift, I stood with Davy's blanket wrapped like a cloak about me. Mr. Asher eyed me up and down with the same lecherous stare he'd given me at the pier. He took a step toward me, as if to help me, but I think he had it in mind to tear the fabric from my hands. I stepped back.

Mistress Asher stirred the fire so vigorously it sent up a cloud of ashes.

Mr. Asher retreated, coughing. "I'll eat in the tavern this morning."

After he had gone, Mistress Asher let the smile drop. She glared at me. "I've warned you. Don't take that lightly."

I did not intend to. Mr. Asher clearly had a roving eye, and Cora had been in his sights. But I had done nothing and had nothing to answer for.

I would not fall in Mr. Asher's path. I folded up the blanket and set it in the corner, then pulled on my skirt and laced up the bodice. The seam on the side tore a little more. If I didn't get something to wear soon, I would be tempting Mr. Asher in my shift day and night, willy-nilly.

After everyone had eaten breakfast, the next task was scrubbing the dishes, a great pile of them. Nearly every plate, platter, trencher and pot in the house was dirty. Apparently, scrubbing dishes had been Cora's job, along with the morning fire. As Lydia said with a shrug, "No one else saw fit to do it. Except Chloe there." She nodded at the round young woman who sat in the rocker, nursing one of the boys. "And she's about as much use as a three day old dumpling."

Mistress Asher laughed and slapped a hand against a thick thigh. "That's my dumpling," she cackled. "Three days old and still wet and doughy."

Chloe's milky white face turned pink. She did not laugh.

It was hard to sort out who was who in this house. I could see Mistress Asher was in charge, at least of the kitchen, and Chloe looked so much like her anyone would assume her to be a daughter, even if she had not spoken of Mama. So then who was Lydia? I had thought her to be a servant at first, but she ate with the family, and no servant would make such jokes about the daughter, not if she wanted to keep her position. In addition to the three women in the house, there were the two baby boys, and three men. Mr. Asher and his son, Ethan, had both been at the docks. Another young man, named Tom, had been at the table the night before, though I had been too tired to take much notice of him, and he had not spoken to me.

I was even more confused the next minute. Mistress Asher had one of the two babies on her lap, playing piggy toes with him, but as soon as he started fussing, she stood up abruptly. "Here, Chloe. What is taking so long? Don't let Jeb be such a greedy bastard."

Chloe colored again, clearly embarrassed. Gently, she pried the little one from her breast. The baby cried once in protest, but like Chloe he seemed used to this arrangement. Mistress Asher handed her the second baby, and she began nursing him. The boys were nearly identical, I realized, dressed in plain white shifts. Twins? But clearly this boy was Mistress Asher's favorite. Instead of picking up poor Jeb and playing with him, she left him on the floor at Chloe's feet.

Chloe finished nursing before I finished scrubbing the pots, but Mistress Asher stopped me. "Lydia's going to take you to market now and show you what we need," she told me.

Lydia pouted. "It's too hot to walk to the market this late."

"Then you watch the children while Chloe takes her."

"No, Mama. I'm meeting with Alice to study. You know how the children annoy her."

Mama? So Lydia was the daughter of the house.

Mistress Asher sighed and took the boy Chloe had been nursing. "I suppose I'll have to watch them. Don't dawdle, Chloe."

"Yes, Mama. I'll just put Jeb in his crib." She bent to pick him up.

Mistress Asher waved her free hand. "No, leave him. He'll be fine sleeping where he is."

"You won't let him roll into the fire?" Chloe hesitated.

"What do you take me for?" Mistress Asher said angrily. "As if I haven't been minding children since before you were even born. Hurry up now so you can get back before the little bugger is hungry again."

Chloe ducked her head as if she had been hit. Without a word, she picked up her kerchief, tied it about her shoulders and stepped briskly out the door.

I scrambled to catch up to her. "It must be hard having twins," I said in an effort to be friendly.

"Twins?" She looked at me, startled out of her silence. "Oh, you mean the boys. They're not twins. Jeb is my own son. Gideon is Mama's baby. He was born just two weeks after Jeb."

She didn't add any more to that, so I tried another avenue. "Are you really Lydia's sister?"

She smiled at this, and I realized it was the first she had done so. She was really quite pretty, the smile lighting up her face, giving her pink cheeks life and making her eyes sparkle. "No, not at all," she said. "Mama was wet nurse to Lydia when we were both babies. Lydia is Ethan's sister." The coloring in her cheeks flushed even more. "It's Tom, and of course Gideon, who are my brothers, or half brothers really."

So Tom was her brother, not her husband. Where was her husband then? If he had left her, or if there was no husband at all, that would explain her embarrassment over her mother's name-calling.

By the time we returned from market both babes were bawling, Lydia was nowhere to be found, and Mistress Asher scolded Chloe and me in equal measures for our lackadaisical tardiness. We were late putting dinner on the table, and everyone scowled throughout the meal.

The afternoon was filled with more scrubbing; first dishes, then floors. The white pine boards, Mistress Asher insisted, had to be scoured with sand. My hands puckered like week-old cherries, and my knees ached from kneeling on the hard wood. That work was interrupted only to serve the family supper. Of course, that meant more dishes. By nightfall, I never wanted to look at another dish of any sort. Finally, I threw the last bucket of hot water out the door and slammed the empty pail upside down beside the hearth.

Just let anyone tell me to do one more, I thought mutinously, and I'll scream the truth out and be damned. But no one from the family came near the kitchen, and I was far too tired to stay angry. I was just grateful to seek my bed, even if that bed were no more than a cloak spread in front of the hearth. I banked the fire and lay down, falling asleep almost instantly.

CHAPTER 10

In the middle of the night, the front door burst open, jerking me awake. "Where's my wife?" Samuel Asher bellowed, clomping down the hallway.

Mistress Asher slept in the parlor across from the kitchen. Her door creaked open.

"There you are. Give us a kiss, Joggy. You've been a long time coming." Mr. Asher snorted in laughter at his own crude joke.

"Hush. You'll wake the neighbors." Light from her candle flicked through the cracks in the kitchen door.

Samuel Asher's voice, slurred with drink, grew louder. "Damned if I care about the neighbors! Come up to bed with me, Joggy."

"Don't call me that. She's been dead near twenty years." There was a shuffling sound, like someone backing up quickly, then a pause.

"Well you comforted me then," Mr. Asher wheedled. "And I wed you to save you the shame."

"It was no shame for me."

"No? A wet nurse pregnant with the master's child? Where could you have gone if I'd turned you out?"

"I never wanted that child," Mistress Asher said harshly.

Another bit of scuffling in the hallway drowned out some of his words, but the next were clear. ". . . wanted *me* right enough. Me and my house and my fortune. You opened your legs wide then, and you can do it now."

"You're drunk." Mistress Asher bumped up against the kitchen door. I could hear her fumbling for the latch.

Both seemed to have forgotten me. And I would just as soon keep it that way. Neither would be happy to find me overhearing this quarrel.

I pulled my blanket around me and crawled away from the fireplace to the pantry.

Mr. Asher's fist hit the door. It flew open. Mistress Asher fell backward into the kitchen with a squeak and dropped the candle.

"You're my wife," he roared. "If I want you in my bed, you'll be there." The candle had gone out, but I could see them silhouetted by the moonlight, a gaunt, black crow looming over a plump sparrow.

Mistress Asher scuttled to the far side of the table, moving quickly in spite of her bulk. With the table between them, she spoke boldly. "I was wife to you any time you wanted, even before it was legal between us. But since it's never mattered much if the one you're bedding is wife or not, I'll not stand as your piss pot. Go find yourself a whore."

He feinted toward the right, then lunged left, but she kept the table between them.

He laughed. "Someone like your daughter, you mean? Ah, Chloe . . . she's a warm handful." He lunged left again, but she circled the table, grabbing up a knife from the counter.

"I'll kill you if you come near her." She waved the knife like a flag. Even I could see she hadn't the slightest idea how to use it.

Samuel Asher's teeth flashed in a mock smile. He leaned right, then dove across the table, grabbing her wrists. He slammed the one holding the knife against the table edge. She cried out and let go. The knife clattered to the floor and lay two feet from the dark corner where I hid. Mr. Asher jerked her closer and grabbed her hair, pulling her head back. She stopped fighting him. I saw her go slack in his arms, suffering him to kiss her like a rag doll.

He shoved her away so hard she fell to the floor and lay there without moving.

"What kind of a wife are you?" He spat on her. "More like a cold fish without a drop of blood in your veins. It's your own fault if I have found a bit of warmth in another's bed."

He kicked her, bringing out a sob of pain. But the fight was gone out of her, her moment of bravado evaporated. He kicked her again, but she lay like a moist lump, crying and sniffling. With another oath, Samuel Asher stomped out of the kitchen. The front door slammed.

I came out of my corner and put my hand to the poor woman's

shoulder. "Are you hurt badly?" I whispered. The blows had been hard enough to break bones.

She reacted to my hand against her shoulder as if it were a red-hot poker from the fire. "You." She spat out the word like an oath. "It was buying you put him in this state." She regarded me with pure hatred. "Just be thankful he was too drunk to remember you. You'd better forget what you saw tonight." She pulled herself to her feet and limped out of the kitchen.

No, I thought. Tonight was something I would be wise to remember. I took up the kitchen knife from the floor. It was a small knife, not too heavy. The blade gleamed in the glowing embers of the hearth fire. I picked up a rag from the scullery, wrapped the knife in it, then pushed the bundle deep into my shift pocket. Finally, I slipped out the back door of the kitchen to the stables. The horses weren't the best smelling company, but I would not make it easy for Samuel Asher to find me. And if he did, he would find me a tougher quarry than his wife.

After a night in the stable, I was up and tending the fire long before dawn. Mistress Asher did not come down that morning, and Mr. Asher barely spoke. Lydia, the only other family member up for breakfast, chattered through the whole meal as if she didn't notice the way he held his aching head.

I expected Ethan to provide writing materials that day, but he was also absent from breakfast. Writing Grandfather and Mam was proving much more difficult than I had imagined. At home, Grandfather had a ready supply of quills and paper, and Mam bought ink and pounce for drying it at the shop. Here I had no access to such luxuries. I had seen a stationer's shop near the market when I went with Chloe, but I had no coin to purchase supplies, and I doubted anyone would be inclined to offer me credit, looking as ragged as I was. Ethan had promised to supply me with the necessary articles, but he seemed to have forgotten. I would have to remind him, as soon as I could find him.

When Mistress Asher came down around midmorning, she held one arm tightly against her side and favored her left ankle. She glared at me, one eye blackened and swollen nearly shut, and the other full of anger. Neither Chloe nor Lydia made any comment about her injuries, but I noticed Lydia was quieter than usual and brought the mistress a cup of tea before anyone asked. Chloe gathered up both babies to feed them upstairs, and I suspect, to stay out of reach of her mother's sharp tongue. I thought about the argument I had overheard. Was it possible Samuel Asher was the father of both babies? If that were true, it explained why Chloe refused to name her lover, in spite of the shame she faced keeping silent.

Ethan came to dinner that noon but he was so rushed I had no chance to talk to him. After another afternoon of scrubbing and cooking under Mistress Asher's baleful glare and sharp-tongued criticism, I was ready to demand writing materials from Ethan no matter who was listening. But Ethan left before I had even finished clearing supper, and I went to bed no closer to writing Grandfather than I had been that morning.

Late the next afternoon I decided to find Ethan myself, since that still seemed easier than finding the writing materials. I waited until Mistress Asher dozed off in the rocker, and Chloe was busy with the two boys. Lydia had gone off somewhere.

Swiping my hands on my borrowed apron, I slipped out the kitchen door and up the stairs. On the second floor, four doors stood opposite each other along a central hall, but all were shut. One was likely to be the master's bedroom and another his study. Where would Ethan be?

I hesitated, chewing on my lip. I could hardly wander about the house as if I owned it. I hadn't thought to bring a tray of tea or coffee as an excuse. I would just have to pick a door and knock on it. If it were the master, I would pretend I had come to see if he wanted anything. With this resolve, I had taken two steps toward the first door and raised my hand, when it flew open. I stared stupidly into Ethan's face, my mouth open and my hand in the air as if I meant to hit him.

Ethan seemed unperturbed by my sudden appearance. He smiled his wide warm, smile. "Looking for me, are you?" He stepped aside as if to invite me into his room.

"Yes. I mean no, not exactly." Something about Ethan's presence took my breath away and left me tongue-tied in a way Grandfather would never have believed. I blushed, took a deep breath and tried again. "Paper," I squeaked. "And quill and ink. I need to write my grandfather."

"Of course. How rude of me to forget." He took my hand in his and drew me into the room. He raised my hand to his lips. "But I've not forgotten you're a lady." He kissed my fingers.

I flushed with an unexpected heat. "Please," I said, not sure exactly what I meant.

Then Mistress Asher loomed in the doorway. I had not heard her on the stairs. Neither, apparently, had Ethan heard her coming. For the briefest moment a look of intense rage crossed his face. Startled, I jerked my hand free and stepped back, treading on the hem of my skirt and tripping over it. I fell to the floor with a thump.

Instantly Ethan was beside me, helping me up, all smiles and solicitousness. "Not the handiest of housemaids Father has found, is she?" He smiled as if he meant to share the joke, but the words stung.

Mistress Asher did not smile. Her eye was still swollen shut and rimmed with black and green bruising. "A word with you, Ethan? You've work in the kitchen, girl!" Her anger was neither brief nor hidden and far beyond anything rational.

"Yes, ma'am. I mean, no ma'am." I bobbed a hasty curtsey and retreated downstairs.

In the kitchen Lydia, back from her errand, smiled sweetly, like a cat that's been at the cream. "Mama Bess did warn you." She pulled off her gloves, one finger at a time. "I suppose she could have you flogged. They did Cora." She laughed, tucking the gloves away in her pocket. "Though it didn't really matter in the end."

"I've no idea what you are talking about." I picked up the basket of green beans by the table and sat to snap them.

"No?" Lydia arched an eyebrow and pulled out a black lace fan. "A bit slow, are you?"

Unfortunately, I was beginning to understand. Ethan had a charm that made my knees weaken. Whenever he was near, I forgot everything else. Had he had the same effect on Cora? Had she tempted both Mr. Asher and his son? But Mr. Asher was a vulture, and Ethan was a gentleman. It was not his fault he was so handsome. He had shown nothing but kindness to me.

Still there was that look, so intense, as if his eyes could burn right through me, transforming his face from handsome to hideous. Or had I imagined it? He'd been startled, just as I was. The more I thought about it, the more ridiculous it seemed. He had nothing to be angry about. I'd only asked for paper and quill.

And come away without either, I thought ruefully. Perhaps I would have to find a way to steal the writing supplies. That was a daunting prospect. I dropped another bean in the bowl and stretched out my hand to stare at it. I had no idea what the penalty for thievery was here, but in Edinburgh, they might cut off a hand; that or seven years transportation to America. Since they could hardly do the latter, I had an uneasy feeling the former would be more likely.

I snapped my fingers shut and went back to the beans. I would just have to see to it I didn't get caught. I wished I could talk to Peg. She would likely have an idea. Unbidden, a picture of Davy McRae, with the wind blowing his hair into a cedar gold mane, filled my mind.

That night I slept in the stable again, but had the fire going and a pot of water set to boil before Mistress Asher came in to check. She was in a sour mood, ready to find fault in all I did. The fire was too hot, the water too cold, the bread dough too sticky. It took a great deal more patience than I usually had to keep from snapping back at her. But I had not missed Lydia's offhand remark about a flogging. I'd seen a flogging once in Edinburgh, a servant girl charged with disobedience. Ten stripes on her bare back drew blood, but her choked screams were worse. The memory helped me hold my tongue.

By the time breakfast was ready to serve, I was seething like the pot of stew I'd set to boil. Just a bit longer, I told myself through clenched teeth. I only had to get the family fed, and I could be off to market. There, at least, amid the bustle of ordinary people, who did not seem bent on vexing me, I could think. Perhaps I could buy pen, ink, and paper on the Asher's account, or convince Chloe to help me with it.

Neither Chloe nor Lydia had come down for breakfast. Mistress Asher sat down at the table with Mr. Asher and Tom, leaving me to serve. I didn't see Ethan come in as I dished out applesauce to Mr. Asher. When he clamped a hand on my shoulder, I spun around as startled as if he had hit me. I dropped the dish I carried. It clattered to the floor and rolled, clanging and splashing applesauce in a circle around the room.

He paid it no more mind than the flies already buzzing in the morning heat. He shoved a bundle of dirty linen at me. "I'll need this washed out today, Sally. See you do it right."

Suddenly I couldn't be Sally MacLaughlin any more. "I'll do no such thing." Fury overrode common sense. How dare he treat me like a servant, when he of all people knew very well I was not? I had instinctively grabbed the bundle as he shoved it at me, and I started to shove it back, when I caught his brief wink. Ethan put his hand on mine on top of the bundle and squeezed. Under my fingers in the folds of cloth, I felt a faint rustle. Belatedly I realized the bundle contained more than dirty laundry.

I looked about me in confusion. Mr. Asher had half risen to his feet, his own face red with anger. Tom leaned back in his chair, balancing on two legs and grinning oddly. It was the look on Mistress Asher's face, however, which actually brought me to my senses. She looked positively delighted. Here was disobedience she could do something about.

"I mean . . . " hastily I tried to cover my outburst. "I mean, yes, sir. You startled me, sir. I'll see to it right away after breakfast, sir." I curtseyed very briefly and fled to the kitchen.

"My God," Tom burst out before I reached the door. "That's fast work even for you, Ethan. Do you want to take a flourish before breakfast? Or have you rogered her already?" He pounded his fist on the table, nearly choking on his raucous laughter.

I didn't hear Ethan's reply, but I heard Mistress Asher screech. "You'll keep a decent tongue in your head or feel the back of my hand."

"Shut up all of you!" Mr. Asher shouted and pounded his fist on the table. "Is it too much to ask for a peaceful breakfast in my own home?"

Back in the kitchen, I shook out the shirt and found a quill, a rolled sheet of paper and a small stoppered bottle of ink. Ethan had not forgotten his promise. There was no pounce to dry the ink but perhaps a handful of sand from the yard would do. Finally I could write Grandfather. I wrapped the stuff back into the shirt and shoved it behind a flour sack in the pantry. Then I went back to clean up the applesauce, endure another scolding from Mistress Asher, and clear away the breakfast things.

I had no time to myself until mid afternoon when Mistress Asher sat down with her spinning wheel. Both Lydia and Chloe sat in the hall, sewing while the boys napped. Now I could write the letter. I spread out the paper on the kitchen table, unstoppered the ink, dipped my quill, and . . . stopped. What to say? I'd been so intent on getting paper, I hadn't thought what to write.

I scratched out a brief note telling them only I was being held as a servant in Philadelphia and to please send sufficient money to buy me back from the Ashers and pay for my passage home again. I promised to explain the whole situation upon my return. Then I sprinkled some sand on it from near the back stoop to substitute for pounce and waved the feather tuft of the quill over it to speed the ink drying.

The next problem was how to get it back to Ethan. I realized by now the whole family took any deliberate encounter I had with him to mean I was falling into the unfortunate Cora's ways. I most certainly did not want them thinking that. I shook out the shirt he'd wrapped the stuff in and decided it was not really so dirty after all. I shook it out to air it, folded it neatly, and hid the stuff between the folds. I thought about and then discarded several plans to deliver the shirt to Ethan, but in the end I just picked up the shirt and marched upstairs with it to knock on his door. He had asked me to wash it, hadn't he? Surely he and the rest of the family would expect it returned when it had had sufficient time to dry.

At my knock, he opened his door. He was fully dressed this time, complete with snowy white stock, velvet frock coat and a stylish powdered wig. He bowed over my hand, his lips brushing my fingertips.

"Ah, the lovely Sally, and my cleaned shirt. You've been very prompt, my dear. Wouldn't you say so, Tom?"

Tom had not risen when I knocked, nor did he answer his half-brother now, but Ethan didn't seem to expect a reply.

"Unfortunately, your timing is regrettable. I'm just on my way out. Any other time, I would ask you in so I could thank you properly."

"Leave it, Ethan." Tom spoke in a lazy, bored drawl. "You can bed her when you're back if you haven't already. You won't lose your parts if you have to wait."

My cheeks grew hot at Tom's crudeness. I focused on Ethan's warm smile. "You're going out now, near supper?" I glanced at the folded shirt set carelessly aside on the lamp table.

His eyes followed mine. "We'll be gone several days, but you've no need to worry. I'll not forget."

Tom, apparently tiring of his brother's gallantry, draped one arm across Ethan's shoulders and leered at me. "Do you think you can wait three days, girl? If not, I can see to you now. I may not have the charm my brother has, but I'm a damn sight quicker." His eyes slowly raked my bodice, taking in every curve showing through the thin, worn fabric.

"Tom." Ethan put a restraining hand on his brother. "You're frightening the girl."

I was not frightened, not exactly. In spite of his brother's comments, Ethan was a gentleman, like those I'd known at home, and Tom was just a rude, crude boy. Still, I did not like the drift of the conversation. I looked again at the shirt. "How long do you think it will be?"

"She's awful impatient for you, Ethan," Tom said, grinning wickedly.

"I'll see it done as fast as possible," Ethan said, ignoring Tom.

Feeling I'd gotten as much promise as could be hoped for, I pulled my hand free of his and hurried away, trying to stop my ears against Tom's increasingly bawdy remarks.

CHAPTER 11

Tom and Ethan's absence affected the women of the house most. The tension vanished, as if a tight rope had slackened. But the reprieve was short-lived. When they returned a few days later, the bickering resumed, though neither one spent much time at home.

It took days before I found Ethan alone in the hall, coming late to supper, just as I came from the kitchen with a bowl of stewed apples. He stepped past me and reached for the dining room doorknob.

"What news of my letter?" I whispered, plucking his sleeve.

Ethan jerked his arm away and winced. "It's been seen to," he said. His jacket sleeve was torn at the shoulder and a dark blotch stained the fabric. His boots were mud-splattered. Normally fastidious in his dress, Ethan had never come to dinner so travel-stained and rumpled.

"What's wrong?" I asked.

"Be patient, girl!" he snapped. He pushed past me into the dining room

Stung by his words and his tone, I followed him with the apples.

"What's kept you?" Mr. Asher grumbled. "Don't tell me you found the scoundrel that made off with that shipment of Bordeaux wines from last week."

"What's happened to you?" Mistress Asher interrupted and half rose from her seat.

Ethan sat down without answering either of them.

Tom reached across the table for the bread. "If he had found the shipment, he would never come skulking in here late like this." He tore off the end of the loaf.

"You haven't fared any better," Ethan said.

Every meal brought the same accusations, the same talk of missing shipments, smugglers, and bribes. Mr. Asher served as customs agent for the region, though apparently Ethan and Tom did most of the work, checking arrivals, patrolling some of the private wharves along the Delaware River, and collecting the tax revenues. Mr. Asher also had his own shares in various shipping ventures and served as factor for several other merchants. Throughout the day, sea captains and merchants came to call on him in his office upstairs. From the shouting, I knew Mr. Asher had many business problems.

"You're both bumblers," Mr. Asher said. He leaned back that I might ladle the apples onto his plate. "I might as well do it myself for all the good the pair of you have done."

I offered the apples to Lydia, but she waved me away. Carefully stepping around the boys playing at her feet, I took the bowl to Chloe. She helped herself to a large dollop, then looked at her mother. Mistress Asher was still trying to get Ethan's attention and wasn't watching Chloe. Chloe took another spoonful before waving me on.

"What did happen to you?" Tom asked. "Fall off your horse? You're not called on to drink the goods you find."

Ethan scowled. He was having a hard time cutting his meat with one hand. "The scoundrel shot at me."

"Oh my," Chloe and Mistress Asher echoed each other.

Ethan ignored them both. "It's just a scratch, but the damned horse shied and threw me."

Tom laughed, the sarcasm in his voice tinged with scorn. "So of course the other fellow got away. Good job, dear brother."

Shot at? No wonder the poor man had no time for me. I returned to the kitchen and resolved to be patient. It would be weeks before any answer came.

The next morning was marketing day. Mistress Asher wanted Lydia to go with me, but she refused, saying, "She can do it herself."

Mistress Asher grumbled. "She'll run off sure as anything."

"She would be a fool to do so, with no place to go and not even a ha'penny to her name." Lydia eyed me speculatively. "She's dirty as a beggar, but not much of a fool."

Since Chloe had to take care of the boys, the mistress reluctantly gave me the chore. "But see you hurry back! Don't be lollygagging."

After days of unseasonable heat, the sky was overcast with the damp chill of spring. Rain threatened. But in spite of the gray sky, I rejoiced in the chance to be alone, away from the constant bickering, Chloe's whining, and the sharp, stupid orders from Mistress Asher. I found my way to market without difficulty, and finished shopping quickly.

With time to spare and no desire to hurry back, I strolled on past the market sheds on Second Street. The streets were wider here, with cobbled footpaths along either side of the pothole-ridden, dirt thoroughfare down the middle.

A spattering of rain left dark spots in the dusty street. I looked skyward to gauge the coming storm. Quilted clouds framed the tall, thin spire of Christ's Church. This was one of the four spires I had seen from the ship, finished only a few years earlier.

Indeed, everywhere I looked, I saw evidence of new building. Stacks of gleaming white timbers lay beside a partially framed house on one corner, while masons slapped mortar to bricks just across the street. I could grow to like the place. There was a vibrance here, a sense of living that Edinburgh's old cobblestone streets never had. And the people! Never had I seen so many differences within the human race. Skin tone alone ranged from a deep dusky black of a dockworker, laboring shirtless in the sun all day, to the translucent pink, of a bonneted, blond child. They dressed in all manner of garb from simple shifts to fashionable elegance to ragged furs. A morning spent going to market felt like a day at the fair.

Unfortunately, as I wandered, I lost track of my way. I've never been very good with directions, but in the familiar streets of Leith, it never mattered. I wandered for some time before realizing I was completely lost. I turned, looking back the way I had come. A maze of unfamiliar farmers' carts, shops and people filled the avenue. Had I come up the street that way, or had I turned? I couldn't remember.

I turned about in a sudden panic and stepped smack into Peg Willet.

"Watch yourself," she started. Then she recognized me, clapped her arms about my shoulders and hugged me. "Callie, ye are looking . . . " she stepped back, lifted one eyebrow as she regarded my ragged skirt, torn bodice and dirty chemise. "Well," she said with hardly a pause. "Maybe ye have looked a bit better in the past, but it's good to see ye nonetheless." Her broad grin was as infectious as ever.

What a relief to see her! She looked as if Philadelphia agreed with her. Her cheeks were plump and rosy, and she wore a crisp, white apron over her worn skirt.

Peg looped her arm in mine. "Come along with ye then. Let's sit a bit and catch up with each other. There's a coffee shop not far from here. We'll stop and get a cup."

"Coffee?" I had heard of it, but had never tried it.

"Oh, aye, it's better than tea by a long shot. Everyone drinks it."

I hesitated. "I have no coin, and I have to get back."

"Dinna' fash yourself. It's my treat." Peg pulled me on across the dusty square. "And we won't take a minute."

The small shop was dark inside, with a half dozen tables, most filled with merchants. A few journeymen in working leathers crowded around one table, and a couple of fresh-faced apprentices hung by the door. A young girl brought us two mugs of hot liquid, blacker than any tea I'd ever seen, steaming with a delicious, pungent aroma.

Peg sipped her coffee. "Now, tell what ye have been doing and how ye are getting on," she said. "I thought sure ye would be on your way back by now. At the very least, I thought to see ye decently dressed."

I took a tentative sip of the coffee and frowned. It was terribly bitter. "How would I have managed that? No one gives away clothes here, any more than they did in Scotland."

"Did your mistress not give ye a new dress?"

I shook my head. "Why would she? She has no liking for me."

"Callie, I may not be able to read a word, but I know what I put my mark to. My papers say I'm to be given room and board and decent clothing. I'm thinking yours do the same."

Of course, I had never seen my own papers, false as they were. "I didn't sign anything," I reminded her.

She waved her hand dismissively. "It doesn't matter if ye did or did not. They think ye did, so they owe ye what they have promised."

I wasn't sure how sound her logic was, but didn't argue. The second sip of the coffee was better than the first and the third a bit better than that.

Peg, it turned out, had landed in an ideal situation. She worked for a family who owned a prosperous tavern in the Northern Liberties, not far from Vine Street. "A family with four grown sons, all to home, and all looking for a good wife," she said, glowing with excitement. "I'll have my pick of the lot. Not a bad looking lot either."

"Peg! You're not serious. You can't pick a husband like that!"

"Do ye have a better way for a girl with no money or family?" She patted my arm in what was meant to be reassuring. "Don't worry about me. I'll bide my time well enough and pick the best one. Now tell me about your own self."

I told her about the Asher family and my letter to grandfather and Ethan's help. "So even now my letter must be nearing Scotland."

"I'm glad for ye," Peg said simply. "I never thought ye could be kept here against your will. And what will ye do in the meantime?"

"Go on playing the part of a maid, I suppose." I shrugged. "What else can I do?"

"Ye could set your cap on winning Master Ethan Asher. It sounds as if the job's half done already."

"Peg!" I protested, then stopped. She was only teasing. "Have you heard news of Mary and the bairns?"

Peg's grin disappeared. "Oh, aye, though there's little good news there."

"What?" Immediately I feared the worst. "The bairns? Are they ill?"

"Nae, they're right enough for the nonce, but it canna' last. No one wanted to take on the contract of a widow woman with two bairns and the passage of a dead husband to pay for to boot. Mr. Shakleton took her on himself." Peg frowned at her coffee. "He's a cowardly spawn of the devil, that man. He means to work it out of her before she dies. He keeps her busy dawn to dusk and leaves Leah to mind the babe. When the poor bairn cries for his mam to feed him, the master beats the wee lass for not keeping him quiet. Mary's beside herself with worry for the pair of them and dead tired from working, too." Peg shook her head. "She's that close to running off—though she would never last long, what with two bairns and one not yet walking. She needs a friend more than ever."

As it always did, news of Mary's plight made my own hardships seem trivial. I vowed to visit her as soon as I could get away. Just then the church bells rang noon. I jumped up in alarm. "I've got to get back or there will be a fine to-do!" I rushed out, then stopped short. "Peg, you don't know the way back to Bell Court do you? It's close to little Dock Creek, but I'm all turned around."

Peg laughed and took my arm. "That I do, Callie. Ye would get lost in your own kitchen, did ye close your eyes a moment. Truth to tell, ye are not far from Shakleton's house, where Mary landed. They are just off Second Street, a block or so closer to the river than you."

Peg walked with me, chattering about this or that shopkeeper as we passed, commenting on the one who gave fair weight and the one who always set his hand on the scale if you didn't mind him. She pointed out the farmwoman whose cabbages were always wormy and the chandler whose candles lasted a good hour longer than any other because he used more beeswax than tallow. I marveled at how she knew so much. She had arrived in Philadelphia the same time I did, yet she knew far more about the place. A servant all her life, Peg had never had any kind of schooling, but she was used to doing the marketing and pleasing the master.

Peg walked with me to the corner of Market and Third Street. "I have to get back too." She kissed both my cheeks. "Look for me the next market day."

I had only a little further to go, but the light drizzle of the morning turned to real rain. I came in drenched, to find Mistress Asher in a fury.

"Where have you been, girl? You should have been here two hours ago." She slapped my cheek. Startled, I dropped my bundles.

"Clumsy wretch." She drew back to hit me again.

I caught her arm. She grunted, not expecting me to resist.

I held her wrist and twisted it enough to pain her. "You will not strike me!" Without thinking, I spoke to her as if she were the servant, and I the mistress. Her first blow had surprised me. It wouldn't happen again.

Mistress Asher's small eyes sparked anger, but I held her wrist until she dropped her eyes and twisted free. She backed away.

Still wary, I bent to pick up the bundles I had dropped.

Lydia sauntered in at that moment. She shook the rain off her cloak as she looked from her stepmother, rubbing furiously at her wrist, to me with my cheek still red from the blow.

She picked up an apple from the bowl on the table and rubbed it on her skirt. "You've been long enough at the market to grow radishes," she remarked. "What happened?"

"I was lost." I wouldn't tell them of meeting Peg. I may have won this little skirmish with the mistress, but sure enough, if she hadn't hated me before, she hated me now. And she had the power to win the war, no matter how many battles I won. As for Lydia, I didn't know. Her face always showed a bland mask of disinterest, betraying no anger, no love, nothing. But I was sure that behind those dark, masked eyes, a cauldron seethed.

The rain continued on and off for a week, and I had no chance to see Mary or Peg. But by Sunday night the rain stopped, promising a clear Monday. Mistress Asher came into the kitchen as I lit the morning cook fire. Already sweat beaded on my forehead. I think she hoped to find me still abed, for she grumbled irritably to herself before getting down to business.

"I've told Tom to drag the wash pot into the yard." She pinched the bread I had set to rise, testing it. "We'll wash today; all the linens and such." She sniffed at the tea I had brewed. "It's weak still," she said, finding at last something to complain of. "You should start earlier."

Right after breakfast, she bullied Tom into dragging the big iron pot out into the yard and hanging it on a hook, then ordered me to fill it with water, start the fire, and stir the wash. Chloe stripped the sheets from each bed in the house and brought me piles of table linens, toweling, and undergarments to boil, rinse, and hang. It was backbreaking work, and the longer I stirred and pounded, the angrier I became. Here I was, washing the entire stock of family linen, and my own dress was ready to fall off my shoulders. By the time Mistress Asher came out to check on my progress near noon, I was steaming to match the boiling brew in front of me.

"I need a new dress," I demanded. "You'll give me coin tomorrow to buy myself cloth at the market." I plunged the dasher into the kettle and plowed on. "My own is about to fall to rags." Then, inspired by my talk with Peg, I added. "It's in my contract you know."

She narrowed her eyes. "Eh, what?"

"My indenture promised clothing. If it is not provided, the contract is void." I highly doubted this last was true. While most indentures required that food and clothes be provided, there was actually little enforcement according to Peg. Even though I didn't really know what my papers stated, since I had never read them, I was reasonably sure Mistress Asher had not read them either, because she couldn't read. She had barely glanced at the receipts I brought from marketing and turned them over to Lydia.

"Ask Mr. Asher or better yet, ask Ethan. Either of them would know," I said smoothly. She would never risk rousing their irritation with a minor household matter. By now, I knew the limits of her power did not extend beyond the kitchen.

Her lips pursed in a frown. I could almost see her thinking. She worked her fingers back and forth with the effort. "You would like that, wouldn't you?" she said finally. "Making me look bad so as to work your own way into his heart and who knows where else. I warned you'd be sorry if you took after Cora." Suddenly, a gleam lit up her eye. "I've just the thing. Chloe," she screeched. "Fetch the bundle from the morning room chest."

A few minutes later, Chloe handed her a bundle, which she in turn shoved at me. "This was Cora's." She chuckled. "She'll not be wanting it now."

The more I heard of Cora, the less I liked her. Whatever had happened to Cora, I didn't want happening to me.

The bundle contained a dingy, blue striped short gown, a dark brown bodice and a dimity petticoat that had once been the color of new butter. Wadded up inside was an unbleached cotton shift, only slightly less dirty than my own. It wasn't exactly what I expected for new clothes, but it would give me something decent to wear. First, though, the clothes would need to be washed. If Cora had included a company of lice along with her other faults, I didn't need to share them.

A pale round moon of a hot summer night hung low in the sky before I finished washing everything, including my new clothes, and hung each garment on the long lines stretched across the yard behind the kitchen near the garden. I pressed my fists into the small of my back, and lifted my aching shoulders. It was late, but I decided to stop in the kitchen and look for a heel of bread or an apple to eat before going back out to the stable to sleep. As I turned, a flicker of movement caught my eye at the far edge of the yard. I stopped and peered into the darkness beyond the wet sheets hanging wraithlike on the lines.

A form, human in size and shape, paused in the shadow of the trees. The figure took a few steps and stopped again, watching, I felt sure. But for what purpose? Watching me? 'Twas unlikely. The sheets hid me for the most part, but I had no idea how long the watcher had been there, spying on the house. With a sudden irrational fear, I dashed across the yard and into the kitchen, dropping the bolt in the door behind me. I leaned against the solid wood door and tried to still my heart. The kitchen was dark, except for the low coals of the fire on the hearth. The family had all gone upstairs to bed.

A stick cracked in the fire. I jumped at the sound, then realized what it was. "Don't be ridiculous," I told myself firmly. There was no sense letting bumps and shadows frighten me.

Just then the front door slammed open. A familiar, drunken voice shouted, "Where's my Joggy?"

I didn't take time to think. Better face a phantom than let the master find me alone. I scrambled to unbolt the kitchen door and race across the yard to the stable. I waited just inside the door, gripping the stolen knife in one hand, until the pounding of my heart stilled.

A deep quiet surrounded me, punctuated with nothing more than the tiny chirpings of crickets in the grass. No one, shadow or human, followed me.

Up in the loft, I kept a tense watch for awhile, but I was bone weary. Eventually my eyes closed of their own accord, and I fell asleep.

The next morning I walked along the back edge of the yard, but saw no footprints. I must have imagined the watcher. Why would anyone spy on the Ashers?

I made breakfast, took in the laundry, and dressed in my new clothes before I began sweeping the hall. I threw a handful of wet sand over the floor to dampen it, then started at the end closest to the front door. I had not spent much time sweeping at home, but it's not a difficult job. I liked the careful, methodical gathering of dirt, so orderly in a life turned upside down. I thought of Mary. I wanted to visit her, but couldn't see how to get away without bringing trouble to both of us.

Suddenly the front door flew open and Mr. Asher, Ethan, and a third man tromped in, swirling the dust across the clean floor.

"Watch out there!" I said, irritated. Then I saw who the third man was. Davy McRae.

My scolding turned into an incoherent squeak. He saw me in the same instant and shook his head slightly. Then quite deliberately ignoring me, he followed Mr. Asher and Ethan upstairs. Neither of them had given me a moment's glance. I might as well have been invisible.

I closed the door behind them and started sweeping again, my thoughts as scattered as the dirt. What was he doing here? What sort of man was he after all, dealing with Mr. Asher? And though he said it was at his father's bidding, he had been working with that cockroach, Mr. Shakleton, too. Was he a scoundrel after all?

I shook my head. I couldn't believe it, not after all the kindness and generosity he had shown aboard the ship. I didn't know what he was up to, and maybe it was better that way. I had best follow Peg's advice and forget about Davy McRae.

I did try, but he came up behind me while I was digging onions in the herb garden an hour later. Startled, I dropped my basket.

He stooped to help me pick up the spilled vegetables. "Ye should not be here," he said.

"What?" I gaped at him. Of course I shouldn't be here. I should be in Scotland, with my family, perhaps going to a summer ball with Elspeth. Was he joking? But no, his tawny eyes were dark and serious.

"Well, that's no news to me!" I said, fighting anger. I snatched the basket and stood up. "Isn't that what I've been saying for months now?"

He stood too, dropping the last couple of onions into the basket. "That's not what I mean. Callie, listen to me. This family . . ." He seemed to be searching for words and found none. "Callie, they're no good."

I choked off a laugh. "Haven't I been living under their roof these past weeks?" I stepped across the rows of onions, and stopped to dig a couple of carrots. "Besides," I added without looking up, "you're dealing with them, aren't you?"

"Aye. But I'm doing so with my eyes wide open and a hand on my dirk. I've seen ye have sense enough to sleep in the stable, but ye dinna' know what ye are up against."

"What?" I sat back on my heels to stare up at him. "How do you know where I sleep?"

"I've been watching the house from time to time," he admitted. "I've told ye. Mr. Asher is not a man to trust."

I pulled up a carrot, brushed the sandy dirt from it, and laid it in the basket atop the onions. If Davy had been watching, that explained the figure in the shadows. A man spying in the dark was no one to trust, but somehow I felt safer knowing it was Davy. Still, I had to live with the Ashers, at least until Grandfather answered my letter. I reached for another carrot. "It doesn't matter they are no good. I've no choice."

Davy stepped over the row of carrots to face me. He took the basket and set it down behind him. Then he took both my hands and pulled me to my feet. "Ye could come away with me. I offered it before and I mean it. I would see ye safe."

The last time he had made the offer, I'd been angry at what I took to be teasing, but there was no mockery this time. His shirt sleeves were open and rolled back, revealing strong, bronzed arms, a shade darker than the burnished gold of his hair. The spell of his words washed over me. Freedom, his words promised, and safety. I remembered the feel of his arms holding me the night of the storm. I wanted to fall into those arms and let him care for me.

I tried to order my thoughts. I knew very little about Davy McRae, but clearly he was in some kind of trouble. By his own admission, at least one man wanted him dead. Likely he did mean to help me, but what could he do, really? Ethan, a gentleman with property and connections, seemed a much safer bet, in spite of his family.

Abruptly, I shook my head. "And risk a flogging for running away? No, thank you. I've written Grandfather. It can't be much longer 'til he replies and I can go safe home."

He stared at me a moment longer, his gaze as unblinking as a cat about to pounce. "Perhaps ye are right. But promise me this. Ye will send word to me do ye need my help."

"How am I supposed to do that?" I kept my voice light. He seemed so serious, so unlike the joking, smiling Davy who asked me to come away with him before.

"Come down to the wharves. There's a ship there, a small one near the far end. She's called *Le Rossignol*. Ask for Davy McRae. Ye will find me."

I didn't think wandering alone by the wharves day or night asking for Davy or any other man was a good plan. I saw more sense in shouting to the world, "I'm alone and helpless; do you what you will with me," than in following his suggestion.

Davy was waiting for an answer. His grip on my hands tightened. I winced. "You're hurting me."

He let go of me as suddenly as if I it had bitten him. "Don't forget," he said. *"Le Rossignol."* Then he walked away with a graceful stride that ate the ground as if he was running.

I rubbed my hands together, looking after him. His warning frightened me. What did he know that I did not?

CHAPTER 12

In the morning when I came in from the stable, Chloe stood in front of the hearth, balancing a baby in each arm. "You're out early."

Without answering, I added a couple of sticks to the fire. Chloe irritated me no end. She always looked as if she expected a beating, with her head down, her shoulders hunched, and her eyes weepy. A single woman, with a bastard child and a bully for a mother, she deserved some pity, but I wanted to shake her. Just being near her made me feel mean-spirited.

She set Gideon down on the floor to play with a wooden spoon, then looked around nervously. "Mama's not up yet, is she?"

I shook my head.

"All right then." She settled into the rocker to feed Jeb. "He's my own son after all," she said, as if to justify giving him the first turn. But son or not, I knew if Mistress Asher came in Jeb would lose his place.

Once breakfast was served, I hurried through the marketing, so I could squeeze in a visit to Mary. Peg had given me directions to a house not far from the Asher's. Mary was glad to see me, but frazzled. She nursed Rabbie while she stood, stirring a pot of boiling water. Leah helped by dropping in handfuls of oats to make the porridge.

"I hate to let her so near the fire," Mary confessed, "but if I don't feed the babe before Mr. Shakleton returns, she'll never keep the wee thing quiet."

I took over the porridge to let Mary nurse in peace and give Leah a rest. The poor girl's legs were covered with bruises in shades of green and purple. Mary still fidgeted, fearing Mr. Shakleton would find me there and fly into a fury, so I kept the visit short.

Mary squeezed my hand as I said goodbye. "I thank ye," she said. "Ye are a comfort." She gave Rabbie to Leah and took the spoon back.

In the following weeks, I managed to visit Mary another time or two. She never said much but just closed her eyes for a few precious minutes, thanking me when I left. Peg and I met more often. She was always bubbling with scandalous gossip. For someone who couldn't read a scrap of print, it was a marvel how she knew everything. Sometimes her news was of the broader world and political affairs. In July, she said that Virginian, Colonel Washington, had surrendered to the French at some place called Grand Meadows. She proclaimed that meant that any day now the Indian allies of the French would descend on Philadelphia and scalp us all. She told of women captured by the Indians and sold to the French. "Can ye believe it, Callie? Those poor girls sold as slaves to the Frenchies?"

I had overheard talk of Colonel Washington's defeat, but the Ashers had not mentioned this plan for enslaving girls. Of course, they would hardly object.

"That sounds like my indenture."

"It's no very Christian, if ye ask me," Peg insisted.

The next week she was reassured. "That Mr. Franklin, ye know that clever fellow who puts long poles on houses to catch the lightning? Well, he's been up to Albany, figuring out some plan to join all the colonies against the French. He'll see Philadelphia stays safe from those heathen marauders."

Most of her gossip was unimportant trivia about folk I didn't know, like the scandal over the cooper's daughter, who ran off with their most trusted servant. Usually I let it slide in one ear and out the other, simply enjoying the company of a friend and the familiar lilt of home instead of the flat English I heard day in and day out.

For four weeks, nothing changed. I visited Mary a few times, and chatted with Peg in the market. But one day I met Peg near the coffee house. "Ah, Callie, here ye are." She caught my arm to stop me from going inside. "I've been worritin' and worritin' ye wouldn't come today."

"What is it?" I paused beside the door. I enjoyed our occasional cups of the bitter drink.

"It's Mary," Peg went on breathlessly. "Wee Rabbie has a fever and the master won't have him in the house. He's put both bairns in the stable and keeps Mary working inside. He's afraid she'll sicken and be no use to him. She's fair crazed with worry."

"Poor Mary! What will she do?"

"Ye'll have to help." Peg tucked a loaf of bread in my basket, alongside the roast and cheese already there. "For Mary. I know broth would be better, but I couldn't manage that."

"Me? What can I do?" It came out as a squeak.

The coffee house proprietor looked up, a steaming pot in one hand, and mug in the other. "Come in or move out!" he barked. "Don't just stand there blocking the door."

Peg tucked her arm in mine and led me down the street. "I dinna' know precisely, but ye promised to look out for them. Ye can write, can ye not? Surely that's good for something?"

I didn't know how writing might help, but Peg was right. I had promised. There would be no coffee that morning.

It was two miles from the market to Mr. Shakleton's house. I hurried along the unpaved street, flanked by a swarm of flies buzzing in the heat. At the corner opposite Mr. Shakleton's narrow, brick house, I paused to mop my face with a hem of my apron.

Mr. Shakleton kept his offices on the street level and his living quarters upstairs. A painted wooden sign hung over the front door announcing Shakleton Enterprises. Next to the side door, a horse, hitched to a wagon, lazily switched his tail.

The sight of the wagon brought me up short. Mr. Shakleton's business hours were erratic. Mary always worried he would come in unexpectedly. He had a terrible temper, she said. I hesitated, fanning away the flies. I couldn't let him see me.

"Here, missy, what are you doing, cluttering up my stoop?" The squeaky voice of a wizened old lady in dusty mob cap startled me out of my reverie.

"Nothing, " I stammered. "I mean, I'm sorry . . ."

"Move along then." She brandished a large pair of iron scissors.

I stepped away, but she clutched my skirt

"You want a seamstress, missy." She rubbed the thin fabric between her fingers. "Surely, a fine lady like yourself wants a better shift than this.

I could make it up for you in no time. Come look. I've fine goods for you to choose from."

I snatched my skirt away from her. "I don't want . . ."

"Don't tell me you're not a lady." She cackled like an old biddy hen and caught my hand in her own hard claw-like fingers. "I see those hands. Raw and rough they are now, but not so long since you kept them in fine gloves. What made you lose your fine gloves, Missy, and start dipping your lovely hands in hot dishwater instead of perfumes?"

I shook loose, stepping off the stoop to cross the street, but just then Mr. Shakleton's front door slammed. I heard the angry voices of Mr. Shakleton and Mr. Asher, arguing. I couldn't let them see me. I whirled back to the old woman. "What have you got for muslin? No, make that dimity." I pushed past her into the shop and began fingering the goods.

The old woman's shop was full of dust, and too dark to see any color in the worn pieces of gowns she offered as fabric. I stood near the door to look at her samples in the light. While I pretended interest, I could still hear parts of the argument as the men rounded the corner.

Mr. Shakleton's nasal whine was unmistakable. " . . . not likely to get my cost out of her before she dies, and with the passage of two sniveling brats and a dead husband to pay off, it's poor business prospect for me all around."

He was talking about Mary! I shoved the bit of yellow muslin back at the shopkeeper, angry enough to confront Mr. Shakleton right there.

But the old woman stood between me and the doorway with another piece of cloth. "Perhaps this lovely linsey-woolsey? It's just the right blue for you."

A row would only cause more trouble for Mary. Reluctantly, I took the linsey-woolsey and held it up, still trying to eavesdrop on the men across the street.

Mr. Asher was doing the complaining now. " . . . last three loads the count has come out short." He lifted the canvas tarp covering the wagon, peered at the goods and tied it back down.

Mr. Shakleton kicked out the wheel chocks, and untied the horse. "I swear everything has been delivered correctly from this warehouse. If you're looking for a thief, don't look any further than that damned Scot. He's always where he isn't wanted."

"I thought you meant to dispose of him this last voyage." Mr. Asher climbed up on the wagon seat and took the reins.

"I tried. The fellow is slipperier than an eel in a barrel. You just watch out for him." Mr. Shakleton slapped the horse on the rump. He watched as Mr. Asher drove away, then went back in the house.

They had to mean Davy McRae. I remembered the sailor in the rigging. Davy had said the fellow was trying to murder him on Mr. Shakleton's orders. So he had been telling the truth.

"Try this one, missy." The old woman had a piece of green silk that must once have been part of a quilted gown.

I waved it away. "I've changed my mind. I don't want anything after all." I pushed past her and went out. There was no use trying to see Mary with Mr. Shakleton there. I would just have to try again later. I walked away with the old woman's shrill complaints following me down the block.

I was hot and tired by the time I reached the Asher's kitchen.

"What is the matter?" Chloe poured me a glass of cool water from the pitcher.

Lydia watched, a sardonic smile tilting her lips. "Had a bit of a romp, have you?"

I realized my cap was awry and bits of dusty lint clung to my skirt.

"Ethan's still gone," Mistress Asher said sourly.

Lydia laughed. "There's more fish in the sea than in this house, Mama. Just ask Sally."

I didn't respond. After all, what could I say? "I wasn't dallying with your son or anyone else. I was eavesdropping on your husband." Without a word, I accepted the water and drank it before unpacking the day's marketing.

The worst of it was I had not managed to see Mary. I thought to try later, but all day Mistress Asher kept a suspicious eye on me, fussing at every chore until long after supper was served and the dishes were washed. It was full dark when she finally took herself off to bed, and I slipped out to the stable. I meant to think of a plan to help Mary, but after such an exhausting day, neither the heat of the night, nor the shuffling and stamping of the horse, nor even the worries about my friend could keep my eyes open.

CHAPTER 13

I slept late the next morning and fell behind in my chores. It was long after breakfast before I ventured upstairs to empty the chamber pots. I hated this task at the best of times. With hours to ripen in the heat, the family's nightly leavings were even less pleasant. Briefly, I considered running away and risking a flogging. But only briefly. One couldn't die of the noxious odor of a chamber pot after all.

So with an extra rag to hold against my nose to block the smell, I took up the pot from the master bedroom first. As I left Mr. Asher's bedroom, I heard Mr. Asher's deep voice shouting from Ethan's study across the hall. "You and Tom think I've one foot in the grave. Well, you've a long wait for that! Tom will kill himself with whoring and drinking before he even comes of age. And you . . . " The scorn thickened his voice like mud choking the street's gutter. "Just wait. Gideon will get it all. The only one of my three sons worth anything."

"Not son. Grandson," Ethan said. His voice was low, almost inaudible through the heavy door. Had I heard him right? Did he mean Jeb? No one ever paid poor wee Jeb any mind. I had no time to wonder what he meant, though, for at that moment there was a resounding thud and a crash. The door sprang open under my fingers, and I leaped backward.

Not soon enough.

Ethan crashed into me, tromping on my foot and tripping me up. I fell. The chamber pot crashed against the floor, spilling its nasty contents. With his eyebrows drawn together in a scowl of black fury, Ethan swept past me as if he were blind. His cheek was red, and tiny beads of blood oozed from a small cut on his lip.

Samuel Asher was at the door after him before I could rise. He saw me and stopped short.

"What did you hear?" he demanded, making no move to help me up. His powdered wig had slipped back, baring the broad expanse of his sloping forehead, wrinkled now in disgust. Whether from the noxious smell or the interruption, I couldn't tell.

"Nothing," I said truthfully. At least, I hadn't heard anything that made sense. "I only just came up. For the chamber pots."

He loomed over me like a vulture, his black eyes glittering with suspicion. Then, stepping carefully over the puddles, he went downstairs after Ethan, muttering. "One day he'll go too far."

I surveyed the mess. Some of the strong liquid had spattered the wall and my skirt, but most had splashed on the smooth wooden floorboards of the hallway. I set about cleaning it up.

The rest of the day was no better. Nothing went right. The fire smoked and burned slow all day. Both dinner and supper were late, and when I went to scrub the dishes, I dropped Mistress Asher's best porcelain bowl. It struck against the iron spider and shattered into pieces. By that time, I didn't even care about the scolding Mistress Asher would give. I just swept up the pieces and dumped them with the rest of the rubbish.

I was exhausted when I finally went out to sleep. A cool breeze tickled the leaves of the oak trees lining the yard and wispy clouds scudded across a dark sky. Tired as I was, I let the breeze play with my sweaty hair, before visiting the necessary and turning toward the barn.

A sound, like a sob or a sigh in the wind brought me up short. I peered into the darkness beyond the garden, but I couldn't see anything in the shadows. I carried no lantern, since I never wanted it seen from the house. No one had guessed yet that I was sleeping in the barn, and I would just as soon leave it that way.

I took another step. It wasn't full dark yet. A deep twilight lingered, turning the sky to indigo. For a moment, I saw a white ghostly shape wavering at the edge of the yard. My hands felt clammy. "Davy?" I whispered, but the figure was too small to be a man. Was it a dog? There were far too many half wild dogs in the city, vicious and hungry things, with little fear of humans. But this shape seemed too fey, too ephemeral for a dog.

"Hello?" My voice wavered.

Suddenly the shape separated itself from the darkness and hurtled toward me. My first reaction was fear, throwing up my arm to ward it off. Then I realized it was no dog, but a child.

"Leah? What are you doing here?"

She was crying too hard to answer. I stroked her hair and murmured, kneeling to wrap my arms around her. The damp from the grass seeped up, soaking my skirt.

"It's Mam. He's taken her." Her voice was a breathy whisper that shuddered into a sob.

She meant Mr. Shakleton, of course. I held her close and rocked with her while her breath caught in her throat. Leah made almost no sound as she cried. I could hear the crickets singing in the dark night over her ragged gulps of air. "There, there," I crooned. "You're safe now, lass."

Finally her body stopped shaking, and she sagged against me, her wet face buried in my shoulder.

"Tell me what's happened. Where's your brother?"

"Dead," she whispered. "He's dead." She took a deep breath and shuddered with it, but held back her tears.

Dead? I rocked back, as if I'd been hit. "Tell me." I bent close to hear her.

"All night . . . He was so hot. I tried to keep him quiet like that man told me. I tried." She trembled with the effort of holding back a sob.

I patted her back gently. "I know you did."

"'I never put him down, not even a moment. But Mam didn't come and didn't come. And then when she did, it was too late."

"And then?" I prompted.

"We ran. It was so dark, and I was that scared, but I never cried. We ran and ran. But they caught up anyway. Mam shoved me down in the hay and bid me stay till all were gone and then come to find you. I came as quick as I could, but there were dogs, and I'm so hungry."

"How long ago? How long since Rabbie died?"

She swayed a bit. "I dinna' ken."

I caught her to keep her from falling. She weighed so little in my arms, I thought she might drift away like the feathers of a dandelion clock. I did a few quick calculations in my head. Peg had seen Mary three days ago, when Rabbie was sick. If he had died that same night, it would mean she'd been two days without food. No wonder the poor child was faint.

First things first. I had to feed her and then find Mary.

I glanced back at the house. Lantern light showed from one upstairs window, the master's study, but the rest of the house was dark. I knew Tom and Ethan had gone out for the night, and the others would be asleep. Still, I couldn't risk bringing her into the house with me.

I carried her instead into the stable. Though I slept there at night, I took care never to leave my cloak or any sign of my presence behind. Tom cleaned the stable daily, fed and watered the horses, but he was not a particularly early riser, especially when he'd been out late. So far at least, he'd seen no sign of me there.

Tom and Ethan would not likely be back soon. Usually they came in late, stabled their horses quickly, and stumbled half drunk into the house, never knowing I slept in the loft. Leah could spend the night with me there.

"Up you go, lass," I said, setting Leah in front of the ladder. "I'll be back with a bite for you faster than you can blink twice."

I gathered up a half loaf of stale bread and several apples. There was a bit of cheese in the pantry saved for the master's breakfast. On impulse, I took that, too. I would think of some excuse to explain its absence later.

Leah ate greedily without a word and fell asleep with the last apple still in her hand.

I put the apple in my pocket for later. Such a precious child. How could anyone think to hurt her? And poor Mary, one child dead, the other lost. She must be insane with worry. I had to get word to her that Leah was safe.

But first I would have to find a place where Leah would be safe. I couldn't keep her here. The Ashers were no more likely to help a stray waif than Mr. Shakleton. Ethan might help. He had helped me with the letter after all. But Ethan would be out late, and when he came back he would have Tom in tow.

I thought of Peg. She had spoken well of her master. But I had a deep distrust of all masters by now. More practically, Peg's house lay six miles away, the other side of the market, a good two hours walk in the dark. Leah would never make it that far.

There was only one other option. Davy McRae. He had offered to help that day in the garden.

Leah slept, her head resting in my lap, but I could not. I leaned back against a mound of hay and tried to think. Only one thing stood sure. I could not let Leah be found here in the morning. I would have to take her to Davy tonight. I could wait until the moon rose. Surely it was less than a mile to the wharves, and I didn't think there were very many turnings.

I let Leah sleep until the moon shone through the cracks in the wood slats of the barn walls. Then I gently shook her awake. "Come child," I whispered, "We have to go now."

She sat up obediently, blinking at me like a tiny disheveled owl. Without speaking, I helped her down the ladder and hurried away as fast as we could. I tried not to think about the penalty for running. I would be back before morning. Long before morning. No one would be the wiser for my midnight excursion.

Leah stumbled after me. I kept a tight grip on her arm and didn't let her slow down until we were far enough away I could not see the house anymore.

The street was unpaved, and moonlight cast deep shadows in the ruts, making it hard to judge where to put my feet.

Leah walked with her eyes half closed, whimpering a bit now and then. The sound tore at my heart. What had happened to the bright, cheery lassie who played cat's cradle with me?

We crossed the stone bridge over Dock Creek. I turned, thinking to follow the brackish smell of mud and rotting garbage to the river, but the street dead-ended. Leah's legs folded up and she sat down. I gave her the apple I'd saved. Obediently, she took a bite, then let it drop in her lap. The poor thing was worn out. I would have to carry her.

"Climb on pig-a-back," I told her. I laced my arms around her legs, and retraced our steps. With Leah on my back, we moved faster, but I still had to watch my feet constantly to manage the rutted ground. Soon, Leah lay her head on my shoulder and slept, growing heavier with each step until my shoulders burned with the strain.

At the next turning, I hesitated. Everything looked unfamiliar in the dark. The moonlit houses loomed overhead, seeming to sway and clutch at me, instead of standing square and tall as houses were supposed to do. "Don't let your imagination run away with you here, Callie my girl," I told myself. "Finding Davy is the only practical answer, and you've got to be practical." But how was I to find him, when I couldn't even find the river? I peered up and down the street. In the distance a lone street lamp flickered. Recently more people had installed such lights in front of their houses in our neighborhood, but there weren't many along this stretch of road. I stood still, considering if this meant I was going the right way or not. Then I heard waves lapping against the shore. I followed the sound downhill.

Soon the scent of fresh water and tar replaced the stench of Dock Creek, and the sounds of creaking wood and slapping ropes mingled with the sound of waves. Then more disconcerting noises wafted through the darkness. Bursts of raucous laughter and snatches of disharmonious song reminded me the river front was a part of the city unlikely to keep civilized hours. I didn't want to be caught out by a watchman or a randy, drunken sailor.

Moving cautiously and keeping to the shadows, I reached the end of the street and saw the moon shining on water. The wharves stretched both north and south. I leaned back into the shadows beside a deep doorstep and slid Leah off my aching back. She muttered a whispery complaint, but didn't wake. I rolled my shoulders to ease the stiffness and surveyed the scene.

My heart sank at the sight. Though quieter than in the daytime, there were any number of men awake. Here and there lantern light flickered through the unshuttered window of a tippling house or the open mouth of a groggery carved into the caves in the riverbank. In two or three places clumps of men gathered round a small fire, passing a bottle. Even more disheartening than the activity along the waterfront was the sheer number of wharves. They stretched in both directions as far as I could see and over a hundred ships lay beside them.

How in heaven's name was I to find Davy? He had said to ask for him. I eyed the various men I could see from shelter of my hiding place. One fellow lay in the gutter not far from me, snoring. Not far beyond him five ill-kempt sailors lounged in front of an open doorway. Downwind of them, I could tell they had been a long time at sea. One of the crew kept trying to sing "The Three Ravens," a song I'd heard often aboard the ship, but this man kept getting stuck on the "down, derry, derry, downs" and his companions ignored him. I remembered Hairy Hands from the ship and shuddered slightly. That was not the place to ask for help.

I chewed on my lower lip. Perhaps I could go along by the water, keep to the shadows, and try to read the names painted on the ships' hulls. His wouldn't be a big ship, I reasoned. He wouldn't have sailed the ocean with us if he had his own vessel to do it in. His ship would be smaller, built for coastal waters. Here, near where I hid, the ships were huge, as big or bigger than the one that had carried me. I turned my steps away from the fight in the tavern, toward the far end of the wharves where the ships were smaller. There were fewer taverns in this direction and even less light, as the clouds drifted in, covering the moon. My arms ached. Every time I stopped to rest, Leah slipped off my back, and I had to haul her up again and go on.

'Twas hopeless. Ship after ship lay at harbor, some with names clearly painted and others too dark or dirty to see. On some, sailors stood guard or lolled about on deck. At others, I could hear the drinking and partying below decks. But there were too many.

I let Leah slip off my back and sank down against a pile of boxes stacked near the water. I had failed. I couldn't save Leah from Mr. Shakleton or myself from Mr. Asher, and I couldn't help Mary. I drew my knees inside my skirt, dropped my head to my arms against them and swallowed a sob of despair.

Then I heard faint music. Not raucous, drunken song, but real music. A thin piping sounded the Scots love ballad of Tam Lin. Over the piping rose the rich, mellow voice, "Janet has kilted her green kirtle, a little aboon her knee . . . " I knew that song. More important, I knew that voice.

I jumped up, hoisted Leah on my back, and stumbled toward the sound.

The guard posted at the gangplank leaned against the railing with his eyes closed and his cheek propped up by his hand. I studied him from the shadow of the shack at the end of the pier. A glint of gold in one ear caught the moonlight. He seemed to be dozing, or at least paying more attention to the music from below deck then to his duties, but he jerked upright as I set foot on the gangplank and stood to block my way.

"Ye canna' go there, miss," he said in a broad Scots accent that was as much music to my ears as the piper aboard the boat.

"Aye, I can," I said stubbornly trying to push past. It was no good though, as he stood solid as a rock, arms crossed. I saw now he only had the one ear, from which the golden earring dangled. "It's Davy McRae I need, and I'll thank you to get out of my way and let me to him." I was not about to let anyone stop me now, so close. If I didn't think I would drop Leah, or tumble over myself, I would have kicked him.

"Captain Davy?" His manner changed completely. "Well, why didn't you say so?" He put out a broad beefy hand to help me up the narrow gangplank and pushed me toward a covered barrel. "Just wait here," he said. "I'll fetch the captain."

Captain? That was a surprise. I eased Leah off my back once more and sat on the barrel, holding her in my arms. The ship swayed comfortably beneath me and the breeze played with the ropes, gently slapping them against the masts. I closed my eyes, wishing I could sleep as easily as the child. The music from below stopped abruptly. Shortly, the piping resumed, without the singer.

Then Davy McRae was there, lifting the child from my lap. Never was the sight of any man so welcome as that. I wanted to fall into his arms and weep with relief, but he had Leah there now.

"Callie, what in God's name are ye doing here at this time of night?"

How could I explain? I hugged my arms tight across my chest, hunching my shoulders against the ache. "You told me to come to you did I need help. I came."

He whistled, whether in admiration or disapproval I couldn't tell. "Aye, that I did. Still, I hardly expected ye in the middle of the night. And this is Leah, no? Mary Rawles' child?"

I nodded. Why was I so much more tired now, when he held Leah?

"I'm thinking ye have a story to tell me, lass, but it will wait. Come into my parlor, and I'll give ye a wee drop. Ye carried the child all the way, have ye? She's not ill?"

"No, just tired and frightened." As was I. Was it foolish to wish I could trade places with Leah? I shook my head and followed him into a cabin, tidy and well appointed, though not lavish. Davy settled Leah on the bunk.

She roused a bit. "Mr. McRae. Tell me a story."

"Later, lassie." He covered her with a light quilt. She was back asleep without ever having truly woken. Davy opened a cupboard behind the door, took out two glasses and a bottle of whisky. He poured a generous portion for each of us and sat at the small table opposite me.

I told him how Leah had come to me and what I knew of Mary as I sipped the fiery liquid. It burned, leaving a warm glow in the hollow of my stomach.

Davy drained his glass in one gulp, then jumped up and paced back and forth across the cabin, increasingly restless while I talked. The candlelight cast grotesque shadows on the curving wall. A stubbly growth of beard darkened his face, and his eyes burned with amber fire.

"The child needs a safe place to stay," I finished. "I didn't think I could trust her to Mr. Shakleton."

Davy's fist hit the table, interrupting me. "That man's a snake. No one in his right mind would think to leave a child with him."

"I was just telling you the same thing." I stood up. "I took you at your word to help, but if you cannot, well, I'll just take her off again."

"Sit down, lass. Don't be a fool." He refilled both our glasses and handed mine back. He took a sip, then spoke again in a calmer voice. "I can help ye, just as I said. It's a surprise to me, but I know a place to take the lassie." He spun a chair and straddled it. "There's a woman not too far from here. She'll do."

What sort of a woman? I wondered, with a wave of irrational jealousy. I had no business thinking of the women he might know in Philadelphia.

"Where is she?" I asked, keeping my voice steady. "I'll have to tell Mary."

"I'll see to it Mary knows she's safe," Davy shook his head. "Best ye don't know where I put her. Mr. Asher and Mr. Shakleton are thick in all this business. If ye talk to Mary, they're bound to suspect something's up. Ye can't let slip what ye don't know."

There was a knock at the door just then. At Davy's gruff command, another sailor entered with a tray, containing sliced cheeses, biscuits, and a bowl of steaming broth.

"'Tis not much, sir," he said. "But I thought as the lady could do with a bite, her looking so worn out and all."

"Thank ye," Davy said, taking the tray from him.

I didn't want to admit it, but Davy was right. Leah might be safer if I didn't know where she landed, but I still meant to reassure Mary.

I took up a slice of cheese and broke off a chunk of biscuit to go with it. "Is this really your ship?"

"'Tis my father's." He smiled a crooked smile, one corner of his mouth lifting higher than the other. "Though as he's in Scotland and I'm here, ye might say as she is mine to master."

"Oh." I had thought Davy McRae to be a man of no consequence, like Mr. Rawles, or the others in the crowded hold. It upset my whole view of him to find him a ship's master.

Davy sipped his whisky, a slight frown drawing down the corners of his mouth.

I pushed the empty glass away and rose. "I have to get back," I said. "They'll say I ran if I'm not there when the family wakes."

Davy caught my arm. "Ye don't have to go back, Callie. I would see ye safe as well as the child."

The thought tempted me. For a moment I closed my eyes and imagined what it might mean to stay aboard this ship. No more scrubbing the Asher's dishes for a start! Could Davy actually take me back to Scotland?

No. Davy's ship was far too small to make an ocean voyage. Davy had helped any number of times, but he didn't have the means to see me safe. I shook my head. "The letter from Grandfather will be here any day now. I'll bide with them 'til I've a passage home. That's the better way."

Davy's lips tightened. He took a breath as if he meant to argue, then let it out in a sigh. Without a word, he followed me on deck.

Outside, the air stank of rotten fish, mud and weeds, but it was cool and refreshing in spite of that and far away from the intrigue of the Asher house.

Only, I realized with a start, I didn't know quite where that was. The wharves were dark now, with very few lights shining at windows or open doors. The alleys and roads to the wharves were straight enough, if only I could remember which one I'd come down. I turned back to Davy. "Please. Could you just tell me the way I need to go?"

Davy laughed. "Oh, Callie. Ye do give me a thing to smile at."

The walk back seemed much shorter, now Leah was off my back. I walked beside Davy, holding his arm for support but thinking of Leah, asleep on the bunk. What would become of her? What was I doing, abandoning her like this? But she wasn't alone. She had Davy McRae to take care of her now, and God forgive me, that would have to be enough.

It was still dark, but already there was a lightening in the east, a nearly imperceptible fading of black to gray, and the first twittering birds were waking. The looming shadows of the houses receded and the eerie pools of light from street lamps lost their sinister aspect.

I sighed. Less menacing or not, the closer we got to the Asher's the more miserable I felt. I thought of Leah, safe asleep on Davy's ship in spite of her uncertain future. Wasn't it better to have no idea of what was to come than to return to certain misery?

Then I shook myself. That was romantic twaddle. The child was hardly safe without her mam. And if her present situation was unhappy, her future looked even more chancy. Miserable as I might be at the Asher's, I meant to go back to Scotland, and that was the way to do it.

Davy stopped a short ways up the street from Asher's. "Best not be seen with me, not at this time of night. There would be too many uncomfortable questions."

I took a step forward, then turned back. "Thank you. You'll let me know . . ."

"Aye, and I'll get word to Mary the bairn is safe."

There was nothing more to say. I turned to walk the rest of the way, but Davy put out a hand to stop me. "Ye dinna' have to go back."

I couldn't look him or I would never be strong enough to say no. I twisted the ends of my kerchief into a knot. "I must."

It was his turn to sigh. "Well, see ye dinna' get lost."

"What? It's only just over there!" I looked up indignantly. "I couldn't get lost in that stretch."

"Even so." His eyes sparkled. "Hush," he added putting a finger to my lips to stop my protest. "I just wanted to see ye look at me once more." His hand brushed my check as he tucked a stray wisp of hair behind my ear. My knees wobbled. Then he bent and kissed me, quickly and fiercely, a meeting of warm lips. I could taste the whisky still lingering in his breath. I closed my eyes. Then just as suddenly as he'd started, he broke off the kiss. Without another word, he strode away. His boots thudded quietly in the packed dust of the street.

I stood still, watching after him until he turned off the street without looking back even once. Ah, Davy McRae, I thought. You're right. I could get lost, even this close.

CHAPTER 14

There was no point in trying to sleep. It was already time to be in the kitchen, stirring up the fire and starting the bread. I went around to the back of the house and came in through the kitchen door.

Lydia sat in her mother's rocker, twirling a ringlet of her dark hair around a finger. "Up early? Or is it out late?"

I turned my back to her and bent over the hearth so she couldn't see the sudden flush I felt across my cheeks.

"I told Cora," she went on in the same bored tone, "my room has a window on the street."

"Oh?" The hearth shovel shook in my hand as I dug a live coal out of the ashes. Just what had she seen?

"Cora tried hiding in the stable too." The floorboards squeaked as Lydia rocked slowly back and forth. "It didn't do her any good in the end. Of course, she had only the one lover."

I spun around to glare at her. "What exactly are you saying?" I demanded.

Lydia smiled wryly, but the smile did not reach her eyes. "I'm just talking about balance." She held up her hands, palms flat, as if weighing one against the other. "Cora couldn't manage it with just one lover." She curled up her hands into fists and let them drop in her lap.

I leaned the shovel against the side of the hearth. "Just where is this mysterious Cora? Maybe I should talk to her, so she can tell me herself what it is I'm supposed to be mindful of."

Lydia stood up, all pretense of a smile gone. "Cora's dead," she spat. "And the baby she carried too." She stalked out of the kitchen.

Dead? Lots of women died in childbirth, of course, but something about Lydia's warning made me think that wasn't Cora's fate. For a moment I wished I had agreed to stay with Davy. But that would be equally dangerous, I suspected, and offer far less chance to get back to Edinburgh. I would just have to be careful.

At breakfast an hour later, Mistress Asher announced the day would be spent cleaning the hearths. "Who's to help?" she asked.

Ethan held up his hands. "Not me. Father and I have a new shipment to see to at the docks."

Lydia stood up. "Alice is expecting me this morning." She followed her brother.

That left the mistress, Tom, Chloe, and me to start the chore as soon as breakfast had been cleared away. We raked out some coals and put them in a bucket, covering them with ash before we drowned all the hearth fires. In short order it became obvious Chloe would be no help at all. First Jeb knocked over the ash bucket, blackening himself and the floorboards. While Chloe picked him up and swept ineffectually at the mess, Gideon tripped over the fire poker, knocking himself in the head. He started howling.

I took the broom from Chloe. "I'll do that," I said. "You had best mind the lads."

Chloe scooped up both boys and took them out to the garden to stay out of the way. That left Mistress Asher to direct the work and Tom and me to do it.

Tom's job was to catch a couple of chickens and drop them down the chimneys so that their frantic fluttering wings would brush the chimney soot loose. My job was to clean up the mess after them. After the chickens had done their part, Tom sat on the edge of the table, ready to carry the full buckets of ash and water out and even more ready to annoy his mother. He joked about his sisters, his brother, and my rump as I knelt on the hearth to sweep out the corners.

Mistress Asher grew more and more irritated with him. Finally she snapped. "Shut up, boy, or take yourself off. Surely your father or brother needs some kind of help."

Tom set the bucket of dirty water he was carrying down in the middle of the floor and made an exaggerated courtly bow to his mother. "I beg your pardon, mother," he said with a sardonic grin that made a mockery of his words. He turned to me and bowed again, with a rude wink. "I hope I've not offended you, sweet lady," he said mockingly, "by carrying slops for you. I'm sure if it were Ethan doing the service, you'd be more congenial."

"If it were Ethan, he would be gentleman enough to . . ." My voice trailed away. To do what? Carry me away? Stop this obnoxious work? Truthfully, in spite of his promises, he had done none of that.

"To take you to bed?" Tom finished for me.

"Shut your filthy mouth," Mistress Asher screeched.

"Your pardon again, Mother. I'd forgotten your . . . " He eyed her as rudely as he had eyed me. "Your fondness for your stepson."

She threw the poker at him. He ducked and it hit the far wall of the kitchen, clattering against the copper pans hanging there.

With a laugh, Tom grabbed a biscuit from the bowl on the table and sauntered out of the kitchen in search of other mischief.

Mistress Asher had me serve a cold lunch and continue cleaning the upstairs fireplaces. My eyes, already heavy with lack of sleep, burned from the gritty soot and dust. I scraped out piles of ash and carted them out to the barrel in the yard, where the rain would seep through the ash to make lye water for soap. As I worked, I fretted about Mary. Was Davy getting a message to her? Was Leah safe?

By late afternoon, I knelt in front of the last hearth in the master bedroom. I swept out the ash, then picked up a damp rag to wipe the bricks clean. As I bent over, I heard footsteps on the stairs. The door to the study slammed and the master's voice rose in anger.

"That scoundrel is robbing me right under my nose, and you're too weak-kneed to stand up to him," Samuel Asher snarled.

I stopped. The chimney in the room where I worked connected with the chimney of the study. I could hear the voices, a bit muffled but mostly audible. If I could hear them, they could hear me. I didn't want Mr. Asher to find me alone upstairs. Lydia's warning about Cora's fate was still fresh in my mind.

But the answering voice was Ethan's. I let out the breath I'd been holding. If Ethan was with him, I had little to fear from Mr. Asher. Ethan's reply was too soft to catch the words, but it clearly did not please his father.

"I don't trust that man," Mr. Asher continued. "And you are a fool if you do."

Who were they talking about? Mr. Shakleton? Davy? Another business partner? As the only customs agent in the whole colony, Mr. Asher worked with a lot of people, few of them trustworthy.

I missed the next bit, but then Ethan spoke sharply. "I'll see to unloading that ship from Edinburgh myself. Here are the bills and letters from the captain."

"And what good will that do, boy? You've missed every theft of goods so far. You won't see as much as a blind man in a cave without a candle. Here. Give me that. I'll take care of it and figure the tax."

I sat back on my heels. A ship from Edinburgh, he'd said, carrying letters. Even now, the letter from Grandfather promising payment for my safe return was sitting on the other side of the chimney. I could hardly believe it.

With renewed energy, I set to finish my task. Now Ethan would show his father the letter, and I would shed my guise of Sally MacLaughlin and be on my way home. No more Cinderella and the wicked stepsisters for me. My prince was about to rescue me.

I finished that last chimney and took the ashes outside. I washed my soot-streaked hands and face and rinsed out my smudged apron. I stirred the stew and sliced bread for supper, expecting at any minute Ethan would come into the kitchen to share the news. But no one interrupted the meal preparations. My stomach churned with impatience as I served.

Mr. Shakleton had come as guest to supper. As usual, he talked of what ships had docked and what they brought. Ethan stayed silent and brooding. Several times I started to ask about the letter, but each time his forbidding expression stopped me.

I decided to wait and catch Ethan on his way out. I meant to sweep the hall as a pretense for lingering near the door, but instead I leaned against the wall in the hall outside the dining room. I was so tired; my eyes kept closing even while I stood there. I shook my head to try to clear away the cobwebs and propped my chin atop the broom handle to stay awake

Lydia chattered on and on about a new dress pattern she'd borrowed from Alice. No one answered her except Tom, who told bawdy jokes about her friends. When Lydia ignored his bait, he turned to the topic of Chloe's absent beaus and poor Jeb's absent father.

Chloe excused herself. Sniffling, she brushed past me without a word, balancing a baby on each hip as she took them up to bed.

Tom turned next to teasing his mother until Mr. Asher bellowed at him to shut up. I wished they would all be done with the meal and leave me to talk to Ethan. Why wasn't he saying anything? He couldn't have forgotten me. Perhaps he was waiting until his father was in a better mood. By now, Mr. Asher was drowning out even Tom's rude jests with his tirade about thievery. To hear it from him, every merchant in the city was stealing from him, and his sons were nothing but incompetent, lazy nincompoops who helped the wily thieves more than stopping them.

"Leave off your whining, Samuel," Mr. Shakleton said in his high, nasally voice. "You want to know thievery? Just look at that damned freight I took on." His next words were muffled as he took a bite and chewed. ". . . no good to anyone since the flogging. Fact is, she's likely to die before I've any return on my investment."

Die? The word shook me out of my stupor. He must mean Mary. He'd had her flogged. Of course, that was often the punishment for running. I shuddered, and the flesh on my own back tingled as I thought of the whip biting into bared skin. Poor Mary. All she'd ever tried to do was care for her family. I squeezed the broom handle, wishing I had a sword that I could run through Mr. Shakleton. Somehow, I vowed, I would see a way to help Mary before I went home.

I took a deep breath. No wonder Ethan thought it best not to say anything about the letter in front of Mr. Shakleton. Peg had called him devil's spawn. I thought the term too kind.

Mistress Asher rang the bell for me to clear the dishes. She and Lydia went up to bed, but the men went on talking while I cleaned up. I tried to catch Ethan's eye and signal him to meet me later, but he was not paying the slightest attention. I finished all the dishes, and still Mr. Shakleton, Mr. Asher, and his sons drank and smoked their pipes. I fretted in the kitchen for an hour, then stepped into the hall.

The men showed no sign of tiring. Their voices rose and fell in animated conversation behind the closed door of the dining room. They weren't likely to finish any time soon. A light, rhythmic snoring from Lydia's room meant she had drifted off to sleep instead of reading as she had planned. No sound came from the room with Chloe and the boys. It was tempting to dash up the stairs and find the letter now.

I had put one foot on the lowest step, when the door to the dining room creaked. I leaped off the stairs and snatched up my broom just as Tom came out, empty wine jug in hand.

"Bit late to be sweeping, isn't it, girl?" He leered.

I felt the heat of a deep blush of fear. Another step and he would have caught me.

Tom, undoubtedly mistaking my blush for something else, slapped his knee. "Or are you waiting for dessert? I'll warn you, my brother is not in best form just now, but I would be more than happy to stand in." He made a rude gesture. "If you think you can handle it."

"I . . . I. don't want anyone, least of all you." I stammered. Then using the broom as a shield, I pushed past him to the kitchen.

Tom laughed all the way down to the cellar.

I stood in the kitchen, shaking. Mary had been flogged for running. What would they do if they caught me reading Mr. Asher's private papers?

The fire on the hearth burned low, but the kitchen, with the door closed against the darkness, was still warm and stuffy. I took off my short jacket and fanned myself with the dishcloth. After precious little rest the night before and the heavy work of the day, I was too tired to think clearly. I desperately wanted sleep, but even more desperately, I wanted that letter. I propped myself up with my elbows on my knees. They couldn't be much longer.

I must have dozed, for I woke with a start. My arms had gone numb, and pins and needles shot through them as I jerked awake. The hearth fire, with few ashes to bank it, had burned out, and the coals were black and cold. I'd been asleep for at least a couple of hours. The house was silent and the darkness so thick I couldn't tell how long I'd slept.

But something had wakened me, a sound of some sort. A small sound, like a child crying in the night. A foot on the steps perhaps? Or a door closing? I listened even more intently, my ears straining till I could hear my own heartbeat.

I had no idea who was home. Had Tom and Ethan gone out as usual? Had they returned? Had Mr. Shakleton left? What of Mr. Asher? There was no way of knowing. A mouse skittered across the wood floor. Upstairs someone turned in bed, rustling the straw tick. But it was no good. The barely audible creaks and groans of a house asleep revealed nothing.

I stood up. I would have to risk searching the study now, while everyone slept. Safer that than wait until tomorrow. I patted the pocket I wore under my petticoat to make sure of the knife I had stolen the night Mr. Asher had come after his wife. I wasn't sure what I meant to do with it, but the solid weight gave me some comfort.

Not daring to light a candle, I crept up the stairs. Down the hall in Chloe's room one of the babes fussed. I heard Chloe stumble to his cradle, crooning softly as she took him to nurse.

At the top landing, I paused. A breeze rattled the window, open to the cooling night air.

The door to the study squeaked as I slowly pushed it open and slipped inside, shutting the door carefully behind me. I stood with my back pressed against the solid wood while my eyes adjusted. Something was wrong. The odor of something rank filled the room. The candle had guttered out and the night was dark, with shifting clouds hiding the moon and dimming the stars. The curtain fluttered, but nothing else stirred. The clouds slowly drifted past like the wispy rags of a shroud. A stray bit of moonlight shone on the white plume of a quill pen on the carpet. I caught my breath. Samuel Asher was many things, but never careless. He would not leave a quill on the floor. Still holding my breath, I glanced from the quill to the desk, and then to the bulk in the chair beside the desk. The room was not empty.

He lay slumped over, unmoving. My hand still on the latch, I stared at him. Downstairs in the hallway, the grandfather clock ticked.

Was he drunk? Passed out? But he always snored, a great rumbling sound that shook the bedstead.

I had to breathe. Slowly, I let out the breath I'd been holding and just as slowly took in air. The curtain at the open window moved, but Mr. Asher did not. There was no rise and fall of his shoulders. My palm, suddenly slick with sweat, trembled on the latch. No one could stay that still, that long. Not sleeping then. Not drunk. Dead.

I should have left right then, slipping out as quietly as I had slipped in. Let someone else find him in the morning.

But the letter from Scotland meant freedom. And an end to hiding.

Help for me and Mary, and a return to all I wanted. I had to find it. Still, none of that made me easy about searching a dead man's room, especially with him still in it. I took a deep breath. I could not stand dithering by the doorway all night. I would not let a dead man frighten me. He could no longer be a threat to me or anyone else. But the longer I dawdled, the greater my risk of getting caught by one of the others.

I tiptoed across the floor, wincing with each creaking whisper of wood. Mr. Asher's hand lay flopped across the desktop, still clutching at a wrinkled paper. Tentatively, I touched his hand. The fingers felt cool and waxy, but not yet stiff. Holding my breath, I teased the paper out of his grasp and held it up. The sheet was blank.

More papers lay scattered across the desktop mashed under his face. It was too dark to read any of them. I would have to take them over by the window to find the letter from Grandfather, and to do that, I would have to move him. With a shudder of distaste, I put my hand on his back, thinking just to shift him over a bit. The cloth of his frock coat was wet with something thick and sticky. My hand slipped as I pushed and suddenly bumped up against something long and hard lodged in his back. A knife. I flinched with the sudden realization of what that meant. He was not just dead. This wasn't a heart attack or a drunken apoplexy. Someone had stuck the knife in his back. Someone had murdered him.

My knees buckled. I fell against the dead man. He tumbled over, off the chair, hitting the floor with a loud thud. Silence filled the room. I stared at the quivering handle of the knife and the dark stain spreading across Samuel Asher's pale waistcoat.

Suddenly, a shadow in the window blocked the moonlight. Alarmed, I grabbed the knife and scrambled to my feet. Wraithlike, the figure slid inside. He wore dark clothing and his face was hidden, but I recognized him anyway.

"Davy McRae! What are you doing here?" I whispered.

He looked from me to the fallen body of my employer and back to the knife. "I think the more pertinent question is, what are ye doing here?"

Startled, I realized how it must look. I dropped the knife. "How can you even think . . ." I started angrily.

In two steps, he crossed the room, threw an arm around me, and clapped a hand to my mouth. I frantically struggled to free myself.

"Hush," he whispered, his breath tickling my ear.

Fear choked me. Maybe he had killed Mr. Asher, and I had interrupted him. He had my arms pinned, but I aimed a kick at him and tried to bite the hand smothering me.

He shook me, squeezing harder. "Stop it, Callie," he hissed. "Ye know I'll not hurt ye."

As suddenly as it had come, the panic fled. I did know he wouldn't hurt me. I stopped struggling and nodded to show I understood him.

He loosened his grip slowly, and we stood eyeing each other suspiciously. "It's no good. Ye have made enough noise already to wake the dead." He shot another glance at the dead man lying at our feet. "Or at least the household about him, drunk or no." He stood up, stepped over the body and turned the key in the lock on the door.

He was right. Already I could hear a confusion of voices as each member of the household flung open a bedroom door and demanded to know what was going on. In a heartbeat, they would gather enough sense to realize who was missing and come looking. I would have no chance to get past them to the kitchen. Desperately I looked around. Where could I hide?

Still ignoring the dead man, Davy grabbed a handful of papers from the desk and stuffed them inside his shirt. He shoved me toward the window. "Ye can't let them find ye here. There is a rope."

Feet pounded toward us, and fists rattled the door. I had no choice. When they found a servant in the master's study at this hour . . . I doubted they would even bother with a trial. I dangled my legs over the windowsill and took hold of the rope Davy had tied to the trellis.

"Hurry," Davy instructed. "Hand over hand. Dinna' let go until ye reach the bottom." Then he gave me a little push, and I was out the window.

I couldn't hang on. The rope slid painfully across my palms as I plunged down and my skirt ballooned upward. The billowing fabric caught and held on a loose nail in the sash. I gasped, hanging dizzily for a second or two. Then I heard an ominous ripping sound. I tumbled to the ground, hitting it with a thud that knocked the wind out of me.

Before I could get up and run to the stable, Davy was on the ground beside me. "Easy, lass. I meant ye to climb down, not dive out the window." He pulled me up and half dragged me across the garden toward the gate.

Light flared in the window behind us. "Stop!" Tom yelled out the window. "It's Sally." A pistol shot rang out, the ball smacking the ground to the left of us. Fear coursed through me and I ran, my bare feet scarcely touching the damp ground.

Davy had a horse waiting in the shadow of the trees. Without a word, he leapt up into the saddle and reached a hand down to pull me up behind him.

"Hang on!" He touched his heels to the horse's flanks.

I barely had time to clutch him around the waist before the horse leapt forward and away.

So I found myself galloping into the darkness, my petticoat torn and indecently hitched up above my knees, my flesh goosepimply with cold and shock, fleeing the scene of a murder.

Perhaps fleeing with the murderer himself. Questions beat against me as the horse's hooves pounded the road. Why had Davy been at the window? Had he killed Samuel Asher? He had worked with the man and even supped with him. It seemed an odd way to do business, killing your partners. Still, Davy had killed at least once before. There was that scuffle with the sailor on the boom. Davy claimed that had been to save himself, but killing a man in his own study could hardly be thought self-defense.

I should have been worried. Really, I should have been terrified. Riding off with Davy McRae was as crazy as boarding a ship to cross the ocean.

But what I actually felt was quite different. I lay my head against Davy's strong back sheltering me from the wind, and I felt free.

Part 3

Complications

Pennsylvania and Maryland, August 1754

CHAPTER 15

W e rode hard leaving Philadelphia, but beyond the gas lights of the city, the horse's pounding hooves slowed until a steady clip-clop punctuated the silence. The country grew rougher, with croplands and pastures giving way to stretches of wooded hillsides. I thought about asking Davy if he had killed Mr. Asher, but I wasn't sure I wanted to hear his answer. I settled for asking him where we were going.

"Baltimore," he said.

I 'd never heard of Baltimore and had no idea why we would go there, but I was too tired to ask. I closed my eyes, then jerked awake as I felt my grip slacken.

Davy must have felt me slipping. We stopped by a split rail fence to shift positions. "Ye are shivering, lass."

"I'm all right." I wasn't really cold, but I couldn't stop shaking.

Davy didn't argue. He put me in front of him, bracing me against his left arm while he held the reins in his right. He was so close I could feel his breath tickle the back of my neck. When he squeezed his thighs to signal the horse, the ripple of his muscles against me sparked a warm glow in the pit of my stomach. My shaking turned to trembling of a different sort as my heartbeat echoed his. Wrapped in the safety of his arms, I no longer cared where we were going.

Gradually the sky lightened, imperceptibly at first. Before the dark faded, a few clear, jerky notes of a warbler announced dawn. The wheezy voice of a siskin joined in and soon the air was filled with a cacophony of chirps, trills and whistles, promising a bright and glorious day. Davy whistled in imitation of one persistent bobolink, and the two continued an animated conversation until we passed out of range. In the growing light, I could see that even the horse had pricked up her ears and lightened her step in anticipation of the coming day.

I could muster no such energy. Gone was the euphoria of freedom, replaced with the lethargy of sheer exhaustion. I slumped against Davy and concentrated only on staying upright.

Finally, Davy turned the horse off the road and into a small copse of woods. "Just a bit further, lass," he murmured into my ear, in the voice used to calm a fractious horse. We stopped beside a patch of bracken under a great hemlock tree. Davy dismounted and reached up to help me. I tumbled into his arms, stiff in every bone of my body after hours of unaccustomed riding. My feet touched the ground, and my knees buckled. Davy caught me by the elbow and guided me a few steps to a mossy hillock. I sank into it.

He stood over me, rubbing his chin. My eyes closed.

"Callie." His voice was soft and very close. "Callie."

I opened one eye. I realized he'd been talking to me. Something about horses.

He squatted beside me. "I know ye are chilled and wanting a fire to warm ye, but ye must wait a bit more. Can ye do it?"

Wordlessly I nodded. As long as he didn't ask me to climb back up on that dratted horse, I didn't much care about a fire or anything else. I closed both eyes again.

"Bide ye here then. I'll no be long." He put his hand on my shoulder and squeezed briefly. I felt him stand up and heard the quiet pad of his footsteps receding. Then I heard the squeak of saddle leather as he mounted.

Suddenly, the sense of what he'd said penetrated and I realized he meant to leave me alone in the woods. Both eyes flew open. "Wait!" I struggled to stand up.

He had already drawn up the reins. "I'll no be long," he repeated. "Dinna' worry." Then, touching his heels to the horse's flank, he rode away.

I swayed unsteadily on my knees. I meant to run after him, but my legs were too heavy to move. I couldn't even find the energy to scream. I sank back to the leaf-strewn ground. Fury and frustration at Davy's leaving me warred with fear at being alone in the woods. I leaned against a mossy rock, intending only to rest, until I could sort out the jumble of emotions. It was no use. Exhaustion won. My eyes closed of their own volition and I fell asleep.

When I woke, the sun had climbed high, and the chorus of bird song had dwindled to a midday patter. I sat bolt upright, realizing Davy had been gone for hours. What if he didn't come back? If he had killed Samuel Asher, I was the only witness. But, I told myself, trying to fight rising panic, wouldn't that argue for killing me on the spot, not taking me along? Perhaps he meant only to lose me. After all, if I starved, or hopelessly lost myself in the woods, who would ever find me? With the sun straight overhead, I had no idea where I was, or which way led to Philadelphia. I squeezed my eyes shut, trying to recall. Had we been riding toward the soft glow of the dawn, or alongside it?

Other questions crowded out any sensible answer. Was I going to die out here like an animal in the wilderness? Would savage Indians find me defenseless and carry me off or murder me? I had been cold and miserable on the ship, and I had been tired and overworked at Asher's, but always I had been in the company of fellow humans. Now I was utterly alone, a fugitive from the law. For even though I most certainly had not killed Samuel Asher, I had no way to prove it unless I found out who had killed him.

I stood up abruptly. There was no point sitting here waiting like a helpless ninny for some ne'er-do-well vagabond. A little investigation of my surroundings revealed that Davy had left me in a narrow band of woods, tucked between a one-lane road and a small, rocky creek. Across the road, woods continued as far as I could see, an impenetrable tangle of sycamores, beech and chestnuts. The opposite bank of the creek was no different, save the underbrush was thicker. Other than the road itself, no cabin, clearing, or fence marked any evidence of human habitation.

I stood on the edge of the road, comtemplating my only link to civilization. A narrow, dusty path, wide enough for a set of wagon wheels, curved off into the woods in both directions. Grassy patches grew between the ruts. It was not well-traveled then. Quite possibly no one except us had set foot upon it in months. Nevertheless, the road surely had come from Philadelphia. The only question was, which way led back?

I retraced my steps to the creek and knelt along the bank to scoop out a few swallows. The water was cool and refreshing without the brackish taste of well water I had become accustomed to in Philadelphia. The overhanging trees offered some shade from the hot sun and cloudless sky. I dipped out another double handful of water and splashed it on my face.

Just then a frog jumped and landed with a plop in the creek. Startled, I jerked backwards, my heart pounding. I sat heavily in a puddle of mud along the bank. Wetness seeped through the thin fabric of my torn petticoat.

"Think, Callie," I told myself, standing up and brushing ineffectively at the mud. Only a bairn frighted at bumps in the night, and here it was broad daylight. The sleepy drone of insects mingled with occasional bright birdcalls innocuously filled the woods. No wild Indians hid behind the trees and no wild animals, save the frog, lurked in the shadows. It was time to make some sort of a plan.

Fleeing with Davy may have been one of my more foolish mistakes, I reflected. After all, I had done nothing wrong. But there had been no choice, really. Anyone who found me in the room would never believe Mr. Asher was dead when I came in. Then too, if I had been faster getting out the window, I might have made it to the stable without being seen. As it was, Tom had recognized me. Perhaps it did make sense to run, but I had to admit that the real reason I fled was simply because Davy had filled me with a breathless excitement that drove away all rational thought.

Well Davy wasn't here now to cloud my reason. I had to go back to Philadelphia. I needed to find that letter from Scotland, and I needed to talk to Mary. I didn't know what I might do to help her, but I couldn't just leave her there.

I just wasn't sure how to manage it. I walked back to the road and listened. No clop of hooves, no squeak of wagon wheel broke the quiet hum of the woods. The road lay as empty and deserted as it had all day, with no clear marks of anyone passing from either direction. I supposed I could wait for Davy. I didn't really believe he would just leave me alone in the woods. Eventually, he would return. But when? I looked to the road, winding into the woods a hundred yards in either direction, beckoning me to follow it. Just see what's beyond the next bend, it seemed to promise. Surely something there would show the way.

I hesitated a moment longer. I had left Grandfather's house in Leith and the Asher home in Philadelphia without a moment's thought, and neither venture had proved auspicious. Walking barefoot, without food or water, along an unknown road, could hardly turn out better. Still, to my mind, doing is always better than waiting. I meant to head back to Philadelphia. With a final shrug, I set out walking.

The sun burned hot in the late afternoon sky without any breeze to soften it. The road more or less followed the creek. I paused now and again for a drink of water, then plodded doggedly onward. I had been walking for several hours when I heard the sound of approaching hooves. I stopped in the middle of the road. I probably ought to have hidden to see if the rider looked like a gentleman who might help. But my belly felt as hollow as an empty drum, and my feet hurt. I was in no mood to wait for anything.

Soon the horseman came into view, trotting toward me down the road. I saw at once it was Davy McRae, riding the same horse he had been riding the night before and leading another horse, a small, compact bay. The setting sunlight shone on his hair like a golden mantle. In spite of myself, I smiled at seeing him, but my pleasure was short-lived.

He was whistling. Whistling! As if he hadn't a care in all the world. All my frenzied fear and worry from the past twenty-four hours transformed into anger, a black fury at the entire world of men who kept me from my purpose. I took a step forward, meaning to tell him just what I thought, and trod on a sharp rock. With a cry, I snatched up the stone and hurled it at him.

It fell far short of its mark. Davy jerked back on the reins, and his horse danced away.

"How dare you?" I began, reaching for another rock. I stopped suddenly, swaying as a black pounding behind my eyes made me quite dizzy. I sat down with a thud.

Davy touched his heels to the horse's flanks and rushed to my side. He knelt beside me. "Hold there, lass, easy now. Put your head between your knees till it passes."

I meant to berate him for leaving me in the woods, to demand he take me back to Philadelphia this instant. But instead I said, "I'm so hungry!"

Davy's worried face relaxed, and the gold flecks in his eyes twinkled. "Well then, lass, ye have come to the right man. I'll see ye dinna" go hungry for long." He pulled a loaf of bread and a wheel of cheese from his saddlebags. Washed down with cool creek water, it was the best meal I'd had in days.

Surprisingly, I felt much better as I ate. Davy didn't say a word until I finished. Then he stood up and pulled me to my feet. "All right then, lass. Are ye up to riding now?"

"But it's getting dark."

"Aye, but darkness won't stop the watch. They'll be coming for ye, night or day."

"What?"

"There's murder been done, and the hue and cry out for ye. Did ye no think of that?"

Actually, I had thought we were well and truly away. I hadn't thought of anyone coming after me. But of course they would. No matter how far, or how long I ran, they would hunt for me. That complicated things considerably.

"There's a fair description posted of ye down to the last stitch of your clothes, such as they are," Davy continued. He checked the cinch on the mare, then motioned for me to come over and mount while he held her.

I didn't move. "I have to go back." I would have to be careful, of course, to make sure no one saw me. But I had made a promise to help Mary, and done a right poor job of it so far. I couldn't just abandon her.

"Don't be daft,'" Davy said impatiently. "I've just told ye, ye are wanted for murder. Isn't that reason enough to stay away from the place?"

"I know that." I put my hands on my hips. "But I didn't kill anyone and so I've got to clear my name. There's no other way for me. No one is going to let penniless Sally McLaughlin board a ship. Ethan said there was a letter from Grandfather. It's bound to carry promise of payment."

Davy looped the horse's reins around a branch. "Was that before or after ye found the elder Mr. Asher with a knife in his back? No one is going to let the murderer of Samuel Asher board a ship, whether ye be penniless Sally McLaughlin, or Callie Beaton with money to spare."

"That's why I have to prove I'm not the murderer. I can't do that in the middle of the woods."

"Ye canna' do it in jail either."

We glared at each other while the horses pawed the ground. The bay mare bent her neck and pulled at tufts of grass. This was getting us nowhere.

I looked away first. Even with the anger sparking between us, it was hard to resist him. I bent down and picked up a dry stick at my feet before facing him again. "Where did you say we were going instead?"

"Ye will not have heard of the place. It's south of here, in the colony of Maryland, on the Chesapeake Bay. It's not far from a little place called Baltimore. Mount up." He held his hands cupped to give me a leg up.

"I can't go there." I took a step back, horrified at traveling as far as yet another colony.

I supposed I could get a ship from this place, Baltimore, if they hadn't heard of the murder, but the letter from Grandfather, which would undoubtedly guarantee payment for my passage, was in Philadelphia. But most of all, I couldn't stop thinking of Mary. "I've got to help Mary somehow," I said.

"And just how will ye manage that?" he said. "It'll be no comfort to her to have ye taken up by the constables."

It was no use arguing with him. It wasn't that I didn't worry. I had no wish to be jailed and held for murder, but I couldn't figure out any other way to keep my promise. I whacked the stick against the nearest tree. It broke with a sharp, satisfying crack. "I am going back to Philadelphia, whether you want to or not. I'll walk there myself if you won't help me." I spun away from him and started down the road, in the same direction I'd been going before Davy came back.

I could sense Davy's eyes on my back for a moment or two before he grabbed up the reins of both horses.

He caught up and fell into step alongside me. We walked in silence for a bit. When he spoke his voice was as bland as unsalted porridge. "Do ye not know, lass, that they hang murderers?"

"I didn't kill anyone." I whirled to face him. "You know I didn't."

He sighed. "'Tis no matter what I believe, ye ken. 'Tis what the judge believes. And the word of a runaway servant willna' count for much in the eyes of the law."

"I don't intend to let anyone catch me," I muttered, stepping out again. I was sure I could devise some plan before I got back to the city. I didn't mean to just waltz into the Asher house and demand the letter after all. No one would notice one more servant in town. I would talk to Peg first. She would likely have some idea what to do next.

We walked on in silence for another ten minutes or so. I kept trying to figure out how to help both Mary and myself, without getting caught, but I was finding it harder and harder to ignore my sore feet. No matter how carefully I watched, with each step I seemed to find the sharpest rocks. I limped on first one foot, then the other.

"As long as we've the two horses," Davy said finally, "it seems a bit of a waste to be walking. Perhaps ye would find no objection to riding just for a bit."

I hated to admit it, but he had a point. My feet would give out long before we reached the city. With a scowl, I allowed him to help me mount and we set off again. I settled into the saddle, shifting about to try to find a comfortable seat. I was still sore from the ride the day before, but even that soreness hurt less than my poor bruised feet.

We hadn't gone far however, when another thought occurred to me. I pulled back on the reins and stopped abruptly. "Is this the way to Philadelphia?" I demanded.

Davy's maddening, crooked smile lit his face. "Well, not exactly. Lest ye intend to go right around the world."

"You . . . you . . . " I sputtered, then jerked back on the reins to turn her, and kicked my heels into my horse's sides. The little mare, startled out of her placid nibbling of tender roadside greens, snorted and leapt forward in a dead run. I gasped, grabbed wildly for her mane to hang on, and dropped the reins. The mare, in total panic, barreled down the road with me clinging precariously to her back. Her mane whipped into my face, stinging my cheeks. I closed my eyes, expecting any minute to be dashed to death.

Davy wheeled his own horse and spurred it after me. He caught up as my own mare began to slow. A mild-mannered beast, she had no heart for running and had only done so in surprise. I opened my eyes as Davy bent down and snatched up the trailing reins, pulling her to a stop. He leapt off his horse, no longer smiling. The gold flecks in his eyes burned with anger. He jerked me off the horse and pushed me roughly aside. "Easy now, easy there," he murmured to the horse as he ran his hands up and down her legs.

I sat beside the road where I had fallen the minute my sore, swollen feet touched the ground.

Davy finished his inspection. Apparently satisfied, he strode over to me and stood, hands on hips, glaring. "Are ye daft?" His voice was not loud, but sharp with anger. "She could have broken a leg, or tripped and killed the both of ye."

I didn't answer. Miserable, I hugged my knees to my chest.

Finally he puffed out his breath in a deep sigh and let his arms drop. "Are ye hurt, lass?" he asked finally.

I shook my head.

"All right, then. No harm done." He held out a hand, as much a gesture of peace as an offer to help me up.

I pressed my lips tight together and refused to look up at him. "Will you tell me the way to Philadelphia?" I asked. He might be ready to let go his anger, but I was not. He'd tricked me into coming this far. The only gentlemanly thing for him to do was help me return.

Davy muttered something inaudible. He stomped away. I sat without moving while he tied each horse securely.

It was ten minutes before he left the horses and came back. He sat down beside me on the grassy verge. "Look, Miss Beaton, I havena' ever lied to ye, and I won't now. I'll no tell ye how to get to Philadelphia, because I've no wish to see ye hang. But I'll make a bargain with ye if ye will take it. I'll promise to bring ye back as soon as we've met my ship and I've done my business in Baltimore. Will ye come with me then?"

I picked at the burrs stuck to the raveled edge of my petticoat. Perhaps Davy hadn't ever lied to me, at least not that I knew about. But it wasn't his honesty that convinced me. My feet were so sore already, I knew I would never be able to walk barefoot back to the city whether I knew the way or not.

"You won't give me the horse to go there on my own, will you?" I asked.

"Nae," Davy said. "I will not."

"Why should I believe you?" It wasn't much of a question. I already knew there was no other choice.

He shrugged. "Ye trusted me with Leah, did ye not? And she's safe enough."

I pulled off another burr. "I've only your word on that."

"My word is all I've got to give ye." Davy ran his fingers through his tangled curls as if straightening his hair would clear up the tangled mess we were in. "It will have to do."

"I suppose it will." There were too many burrs to pick off. I gave up the job and stood up. "I'll go along to Baltimore, and then you'll take me straight back to Philadelphia."

Davy stood up too. He took my hand in his and made a formal bow, his lips brushing my fingers. "I give ye my word, lass."

Many men had bowed over my hand, in drawing rooms and at balls. But never had a man done so on a deserted lane in the green woods. Such a bow might seem ludicrous, coming as it did from a man whose woolen waistcoat was laced up with a bit of twine, but there was nothing laughable about Davy McRae. His form was flawless and his sincerity far less questionable than the dandies who had paid me court in Grandfather's house. I had no doubt he meant what he said.

CHAPTER 16

We rode for some time in silence. I was in no mood to talk, and Davy did not interrupt my thoughts. I had accepted the necessity of riding away from Philadelphia, but I was not pleased. I ached with worry for Mary and frustration that even now Grandfather's letter sat unnoticed on the desk of a dead man. All my glorious feeling of freedom at leaving the oppression of the Asher household evaporated with each step away from my goal.

The sun set, but the soft twilight of a summer eve lingered. The road turned, and we left the creek behind us. Soon the hum of crickets and katydids replaced the murmur of trickling water.

Gradually, the air grew cooler, and a soft breeze rustled through the leaves. One by one, stars winked on and the moon rose. The narrow road wound though the underbrush. I wondered how Davy knew to follow it. Dappled shadows through the arching latticework of branches overhead drained all color from the landscape, and the pale fabric of Davy's shirt fluttered like a will-o-the-wisp among the trees. Will-o-the-wisps are tricky spirits who dazzle the wanderer into following the fairy light, only to drown the unlucky traveler in a marshy pool in the heather. I'd heard that once you found yourself bedeviled by one, there was naught you could do against it. A shiver ran through me. Was I following a man or a spirit?

"That's foolishness!" I told myself firmly. Davy had been solid and steady enough to lean against when we rode together the night before. As soon as the road widened a bit, I kicked my horse to spur her alongside Davy. I was anxious to hear the very real sound of his voice to break the spell of the night. "Davy, you never did tell me what you were doing in Mr. Asher's study."

"Ahh." His voice floated across the darkness. "I thought ye would come to wonder did I kill the man."

"Did you?" I could ask the question now when I couldn't see his face.

"If ye dinna' already know that, lass, I doubt ye would be riding beside me."

That was true enough. I never really believed Davy had killed Samuel Asher. I just couldn't imagine him stabbing a man in the back. Still, he could have had no *lawful* business at that time in that place. I remembered the papers he had taken from the desk.

A passing breeze rattled the leaves of the trees overhead, and twigs on the path cracked under the horses' hooves. Off to the left of us, an owl hooted. My mare skittered sideways, then settled back to a nervous walk.

"Where did you take Leah?" I asked to get him talking again. He may be able to ride in the dark for hours, but I found it unsettling.

"Godwin's Landing," he said.

"Where is that?"

"Not far from the city, along the river. I know the people there. The lass will be safe enough and out of reach of Mr. Shakleton."

I couldn't argue with the sense of that. Then another thought struck me. "If it's so close, why aren't we going there? Couldn't you leave me with these friends of yours?"

Davy chuckled. "Ye would not like it. In any case, it's a bit too close to the city. They can hide a wee lass there well enough, but I'm none too sure ye would be out of reach. It's where I got the horse, ye ken."

"Oh? You didn't steal it?" I was only half joking. Whatever Davy did, he seemed mixed up with some sort of trouble.

Davy shook his head, somewhat sorrowfully, I imagined. "Nae. I supposed that when ye are wanted for murder, the theft of a horse is of no real matter. But since 'tis ye would hang for the murder and me 'twould swing for the horse, I thought it best to buy the beast."

I laughed in spite of myself. "Oh, you did, did you? Downright selfish, I'd call that!" Davy was a rogue, all right, and likely bent on mischief. And I was undoubtedly a fool to trust him, but trust him or no, I had to admit his laughter chased away the phantoms of the night.

We rode for several hours, stopping before dawn. By that time I was too weary and sore from riding to care whose company I kept. When

Davy called a halt, I slid off the saddle gratefully. But I was as wobbly as a newborn kitten. My feet hit the ground, and I sagged against the mare's belly.

"Steady there, lass." Davy helped me to a rock nearby. "Not used to riding are ye? We'll get a bit of sleep." He lay out his traveling cloak on the ground before he pulled the saddle off my horse, slipped off the bridle and set about putting fetters on her front legs.

I eyed the cloak dubiously. Not that it didn't look inviting. I think I could have slept on a bed of rocks at that moment. But the cloak was not very wide. Sleeping on it, beside Davy . . . I shook my head. "We can't both sleep there," I said. "It's not . . . proper."

"What?" Davy put down the mare's hoof to stare at me. He cocked his head sideways, as if a different angle would turn my words into sense. "Ye have ridden abroad in the countryside with a skellum like me for a day and a night, and ye have the watch after ye for murder," he said. "Do ye mean to say ye are fretting about propriety now?"

I tilted my chin up, set my lips, and nodded without saying anything more. I was too tired to explain it to myself, let alone make him see my point.

He shook his head. "Miss Beaton, I've managed to keep out of your skirts, such as they are, for these two days. Ye may recall, I never touched ye the last time we found ourselves . . . compromised by circumstances."

I shivered. I knew exactly what he meant, remembering all too well the warmth of his arms around me under the tarp in the boat during the storm. My heart beat a little faster thinking of it. It was exactly that feeling that made me wary now. I looked down at my toes. I couldn't look into his eyes, even dark and hidden as they were in the predawn gloom.

Davy waited a moment, but when I didn't answer, he went on. "I'm thinking ye have little to worry on that account. There's only the one cloak, do ye see?

I didn't look up.

I heard the whoosh of his breath as he let out a sigh. "Very well. If ye prefer, I'll sleep on the opposite side of the tree."

"Thank you." I lay down on the cloak. I felt a twinge of guilt at making him sleep in the bracken, but I clamped my lips tight and kept silent.

Davy took some time settling the horses to graze. I kept my eyes closed and listened to him whispering to them in Gaelic. Then his boots crunched on the leaves near my head and passed by. I heard him lower his body to the ground and stretch out. He turned once or twice and then was still.

Even exhausted as I was, I shivered for a long time. Not with cold, nor even fear now. The murder and flight seemed no more real than anything else in a whole list of unbelievable events. No. It was Davy McRae lying on the far side of the tree keeping me awake, his breathing soft and even as an innocent baby. He had enough charm to set me at ease and the guile to steal his granny's drawers. He drew me toward him like a moth to a candle flame.

I turned over, trying to get comfortable. How in the world had I managed to get myself hiding in the woods as a fugitive, listening to Davy McRae sleep? I shifted again. The leaves crackled under me, sending a pair of squirrels scampering. The horses, grazing only a few yards away, stomped. Davy did not stir.

I sat up, straightened the cloak underneath me, and lay down again, my mind a-whirl. What should I do once Davy got me back to Philadelphia? First I would find a way to help Mary and then find Grandfather's letter. But if I wanted to stay out of jail, perhaps the first thing to do was find out who really killed Mr. Asher. Once my name was cleared, then I could see to the rest.

A stick cracked nearby, startling me, but it was just deer stepping daintily among the ferns. The horses snorted and went back to nibbling at the browse. I lay down again. Something noisy scurried through the underbrush. Fearing a snake, I jerked upright. Davy still hadn't moved.

I curled up in a ball, closed my eyes, and stuffed a finger in each ear. Then a tree frog croaked a heartfelt, booming love song. My eyes flew open.

It was no use. I crawled around to the other side of the tree, dragging the cloak with me. I spread it out and lay down close to Davy, my back against his. I thought I heard a chuckle, but I must have been mistaken, for Davy's breath was just as slow and even as before. Surely he slept. Feeling a bit safer, I finally relaxed and drifted off to sleep.

Davy roused me after sleeping only a few hours. He made no mention of the altered sleeping arrangements, as he set about building a small fire and cleaning a pair of trout he caught while I was still sleeping.

I stood up, bleary-eyed and still groggy. I smoothed out my shift and inspected the damage to my skirt. The rip had started well below the waistband and ran in a sideways slash to the hem. Now after a day and a night walking and riding in the torn garment, the trailing ends had raveled and dragged through the mud. It looked more like a gypsy's rags than a skirt. I knotted the two longest pieces together to keep from tripping on it. Then I turned my attention to my hair and ran my fingers through the snarls. Not that it did much good. Without a comb, the tangled mass on my head resembled a poorly made bird's nest more than anything else. Davy had hung a waterskin on a branch beside me. I took a long swallow, then poured some into the palm of my hand to splash on my face. The water washed the sleep from my eyes and the dust from my skin, but with nothing better than the hem of my filthy shift to dry it, I was glad I couldn't see the results. With this very unsatisfactory toilette, I turned to look at Davy.

He had taken up the cloak we slept on and was shaking out the leaves before folding it. A rough stubble of a beard, darker than his hair, covered his face and his shirt was rumpled and dirty, but he whistled as he stowed the cloak in one of the saddlebags. What was he so cheerful about? Didn't the man ever need to sleep?

Davy spitted the trout and hung them over the fire. Soon they dripped and sizzled with an aroma that made my stomach moan in anticipation.

I sat on the ground beside the fire. After all, my gown could hardly get any muddier than it already was.

"Tell me, why are we going to this. . . Baltimore, is it?" I asked.

"Well, that's a bit . . . complicated, ye see." Davy poked at the fish, then leaned back against a tree and stretched his legs out. "How much do ye know of Mr. Asher's business?"

"Not much," I admitted. I had heard him arguing with his sons and with Mr. Shakleton about shipments, especially shipments gone missing, on several occasions, but my concern had always been for the letter I expected from Grandfather. "Isn't he a customs agent?"

"Aye, he is that, and a merchant himself. He's been partners with Mr. Shakleton on some ventures, but each of them has their own concerns as well."

I nodded. I knew the two men were partners. Mr. Shakleton often visited or joined the Ashers for dinner. "But what does all that have to do with your business in Baltimore?" I asked. Then I remembered Davy had been to the Asher's for dinner at least once himself, and I'd seen him in Mr. Shakleton's cabin aboard the ship. I frowned. "Are you working for one of them?"

Davy grunted. "That depends on whom ye are asking."

"I'm asking you."

Instead of answering, Davy leaned forward and took the first fish off the spit. He wrapped it up in a huge leaf and handed it to me.

I balanced the leaf on one knee. The steam rising from the soft flesh smelled delicious. I picked off a chunk and popped it in my mouth, burning my fingers and my tongue in the process. It tasted every bit as good as it smelled.

Davy finished his own share before resuming the conversation. "I suppose ye have the right to ask." The gold sparks in his eyes darkened, hiding something. "Seeing as how ye have put your safety in my hands. I'll tell ye what I can. Ye should know that Mr. Shakleton is my father's factor, or he was so until my father sent me along to help him."

"Why would he do that?"

Davy shrugged. "My father prefers to send me far away whenever he can. But this time he had some reason. He had cause to question the accuracy of the accounts. A shipment of wine from France sent here last year has disappeared. Mr. Shakleton swears he brought it over and that Mr. Asher took it as customs duty. Mr. Asher declared he never saw it at all. My father wants me to help them find it. The two of them want it found sure enough, but not by me."

"So you're not very popular with either one. It's a wonder you haven't been murdered." The memory of the two men struggling in the ropes high above the ship came back to me. Davy had good reason to believe the man had been sent to kill him. I finished the fish and wiped my fingers on the hem of my shift.

"Ye have the right of it. One or both of them is lying for sure. They would both sooner see me dead than meddling in their arrangements, even when those arrangements are with my father's money."

"But I still don't understand why you would want Mr. Asher dead," I said. "If he is the one lying, don't you need him to find the shipment?"

"I dinna' want him dead." He reached forward and stirred the fire. "He was a cheat, with deep pockets and a stone cold heart, but now the customs post will likely go to his son. There's only the one customs agent in the whole colony, and he is appointed by the governor. He'll give it to Ethan Asher. Now there's a man with a soul as black as tar and hands just as sticky. I had no liking for the elder Mr. Asher, but I'd a clear sight rather deal with the father than the son."

"What? Ethan?" I stood up and brushed the leaves from my skirts. "There's a lot of talk against him, but he's been kind to me. He helped me write to Grandfather."

"Did he now?" Davy's voice was full of skepticism. He stood too, eyeing me speculatively, from my bare feet and torn petticoat to the ragged edges of my shift ruffling over the top of the second hand bodice. "And ye never gave him any favors in return?"

I slapped him, the shock of his words jolting me to action. My hand stung and my face burned as hot as his cheek. It was exactly the sort of thing Tom would say. I'd wanted to hit Tom since the day I'd met him.

Davy rubbed his face. "I suppose I deserved that. I meant no offense, lass. Only ye ken, no doubt, the man has been known to offer a bit more to the ladies than they seem to want."

I frowned and turned away. Ethan had been kind to me. I'd worried a great deal about Samuel Asher's advances, and Tom had been crude time and again. But Ethan had done no more than kiss my hand, as any gentleman courting a lady may do. His mother and his sister had warned me against him, but that seemed more designed to keep me away from him than vice versa. No matter what anyone said, the man had helped me, and I was still counting on him. I could not believe ill of him.

I busied myself with trying to comb out my hair while Davy kicked apart the fire and smothered it with dirt. For five minutes neither of us spoke.

Finally, after he had saddled the horses and cleaned up camp, he turned to me again. "We'll have to find ye some other clothes," he said, as if nothing had come between us. "The warrant describing ye will have gone by post and reached the inns ahead of us. Can we make ye into a lad perhaps?" He dug in his saddlebags, pulling out his own spare shirt and trousers.

Davy was not a big man, but he was still a good four inches taller than I. His shirt was large and blousy on me and the trousers dragged the ground.

"Ye don't look much like a lad." Davy regarded me critically. "But with a hat pulled down over the eyes, maybe ye will do. Don't walk so straight. Can ye no slouch a bit? Let your arms dangle and your mouth hang open like a farm boy bedazzled by the sights of the town."

I tried dropping my shoulders and slouching, but my efforts only made him laugh.

I straightened up and glared up at him. "For nearly twenty years Mam has been scolding me to stand up straight and keep my mouth closed. I can't stop now."

Davy wiped the tears of mirth from the corners of his eyes. "Aye, I see that. Dinna' fash yourself, lass. Ye have too many curves anyway to fool ought but a blind man. Still, with an oversized coat, perhaps a hat, in the dark of a taproom . . . Well, there's naught to do but try."

As it happened, the first place we came to toward evening was not an inn, but a farm. The road we had been following, such as it was, ended abruptly as it ran into a split rail fence. Across the fence was a section of partially cleared pasture. A couple of scrawny cows grazed between the stumps that still dotted the field. Davy turned his horse and followed the fence until we came to the other side of the field and not far beyond that, a cabin.

It was a small place, but neat and well tended. A half dozen apple trees heavy with ripening fruit stood to one side of the house, and a patch for a garden had been cleared on the other side. The clear, rhythmic thumping of an ax hitting wood grew louder. The woodchopper, a giant of a man, with short-cropped blond hair and a thick blond beard, stopped when he saw us, his ax held lightly in one hand. Then apparently deciding we were harmless, he buried the ax head in the chopping block and came forward to greet us.

"Good day to ye, sir." Davy dismounted and shook hands with the farmer. "Do ye mind if we get some water for the horses?" I dismounted too, letting Davy take the reins of my horse.

The farmer's wife appeared at the door, wiping her hands on her apron. She too was pale blond, like her color had been washed away. A pack of blond-haired bairns clung to her skirts and peered around her at the strangers in their yard. She spoke to her husband in a language I didn't understand - Swedish, I guessed, by the musical sound of it.

He looked at me, shrugged, and then answered her briefly in the same tongue.

The woman shooed the children back and took my hand to lead me into the house.

Davy winked. "I said ye would never fool anyone by light of day." He went with the farmer to tend the horses.

The woman began talking before I'd even entered the cabin. She spoke no English, and I could not understand a word she said, but that didn't seem to bother her in the slightest. "Etta," she said, pointing to herself. "Etta Jurgenson."

"Callie," I told her in return. "Callie Beaton."

Introductions complete, she took my elbow and directed me toward the single chair beside the table. She patted my hand before pouring out a cup of cool buttermilk for me, not in a tin cup as I might have expected, but in a small china teacup. It dawned on me that I was being invited in for high tea; the type of affair Mam had insisted was the proper time and place for women to socialize. What would Mam think to see me now, dressed in a pair of ragged trous and an oversized sark, having tea in a dingy cabin in the middle of the wilderness? Mam had never envisioned such a tea, but I meant to do her proud in any case. I praised Etta's offerings, admired her china, and listened attentively, though neither of us could understand the other.

She had four boys, blond stair-step reproductions of their father. By signs, she led me to understand she was expecting another and that she hoped to God it was a girl this time.

I nodded in sympathy. I could only imagine a life with no womenfolk around.

Still she seemed content enough, and the little boys, once they got over their shyness, helped her in small ways like fetching some water or a bit of kindling.

Davy and Leif Jurgenson came in after an hour or so. Apparently, Leif, who spoke more English than his wife and understood her need for company, had invited us to share their supper and spend the night.

"It's safe enough here," Davy explained when I questioned him. "Besides, I thought ye might like a roof over your head tonight. I know ye are not used to sleeping rough."

I couldn't help smiling, thinking of all the rough places I had slept since leaving Grandfather's house. It had been so long since I'd slept in a real bed, I wasn't sure I even knew what it felt like anymore.

Etta stood up to start supper. I rose to help her, but Davy caught my arm and shook his head ever so slightly. "Ye are likely the first guest she's had in a long while," he whispered. "She'll want to serve ye proper."

Dinner, a simple stew, probably squirrel thickened with corn meal, was delicious and abundant. There weren't enough chairs to go around, so the men pulled the table closer to the single bed on one side of the cabin, and after serving, Etta sat there. I stayed in the one straight-backed chair I'd been seated on earlier. Davy was given the stool. Leif set up a small keg on one end, and the little boys stood around the table. Etta beamed with pleasure as I smacked my lips and asked for seconds.

After supper, guest or no, I pitched in and helped clear the dishes and wash up. Etta scrubbed the boys' faces and piled them onto the bed, where they tumbled about and wrestled like so many puppies until they grew tired. Etta poured out mugs of hard cider for the four of us. Leif got out a pipe and a pouch of tobacco, and Davy pulled out his fife. He played a couple of simple tunes first, then set into a foot-tapping jig. Whether it was the effect of cider, or the delicious feeling of safety, I found I couldn't keep still. I jumped up. Pushing the chair and the stool to the edges of the room, I kicked up my heels in time to the music. At the end of the song Etta clapped in delight. I grabbed her hands and pulled her up to join me. Davy obligingly played a slower tune, while I showed Etta the steps. The two of us whirled and stomped to the delight of the children and the smiles of the men, until Etta, breathless, stumbled over her husband's big feet. He caught her as she fell and pulled her onto his lap, where she seemed content to rest.

Davy lifted his eyebrow to me in mute question. Was I ready for more?

I nodded, and he started in on a reel this time. It had been months since I danced, and I reveled in the sheer joy of it. Davy played faster and faster. With a toss of my head, I met the unspoken challenge until my feet tapped out the staccato beat in a blur of movement. Just as it seemed I couldn't move any faster, Davy finished the song with a musical flourish. I made a sweeping curtsey to the company, then collapsed onto the chair reserved for me. Everyone clapped, and Etta jumped up to pour out another round of cider. Davy lifted his mug in tribute, and for a moment our eyes met. Already giddy from the dance and the company, I felt the spark flash between us. Then Davy took a deep swallow, breaking the spell.

After the dance, Leif sang a couple of ballads in a strong, deep voice, and Davy, after listening to a few measures, played an accompaniment. It grew late and the little boys, tired of their roughhousing, fell asleep on the bed. Leif started in on one last ballad, slower, softer than the earlier ones. Etta joined in on the choruses. I had no idea what the words meant, but it was obvious the song was a love song, and the story it told was their own. Etta might be alone among the men on this farm in the wilderness, but clearly she was here of her own free will. Lonely for the company of women perhaps, but nevertheless she had what she needed in her man.

Later, as I lay wrapped up in a blanket on the floor in front of the hearth, I remembered the look that had passed between them as they sang to each other; guests all forgotten in the depths of their love, and I felt an odd sort of longing. Not for Mam, Grandfather, or Elspeth. Not for home. For something else entirely.

CHAPTER 17

We left early the next morning after a breakfast of cold cornbread. Etta clicked her tongue in disapproval over the shirt and trousers I wore, but there was nothing that could be done about it. Like so many of the servants in Philadelphia, she had naught but the skirt and bodice she wore, and there was no merchant within miles selling either clothes or cloth. I was beginning to think that the American colonies were truly the wild, uncivilized place they talked about in Edinburgh, not because of savage Indians and fearsome animals, but simply because finding a decent set of clothes was well nigh impossible. I remembered the shipment of woolens in the hold of the ship transporting me across the ocean. Valuable cargo indeed for a country so poor in cloth. I thought, too, of the length of it draped over me in the cold ocean night. How had Davy McRae gotten hold of such a piece?

I clucked to the horse, shaking off the unanswered questions. The morning was far too bright to worry about a length of woolen cloth left behind at the Asher's house.

The night with the Jurgensons had done wonders for my spirits. A hot meal, the music and easy company, and a restful sleep restored my good humor. I set out with a light heart. Four or five days riding, Davy had said, then back to Philadelphia. In the meantime, the air was fresh, birdsong chorused throughout the woods, and I could think of much less pleasant things than riding behind Davy McRae in the dappled forest sunshine.

Shadows were growing long by the time we reached a tavern, set amidst a collection of squat, ramshackle log cabins too small to even call a village. Hugging the side of the road as if to snare any reluctant traveler, the tavern was indistinguishable from the other buildings save for an open door and a wooden stoop before it. Just beyond the tavern a tumbledown fence enclosed a muddy pasture with a rickety stable leaning into one corner.

Davy stopped his horse before the small clearing. "I dinna' like the look of the place."

"We don't have to stop here. We did all right sleeping out. And besides, it's early yet, isn't it?"

"Aye, 'tis not past four o'clock. But take a look to the sky, lass. There is rain moving in."

Dark, heavy clouds hung on the edge of the horizon. "Those aren't rain clouds." I squinted at them. "Or if they are, they're too far away to bother us."

Davy rolled his eyes at me. "Do ye have to argue with everything I say? I'm telling ye, we'll have rain in an hour or less."

"I'm not arguing," I protested. "I'm trying to help. You said you didn't like the place."

Davy shook his head. "Well, like it or no, we're stopping here for the night. And ye had best keep quiet." Davy touched his heels to his horse's flank and moved on.

There was no sign of life as we approached the tavern, but at the sound of Davy's hallo, a large man, dark hair hanging in rat tails, came out on the porch, wiping his hands on a dirty towel tied round his waist as an apron.

"We're looking for supper and a place to sleep," Davy said without dismounting.

"Just the two of you?" The innkeeper directed his words to Davy, but stared at me. I wasn't sure I wanted supper from such a filthy cook, but following Davy's advice, I kept quiet. The innkeeper's gaze unnerved me. I wore a limp felt hat, courtesy of Leif Jurgenson, with the brim pulled low over my eyes and my hair tucked up inside it, but we hadn't found a coat, and my disguise as a boy only worked in dim light.

"That will be six pence pay as money, or four pence pay as hard money." The innkeeper stuck out a thick calloused hand, palm up. "In advance."

"I've English silver," Davy said and dropped four coins into the open palm.

The innkeeper bit each coin, then nodded. "Come in and wet your whistle. You can hobble your beasts in the pasture. Don't turn 'em loose. The fence is down at the far corner. It'll be another halfpence each if you want them in the stable."

"The pasture's fine," Davy said, swinging down. He motioned for me to dismount, then thrust the reins of his horse at me. "Hobble 'em good, boy," he ordered in a rough voice. Then, with his back to the innkeeper, he lowered his voice to a whisper. "Don't come in before I come out for ye." He strode across the porch and disappeared into the dark maw of the open door behind our host.

I took the reins and led the horses over to the gate. I liked the placid mare I rode, but I wasn't so sure of Davy's mount. Luckily, both horses were hungry for the grass on the other side of the fence and followed readily enough. Once inside the pasture I tied them to the fence rail. I wasn't sure how to hobble them, so I unsaddled them and heaved the saddles up on the fence rail. Davy's advice to stay outside made sense, so I rummaged around in the saddlebags to find the brush Davy had used. I'd never brushed a horse before, but it couldn't be much different than brushing hair.

While I worked, another party of horsemen arrived. They stripped their horses and swatted them loose in the pasture, with no regard for the fence rail down. I stayed behind the horses, mostly out of sight. Not long after that, a peddler carrying a heavy sack on his back ambled up the road and went inside.

The sky grew darker and a rumble of thunder echoed the growling in my stomach. Then a spattering of raindrops swept across the pasture, splashing on my nose and cheeks and leaving dark spots on the saddle leather.

I frowned at the sky. Davy's warning or no, I was not about to sit in the rain like an idiot. I shoved the brush back in the saddlebags and turned to go inside. Davy's horse stamped nervously. The air itself seemed charged with energy and ready to explode. Just then, lightning crackled overhead, blinding me for an instant. In the darkness following, a hand touched my arm.

I shrieked, but the sound was lost in the thunder as I stumbled backward into the horse. The horse snorted and shifted away.

"Easy there." Davy's voice was calm. I wasn't sure if he meant to soothe me or the horse.

"Don't sneak up on me like that!" I said, as soon as I caught my breath.

Davy didn't answer. He hobbled the horses quickly, then slipped off their bridles. When he saw where I'd put the saddles, he gave a small grunt of approval. He slung the saddlebags over his shoulder before turning to me. "Do ye have the knife still?"

My hand went to the hard lump in my pocket. "Why should I need a knife?" I asked, pulling it out. It was still wrapped in the rag and tied with a piece of twine.

"Chances are ye won't." He took it from me, unwrapped it, and handed it back. "Put it in your belt, where ye can reach it quick. There are some very nasty men here tonight."

"What sort of men?" I adjusted the belt so the knife was secure. The hard handle pressed uncomfortably against my side. A chill breeze blew over us, carrying a fresh ripple of droplets.

Davy pushed me toward the tavern as he answered. "Deserters, likely. Heading home for the harvest after fighting the French out in the west of Pennsylvania. The tavern keeper is a suspicious lout. He'll turn us in, if he thinks to gain by it."

The wind swirled into a dust devil as Davy hurried me across the yard. We ducked into the taproom just ahead of the downpour. Inside, it was dark and smoky, lit only by a couple of punched tin lanterns and the fire on the hearth. Even with my hat low and my shoulders hunched, I could feel the eyes of the men on me as I crossed the room to an empty table against the wall opposite the door. The innkeeper plopped a couple of wooden bowls and a half loaf of dark bread in front of us. In the bowls steamed a thin, greasy stew of indeterminate meat. It smelled slightly sour, as if the cook just kept adding to the pot, and so the contents of the stew pot included remnants not only of last night's supper, but last year's as well. Hungry as I was, I didn't eat much. The tavern keeper slopped my uneaten portion back into the iron pot hung over the fire. He swiped out the bowl with his dirty apron and placed it back in the stack beside the hearth.

By the time we finished eating, rain drummed against the roof. The tavern was so small that it had no private rooms, and we had paid only for a place on the floor.

I was tired, but the others showed no sign of turning in. The peddler opened his pack and spread out his wares for the tavern keeper to look over. Some of the other men crowded around examining the bullet molds and ax heads he carried.

I was drawn to a cloth with a dozen or so brooches pinned to it. They were gleaming silver, catching the firelight. Most were roundels and rings, but one stood out from the others. It was a pair of intertwined hearts, with a crown on top, a luckenbooth brooch, like the ones in the shops in Edinburgh. I leaned in for a closer look, when Davy punched my shoulder playfully, but hard enough to hurt.

"Ouch," I squeaked, pulling back.

"Ye have no money to buy your sweetheart a token, lad," he said in a loud voice. "So there's no sense even looking."

"Oh. Oh, right." I suddenly remembered I was supposed to be a lad.

"Sweetheart?" One of the men guffawed. "He ain't but just weaned hisself."

Everyone laughed. With cheeks burning in embarrassment, I retreated to the dark corner by the fireplace. Davy didn't look at me. Instead, he laughed with the others. When the peddler pulled out a pack of playing cards, Davy joined the game.

I curled up in the cloak on the floor with my back against the wall and pretended to sleep. The embers burned low and still the men drank and slapped the cards on the table, with Davy among them. I felt very much alone in this alien world of men and drink and cards.

I hadn't even realized I had fallen asleep when I felt someone's rough hand shaking me. My eyes flew open to the inky darkness of the room. Immediately the hand was clapped over my mouth, and Davy whispered, "Hush, lass. It's only me."

My fear evaporated. I nodded to show I understood. Davy loosened his grip. "What do you want?" I hissed.

"Follow me." He breathed the words more than speaking them. He led the way around the rough men sprawled across the floor. Davy's step was light and sure, as if he had cat's eyes to see in the dark. I stumbled along as best I could.

Without a word, Davy saddled the wet horses quickly and helped me mount. The rain had stopped, but the ground was sodden. We rode hard for at least a mile, before Davy explained. "They didn't get a good look at ye in the dark, but I'd not trust our luck in the light of day. They heard ye right enough, when ye pined over the trader's baubles. They're crude, ye ken, and outlaws for sure, but they're no stupid. They'll have figured ye to be a woman and hiding something."

"Will they follow us?"

"Not likely. I won fair and square, so they've no cause there. And since the lot of them are on the run, they'll think twice before chasing after us. Besides," he grinned mischievously, "'ye will maybe not have noticed, but we're not taking the main road. There's a good chance they'll never find us along these back ways."

Morning light found us still riding. Davy called a brief halt for breakfast, a chunk of bread washed down with water. We ate quickly, without much talk, but when it came time to mount up again, Davy took my hand in his. He pressed something hard and metallic in my palm and closed my fingers over it.

I opened my hand. "It's the luckenbooth brooch," I said. The twined silver hearts gleamed. "How did you get this?"

"I told ye, I won," Davy said. "Think of it as a down payment on your half of the winnings."

"I didn't win anything," I protested.

"Aye, but since we're traveling together, I count us as partners." Davy put a finger to my lips. "Just take it and pin it inside your shirt. It's a charm, ye ken. It'll keep the fairies away."

I knew the legend that claimed a luckenbooth brooch kept the wearer safe from the evil eye. But there was more to the story than that. The part I knew told how a man gave it to his sweetheart when they were betrothed. Did Davy know that as well? He wasn't looking at me any more, but had turned to check the cinches. Surely it didn't mean any such thing to him. I put the brooch inside my pocket. We mounted and rode on.

The day was overcast and gloomy, with showers off and on, but the heavy rain was over, and it was warm enough that the damp didn't bother me. We camped that night near a river. We'd have to cross it come morning, Davy said, and with no bridge nearby, he didn't want to try swimming it in the dark. Davy gathered wood for a fire, while I took the canvas bucket to the riverbank to fetch water. The sun was just setting, casting an orange glow in the sky and shimmering in its reflection in the softly rippling current. I knelt to scoop the bucket full, then splashed a double handful on my face. The cool water ran down my cheeks and dripped off my nose, sluicing away the dust and grime from the road. It would be lovely to feel that clean all over, I mused. And why not? Davy was busy up at the fire, and there was no one else about for miles. If I hurried . . .

I stripped quickly and stepped into the water. The bank was a shallow shelf of rocks and gravel that sloped into the deeper current. A half dozen steps brought the water up to my thighs. The cold touch of it against my bare skin made me shiver, and tiny goose bumps rose on my arms and belly. I hesitated only a moment, then ducked down so the water came up to my neck. The current gently tugged at my hair. I closed my eyes, savoring the gentle caress of water flowing across bare skin.

A voice from behind the screen of trees up the bank interrupted my dreaming. "Do ye know, lass, there's snakes in there? Copperheads, likely."

I shot up out of the water, stumbled on a rock in the sandy bottom, and fell forward. Panic-stricken, I scrambled up the bank, only belatedly remembering my nakedness. I spun around to face the water, with my bare back to the trees. I crouched, arms crossed.

"Go away!" I shouted.

"There's supper ready," he shouted back, as calmly as if he were announcing dinner at a ball. "Do ye want one of the fish, or do ye have a mind to catch your own?"

"Go away! I'll be up directly."

There was no answer. Not a sound; not even a rustle of bushes indicating he'd gone. I knew Davy could move silently when he wanted. Had he gone back?

A mosquito whined near my ear. I swatted at it. I could hardly sit bare-arse naked on the bank wondering if he still watched. I snatched up the clothes I had set out on a rock and wiggled into them as quickly as possible. Even oversized and blousy as they were, it wasn't easy getting them on over wet skin.

Davy was seated by the fire, his back against the tree. Without a word, he leaned forward and deftly skewered the remaining fish, offering it to me.

I took it, sat down on the far side of the fire, and began eating. I avoided looking at Davy, but I could feel his eyes on me as I ate, as if he could see right through the clothes I wore. I'd never made much use of fans in the ballrooms of Edinburgh, but just now, I sorely wished I had one to hide the hot blush I felt burning my cheeks. "Are there really snakes?" I said after a bit.

"Aye, though I doubt they'd bite such fair skin as your own. They'd be enchanted just as much as any poor fool."

"You were watching me," I accused.

"Indeed I was, and still am, to be sure."

"You . . . you're no gentleman!"

Davy raised an eyebrow. "Don't ye see me sitting here, on this side of the fire and yourself on the other? But gentleman or no, I am a man who appreciates beauty, and a fair lovely sight I've had tonight."

I didn't know whether to be flattered or angry. We finished the meal in silence. Then I cleaned up while Davy spread out the traveling cloak next to the fire.

"Ye had best get some sleep, lass," he said. "We've a long ride tomorrow."

My clothes were still damp, and the night air had turned chilly. The thought of Davy's warm body beside my own sent shivers up my spine.

But Davy made no move away from the dying embers of the fire.

"Aren't you going to sleep?" I asked after a moment.

"Not just now," he said, his face hidden in the shadows.

"But you were awake half the night last night," I protested.

"Aye, but I'm no made of stone. If I'm to stay a gentleman, as ye call it, I'd best keep the watch tonight."

I woke to the sound of Davy's whistle.

He smiled mischievously down at me. "Did ye know ye smile in your sleep, lass? It's quite becoming. Ye may want to try the habit when ye are waking."

"You're supposed to be keeping watch," I said irritably. "Not watching me."

"I've managed to do the both of them, the more pleasure mine."

We picked our way along the riverbank until Davy found a spot suitable for crossing. "It's no very deep," he said frowning, "but the horses will have to swim a bit, just in the middle."

We mounted and he turned his horse into the water. My own mare snorted and shook her head, clearly unwilling to follow. "I don't blame you one bit," I muttered to the mare. "It's not my idea of fun either, but you don't want to stay here alone, do you?" I drummed my bare heels into her flanks. She danced sideways, tossing her head.

"Davy!" I called.

He turned, saw my trouble and came back, going round behind my horse. "Hang on." He slapped my mare's rump with the ends of his reins.

She leaped forward like a flea in the fire, nearly leaving me behind. I slipped half off the saddle. Dropping the reins, I twined my fingers in her mane. "Whoa," I called, but once going, she was not about to stop. She plunged into the creek, slowing as the water reached her chest. I felt the change as she began swimming, her powerful shoulders working hard. Horses are not natural swimmers, and I felt a great deal of sympathy for her, forced into this unnatural environment. "But you'll carry me with you, like it or not," I told her and hung on.

We came out on the far side, streaming water. She shook herself like a dog, and me with her, then stood still as Davy handed me the reins. With some difficulty, I loosened my fingers from the mane and took them. I was nearly as wet as the horse, with no way to shake myself dry.

He smiled. "Well, she's no water horse, for sure. Ye have naught to fear about this one taking ye down to the depths." He shook his head with a mock frown. "And as for ye, lass; I wasna sure did ye plan to swim or ride across."

I didn't want to do either, but there was no help for it. We crossed another shallow creek later in the day. The mare didn't have to swim, but she was still nervous about getting her feet wet. Davy took the reins and led her across, saying it was probably easier than fishing me up out of the water. By mid-afternoon, the track Davy followed joined onto a bigger trail, wide enough for a wagon. The shadows were stretching across the road when we reached a third creek, an easy sandy ford, with a wide, shallow bank.

Davy reined up short of it.

"I think we can manage this one," I said, as he reached for my reins.

"Hush," he said in a low voice as he swung off his horse. He slid his hand down the mare's leg and lifted her hoof as if he were checking for stones.

"What is it?"

"Can ye no hear? The birds have gone quiet. Something has frightened them."

CHAPTER 18

The forest held an ominous, unnatural silence. Davy loosened his pistol, then remounted. "Ye have the knife handy?"

"Yes." It was still in my belt.

"All right then. If I shout to ye, kick your horse as hard as ye can and run her like the devil himself is after ye."

He led the way into the creek. At the far side, we stopped again. Davy listened intently. I reached forward and patted my mare's neck.

Davy's shout of alarm broke the silence just before the attack came. A horde of mounted men bore down on us.

I jerked the mare's head to turn her and fly back across the creek. But having crossed the creek once, she was not about to go back, no matter how hard I kicked and screamed at her. She tucked her nose and spun in a circle, dancing away from the water's edge. Then a crack of gunfire exploded. The mare leaped forward, into the creek. From the corner of my eye, I saw Davy's horse fall. Two men went after him, and the other two came at me.

"Davy," I screamed and pulled back on the reins. I couldn't leave him behind. Another shot exploded. The mare reared, her legs pawing the air and eyes rolling back in alarm. She came down, all four feet splashing in the water, and hopped sideways, stiff-legged and frantic to get away. But there was no escape for her now. The two men and their horses crowded her from either side. Rough hands grabbed at her reins and pulled me down.

I slid into the shallow water churned into a murky pool by the frenzy of hooves. I twisted away from the mass of horses and men and grabbed the knife. A fox-faced, filthy man slashed at me with a knife the size of my arm, but missed his mark as I scrambled backwards.

His partner aimed a long barreled pistol at my head and cocked it. I rolled just as he pulled the trigger. With a roar, the ball plowed into the gravel bank beside me, kicking up a stinging spray of pebbles. The man swore, dropped his empty pistol, and kicked his horse toward me, clearly intent on riding me down.

I scuttled crab-legged away. My hat fell off and my hair tumbled loose into my eyes.

The man, seeing my hair, hesitated no more than the space of a breath. Then he grinned an evil, gap-toothed grin, jumped off his horse and came at me again.

I floundered out of the water and got my feet underneath me. Knife in hand, I braced as he grabbed for me. With the force of panic, I thrust the blade into his belly, driving it upwards.

He fell to his knees. One hand clutched his midsection, the blood flowing out between his fingers. His eyes registered shocked surprise. Then he fell into me, his hand clawing at my shirt, tearing it open. His eyes dulled, and he toppled over, bearing me down beneath him. His fingers twitched convulsively, squeezing my breast in a horrifying parody of lust. I shuddered and pushed at him, trying to wriggle out from underneath the dead weight. Dead. He was dead. I couldn't get past that word. I shoved him off me and crawled away. The sharp gravel bit into my knees. I stopped, unable to pull my gaze from his leering face. Dead. The vacant eyes were still open. I closed my eyes and retched.

I was still vomiting when Davy reached me. Blood seeped from a gash across his temple. His shirt was torn and bloody. "Are ye hurt, lass?" He brushed the hair back from my face, touching my cheeks, neck, arms, legs, checking for soundness I supposed, like he'd done with the horse. I couldn't stop trembling. He gathered me into his arms and held me, rocking slightly.

Trembling, I lay my head against his chest, listening to the beat of his heart.

"Lie easy, lass," he murmured.

"Is he dead?" I asked, though I knew the answer. I had seen his eyes go dark.

Davy stroked my hair. "Aye, lass, and ye are not."

I started crying, tears spilling unchecked as Davy kissed my cheeks.

"Hush, ma cushla," he whispered, his lips brushing my ear. "Ye are safe now. There's no more of them."

The woods, which only moments ago had been a crush of squealing horses and swearing men, had gone quiet, save the gentle murmur of the creek and a lone bird, untroubled by our presence. I didn't ask about the others; fled or dead at Davy's hand. Instead, I concentrated on the touch of his fingers on my icy skin. Slowly, the trembling horror of death faded.

Davy's lips found mine. I tasted blood and tears mingled with desire. I twined my fingers in his hair, pulling him close, wanting only to be with him.

He broke off the kiss and crushed me to him, the rough stubble of his chin scraping my forehead. "Callie," he groaned. "I want ye more than I can say. But not here. Not on top of a dead man."

He moved as if to stand. I clung to him. "Don't leave me, Davy," I cried. The world around me was spinning. I needed Davy's touch to steady me.

He stroked my hair again, his finger tracing a line from temple to cheek. "I'm no going anywhere without ye, lass," he said, then pulled me to my feet. He led me to the horse, which stood calmly cropping grass along the road, unconcerned about the two dead men sprawled nearby where Davy had dispatched them. I couldn't take my eyes off them. One lay face down with the back of his head blown open by the musket ball from Davy's pistol. The other sprawled on his back. Hungry flies already blackened the blood trickling out of his mouth.

Davy hoisted me up into the saddle of his horse.

"Where's my horse?" I asked, wrenching my eyes away from the two dead men and looking toward the creek. Blood stained the gravel, and the body of the third thief lay half in and half out of the water. There was no sign of my horse or the fourth robber.

"Gone." Davy strode toward the bank, retrieved the knife from the dead man's body, cleaned it on the grass, then offered it to me.

I shook my head emphatically. I had killed a man. No matter what he meant to do. No matter I hadn't thought I would be able to kill him. The truth of it was, I had meant to kill him. In the moment when I thrust the blade into his belly, I had prayed I would kill him. And I had.

Davy swung up onto the horse behind me, wrapping his arms around me. "Easy, lass. Ye ken ye had no choice?"

I nodded, unconvinced.

We rode for ten minutes into the forest, off the path, until we came to a small grassy clearing, bordered with a burbling creek half the size of the river we'd crossed. Davy pulled me from the horse and into the creek.

A dozen small cuts stung on my face where the pebbles had hit me. Thick mud mingled with the dead man's blood stained the tattered remnants of my borrowed shirt. Davy looked even worse. His hair lay matted at the temple line where the first bullet had grazed him. A bright red smear covered his sleeve and shoulder, and scarlet droplets were spattered across his chest.

We washed away the blood and grime until there was nothing left but the two of us, raw and naked, clinging to each other. I felt his desire, and was surprised at the force of my own answer.

"What are you thinking?" one small part of my mind demanded. "You can't do this." But I could. I would. The whole world of rules and limits be damned. All I wanted at this moment was Davy, and I wanted him with an intensity that drove all else from my mind.

Our lovemaking consumed us entirely, burning away the horror of the attack and binding us together. They were dead, and we were not. Time stood still as life, Davy's life, surged in me and I pulled him deeper. For a moment or an hour or a lifetime, our hearts beat with one rhythm as we drove out the darkness and felt the fierce joy of life.

I felt that moment could go on forever, but a fire so intense must at last burn itself out. Gradually the world returned. The creek flowed once more over the rocks, and the crickets began again their strumming. I shivered. Davy carried me to the bank, where we lay together on his cloak.

He brushed at the tears on my cheek. "Don't cry, lass."

I didn't know I was crying. But once I started, I couldn't stop.

Davy stroked my hair. "I've hurt ye, Callie," he said in a voice full of anguish. "I never meant to take ye like that."

It wasn't that, of course. The pain was already fading. I cried from the unguarded openness of wanting him. All of the past four months crashed in on me, and I wept for Grandfather and Mam and Elspeth, for the months of captivity, hardship and struggle, for the man lying dead at my hand in a creek a mile away. I cried from the final, unarguable knowledge that my world would never again be the safe, simple place it had been when I stormed out of Grandfather's sitting room nearly four months ago.

But I was crying too hard to speak, and so poor Davy, trying in vain to brush away my tears, had no way of knowing why I wept. Finally, drained, I fell asleep, still naked, in his arms.

By morning, my tears were gone. I awoke, slowly coming to my senses without opening my eyes. Birdsong filled the air, and a bit of sunlight filtered through the leaves to warm my cheek. I smiled as the memory of last night came back to me. Still without opening my eyes, I reached out to touch him. But I found no one to touch. I lay alone, wrapped in the traveling cloak. Alarmed, I opened my eyes and sat up.

Davy sat perhaps ten feet away, across the clearing, opposite a small fire. He wasn't looking at me. "Ye had best get dressed," he said. "It'll have to be the shift ye came away in. I've rinsed out the breeches, but the shirt's torn beyond wearing."

I pulled the cloak around me, then stood up and stepped across the clearing toward him. "Davy . . . " I said hesitantly. "What's wrong?"

"There's naught wrong." He kept his eyes down. His face was dark, unreadable.

I reached out to touch his arm. "Davy?"

He flinched from my touch. "The shift is in the saddle bag," he said without expression. "And I've put the brooch ye carried in your pocket along with it. Ye had best hurry. We've a long way to go today."

Hot shame burned my face. So this was what Mam had meant when she warned me. I had foolishly thought his wanting was more than the lust of a moment. What had I done? I had given myself to a man, and now he scorned me. I stiffened my shoulders and spun away from him. Angrily I jerked my shift out of the saddlebag and then let the cloak drop. What did it matter if he saw me naked now? I had nothing left to hide. He'd seen to the depth of my soul and would have none of it. I pulled the shift on over my head. The luckenbooth brooch he'd bought me fell to the ground. Perhaps he counted it as payment for what he'd taken from me. I almost left the brooch in the detritus of the forest floor, a tiny bit of silver as forlorn as I felt. But my skirt was still torn up the length of it. I used the brooch to fasten the fabric.

We ate breakfast without speaking. Davy gave orders to pack up and mount in terse phrases. He couldn't avoid touching me as he pulled me up behind him, but he let go the minute I was settled. He sat, stiff and distant as a piece of wood. For my part, I held onto him as loosely as possible, shrinking away, even as my body stubbornly ached to lean against him and lay my ear against his back to listen to his heart.

I felt as limp and dirty as a wrung out dishrag as we rode on one horse, yet each alone. A stony silence grew between us. As it stretched on into the afternoon, I grew hard myself. I had trusted him. Reluctantly perhaps, hesitantly for sure, but trusted nonetheless. How dare he shuck me off so carelessly?

We rode slowly through thick hemlock forest. The gloom surrounding us deepened as weak sunlight filtered through the ancient branches. Layers of damp leaves and needles carpeted the ground and muffled the sound of the hooves. I closed my eyes and willed my body not to sag.

Then, surprisingly, I felt warm sunshine on my face. I opened my eyes to see we had entered a rocky clearing. Davy abruptly stopped the horse. "Get off."

"What?" I looked about me, dazed. This was no place to camp. "Why?"

He didn't repeat himself, only dismounted and pulled me down beside him. He gripped my arms, spinning me toward him.

"See here, Callie," he began, then stopped, coughed, and began again. "I've been chasing my thoughts round in my head all morning, trying to say this right, but 'tis no use, and I'm bound to say it, right or no."

"What are you doing?" I squirmed, trying to break free of his grip. "You're hurting me."

He wasn't listening. "I'm sorry for last night, Callie. I'm no usually such a randy bastard. It's . . . well, ye standing there in the water, so open . . . so . . ." He stopped and shook his head. "I'll no make excuses. I've done as I've done, and I'm just telling ye I'm sorry."

"Sorry?" I stared at him. "Sorry? You led me into an ambush and let those awful men come after me, then you . . . " I couldn't say it. I shuddered and took a deep breath. "You say you're sorry?" I felt my voice rising hysterically. How could he be sorry? Had our joining meant so little to him? What I thought to be salvation was no more than a moment's satisfaction? Again I struggled to get free of his grip, but he paid no attention.

"What I mean to say, Callie Beaton, is will ye have me now, after I've used ye so?"

I stopped squirming, stopped breathing even, and felt the heat of his desire once more. "Will I have you?" I repeated stunned. "What do you mean?"

"Ach, lass, can ye no hear me? I'm asking will ye marry me?"

The forest seemed to spin around me. Marry him? My knees wobbled. My heart jumped with the memory of our bodies linked. Had he asked me this morning, wrapped in his arms, with the foolish glamour of lovemaking still upon me, I would have said yes. But he'd left me cold before dawn, and I had better sense by full light of day. Now, he offered marriage as a half-hearted apology, a penance for what he had done. What did he take me for? A piece of flotsam to be used or discarded at will?

I jerked away, furious that even now the thought of marriage to him could tempt me. "You forget, Mr. McRae," I said, making my voice as icy as I could. "I'm going back home."

For a moment he looked as if I had punched him. "Callie, I'm begging ye not to judge me from a moment's indiscretion. I can be good to ye. I will be good to ye. Let me prove it."

"A moment's indiscretion? Is that what last night was?" I said bitterly. "If that's the case, it's hardly worth the remembering now, is it? But indiscretion or no, I'm going back home, and you have promised to help me get there. Or have you forgotten that as well?"

Davy's face darkened and his eyes flashed angrily. Then the look passed, and his mouth twitched in a hint of a smile, as if he had just realized I had released him from the worse obligation, in favor of a minor one. He took a step back, boot scraping on rock, and made a sweeping bow. "Thank ye, Miss Beaton, for the reminder. I see I must prove myself. I'll not ask again until I've kept my promise."

With that enigmatic remark, we continued our journey. We still rode in silence, following no discernible track, but there was a difference now. As I held loosely to his waist and swayed to the rhythm of the horse, he was less stiff, less rigidly set against me. After a time, he even began whistling, calling to the birds as he had done the morning of our first ride.

He's relieved, I realized. Relieved to shed me like an old snake skin, without guilt, for he had made an offer. I had been right to refuse him. Ruined or no, I didn't want to be the object of his pity, married out of duty. So I closed a door on that piece of my mind that still longed for the touch of his lips upon my neck and the feel of his hand pressing me toward him. But still, a part of me cried in the silence behind that door.

The shadows of dusk grew thicker, and night came on, yet Davy didn't stop. I shifted uncomfortably behind him, trying to ease the strain of stiff muscles, but I said nothing. If Davy wanted to break the silence as palpable as a wall between as, he could speak first. The horse jounced on and on. I focused on two things—not falling off and not laying my cheek against Davy's back to rest.

The moon rose, a pale half circle shadowed with wispy clouds. Bits of light strayed through the leafy canopy overhead, dappling the stones of the faint track. Then a clearing opened in front of us. Davy stopped the horse with a gentle tug at the edge of the woods and listened. A soft breeze rustled the leaves overhead. Another sound, softer than the breeze, drifted through the night air, the sound of water lapping against the shore. Not a clearing then, a beach. The clouds shifted, and I saw the glint of moonlight on a wave. And not far offshore, a ghost of a shadow against the black sky, a ship swayed at anchor.

Davy's ship, I realized. The one we'd been riding south to meet. But why here, in this deserted cove?

Apparently satisfied that the beach was empty, Davy clucked softly to the horse. We picked our way to the mouth of a marshy creek. The horse's hooves made soft sucking sounds in the muddy ooze.

Suddenly a dark, cloaked figure rose out of the reeds. A hand grabbed the horse's bridle. I gasped. Involuntarily, I clutched at Davy as a vision of the last poor wretch who had snatched at my horse's bridle made me taste bile.

Davy reached back to squeeze my knee. "'Tis only André," he said calmly. He dismounted and shook hands with the man in the cloak. This man moved with the same easy grace and catlike stealth as Davy.

"You're late, mon frère," the stranger said. "We thought to see you before dark."

"There were . . . complications," Davy said, with only a slight hesitation. He raised a hand to help me down from the horse.

Complications? Was that what we had? Complications? I ignored his outstretched hand and slid off the horse by myself.

Davy took my elbow. I wasn't sure if he meant the gesture to support me or prevent me from fleeing. His grasp was gentle, but quite firm.

"Miss Beaton, may I introduce ye to André Guillot?" His voice was as bland and smooth as if he were in Grandfather's drawing room instead of a salt marsh along a wild, deserted shoreline. "André, this is Miss Caroline Beaton, late of Leith, near Edinburgh."

André took my hand in his and raised it to his lips. "Enchanté."

I jerked my hand back. "This is utterly ridiculous!" I stamped my foot and felt the mud squishing between my bare toes. Whirling toward Davy, I jabbed a finger at his chest. "You said we were going to Baltimore."

"Aye, well, it's near enough." He shrugged, then turned to André. "Am I too late?"

André shook his head. "Non, mon frère. An hour, perhaps two. The moon is still high."

Davy nodded. "Will ye take the lass to the ship and find a place to settle her? I'll bide here till ye are back."

André held out his hand. "This way if you please, Ma'amselle. Mind the rock."

I stood between them, looking from one to the other, each obviously expecting me to comply. I clasped both hands behind my back like a recalcitrant six year old. "I'm not going anywhere. Do you really expect me to board a ship in the middle of the night?"

Davy blinked. "Aye. I do."

"With a stranger? Are you daft?"

"Is that the trouble, then?" Davy put a hand on André's shoulder. "Rest easy, lass. André's no stranger. I've known him for as long as I can remember. He's my first mate and my cousin to boot. Ye are safe enough with him."

Again I looked from one to the other. André had pushed back the hood of the cloak. With the moon clear of the clouds and shining on both faces, I saw at once the resemblance: same lithe body, same broad forehead. André's eyes were a shade darker and had none of the gold flecks dancing in Davy's, and his hair was a deep brown. Now he grinned, an echo of Davy's devilish smile, and reached for my hand again.

I took a step back.

"We've no time to play games, lass," Davy said. "Ye will be safe enough aboard the ship. Do ye stay, I can no say the same. In two hours time, there will be a great roil of men here. Do ye really want to meet the lot of them in your muddy shift? I dinna' think I can promise ye safety in such a case."

I crossed my arms defiantly. "You've done precious little to keep me safe till now. I'm tired of being dragged off without knowing what's to come." This whole business was absurd. If he thought he could drag me aboard his ship and leave me there . . . Well I wouldn't do it.

Davy threw up his hands in disgust. "Ye are going, whether ye like it or not. I'll not have ye in my way should a ruckus break out. If ye are too pigheaded to see the folly . . ."

"You'll not have me in the way!" I spluttered. "And isn't it you who dragged me here in the first place? How dare you . . . " Words failed me.

André coughed politely and stepped between. "Ma'amselle, certainement, you have no wish to stay here, standing in the mud with the chill from the ocean to raise the goose bumps on your arms."

I shivered in spite of myself. My arms weren't the only part of me growing cold.

André tucked my arm under his and gently turned me toward the skiff waiting in the shallows. "There is fine wine aboard the ship and perhaps some soup. You are hungry, no?" André patted the hand he held and inexorably drew me a step closer. "You've nothing to fear from me, Ma'amselle. I'm not a barbarian like my cousin here." He inclined his head back toward Davy, but didn't look at him. We had reached the edge of the skiff, and he raised an eyebrow in silent question.

I sighed. I should have been glad to leave Davy behind, but the last time I had boarded a boat against my will, I had ended up halfway round the world. Still, this charming man could hardly be more dangerous than Davy and seemed a good deal more polite. I might regret it in the morning, but just now, supper and a glass of wine seemed like heaven. I stepped into the skiff.

André took his place at the oars. The sea was calm and we reached the ship quickly. One of the crew threw down a rope ladder. I climbed aboard and followed André to a small, comfortable cabin. In a trice, I found myself wrapped in a warm blanket, a glass of strong wine in my hand, and a bowl of hearty soup in front of me.

André set the open bottle of wine on the table beside me and bowed himself out. I lifted my glass. The wine was smooth and heady. I savored the rich, fruity taste before letting it slide down my throat. Grandfather never served wine this good. Who would have thought to find such treasure on a small ship in a deserted bay? I ate my soup and poured a second glass of the wine.

CHAPTER 19

I awakened in the dark. Something had changed. Footsteps clomped on the deck above me, and ropes slapped against the sides of the ship. A heavy hatch door amidships was thrown open with a muffled thud. I stumbled across the cabin and peered out the small porthole. The moon had set and the night was much darker than it had been. I strained my eyes, looking toward what I thought was the shoreline. The light of a single lantern swung once, twice, and then was shuttered. From somewhere on the deck, an answering gleam of light glistened briefly on the water, and then it too disappeared. Sounds of men moving increased, punctuated with low grunts and deep thuds.

I stepped back from the window, aghast as understanding dawned. The ship was being unloaded in near silence, in a deserted bay. I could think of only one reason to unload a ship in the dark. I remembered the muffled thumps the night we 'freights' were locked in before arriving in Philadelphia. Davy had disappeared by morning, and I guessed a good deal of the cargo had too. Everything fell into place. Davy's dealings with Shakleton, his mysterious business, his murder of the poor sailor aboard the boat. Obviously, Davy McRae was no ordinary merchant, but a smuggler in cahoots with Shakleton. I thought of Peg's gossip about the war in the west, and the newspapers posting laws against trading with the French. I had dismissed it as news of someplace far away, of no importance to me. Yet Davy was here, in the thick of it, and André by accent and manners, was clearly French to his core. Where did that leave me?

I shook myself. It didn't matter where I stood. The fact was, Davy was a smuggler and not a man to trust.

Suddenly, a different sort of light flashed, not the diffused light of a lantern briefly unhooded, but a streak like a slash upon a black, velvet sky. A popping sound, like a dull thud, echoed across the water. A second flash and then a third followed close upon the first, each accompanied by the popping sound.

Musket fire, I thought incredulously. They were shooting at each other. But who was doing the shooting? And more importantly, who was getting shot?

I raced out of the cabin and stumbled on deck. The ship was quiet with two fellows lounging against the side. Recognizing Hamish, the one-eyed guard from the night I had brought Leah, I hurried over to them. "They're shooting out there!" I said urgently, straining against the darkness to see the shore.

"Oui, Ma'amselle. " The fellow with a striped shirt spoke without moving. He seemed so unconcerned, I wondered if he actually understood me.

"But someone's going to get hurt." I thought of Davy in the line of fire, too tired to aim properly or even duck. I forgot my earlier condemnations. Worry drove all else from my mind. "What of your captain?" I asked the sailors. "Le capitaine? Shouldn't we go help him?"

Striped shirt shrugged. He turned a patient smile toward me. "Le capitaine would not want us to desert the ship. Right, Hamish?" He looked to his one-eyed friend for corroboration.

"We couldn't leave the lass alone." Hamish's tone showed he was scandalized at the thought, but I wasn't sure if he meant to protect the ship or me.

"Don't worry," Striped shirt said. "Someone is coming now."

"Where?" I couldn't see into the night, but his eyes were better than mine, for in a few minutes, I could make out the dark bulk of a rowboat pulling close with five or six figures in it.

The two loungers loosened the pistols in their belts and stood ready. Then came the familiar trill I had heard Davy whistle so often. Hamish smiled and returned the signal.

In a few minutes, the skiff pulled close. Davy, André and several sailors climbed aboard. I grabbed Davy's arm the minute he set foot on deck. "Not expecting trouble?" I demanded. "I heard shooting. What happened?"

Davy swayed a little, but patted my hand upon his arm. "Not much trouble," he said. There was a fresh, wet smear on his white shirtsleeve and a warm stickiness under my hand.

"You're hurt!"

"Just a bit."

"But you could have been killed!"

Davy stopped, a half smile playing between his eyes and mouth. "Would that matter to ye, lass?"

"Of course it would matter!" I cried and then realized he must be teasing. I drew back. "If you're killed, who will see me to Philadelphia?"

Davy frowned and waved his left hand. "Ye have no need to worry on that account. André will back up any promises I'm prevented from keeping in the case of untimely death."

André. So Davy felt he could cast me off on another man as easily as that.

As if on cue, André took my hand and gently turned me away from Davy. "It's very late, Ma'amselle, and everyone is tired. Perhaps we can talk in the morning? It will be here soon."

Davy did indeed look tired, swaying not from the ship's roll, but as if his legs would give out at any moment.

"Are you sure you're not dying tonight?" I said.

The corner of Davy's mouth twitched. "'I promise ye, lass. I'll not die this night, if I have anything at all to say about it." He wobbled a bit. André dropped my hand and deftly put an arm around Davy's waist, pulling Davy's good arm over his shoulder. Davy sagged against him as the two of them stumbled toward the bow.

I returned to my own cabin. Would it matter to me if Davy were killed? Obviously, I didn't want to be stranded in the wilderness. But beyond that? The way Davy meant the question? I couldn't find an answer. Yet try as I would to ignore it, my mind kept spinning around without reaching an answer.

The next morning I slept late and woke slowly. How delicious it felt to lie in a bed, with covers and pillow, totally comfortable in the slight rocking of the ship. A rap at the cabin door interrupted my sloth. "Come in," I called, irritated at the interruption.

André came in with a gown billowing over his arms, a soft fawn-colored silk embroidered with dark maroon flowers.

"For me?" I asked incredulously, my irritation vanishing in an instant. The gown was not by any means new, but once it must have graced a governor's ball. Even now with the lace sleeves wrinkled and a bit tattered, it was the most beautiful dress I had seen in the colonies.

André laid the gown on the table and held out the rest of the garments he'd brought. There was a blue green satin petticoat and a set of stays. "I thought perhaps it would please Ma'amselle to change out of the . . . gown you have worn here," he said, politely looking away from that garment, which I had slept in for want of anything else.

"Oh, André!" I surprised both of us by throwing my arms around him. André patted my shoulder. Embarrassed, I backed away.

Pretending not to notice my discomfiture, André pushed the stays into my arms and discreetly turned his back.

I took the dress behind the screen and slipped out of my torn petticoat and bodice. I hesitated as I unfastened the luckenbooth brooch holding my skirt shut. What had Davy meant by the gift?

I snapped my hand shut. It didn't matter. I put the brooch in my pocket and then pulled on the petticoat over my shift. "Where is Davy this morning?" I asked as I laced the stays.

"Mon frère is sleeping still," André said without turning around.

"Is he hurt badly, then?" I peered around the screen, the dress momentarily forgotten.

"Non." André waved his hands in dismissal. "A scratch only. Non. He is just very tired. You will know he has not slept much for many days." André kept the laughter out of his voice, but it was clearly there, just below the surface. So Davy had told him what happened.

A hot blush spread over my cheeks and I was glad André couldn't see. I let the dress settle about my shoulders and straightened the lace before fastening the hooks and eyes at the front. Then I stepped out from behind the screen.

André turned. His eyes widened and he whistled. "Ma'amselle! Could mon frère have any idea of the jewel he's caught?"

Oddly enough, the remark pleased me.

André had also brought a brush, along with a small mirror. He waited patiently, chatting of the weather and other minor matters while I attacked the snarled mess my hair had become.

"And now Ma'amselle," André said when I set the brush down. He pulled out a maroon ribbon. "Permit me to help you dress the hair." He took the brush and pulled my hair up and back, tying it with the ribbon.

I tilted my head to look at the effect in the mirror. "Wherever did you learn so much of fashion, André?" I asked, delighted. I hadn't felt pretty in ages.

"There's been a lady or two to teach me how it pleases her," he said, his teeth flashing in an enigmatic smile.

I could guess the kind of ladies offering such instruction. I did not press the issue.

"Shall we breakfast in the captain's salon?" André offered his arm.

In no time, I found myself seated at an elegantly appointed table in an intimate drawing room. A breakfast of porridge, bread and sausages had been laid out on a linen tablecloth. Aside from the slight tilt of the floor and the creaking of ropes and sails, it was hard to remember that I was aboard a ship.

André filled a cup with hot tea and handed it to me. "On behalf of mon frère, le capitaine, bon appetit."

"Thank you." I took a sip. "Why do you call Davy, 'mon frère'—your brother? You can hardly be brothers, with you French and he Scots."

"In truth, we are cousins. My mother is his father's sister," André said. "But we grew up as brothers. Davy came to France as a boy."

"Yes." I remembered now. "His first sea voyage."

"He told you of that? To be sure, mon frère has an easy way with words, but it's not so often he tells his own stories." André offered me another helping of sausage. "Perhaps it's Ma'amselle's charming smile that allowed him to speak so frankly."

I thought of the chill dark under the lifeboat during the storm and doubted very much Davy had been able to see my smile, let alone be charmed by it. I'd been shivering, from fear as well as cold. Davy had held me close and whispered his stories in my ear, calming me . . . and, I thought, caring for me.

I shook my head. Things had changed. I didn't want to think about that night, or any other night Davy had wrapped his arms around me. I stabbed a sausage. "Did you sail with him?" It was far safer to talk about André just now.

"Many times. My sisters always said he could smell trouble from five miles away, and it drew him like a magnet." He lifted one shoulder in a half-hearted shrug. "And where Davy led, I was never far behind." He paused to refill our cups. "I have three sisters. They have no sense of adventure. . . When Davy came to us, two years older and full of ideas, is it any wonder I followed him?" André smiled in some private boyhood memory. "We are brothers. We have shared everything." He winked at me. "Including whippings for the trouble we found."

I imagined Davy as a boy, tousle-haired and grinning, even as he took his punishment.

At that moment Davy stumbled into the salon, tousle-haired to be sure, but decidedly not grinning. He was shirtless, arm bound in white linen. The sight of him set my heart racing. "He's a scoundrel," I reminded myself, "and a smuggler to boot." But my heart wasn't listening.

Davy obviously did not expect company in his salon. At the sight of me, he stopped, hand half raised to comb his fingers through his unruly hair. He stared as if he'd never seen me before. For half a second he seemed at a loss, but almost instantly he recovered his poise and bowed. "Good morrow to ye, Miss Beaton. Ye are looking very fine this morning." His eyes seemed locked on the lace at my bodice. The dress was cut far lower than anything Mam would have allowed in her parlor. I crossed my arms over my chest.

Davy looked at his cousin. "That dress, André?" he said in a strangled voice. "Was there no other?"

"The color suits the Ma'amselle, n'est-ce pas?"

"Oh, aye," Davy said dryly. "It does indeed suit her."

The look that passed between them made me wonder exactly whose dress I wore. What kind of a woman would leave her gown aboard a smuggler's ship? I wasn't sure I wanted to know such a woman.

I took a deep breath, trying for the polite formality Mam had taught me. "Won't you sit down, Mr. McRae." Maybe it wasn't mere pity that had prompted Davy to offer me marriage. When it came to the question, I really had no idea at all what he thought of me. Did he see a whore's dress, settled upon the newest whore? I choked on the bread.

André pounded me on the back and offered me fresh tea once the fit had passed. Davy sat without moving, his face unreadable.

It was an odd breakfast. Though seething with pent-up emotion, anger battling hurt and shame, I did my utmost to play the part of a lady. Davy was uncharacteristically silent and kept his eyes on his plate for the most part. When he did look up, it was no further than the top of my bodice and the revealing view that offered. Each time his eyes slid away from mine, my heart tore and bled a little more. André did most of the talking. Clearly, he was the only one enjoying the meal. Through it all, his face crinkled in silent laughter as he sliced the bread, discoursed on the best sausages, and poured out more tea.

As soon as I could, I excused myself and hurried back to the cabin. I rummaged through the clothes I'd shed earlier and dug out the neckerchief I had gotten along with Cora's other garments. Grimy with sweat and trail dust, the white linen had turned gray, but I wrapped it around my neck anyway. Reluctantly, I pulled the luckenbooth brooch out of my pocket. I ought to give it back to Davy. What would he think if he saw me wearing it?

I shook my head. What he thought didn't matter. I pinned the neckerchief in place with the brooch. Mr. McRae could think what he wanted.

CHAPTER 20

I planned to stay away from both the captain and his first mate, but it proved impossible. I could not stay cooped up in the tiny cabin all the time, comfortable though it might be. Nor could I ask for my meals to be served separately in there. The sailors were busy enough with their own tasks. They had no time to wait on me.

So I joined Davy and André for supper. They were talking business when I entered the salon, something about a wine shipment. André rose to greet me with a bow. Davy did not. He rolled up their papers before glancing at me. His lips curled into an ironic smile when he saw the luckenbooth brooch holding the scarf. Then he lowered his eyes and took a long swallow.

He didn't look at me for the rest of the meal or say a word. I didn't have much to say either. Still, I felt he was watching me. André kept the one-sided conversation going, thanking the sailor who brought in the soup and bread, commenting on the weather, and chattering about other equally inane topics before escorting me back to the cabin after the meal.

I stopped him as he turned to leave me at the cabin door. "André, is there some reason I shouldn't wear this dress?"

André patted my arm. "Non, Ma'amselle, not at all. It is a beautiful dress and you are even more beautiful wearing it."

"Yes, well... but...um . . . whose dress is it?"

"Oh, do not worry about that, Ma'amselle. It belongs to Elise. To be sure, she will not mind you keeping it."

"Elise?"

"Oui. She is a very good friend of mine."

More likely mistress, I thought skeptically, to leave such a dress aboard a ship. I thought again of Davy's reaction. Shared everything, did they? Abruptly, I turned away from André and closed the door of the cabin in his face.

Over the next few days, the tension on the sleek little *Rossignol* continued under the surface. The crew, which numbered five men, mixed Scots and French, were always polite to me, turning from their work to offer greeting when I walked on deck. Renard, the ship's cook, made a habit of bringing a hot drink to the cabin in the evening, at the captain's orders, or so he claimed. Davy and I had little to say to one another, but André never let silence take over. At least, for the first time in many months, I was actually comfortable. The air, so hot and stifling by day on land, was cool, but not cold on the water, and the ship rode lightly in the breeze. The food was hearty and wholesome, not bits of leftovers snatched from the family table. And while this pair of cousins were certainly smugglers, they were not ruffians.

Davy still wore the bandage on his arm, but it seemed the hurt was healing well and in any case had not been severe. On the third evening, after supper, he pulled out his fife and played a medley of songs from *Barbara Allen* to *Fair Janet*. André sang along, rolling the Scot's tunes in a throaty French accent. Under the spell of such music, it was easy to forget my urgency to return to Philadelphia for Mary and myself.

Thus it startled me when Davy traded his fife for a mug one evening and casually announced, "We'll dock in the morning."

"Really?" I said. "In Philadelphia?"

He shook his head and wiped his mouth before answering. "Not in the town precisely, but just south of it. A private landing."

"It is no use to stop at that," André said. "Tell her the rest." A look full of hidden meaning passed between them. Davy shook his head slightly. André shrugged one shoulder.

"Tell me what?" I looked from one to the other. "What do you mean?"

Davy stared into his cup, not speaking.

"She will find out," André insisted.

Davy banged his cup down and stood up abruptly. "'Tis nothing." He strode out of the room.

André rolled his eyes at Davy's back, but loyal as ever, would not say a word more, and I was left wondering what more secrets Davy kept and oddly hurt by his distrust. I had bared my soul to him after all, and he had spurned me in the morning. A niggling voice in a corner of my mind suggested I had done the spurning, but I squelched the thought. Davy McRae had used me and any offer made had been no more than pity.

The next day we turned in toward the shore. We had been traveling up the Delaware River, just as the ship from Edinburgh had. The marshy, tree-lined shore looked no different from the coast we'd been passing for days. Only when we approached closer did I realize a peninsula jutted out from the bank, hiding a small bay. We rounded the peninsula and saw a clearing, with a low, flat landing, sheltered from view of the main channel. A single building stood back of the dock. I was surprised to see it was not a rough, ramshackle structure, but a solidly built, three-story structure of brick and stone. A tavern, by the looks of it, but a much finer one than the miserable place Davy and I had spent the night. A rabble of children tumbling about on the lawn broke off their play as we approached. One ran to the house, no doubt to spread the news of our arrival. The others came to the dock, nudging each other and giggling as we slid alongside the pier, the lines were made fast, and the gangplank set. The children, a motley pack of boys from a wee lad no more than four years old up to a tall fellow of eight or nine, were of all sorts. Two of them had skin the color of black tea laced with cream. A couple of others had the long, black braided hair and rich tan of Indian. The oldest boy's pale skin was sunburned red as his hair. They obviously knew the crew well, for although they stayed out of the way, they called out merrily, with the practiced patter one hears from the beggars on the street.

André turned to Davy. "I'll see she's unloaded, mon frère, and join you at the house. You have introductions to make and explanations, I think."

Without arguing, Davy offered me his arm to steady me on the gangplank.

After a moment's hesitation, I took it and let him lead me up to the house. What sort of introductions and explanations did Davy want to avoid?

A long low porch ran the length of the building. Three dark-skinned women in various states of undress lounged against the railing, while a large, gap-toothed woman leaned back in an oversized rocker, a fan sitting idle in her lap.

"So, it's Davy McRae, come back to us at last," she called out in a husky voice as we approached. "Come up to the house, love, and tell us all the news. We're famished for a bit of gossip here, with the roads empty and the ships few and far between."

I stopped on the path. "What kind of a tavern is this?"

"Never ye worry." Davy pulled me forward. "These are good people."

I wasn't too sure what Davy's definition of good people might be, but mine did not include women who hung half-clothed on the porch railing. "They're not dressed. What if someone comes?"

"Isn't that the point of having a business?"

I stopped again. "What?"

Davy patted my arm and kept walking. "They weren't expecting company just now. There's a road to town, sure enough. Ye maybe don't recall the fork in the road we took just outside Philadelphia. I came here to get the second horse."

Dark hemlocks ringed the clearing, close enough that the rich, cool smell of woodland mixed with the sharp tang of salt marsh as we neared the house. To the right there was a break in the trees that could have been a road. "Not so many folks come out this way," Davy went on, "except when there's to be a race or a cockfight. The road from Philadelphia doesn't lead anywhere else. Most of their trade comes by ship, but not so early in the day. Ye could say they're not really open for business just now."

We had reached the end of the path at the foot of the steps to the porch. Davy let go my arm to make a courtly bow, then stepped up onto the porch and took the woman's fleshy, freckled hand. He kissed it dramatically. "Ye may indeed be famished for gossip, Mistress Godwin, but for naught else, I'd wager."

"Ooh la la, ever the rake!" Mistress Godwin fluttered her eyelashes and fanned herself quickly in a mock faint.

The other women laughed. "No complaints there," one of them called out. "We've enough business to keep us full." This brought forth more laughter.

"Who have you brought along?" the large woman asked.

Davy took my hand again. "Caroline Beaton of Leith, meet Prudence Godwin of Godwin's Landing."

I curtsied. "Pleased to make your acquaintance, madam," I said, relying on the polite response Mam had drilled into me.

Prudence waved her hand. "Ooh, a lady for sure. Where did you find such a prize, Davy? Not your usual haunts, I'd guess." Laughter sparked along the porch rail, but Prudence was not through. She eyed me up and down in a frank appraisal and finally nodded. "She's a mite skinny, though the dress is fine enough." She winked at some private joke only she and Davy shared. "Is she to stay here?"

"She could stay here right enough," Davy said before I could answer.

"You promised to take me to Philadelphia," I interrupted in outrage. "What do you mean to abandon me here in this . . . this . . . " Words failed me. To think he would leave me in a bawdy house! My good name may be already ruined, and my reputation stained beyond all repair, but I wasn't ready to become a bawd!

Davy ignored my outburst and went on calmly and firmly. "As I was saying, she could do here, but 'tis not likely she would agree. She has a few troubles of her own just now."

Prudence raised an eyebrow at this, but didn't ask any more questions. "Well, whatever your troubles, love, you're welcome. This may be a safer place than you can imagine."

"Thank you," I said, somewhat awkwardly. I should have thought before speaking. "I meant no disrespect . . . " I trailed off, unsure what to say.

"Indeed?" Prudence was clearly amused. She let the silence grow.

Davy's attention had wandered to one of the three women at the rail, a woman my height, with a complexion of smooth, creamy coffee. She was strikingly beautiful, the kind of beauty that took men's breath away and set women to grinding teeth in jealousy. Davy had moved over near her and took her hand in his. His head bent to her in quiet conversation. Her thick, dark hair was swept up in a bun, a few curls artfully loosened to frame an oval face. Rich, full lips parted ever so slightly in invitation, an invitation Davy seemed only too happy to answer.

Prudence coughed, wrenching my attention back to her. She had obviously been watching me watch Davy. "That's Elise," she said with a lazy drawl. "You've nothing to worry about there. She won't say a word about the dress you borrowed."

"I'm not worried about anyone Davy McRae has an interest in," I snapped.

Her face crinkled with silent laugh lines. "As you say, love. But come inside and wet your throat. I'm sure a pint or two would ease you. It will take some time for them to unload the ship."

Davy did not follow us in. I settled myself at a table in the corner of the public room and slowly sipped the rum Prudence had a boy bring to me. The air was dead still in spite of two small windows thrown open on either side of the room. I fanned my face with an edge of my skirt, but the effort brought little relief from the heat. I could see why the ladies would wait on the porch where a stray breeze from the river might find them. But I refused to join them. Davy was out there, making eyes at a girl he knew well, and I did not care to witness his flirtations.

The common room held a dozen tables. A huge empty hearth dominated one end of the room. At the wall opposite the fireplace a carved, wooden staircase led to the upper floors, undoubtedly where the ladies' rooms stood ready. I turned my back to the steps, unwilling to think of the business that took place upstairs. When the boy replaced the first drink with a second one, I did not question it. This rum was much stronger than the wine I was used to, but I was so angry at Davy and so frustrated with the whole situation, I hardly noticed. By the time a third drink appeared on the table, I was not thinking clearly at all.

After that, I lost count. Eventually, Davy's crew wandered in looking for refreshment. Vaguely I saw old Hamish sitting at a nearby table with three black men dressed in knee breeches and fresh linen shirts. At first I thought them servants of the house, but they ordered drinks and sat at the table like any other customer. Still, not until I watched a pair of ruddy Indians enter the tavern and sit quietly in one corner did I realize this wasn't any ordinary tavern. Apparently Prudence Godwin ran the place with little regard for the laws against serving slaves, Indians, or apprentices. My opinion of her went up a notch. It's not that I advocated breaking the law. It's just that some laws made less sense than others.

Snatches of conversation drifted my way as I drank another mug. There was speculation on the war with the French and what it might do to trade. Some of them said how such a war opened up all sorts of trade possibilities, but others predicted gloomily it meant more soldiers coming, and trade would be harder to manage. They were both right, I thought wearily, when the trade they were discussing was really nothing more than smuggling. I lay my head down on my arms. What was I doing here, still miles from Philadelphia and even further from home, drinking in a dark, gloomy tavern while my would-be rescuer dallied with a whore?

A light tap on my arm startled me, and I jerked up. A child stood silently at my elbow.

"What do ye think you're about, sneaking up on me like that?" I grumbled, reaching for my glass, which I imagined the girl had come to refill. Then I stopped. Not just any child. Skinny little girl, fine towhead blond, round blue eyes in a serious, elfin face. I shook my head to clear my vision, but the girl remained in front on me.

"Leah. What are you doing here?"

"Did ye bring Mam with ye?" she asked in a whisper.

"I'm sorry." I reached for her.

She stepped back just out of reach and sighed, a whole storm of sorrow held in that frail body. "Mr. McRae said as much, but I thought to ask ye . . ."

"Wait, Leah." I reached for her again, wanting to offer some comfort. But she took another step back and slipped out of the room just as quietly as she had come.

I stood abruptly, knocking over my chair and swaying a little. Anger and rum churned in my belly. So this was what Davy had done to keep Leah safe. He brought her to a brothel. The man had no sense and no morals. Was this what he hadn't wanted to tell me? Well, I had a thing or two to say to him!

I stumbled toward the door. The common room was nearly full by now. Several tables had groups of people seated at them and the talk had given way to singing, playing cards, and drinking. I brushed past them all and pushed my way outside.

Night had fallen. Several couples crowded the porch. I blinked. Davy was not there. How long had I been drinking? Dizzy, I clutched the arm of the nearest man. Hamish, I thought with relief, from our ship.

"Where's the captain?" I mumbled. It was taking more effort than I imagined to make my words come out straight.

Hamish took hold of my arm to stop me from pitching over the rail. "Right behind ye."

I spun around and would have kept spinning, if Davy hadn't been there to catch me. A lot of other people, with faces too dim to recognize, crowded behind him.

"Steady, lass. What manner of devil sent ye flying through the tavern like a banshee out of hell? I thought ye safe asleep in the corner."

I shook free of him. "Do you know Leah is here, Davy McRae?"

"Aye." He took my arm. "Come back inside and sit a bit. I'll tell ye all about it." I could see the amber lights twinkling in his eyes, but I was too angry for his charm this time.

"I'll have no more of your stories, Davy McRae. Have you told Mary you've brought her daughter safe to a whorehouse?" I pulled back my hand and swung, aiming to knock away that maddening smile. I missed, stumbling clumsily into him. I stepped back to swing again, but this time he caught my wrist and held fast.

He frowned at me, his eyes dark with anger. "That's enough, Callie," he said coldly. "Don't be judging a lady before ye know her."

"And I suppose you do know her. I don't want to know your whore, Davy. I don't want anything to do with her. I don't want her dress either."

I pulled at my bodice, desperate to get out of the borrowed dress, mindless of the crowd at the tavern door. I fell to my knees, too dizzy to undo the laces. "She is a lying slut, and you're no better than a bastard."

Davy gripped my arms and hauled me upright. His grasp tightened, bruising my flesh. I squeaked, mid sob. "She's a lady. Have a care what ye say without thinking." He shook me, snapping my head back.

"Stop, Davy. You're hurting me." I tried to twist away from him.

"Have ye no thought to the hurt ye have been dealing?" he said without loosing his grip. He shook me again.

André put a hand on Davy's arm. "This is not the place to talk like this."

"I dinna' think we're talking exactly," Davy's voice twisted with sarcasm, but he let go my arms and took a step back.

I swayed, and André neatly put an arm around my waist. "Perhaps Ma'amselle would consent to lie down. You'll feel better in the morning."

I really didn't want to go with him. I wasn't finished with Davy yet.

But I didn't have much choice. My legs seemed to have turned to jelly and my tongue a wad of cotton. André scooped me up and carried me back to the ship.

I woke late the next morning, decidedly not feeling better. My head ached, and every tiny bob of the ship felt like an earthquake inside my skull. I stayed in the cabin as long as I could, gritting my teeth against the pounding. I most certainly did not want to face anyone who had seen me the night before.

Eventually, of course, my bladder demanded I do something. So I emerged into the daylight. While I slept, the ship had left the harbor and we were heading up the Delaware River again. Just as well, I thought. Except for Leah, who wanted nothing to do with me after I had abandoned her, there was no one at Godwin's Landing I wanted ever to see again.

After relieving myself, I made my way to the ship's galley to beg something to drink. The cook grinned at me. "'Mal à la tête, Ma'amselle?" He brewed me a cup of very strong tea. I hadn't seen him at the tavern the night before, but it hardly mattered. Undoubtedly everyone aboard knew what a spectacle I'd made of myself.

Why hadn't Davy told me the child would be there? But it was not just seeing Leah that had made me so angry. I thought I had banished all feeling for the man, so why had seeing him with Elise made me want to strangle them both? The man had carried away my heart as surely as the ship had carried me from Scotland, but clearly Davy could not be trusted.

I decided to drink my tea in the open air on deck to ease my headache, but as I left the galley, I heard a woman's husky laugh. I peeked around the bulkhead. André stood at the ship's wheel. Elise leaned against him, her dark hair spilling across his chest. So she had not remained behind at the tavern, and my earlier surmise that she spent a great deal of time aboard this ship had been correct. Perhaps it was even her private cabin I slept in. Whose bed did she share now, while I slept in hers?

I turned away. Best drink my tea in the cabin after all.

CHAPTER 21

By evening, my head felt considerably better, but my stomach refused to let me fast in peace. If I didn't want to go hungry, I would have to brave the captain's salon for supper.

I tidied up my hair with Elise's brush. Then I straightened the neck handkerchief and re-pinned the luckenbooth brooch. I pinched my cheeks a bit to redden them and tucked a stray curl back in place. Another curl escaped, but straightening it made it worse. I pulled out all the pins, and redid my hair. My efforts did little to change the results. But with my stomach growling like a hungry wolf, I could think of no other reason to delay. I put down the brush and mirror, closed the door behind me, and crossed the deck to the salon.

The light in the cabin was dim. Low windows at the far end were shadowed by the overhanging poop deck, and the slanting rays of the setting sun shone obliquely. Elise perched on André's lap, whispering something in his ear. Or perhaps tickling him with her tongue. I couldn't really tell.

Davy had his head bent over a roll of charts. He looked up as I entered. I don't know what I expected. I was ready to snap at him if he showed any hint of anger, or if he meant to laugh at me. But he did neither. "Feeling better, lass?" he said in a neutral voice. "Ye will not have met Elise. She's André's fiancée."

Fiancée? That's not what I would call her. Just then Hamish brought in a covered pewter tureen full of a hearty stew along with a good loaf of bread.

While Hamish lit a couple of lanterns, Elise slipped off André's lap to set out bowls and ladle the stew into them. Davy cleared away his papers and we took our places at the table. For a time, conversation was limited to the occasional, "Pass the bread, please" or "Will ye have a bit more wine?"

Elise finished first. She had taken the place next to André at the table. Now she leaned closer to him and laid her hand on top of his. Her fine, dark fingers twined with his rough tanned ones, the two colors complementing each other like two strands in an intricate knotwork. André's fingers tightened to squeeze hers. He blew her a soft kiss, then took another bite of the stew. Elsie turned her head to me. Her full lips stretched into a wide grin as she caught me watching. "I hear tell you come from the same island as Davy do," she said in a rich, musical voice, with an accent that spoke of warmth and sun-filled days. I wondered how she ended up so far north.

"Yes. From Scotland."

"You don' belong dere."

I put down my spoon and sat back. "Of course I belong there."

She shook her head and clucked her tongue, her dark eyes squinted half shut in a frown of disapproval. "Davy say, you be all time looking to go back. Don' you know, what's gone bad by morning can't come good at night? You best look about you, girl, to see what's gone bad."

"I don't know what you are talking about." I pushed my chair back. "Of course I'm returning to Scotland."

"But not just now," Davy said. "Unless ye mean to walk across the water. Have another glass of wine, Callie, before ye get your dander up." Davy filled our glasses before continuing, his words directed to Elise now, not me. "It's no more use talking to her on that account than 'twould be to beg a rock to move for ye."

"A toast," André proposed, "to the lovely ladies keeping us good company this evening."

I didn't want to be the same sort of 'lady' he counted Elise, but neither would I be outdone by her. I tipped my glass toward his.

"What about you, Elise?" I said a moment later, trying to turn the conversation away from my plans. "Is Godwin's Landing your home, then?"

"No. I go time by time to see our boy." Elise stared into her wine as she said this with the kind of look I'd seen on Mary's face when she spoke of Leah or wee Rabbie. A mother then, leaving her child behind.

"Can't you bring him with you?"

"I run Miss Prudence's tavern on the docks in Philadelphia. That's no place for a chil'."

I wondered if the bawdy house at Godwin's Landing was any better, but didn't ask the question aloud. In any case, if Prudence Godwin had a second 'tavern' in the city, I doubted very much all they served was spirits. At least at Godwin's Landing, the child had a safe place to play and a good plenty of playmates.

And Leah among them. Was it possible she, too, was better off out of the city? The thought made me wonder if I'd been rash. But inwardly I shook my head. She might be safer, but not better off without her mam.

Elise stood and laughed as if to banish the gloom settling about us. She trailed a finger along the back of André's neck, then twirled around to lean against Davy, her elbows propped on his shoulders and her dark tresses shining beside his golden curls. "Get out your fife, Davy," she wheedled. "And play us a merry tune."

"As ye wish."

She smiled, kissed him on the cheek, winked at me, and then swirled away, dancing to some music she alone could hear.

I tightened my fists until the nails dug into the palms. André's fiancée indeed! Very slowly, I forced my fists to relax. I had no hold on Davy, nor he on me. There was nothing to be jealous of.

Davy reached for his fife and blew a light trill, testing it. Just then a rap sounded at the door and Hamish came in.

"We'll dock in thirty minutes, sir," he said.

"Thank ye, Hamish." Davy set down the fife.

"Docking? We're back to Philadelphia?" I stood up abruptly, knocking over my chair. "I'll go to see Mary first and then straighten everything out."

"Hold a bit, lass." Davy caught my arm. "Have ye forgotten there's a warrant signed for your arrest?"

I shook free of him and pulled open the door. "Of course not. I don't intend to turn myself in, or let the Ashers or Mr. Shakleton see me. No one will recognize me as the servant girl who ran away." I smoothed out the elegant dress I still wore. "I don't look like a servant any more."

Davy, André and Elise had all followed me out. "That be true," Elise said. "Maybe they think you be something else all together."

I was too anxious to arrive in Philadelphia to let her teasing rile me. I hurried across the deck to the cabin I'd been using.

The others let me go, but Davy dogged my heels. "Ye canna' go into town tonight. Ye will be clapped in jail before ye can blink twice. Do ye want to hang, lass?"

Ignoring him, I stopped in the center of the cabin. What should I take with me? I really had nothing to pack. I spun back toward the door.

Davy blocked the entrance. "Ye canna' go into town on your own," Davy said in a voice with exaggerated patience. "Even ye must see the sense of that. It's dark. Let me see the lay of things in the morning. Tomorrow will be soon enough, no? I'll help ye then."

I tapped my foot impatiently. "You told me to wait 'til morning aboard the ship and look where that got me! You told me not to stay in Philadelphia just that night and look where that got me. I mean to see Mary and I mean to go back to Scotland and the only way I can do that is to go into town."

"Ye will. Tomorrow. I've given ye my word, and that's not a thing I give lightly. Wait for me. Do ye go on your own, ye will be lost or killed for sure." Davy stretched his arm across the doorway. I tried to shove him aside.

He didn't move.

"You brute!" I kicked his shin, bruising my toe. I was so angry I couldn't think straight. "I'm tired of waiting for you to get around to helping me." He could not make me stay. Not now, with town just beyond the docks. "Ethan Asher has promised to help me get home. He'll never believe I killed his father."

Davy stiffened. His eyes darkened, and his voice was cold in its intensity. "Ye canna' go just now."

"Oh? What's to stop me?" I grabbed his arm and tried to yank it free of the doorframe.

"I am sorry, Miss Beaton," he said, without budging. "There are reasons ye dinna' ken, and I say ye must bide."

"What reasons?"

He eyed me, lips pressed together. Then he shook his head. "I canna' tell ye. But I've promised I'd see ye safe to Philadelphia and I will. I've got ye this far, safe and whole. But I'll also promise ye now that do ye try to leave this cabin, I'll tie ye in. Ye will see I keep my promises a damn sight better than Ethan Asher."

"You wouldn't dare!" I scowled at him.

"I would." His anger smoldered just below the surface. "I canna' have ye wandering about, poking your nose in where it's not wanted."

"Some more of your smuggling business tonight?" I snapped.

"Do I have your word ye will bide?"

"You do not."

"'Tis no use talking to a stone," Davy muttered. He ran one hand through his cedar curls, smoothing them back behind his ears. "Well then," he said and left the cabin abruptly.

I leapt after him, but I was too late. The door clicked shut and I heard the key turn in the lock. I pounded both fists on the door. "Davy McRae, you let me out of here!" I yelled. But the wood bruised my hands and there was no answer.

There would be no answer either.

Even though I got on well with the crew, not one of them would go against the captain's orders. Nor could I expect help from André or Elise, both on Davy's side as well. I kicked the offending door locked in my face, but it didn't even wobble.

At least Davy hadn't actually tied me up. Perhaps I could break the door down. What could I use? I took stock of the small cabin. A wobbly table, attached with a set of iron hinges, jutted out from one wall. The chair beside it was a delicate thing with skinny legs and a velvet cushion. Neither offered any help. A ceramic bowl filled with apples and pears sat on the table, along with a pewter plate. Either one of them would break long before denting that solid door. The bunk opposite the door held only pillows and quilts, of no use at all. I cursed Davy for having such a solidly built ship, with no way out of it. I plopped down on the bunk and pounded the pillow in frustration. After a few minutes, I felt the ship bumping up against the dock as we reached the pier. Soon the muffled shouts of the crew faded away. I imagined they'd all gone ashore to wives or sweethearts, leaving only Hamish as watch at the gangplank, and me locked in here.

Gradually, the cabin grew dark and gloomy. I hadn't thought to light a candle, but now a thin glow of moonlight shone through the small porthole over the bunk. I sat up.

The porthole was a window, a window that could open. It was small to be sure, too small for a man, but I just might be able to squeeze through. I jumped up on the bed and pulled it open. Fresh, cool air filled the cabin, bringing the pungent smells of rotting fish and human detritus common to city harbors. I peered down. Black water, cold and fathomless in the pale moonlight, swirled below. There was no escape that way, not down there.

But what about up? I stuck my head and shoulders out the window and looked toward the sky. Overhead, not far from the window, the ship's boat was lashed tight. I could just barely reach it, and from there I could climb over onto the stern. Just the first part would be difficult.

I didn't stop to think. I tied up my skirt, forming a loose trouser. Then I wriggled up through the window and sat in it, clenching the clapboard siding of the ship. While at anchor or docked, I rarely noticed the gentle bob and swing of the ship upon the water, but here, leaning precariously over the murky water below, each movement of the vessel seemed magnified, destined to dislodge me. Slowly, I reached sideways, toward the boat. Too far and I would overbalance. Gripping the window frame with one hand, I leaned a bit more, pressing my heels against the wall to hold me steady. I stretched as far as I could and just caught the edge of the ship's boat. I sucked in air and balanced, half in, half out the window, my right hand firmly grasping the edge of the boat, my legs still dangling inside the cabin. My heart pounded, and my arms trembled from the strain. I couldn't stay like this for long.

Using my right hand to pull and balance, I inched upward, along the side of the boat, drawing up first one leg, then the other, so that soon I stood in the window, facing the ship's hull. I was panting now from exertion and fear. But I couldn't go back. I turned slightly in the window to find some hold for my left hand as well.

I slipped. Grabbing with my right hand and flailing with my left, I kept hold of the boat, but my legs dangled helplessly over the black water. The rough boards of the ship siding scraped at my arms. Dark waves slapped the sides of the ship, like a monster licking its lips. If I fell now, I would sink into the belly of the monster and be swallowed up forever. I scrabbled upward, with no thought of anything save the empty maw waiting below. With fear driving me, I raised myself high enough to throw first one arm, then the other, over the edge. Grabbing the oarlocks, I tumbled into the bottom of the ship's boat.

There I lay trembling. My arms, strengthened by weeks of lifting heavy cooking and wash pots, now felt weak as noodles. For several minutes, I hugged my knees and waited for my heart to stop pounding in my ears.

Finally, my breathing slowed. I could hear again. Even then, I seemed wrapped in a bubble of silence, with sounds of men's drinking and laughter a distant murmur from the shore. The waves, now safely distanced by the solid wood of the hull, kissed the side of the ship in tiny laps like the rough tongue of a kitten. But still I stayed. I was tempted to give up. I could stay where I was till morning light discovered me and wait patiently for Davy to take me into town.

But the idea of waiting patiently for Davy galled me. He had no right to order me to stay. That thought was enough to make me sit up. I had made it this far, hadn't I? I was all but in Philadelphia, within spitting distance of my goal.

The next part was easy anyway. I needn't sit like a ninny in the boat waiting for someone to rescue me. I stepped across the gunwale and over the railing onto the aft deck. It was easy as stepping out to the privy at night. Now, all I had to do was sneak off the ship. I smoothed my skirt out and looked about to get my bearings. Unless I tried to launch the boat I had just come from, there was only one way off the ship, along the gangplank. That, as on my first visit, was guarded by Old Hamish of the one eye, likely drunk by now and soon to be asleep if he wasn't already. I would just wait until he dozed off. Then I could slip past him with no one the wiser.

I looked for a spot where I could watch until I was sure he slept. There was a dark corner by the water barrel. I took a step toward it and froze as a tall, cloaked figure stepped out of the shadow of the cabin. I gasped, a soft sucking in sound, but he, whoever he was, had much sharper hearing than old Hamish and turned to me instantly. There was no use hiding. The man had seen me and was walking my way. His face was deep in the shadows of his hood and he carried a hooded lantern, shuttered now, with nothing more than tiny pinpoints of light slipping through the cracks.

"Davy?" Even as I spoke, I knew it couldn't be. Too tall, too heavy.

The man laughed, an ominous, and yet familiar sound. "Ah, the indomitable Miss Sally MacLaughlin. Always underfoot like some yapping rat terrier. Last seen fleeing the scene of the murder."

"Tom?" I backed slowly until I pressed against the ship's rail.

He kept coming, looming over me, his face a dark mask.

"I didn't kill Mr. Asher," I said, still unsure if it was Tom or someone else. This man sent shivers of fear down my spine. If it was Tom, he must think me a murderer.

"I know that. But we mustn't let such an inconvenient truth get in the way." He was almost on top of me now, and I had no place to go. In the dim light I couldn't see his face, but I saw his smile flash as he reached out a hand as if to take mine and kiss it.

But he didn't. Instead he grabbed my wrist and twisted it painfully, spinning me around and shoving me hard against the railing. My cry of pain was choked off as he crushed my ribs against the wood. With rising panic I realized he didn't mean to stop. He pushed harder on my arm, inexorably twisting it behind my back and lifting me. He meant to shove me overboard. I kicked out and writhed in his grasp, but it was useless. My feet fluttered in empty air. Then, quite suddenly, the awful pressure on my arm was released and I fell. There was nothing to catch. I spun, twisting sideways, plunging downward. I shut my eyes and opened my mouth to gasp in enough air to scream, just as I hit the water with a stinging slap that knocked the wind out of me. The numbing shock of cold water closing over my head filled my mouth and nose and ears and cut off all sound.

Davy had teased I was a selkie and Leah had wondered if he was right. I knew I was not. A selkie knows how to swim. I kicked and flailed with my arms, blinded with briny water stinging my eyes. Totally disoriented, I could not tell which way was up. My lungs hurt with the effort of holding my breath. In another minute, I would drown, alone and unnoticed in the harbor depths. My sodden skirts dragged, pulling me downward.

Down. Yes, down. That meant up was the other way. With a strength aided by fear, I kicked and pulled upward and suddenly my head cleared water. I had just enough time to gulp air before sinking again. But now I knew which way was up. I fought the panic of going under and kicked upward to break the surface. Again I gulped air, before sinking once more. One gasping breath and then the water closed in again. I couldn't keep it up for long. With my skirt dragging me down and my inefficient flailing barely pulling me up, I would tire soon. Then I would just go down. Why not? Why not just let go, let myself sink?

I could not remember exactly what I was fighting against. Was it Davy now? No need to fight him. Or the man I'd killed on the road, reaching for me once more in this inky hell. I felt his gnarled hand on my leg and kicked wildly, gasping for another saving breath, and driving the hallucination away. He was dead; he couldn't touch me any more. But there was something real, something rough and slimy, tangling about my legs.

A sea monster? Fresh panic filled my befuddled brain. Once more I kicked wildly, thrashing arms and legs in a frenzy more violent than effective. But even as I beat at the rough, snaky thing grabbing me, I realized it was not a sea monster, but a rope. Thick sturdy rope, maybe for an anchor or from the side of the ship to the dock. I gasped out a sob of relief and clung to my erstwhile monster, holding my head above the water and gulping air, blessed air.

With the rope's support I no longer was in danger of sinking, but it took some time for me to catch my breath. As the cold settled in my bones, I started shaking. I couldn't call out for fear my attacker would be the one to respond and finish me off. I could only wait, clinging onto the lifeline, as the waves washed over me.

CHAPTER 22

Hamish saw me at dawn. He called Davy and the two of them hauled me aboard. Davy had to pry my fingers loose from the rope, so tightly clenched were they.

Before long, I sat wrapped in warm quilts and sipping hot rum in the same cabin I had started from. Davy, Elise and André crowded into the small space. In spite of the warmth, I couldn't stop the shaking which had started the night before. Elise sat on the bed beside me, chafing my hands to warm them. André leaned his elbows on the table, shaking his head. Davy paced back and forth, a frown darkening his face.

I stared into the hot rum as I explained through chattering teeth how I came to be in the water all night, and why I had not called for help.

"One t'ing puzzles me still," Elise said. "Why don' you swim to the dock and clim' out? Don' you see the ladder, mebbe twenty yards, plain as day?"

I had seen the dock of course, in the long hours when the moon shone on the water. But twenty yards, or twenty miles, it made no difference. "I can't swim," I admitted.

Elise threw back her head and laughed, a rich, throaty sound. She patted my hand. "You be all right, Callie." She stepped across to André. "Come," Laughter still tickled her voice. "'We leave this girl to rest now."

André's formal bow was as polished as ever, but I saw the corner of his mouth twitch as he took Elise's arm and led her out.

Davy stopped his pacing, but he was not amused. His eyebrows drew down in a ferocious scowl and for a moment I thought he would hit me. Instead he wrapped his arms around me in a great hug. I closed my eyes, leaning my head on his chest.

"It's your fault, anyway," I told him. "I would never have been up on deck had you not forbidden me to leave and locked me in. How was I to know Tom Asher might be about, trying to kill me?"

"Ye would never have been on deck if ye had stayed put like I told ye." Davy resumed his pacing. "Are ye sure it was Tom ye saw?"

"Well, no. The lantern was shuttered. I think it was." I shivered, remembering. His face had been hidden in shadows, but I had heard the mocking laugh, as if throwing me overboard was of no more importance than drowning a rat. "Who else would it be? Why was he on board anyway?" I asked, my suspicions returning. I picked up the hot rum and held it close.

Davy rubbed his hand across his brow as if to ease a headache. "Have ye forgotten the wine shipment I told ye of? With Samuel Asher dead now, I thought to treat with his sons. I had meetings with the both of them last night, Ethan first and Tom a bit after. That's why I'm wondering, are ye sure it was Tom? How long do ye think ye were in the water?"

I had no idea. How long had it taken for me to reach the boat, and how long had I lain there? "You should have told me. I would have cooperated better if I knew what was going on."

"Would ye now?" Davy lifted one eyebrow. "Seeing as ye have told me time and again how much help Ethan Asher was to ye. Did I tell you he was coming, would ye not have tried to find him? Gone off with him?"

"Maybe," I said, puffing up with defiance. "Maybe if I had gone off with Ethan, Tom wouldn't have had a chance to throw me overboard." I scowled, but he only stared back at me, one eyebrow still cocked. I let my shoulders droop. I was too tired to argue. I tipped up my mug and drained the rum. "If Ethan is so bad, why did you meet him and his brother?"

Davy took his time answering. He poured another measure of rum in my mug, then plunged the poker from the fire in it to heat it. When the sizzling stopped, he handed it to me. "I dinna' ken which brother is the worse."

"Did you learn anything?" My hand shook as I took up the second mug. The rum had started a slow burning in my gut, like a peat fire banked for the night. The warmth spread gradually until the tips of my fingers and toes tingled. As I relaxed, and my shivering stopped, I felt a heavy exhaustion. Between the night's exertions and the lack of sleep, and then adding the hot rum, I could barely keep my eyes open.

"Ye are cold, lass." Davy took my hand in his. "It's bed for ye now and no argument about it."

I wasn't inclined to argue as I lay down. I closed my eyes, then opened them quickly. "But why would he want to kill me? He knows I didn't kill his father. He said so."

"Aye." Davy nodded grimly. "He knows. But as long as ye are wanted for that murder, do ye think anyone will look elsewhere?"

"Oh." I sunk into the feather mattress and let Davy tuck the quilt around me. His hand brushed my cheek in a gesture that made me catch my breath in sudden longing. "Stay with me." The words came out in a whisper so soft he couldn't have heard.

I slept till late afternoon and woke ravenous. My dreams had been full of Tom at first, then Ethan, and finally Davy, each in turn smiling at me as he threw me overboard. My head was spinning. Someone, André, most likely, had thought I might wake hungry and left a loaf of bread and an apple on the table. Without bothering to look for clothes, which were still wet in any case, I fell on the food. As I ate I tried to sort out the ideas chasing about in my head. I thought of all the help Ethan had given me; supplying paper and ink, a kind word here and there to ease the wait. All of it charming, but none of it very real. Except the letter he had promised to mail for me. That was real. And the answer lay waiting for me on Samuel Asher's desk. It didn't really matter whether it was Tom or Ethan who had tried to kill me. With any luck, I would never see either of them again. What I did need to see was the letter.

I stood abruptly and, hugging the blanket around me, went looking for Davy. "I have to get into Asher's house," I said, when I found him, drinking wine with André and Elise in the captain's salon.

André looked at me askance. "She's not an easy one to keep in clothes, is she?" he murmured, raising his glass in a gesture of appreciation.

Elise laughed. "Dat-shiny eyed girl bring trouble for sure," she said, draping her arm across André's shoulders.

I ignored André and Elise to stare at Davy. I would not be put off this time.

Davy sat back. "Now? Did ye not notice, lass, the man has just tried to kill ye? Will ye no sit down?" He offered me a glass of wine.

I waved the wine away. "Yes, now, or at least soon. Tonight. As soon as it's full dark. Will you help me?"

Davy was shaking his head. "Ye want me to help ye break into the house of a murderer."

"Would-be murderer," I corrected sharply. "I'm not dead yet!"

"Are ye thinking to tell me now he didn't try to drown ye? Maybe it was a sea monster, reached in through the window and dragged ye out, and poor Mr. Asher had naught to do with the whole business." Davy was on his feet, shouting at me now.

I shouted right back. "Maybe he hadn't meant to kill me at all. Maybe it was an accident. Maybe he only wanted . . . " I shook my head. This was ridiculous. The more I thought about that night the more confused the whole thing became.

"Are they always at each other like this?" Elise broke in. "Like a pair of chickens squabbling over the same bug?" No one answered her.

"He would hardly throw the lady in the water, did he just want to roger her," Davy said brutally, taking my words much further than I had meant. He glowered at me, his eyebrows drawn together like a flash of lightning across a storm-dark sky.

André stepped between us, neatly caught my hand and guided me to a chair. "What do you suppose happened to old Mr. Asher?" he said.

I sat down, suddenly realizing what Davy had been trying to tell me all along. "Oh. You think one of his own sons killed him?"

"It does seem likely, doesn't it?"

"But why kill his own father?"

"Well." Davy eyed me speculatively, as if he thought I might explode. "Ethan Asher will likely inherit, not only the house and goods, but his da's position as customs agent as well. As for Tom, well, perhaps he just dinna' like his da very much. Ye have no doubt seen his father had little care for him. Tom would be more his own man, if his brother were in charge."

I frowned. It all came back to the letter, then. Find that and I could prove I wasn't Sally MacLaughlin, and my word was as good as theirs. Then I could swear I hadn't killed Mr. Asher. The word of a lady counted for much more than the word of a servant. I would have to be Callie Beaton if I had any hope of helping Mary. "All right," I conceded. "But I don't need to talk to the man, just get to his desk. With your help, I can do it, Davy. You've sneaked in there before."

"What makes ye think the letter is still there? Won't they have burned it?"

"No. They will have kept it because of the payment promised. Even if they mean to do away with me, they'll want the money from Grandfather."

"It's still a daft idea." Davy raised an eyebrow in André's direction. "Isn't it?"

"Don't look at me." André shrugged. "Have I ever come between you and the trouble you find for yourself?"

Davy drummed his fingers on the table. He wasn't smiling, but the deep frown lines had smoothed. "In and out, ye say? Just the one letter?"

I nodded.

"Likely try it yourself, did I say nae," he muttered. He stood up and clapped his hand to my shoulder. "All right. I will help ye burgle the letter."

It didn't take long to scrounge up an old pair of Davy's trousers. "Ye are a bonny lass and fair swift on your feet," Davy said, "But even a bonnie lass can't run fast enough in skirts, does the need arise."

We waited for darkness and the early moon to set. The night was overcast, with very little light piercing the thick clouds. "The best time for thieves and scalawags," Davy remarked. Once he'd agreed to help me, his anger faded, and he seemed cheerful about the night's plans. No doubt because he was all too familiar with the ways of thieves and scalawags.

The trousers rubbed against my thighs as we walked briskly along the piers and past the empty streets lit by gas lamps. A breeze rattled the leaves of the trees overhead. Sweat dampened my palms and trickled down my back as we turned up a darkened alley. The thumping of my heart seemed loud enough to wake the good citizens of Philadelphia, sleeping peacefully.

Without warning, Davy grabbed my arm and jerked me into a doorway. He put his finger to my lips and pointed to the end of the street. We watched in silence until the night watchman passed. I took a deep breath, thankful for Davy's presence. After all, I had never tried breaking into a house before. Mam and Grandfather had often disagreed on what my education should include, but neither one of them thought housebreaking a skill important for a young lady.

Davy led the way silently through alleys and back yards till I was so turned around, I began to wonder if he meant to just tire me out and never reach our destination. He stopped me once again, with a touch to my wrist. We crouched in a thick hedge at the back of a yard.

"What is it now?" I whispered. I didn't see any watchmen.

Davy pointed to the house.

I sucked in a sharp breath. This was the Asher yard.

"How . . .?" I started in a whisper.

Davy shook his head and put a finger to his lips. He leaned close and whispered in my ear. His breath, warm and tickly, felt like a caress. "Stay quiet and follow close."

He need not have warned me. I had crossed that yard dozens of times in the last few months, but never before in the dark of the moon on an errand of larceny. The trees loomed overhead; the wind rattled the branches like ghostly fingers pointing at me. I stayed so close to Davy that at one point I trod on his heel, nearly tripping him and stumbling backwards myself. He caught me at once, put his arm around me, and breathed into my ear, "Steady."

I took a deep breath and let it out slowly. Then I nodded to show I was ready to go on.

Not surprisingly, the rope we had left hanging out the study window was no longer there. Instead, we crept past the study to the lean-to. Davy boosted me up to the roof, then hoisted himself up after me.

The night was very warm, and the windows on the second floor stood open. From the lean-to roof we pulled ourselves onto the window ledge at the end of the second floor hallway and slipped inside.

A deep silence filled the space, the silence of a house asleep, made deeper by the tiny noises filling it; the creak of a bedspring, the flutter of a curtain. One of the boys cried softly, and Chloe's murmurs soothing him back to sleep were no louder than the purr of a cat.

I found the dark, empty hallway and our unusual entrance disorienting, but not Davy. He stepped confidently, as if it were broad daylight and he had every right to be there. His steps made no sound. The floor creaked under my feet.

At Mr. Asher's study door, Davy paused to listen. Then he tried the knob. It was locked. He took a piece of wire from his breast pocket, twisted it in the keyhole and there was a soft click. He opened the door.

We slipped inside and Davy closed the door and locked it behind us. He went over to the window to pull back the drapes. Pale light from the gas street lamps outside shone through the panes. Davy pointed me toward the desk, while he fastened our escape rope.

Someone had cleaned up the desk and taken most of the papers, leaving only an untidy pile with letters, ledgers and bills all mixed together. I carefully sorted through all the papers left, but found no letter from Scotland.

Davy came over from the window and raised an eyebrow in unspoken question. I shook my head helplessly and prepared to sort everything again. Davy caught my hand and shook his head. "The other office,'" he mouthed. "Across the hall."

By now I felt the whole world could hear my heart beating wildly. My hands felt clammy. I wiped them on my borrowed shirt, then shoved them in my pockets to stop their shaking. I nodded to Davy.

We slipped back out of Samuel's office, leaving the door unlocked, and went across the hall to where Ethan and Tom kept their desks. Ethan's desk was closest to the door. The papers there were organized in neat piles, with bills, inventories, and letters received, each in its own stack. The letter from Scotland lay on the top of this last pile. I snatched it up and carried it over to the window to read it. Davy struck a flint and lit a candle. The writing was thin and wavery in the dim light and not at all familiar. The first lines were a silvery gray, barely readable.

"To the Hon. Sam. Asher,
    In regard to your shipment . . ."

With a sinking feeling, I skipped on down to the bottom. There, instead of my Grandfather's curling signature was the scrawl of one William Kendricks, factor. I'd never heard of the man. This letter wasn't from Grandfather at all. With a cry of disbelief, I dropped the letter and grabbed at the piles on the desk, scattering them all over.

"It has to be here," I muttered, scrabbling through the papers.

Davy caught my hands. "Leave off, lass. There won't be any answer." He pointed to the second desk in the room where he had been looking. Tom's desk. There was another stack of letters there, sealed and ready to mail. At the bottom of that stack was a letter addressed in a familiar hand. I snatched up the letter I had written to Grandfather.

Unmailed. Sitting on this desk for months while Ethan promised me the answer would be coming any day. At that moment I could have committed murder. I looked around, wildly furious with the man I had trusted. I wanted to hit someone, anyone.

Davy pulled me close. "We had best be going, lass. Before anyone hears us. There's naught else here to find."

CHAPTER 23

We didn't speak until we were back at the ship. Once there, my fury bubbled back to the surface. "That two-faced, weasly, slimy bastard," I fumed as I changed back into Elise's dress. The betrayal of finding my letter unsent seemed far worse than the attempt to murder me. I knew it didn't make sense, but there it was. "How dare he lie to me like that?"

Davy pulled out a bottle of rum from the cupboard opposite the door and unstoppered it. He sloshed a healthy measure into each of the two pewter mugs and handed me one before swiveling the chair to sit on it backwards.

I took a big swallow, feeling the burn all the way down.

Raising one eyebrow, Davy shook his head. "Do ye think after breaking into a man's house, ye have the right to fret because he lied to ye?"

I whirled upon him. "Don't you see? Without that letter, how can I help Mary? Without it, I'm still Sally. I'm still stranded." Tears stung my eyes. "Mam must think me dead."

Davy was at my side in an instant. "Hush, ma cushla."

My throat hurt from the effort of holding in my tears. I buried my face in his chest and tried to stop crying.

He held me close, stroking my hair gently. "I'm sorry, lass."

We stood, arms entwined, his heart beating solid and steady, like an anchor holding me fast. "Oh, Davy," I sighed once I had my tears under control. "What am I to do?"

"Stay with me," he said so fast I guessed he must have been waiting for such a question. He held me out a little from him, his hands gripping my arms, his eyes looking into mine.

I wanted to say yes. I wanted to stay wrapped in the comfort of his arms forever, lost in those fiercely burning eyes.

"Callie. I know I've no claim on ye. I am not your brother or your father or your husband to bid ye do this or that. And I've nothing to offer ye, save my love, and I've done little enough to prove that. But do ye stay with me, ye will no regret it. Between the two of us, we'll find a way to help your friend."

I didn't answer. The silken tendrils pulling me toward Scotland wavered. Mam and the others seemed very far away,

Davy's arms tightened as if he didn't mean to ever let go. I held my breath. Perhaps I should stay with him. Perhaps it was not just pity that made him ask.

The door of the salon burst open, and André rushed in. "Mon frère," he began, then stopped when he saw us.

Davy abruptly let go, and I felt cast adrift. I grabbed the edge of the table for support.

"What is it?" Davy drummed his fingers against his thigh.

André paused, looking from Davy to me and back again. The ship rocked gently beneath us, and the lantern hung in the stern window creaked as it swung slowly back and forth. My hand twitched, and I reached for Davy, but drew back before my fingers brushed the soft, curled hairs on his bare arm. If I touched him again, I would lose all will to leave.

André coughed. "Mon frère," he began again. "There's a sailor at the groggery just back from Boston. He worked for Shakleton on the ship that carried the wine. Elise is keeping him . . . entertained until you can question him."

Davy brushed the hair back from his forehead in a gesture of impatience and frustration. "Can ye no just question him yourself?"

André shrugged one shoulder. "He does not like les Français. Elise will try, naturally, but he is not a man to spend much time *talking* to a woman."

"Go with him, Davy," I urged. "He may know where that ship unloaded. You can't let that go."

"Will ye stay here and write your grandfather? I'll send it off at once and then help to see ye home."

I shook my head. "I've got to see Mary. At least tell her I've tried, and give her news of Leah."

"Are ye daft, Callie? Ye canna' go there! George Shakleton will clap you in jail just as fast as Ethan Asher would."

"Would you leave Mary without a word of comfort?"

Davy frowned. "It's not the same."

"Oh? Is your promise more important than mine?"

"I canna' let you go," Davy groaned.

It was the same conversation all over again, but something had changed. Was it Davy? Or me? I wasn't sure. I just knew that something of trust lay between us where it had not before. I tied a kerchief over my hair to hide it, and picked up another to use as a shawl. Davy looked so miserable I took pity and pushed him toward André. "Don't worry about me. Mr. Shakleton will never see me."

Davy nodded reluctantly. "Just there and back, do ye ken? Be careful."

It didn't take long to reach Mr. Shakleton's house. The office windows were still shuttered, and the place looked empty. I went round the back into the kitchen. There was a low fire on the hearth, and bread rising on the table, but Mary wasn't there. She must have already gone to the market. It would be even better to find her there, with no threat of Mr. Shakleton. Confident no one would recognize me dressed as I was, I set off for the marketplace.

Though the sun had barely cleared the horizon, the market square already bustled with activity. Wagons clattered along the dusty street, and hawkers stacked potatoes and apples ready for sale. A woman carrying a bushel basket of pungent onions strode past me to her stand, while a speckled dog yapped at her heels. I walked up and down the street, but I didn't see Mary. Maybe I would have to go back to the house and wait for her there. I scanned the crowd once more, and saw, not Mary, but Peg, an empty basket swinging merrily at her side. I stepped out to greet her.

"Callie?" She stopped abruptly. "Callie Beaton?" She took a step closer, then threw her arms around me. "I've been so worried—Mr. Asher dead and ye nowhere to be found . . . and the hue and cry out for ye . . ."

She stopped, her hands still on my shoulders, and eyed me suspiciously. "Ye dinna' kill him, did ye? I could understand it if ye did, and I said as much to Mary, ye ken, but . . ."

I waved my hand impatiently. "Of course I didn't kill him."

"Well then," Peg said. Her mouth pursed in what might have been disappointment. "Well then," she said again. "Where have ye been? Talk is, ye have run off with Davy McRae and the pair of ye up to no good."

"I have been with Davy," I said. "But I can't talk here. Can we go somewhere?"

Peg twisted her mouth thoughtfully. "We could go into the coffee house, though I've not much cash on me save what I need for marketing."

I pulled back. "I can't Peg. I can't let them see me. I'm not Sally MacLaughlin, as you know well enough, and I didn't kill anyone, but I've no way to prove either."

She shook her head. "Ye have a point there. Ye do get yourself into trouble, don't ye?"

I had no answer to this outrageous accusation. Get myself into trouble? I had no time to get myself into trouble, what with all the trouble other people kept getting me into. Instead, I changed the subject. "Peg, I can't talk about it now. I was looking for Mary."

"Och, the poor woman," Peg said. "They flogged her for running, and she's like a ghost without her bairns."

"I thought I might find her here at the market." We stood in the shadow of a grocer's cart. The square was crowded with maids buying the family dinner, and apprentices running errands.

"'Tis not likely," Peg said. "She's only let do the marketing twice a week, and the cockroach..." Peg spat angrily as she spoke of Mr. Shakleton. "He drags her along with him when it suits him."

I decided I would have to risk the Shakleton house again, and turned to go, when another thought struck me. Peg knew all the gossip. What did she know of the Ashers?

"I know both the sons," she said when I asked. "They come to the tavern where I work often enough. The older one, he's a handsome rake, isn't he?" Peg grinned at me slyly. "Don't tell me ye have got your eye set on him and after two weeks with Davy McRae. It'll take some doing to catch the son of the man ye murdered."

"I never murdered anyone!" I protested. Peg meant well, but her tongue got ahead of her brains too often.

Peg laughed. "I know it, and ye know it yourself, but does he know it?"

I threw up my hands. "I'm not interested in him," I declared, "Or at least not in the way you mean." I felt my cheeks go hot. I had been drawn to him, the most charming gentleman I had met this side of the ocean. Why hadn't he mailed my letter? "Just listen, Peg, won't you?" Sometimes talking with Peg made me dizzy.

"And what do ye think I'm doing?" Peg said, with some asperity.

I took a moment to smooth out my skirts and straighten my kerchief. Then I drew in a deep breath and tried again. "I just need to know if either of them were here the night old Samuel Asher was killed. Do you remember that?"

Peg looked thoughtful. "Two weeks ago, wasn't it? That was the night Peter came back from a trip to Boston. Peter is Master Dodd's second son, ye ken. We met out here in the barn. The hay is a bit scratchy of course, but Lord above, that man can kiss . . ."

"Peg," I interrupted. "The Ashers?"

"Well, yes, they were here. Came in together, they did, and I served them up with beer."

"When did they leave?"

Peg squinted her eyes shut, thinking. "I don't know for sure. I was out in the barn, ye ken. Anne said there'd been a terrible row between them with shouting and all and one stormed out early on. Come to think of it, ye might have to stand in line, do ye want either Mr. Asher. Anne Kramer is taken with one or t'other man, depending on the day, and they both seem to fancy her a bit as well, asking for her when it happens she's working in the kitchen and one of them comes in of an evening, though it's chancy going after a man with such a temper."

"A temper? Which one?"

Peg shook her head. "I'm sorry," she said. "I stayed in the barn a good while. When I came in, most of the work was done, and I just wiped up and went to bed."

So I still didn't know. One of the Ashers had stayed at the inn, drinking long past midnight, and the other had left. Who had gone home and found Samuel in his room, stabbed him in the back and gone calmly off to bed waiting for him to be found?

I said goodbye to Peg. Maybe I could watch for Mary from across the street. I still worried how I could help Mary without the letter. Perhaps if I could find my indenture papers and destroy them, Sally McLaughlin would no longer exist.

With my thoughts full of where the papers might be, I didn't realize I was in front of the coffee house until a hand on my shoulder stopped me.

"I beg pardon." I apologized, thinking I had run into someone as I walked deep in thought, but when I looked up, I stopped. "Ethan." A cold fear gripped my belly. I stepped back onto a portly gentleman's foot. He frowned at me, but made no offer of assistance. I took a deep breath. Perhaps I wasn't in need of assistance. Ethan's hold on my shoulder was firm but not painful.

Ethan's smile seemed genuine, not at all like that of a man bent on murder. It was broad daylight, after all, in the middle of a busy public thoroughfare. Ethan could hardly murder me here without someone noticing. And if he meant to call the guard, well, then I would need assistance, but I would be unlikely to receive any from a casual passerby. "Sally MacLaughlin," he said. "What a pleasure to see you!"

I studied his face without answering. He really did seem surprised to see me, but was it the surprise of a man seeing the girl he thought he had killed, or was it just the surprise of a man seeing the servant who had run away two weeks ago? I couldn't tell.

Ethan seemed oblivious to my suspicions. "I've been so concerned about you, leaving as you did in the middle of the night."

"I didn't kill your father."

"Of course not," Ethan patted my hand as if I were a small child. "Tom had his doubts, of course. Tom always suspects the worst, but I believe I've convinced even him." Ethan shook his head regretfully. "I'm afraid it's only the constables who still think differently. They are bent on finding you."

"You could have told them I didn't do it."

"Of course, of course. You may rest assured I have told them just such, many times in fact, but you running off like that . . . in the middle of the night . . . well, it just didn't look very good for you." Ethan took both my hands in his and stepped closer to me. "Callie. Dear. You must believe I have been concerned about you. Alone and friendless in this land and the law after you. I could only pray you had found someone kind enough to help you."

Ethan's gentle words covered me like a soporific blanket. As he wove the spell around me, I felt a knot of tension in my gut unraveling. I knew I couldn't trust him. I knew he had never sent my letter, but he seemed so kind. Perhaps he really meant to help me.

"Just as troublesome was the thought that I had no way to contact you should the letter from your Grandfather arrive," he went on.

I jerked free of his spell. "There won't be any letter," I scowled. "You never mailed mine."

Ethan stepped back though he didn't let go of my hands. His mouth made a perfect, round 'O' of astonishment. "But I sent it out with Tom that very day, along with a whole packet of letters. Tom was to take it to the brig *Alice*, leaving on the morning tide."

"My letter never went any further than Tom's desk!" I said bitterly.

Ethan raised a quizzical eyebrow. I should never have said that. I thought he meant to ask me how I knew precisely what was on Tom's desk. I wasn't sure how I could answer. Admitting to housebreaking didn't seem a very good way to elicit continued support. But he didn't ask, only stared at me a moment; then he shrugged, apologetic once more. "Tom," he said with a frown. "I'll not speak against my own brother, but were he not my brother . . . well there's one surely headed for trouble no matter what help I give him." He shook his head sorrowfully. "But come up to the house, and we can sort out this whole mess."

I didn't answer. Ethan had the power to straighten out a lot of things now that Samuel Asher was dead, but was he the man to do it?

He must have seen me hesitating, for he went on almost immediately, his voice a gentle purr. "We'll probably even find your papers." He pulled my hands to him, drawing me closer. I had to tip my head back to see him. I felt like a rabbit caught, frozen in the snake's gaze. It was impossible to look away. "You know I've wanted to help you since you arrived. Give me another chance to do so."

The heat of his body, pressed against mine, made it difficult to frame an answer. I couldn't think with him so close.

"Ethan!" Tom's voice cut across the moment like a knife. He clapped Ethan on the shoulder. "Who have you got here?" His tone was light and mocking, as usual. "Wasn't Anne enough exercise this morning? Or have you tired of her already?"

Ethan clutched me tight enough to hurt, his face turning to black anger for a fraction of a second before he released me and regained his bland smile. The change was so fast, I wondered if I had imagined it.

Tom went on teasing. "Ah, but this one's a bitty thing. I thought your taste ran to bigger girls. Let me have a look at this tempting morsel." He put a hand on my arm and spun me around, pulling me free from Ethan's grip. "Why, it's Sally MacLaughlin!" He smiled and held on. "The girl who didn't kill our father, only conveniently ran away the night he died."

Was this the smile I had seen aboard Davy's ship? Tom did not seem terribly surprised to see me, but I could never figure out what Tom was thinking. In any case, whichever of the two had thrown me overboard, he was not likely now to let me walk away now. Any minute he would call the constables and turn me in.

I didn't take time to figure it out. I kicked Tom in the shin. He yelped and let go of me. I ran. I'm not very tall, but even in skirts I am fast. I reached the corner without anyone catching me. I hazarded a look back. No one was chasing me. Ethan had a hand on Tom's arm, restraining him. Or was it Tom holding Ethan back?

I was too frightened to visit Mary just then, but it took a long time to find my way back to the wharves. I found Davy pacing the deck.

He grabbed me roughly and hauled me aboard. "Where in God's name have ye been, lass? I looked for ye hours past!"

I was hot, hungry, and more than a little tired of people grabbing me. "Trying to find my way back here, as I promised!" I said more sharply than I intended.

Davy took one look at my scowl and let go of my arm. "I've a meal set by for ye, if ye have a mind to eat it," he said and strode away into the cabin.

I followed him. While I ate, I told Davy of my meeting with Peg. I hadn't meant to, but I also told him of the encounter with the Ashers. As I thought about it, I was more convinced Tom had killed Samuel and tried to kill me. He probably had my papers too, as Ethan didn't seem to know where they were. Tom had made my life miserable, openly detested his father, and never tried in any way to help me.

Davy was not convinced. "I know both men were on board the boat that night. But Ethan's not the man ye think he is."

"You're just jealous," I fumed, "because he has what you don't."

"What does he have? The guile to capture a girl's heart before he beats her?"

"No," I shouted. What did Ethan have? I didn't know why I felt compelled to defend him. I certainly didn't trust the man, not with so many people speaking against him. "He's a gentleman," I said at last.

Davy laughed, a mean, vicious sound totally unlike his usual merriment. "What promises have ye made the man, Callie?"

I stood up abruptly, knocking the chair over. "How dare you say such? Ethan's asked nothing of me I wouldn't give him." I plowed on, breathlessly, not stopping to think if what I said was true or not. I didn't want Ethan, and I didn't trust him either, but Davy's insulting assumptions drove me wild with anger, and if I allowed myself, fear for the bit of truth in them. I did not allow myself to think. "There have been no promises between us; and no lies. He's never hurt me."

Davy slammed his fist into the table, his face a dark mask. He took a deep breath. I thought he meant to shout at me again, but he did not. Instead, he let the breath out slowly and just as slowly schooled his face to hide his anger. Only when he had regained his calm did he address me again. He took both my hands in his and pulled me back down. "Stay here with me, Callie," he said once more, his voice tightly controlled. "Stay away from Ethan Asher. I haven't got the friends he has, and I haven't got the money he has. So ye have no need to make me any promises." He took another deep breath as if the words would stay locked inside him. "I'll ask nothing of ye. Let me help ye find the papers. Let me help ye to get home. I dinna' know how I can manage it but I will. Just so I know you're safe."

"Safe?" I pulled my hands free, my voice shrill with a hint of hysteria. "Safe, you say? I've not been safe one moment since I set foot on that wretched boat on the docks of Leith, and you kept me aboard. Is that how you'll keep me safe? Locked up? Your own prisoner?" I scoffed, my temper rising. "It's with your help I've been kidnapped, sold at auction, shot at, nearly drowned, and wanted for murder. You're not so very good at keeping a lady safe."

Davy grabbed my wrist, his grip like a band of iron. "I've not hurt ye," he said, his own anger roused. "I have given ye my word of honor to see ye safe home."

"Honor?" I laughed. "Your word?" I had not spoken of what had happened between us in the woods, but the memory of our joining burned inside me with an intensity of longing I could not ignore. Had he forgotten? If that were true, I would not be the one to remind him. I had other charges to lay before him. "How can you speak of honor and promises? You are a smuggler, Davy McRae, a man outside the law."

"And Ethan Asher is a man within the law?" His eyes smoldered now, and his mouth was tight with anger. "Is it his honor ye would trust?"

"He's broken no law I know of!"

"Believe that, lass and ye will have a belly swollen with more than his honor before ye can say him nae, even did ye want to!"

I wrenched my hand free of him. "It's you would make my belly swell with your own bastard, and it's only jealousy another man may beat you there that makes you care now," I screeched.

Davy's eyes flared with angry storms. His teeth clenched tight. He slammed his fist on the table. "I have made ye the offer once, to do right by ye. Do ye think I'll beg ye?"

I'd never seen him so angry, but I didn't care. My own anger nearly choked me. "Let go of me!" How dare he speak to me of honor? Furious, I whirled away from him. Three steps to the door and my hand upon the latch. I tensed, expecting him to call me back, to stop me.

He did not. I pulled the door open and stepped through. Still he didn't move. I slammed the cabin door behind me and walked out into the night.

I walked briskly up the rutted street, plagued with the uncomfortable feeling I had done this before: stormed out in a temper, run from an argument. And look where it had gotten me—halfway around the world, wanted for murder, arguing with a pirate. I tried to tell myself this time was very different. This time, I had a plan of sorts. This time, I was running toward home, not away from it. Trying to convince myself this time wasn't a mistake didn't work very well. My thoughts kept straying to Davy, and as my anger cooled, I could only think of his arms sheltering me. I tried to hold onto my anger at him, but that didn't work very well either. I had never been good at staying angry, only at getting angry. "No help for it now," I told myself. I put one foot in front of the other and kept on, never looking back.

CHAPTER 24

I thought first to find Mary, but Mr. Shakleton would surely be home at this hour, so I decided to go to Peg instead. Twilight settled on the city by the time I found my way to the tavern where she lived and worked. I waited at the edge of the yard. Mosquitoes whined in my ears, louder than the mumble of laughter and voices from the taproom. Hiding in the shadows put me in mind of Leah, who had waited just so for me, confident I could help her and I had taken her to Davy McRae, a self-admitted rogue. Now I stood in need of help, from another such, Peg Willet, who had cheerfully lied to save her friend Sally, while pulling me into this mess.

I sighed gloomily. It was late enough now I dared not go into the tavern to find Peg. Too many people, including the Ashers, could be inside.

A man came out the back door and pissed a long steady stream off the back porch. I sighed again. It could be a long wait.

Several hours later, when the noise from the room had dwindled to near silence and the lamps had burned low, Peg finally came out the back door and headed to the necessary.

I waited until she was within five feet of me, then stepped out of the shadows and called her name softly, trying not to startle her.

It didn't work. She shrieked like a banshee and jumped back, turning to run.

"Wait, Peg," I called. "'Tis me. Callie."

Peg stopped in mid step. "What in the world are ye doing out here in the dark? Ye have taken ten years off my life frightening me like that!"

Serves her right, I thought uncharitably. How much of my life had she taken, pulling me to America? But I hadn't meant to frighten her, and I apologized before asking her to help me find a place to stay at the tavern.

"But how can I hide ye here?" Peg protested. "Both Tom and Ethan Asher come in regularly. They'll see ye surely."

I took both of her hands in mine. "You've got to, Peg. There's no place else I can go."

"Weel, I suppose ye could sleep in Anne's bed back of the kitchen," she said hesitantly. "She's off to see her family for the night, and I could get ye up early enough."

"That would be perfect." I threw my arms around her. "Thank you, Peg."

Peg laughed ruefully. "Don't thank me yet," she said. "I'll have to put ye in the scullery scrubbing dishes to keep ye hid in the morning."

I wasn't about to complain, either that night or in the morning when Peg left me bent over a tub of water with a pile of blackened pots while she went to market. The scullery was a separate room, just off the kitchen, out of sight of the customers. None of the family was likely to come in there since they never washed dishes, and the other servants left that to Peg and Anne, the youngest among them.

Peg had returned by the time the taproom opened about ten o'clock in the morning. Most of the clientele were traders and businessmen. Like other taverns in the bustling city of Philadelphia, this one offered a convenient place for the men to meet, set up trade agreements, close a deal or two, and gather the latest news. Peg and the other serving girls were too busy to ask any questions and no one paid any attention to me.

I had been working a couple of hours when Anne came in. She was a slender girl, not more than sixteen, with mousy brown hair and dark round eyes. She rolled up the sleeves of her chemise and knelt beside me at the washtub. Peg had said something about her knowing the Ashers. I decided it wouldn't hurt to ask.

"What are you offering me in return?" she said.

"I've done half your work here." I waved toward the shiny tin pie plates I had stacked beside the door. "Surely that's worth some information."

She shrugged. "That depends." She eyed me levelly, her blank face unreadable. "I'm not asking who you are, or what your trouble is, though I could make a guess or two. A lot of people talk in taverns, and no one thinks the serving girls have ears. I have information you might want, but there's a price to pay for it."

"What will your information cost me?"

Again, the deep, impenetrable look. "Little enough for now. Time will come, I'll ask for payment."

"I don't like making promises without knowing the terms."

"Nor do I," she agreed. "But there's not always so much choice in the matter, is there?"

I started scrubbing again. "Speak plainly then. I want to know about the Ashers. What do you know about them that could help me?"

She glanced left and right, making sure we were alone in the scullery. "The night old Asher was murdered, both his sons were here."

"That's no news to me." Peg had said as much.

"There's more. I was serving and I heard the pair of them arguing. Ethan, the older one, he was talking too quiet to make out his words. But it made his brother spitting mad. Tom got louder and angrier, shouting about shipments due and business stuff. Ethan never raised his voice. Finally Tom stood up, threw his mug at him and shouted, 'You bastard!' Ethan never blinked, but there was a terrible quiet after Tom's bellow. I heard his answer clear as a bell."

"What did he say?"

She closed her eyes and recited, "'That label, dear brother, is more properly applied to you. In fact, of all the Asher males, I believe I'm the only one who is not a bastard.' With that Tom kicked the bench over and stormed out."

"What of Ethan?" I prompted. "When did he leave?"

Anne blinked. "He didn't. He called for a fresh mug of ale and a rag."

"He must have left some time," I argued. "The taproom closes at midnight, doesn't it? He wouldn't spend the night . . . " My voice trailed off.

"He stayed until the watch came calling for him, as his father was dead. Woke the whole house, they did, looking for him."

"So Ethan could not have killed his father," I said slowly, "but Tom had plenty of time." I felt a sense of profound relief. Even though I had thought Ethan innocent of the murder of his father and the attempt on my life, a nagging suspicion had worried me.

Anne stopped scrubbing and stared at me, obviously searching for words. "I have had both the Ashers to my bed," she said at last. "Neither is a man I would call gentle, though Ethan is the more generous afterwards.

Generous with gifts when he is pleased and, more often, with blows when he's not." Anne pulled down the front of her chemise just enough to show me the dark purpling bruise on her left breast and the fading, yellow green marks on her shoulder.

I sat back, shocked. I knew Samuel Asher beat his wife. I believed Tom Asher capable of any violence, including murder. But Ethan? His smile had always been kind, and his words comforting. "Why do you go with him if he's so brutal?"

Anne shrugged. "At first I smiled at him. I thought him a handsome devil and kind, you know, with a smile for a poor girl."

I nodded. That much at least sounded like Ethan.

"I thought him a solid catch, a good man with means to support me. I went with him willing enough at the start."

"And after?"

Again the slight shrug. "The first time he beat me was because he found out about Tom. I suppose I deserved it then, dishonoring him as it were, with his own brother, though Tom had been first. After that I didn't know how to say no and still see the light of day. Ethan Asher is not a man to be denied."

I thought about Anne's revelations as we finished scrubbing. According to Anne, Ethan Asher was a vicious, evil man, but not a murderer. If he'd been with her all night he couldn't have killed Samuel Asher. It was Tom who'd stormed out. Tom was the one with the opportunity. It was easy to believe Tom capable of murder.

I felt sure I could believe Anne. If she hated Ethan so much, why give him an alibi and not Tom? So it seemed likely that Tom had killed his father and tried to kill me. Ethan had left the ship much earlier, and Tom had come later. Tom wanted me dead; Ethan had been helpful. And the letter to Grandfather, unmailed? Ethan claimed he sent it. And it had been on Tom's desk, not Ethan's. Perhaps Tom had stolen it, trying to thwart his brother.

I slapped the dirty rag into the tub, splashing soapy water all over the front of my skirt. I still didn't know exactly what had happened to Samuel Asher, or where my indenture papers could be, or how to get home.

Peg came into the scullery, carrying a willow basket on her arm. "I know ye want to see Mary. I've made muffins and put by a few for ye to bring her." She thrust the basket toward me. "The mistress will never notice a muffin or two short."

I took the basket and lifted the checkered cloth. A heady steam arose, carrying with it the warm, sweet aroma of fresh baked muffins. "Mmm . . . these smell delicious. But Peg, there's six in here."

"Aye." Peg winked. "I've never said I was very good at counting, did I?" She deftly tucked the cloth back in. "And they'll bring Mary a touch of comfort. The good Lord knows the poor woman needs it."

I gave Peg a quick embrace and set off. The early market crowd had thinned, making it easier to keep a watchful eye out. A little breeze kept away the flies and the heat. It didn't take long to walk across town. No wagon waited beside the Skakleton house, and the place looked empty.

I knocked lightly at the back. "Mary?" I called, pulling the door open. The old woman at the fire straightened slowly.

"Who's there?" she said, peering into the sun which shone at my back and left my face in shadows. She looked terrible, her face gaunt and lined, her eyes dulled with pain.

"Mary?" I moved out of the doorway toward her. "Mary, is that you? It's me, Callie."

Then she smiled, transforming her whole face for an instant into the Mary I knew before the pain returned. She embraced me.

"Callie, so good to see ye. What have you been up to?"

Soon the two of us sat at the kitchen table, snapping beans and enjoying Peg's muffins. Mr. Shakleton had gone out early, she said, and wasn't expected back for lunch. Mary's face sagged with fatigue, but lit up when I told her I'd seen Leah, safe outside the city.

"And what of Mr. McRae?" she asked, going straight to the part I had meant to hide. "Why are ye here, when ye could be with him?"

"Mary, don't you see? He is not the sort to settle down. He has no property or . . . " I couldn't bring myself to tell even Mary about the night in the woods, or his proposal afterwards. Why exactly had I refused him?

"I thought it was your grandfather that cared for a proper match."

I closed my eyes. Just thinking of Davy, hair blown wild in the wind, eyes alight with his merry smile made me tremble with longing. I gripped the table and snapped my eyes open. He was too angry to want to see me again, even if I longed for him. I couldn't think of him now.

"Davy or no, I have to clear my name if I'm to help you," I insisted. "For that I need those indenture papers."

"Don't throw away love so lightly, Callie." She touched my hand. I could see she was thinking of her husband, the baby she had lost, and the daughter out of reach.

What could I say to a mother so bereaved? My own troubles paled compared to hers. I was a woman, not a child. My mother, though far away, had seen me grown. Leah was barely eight. "Oh, Mary."

She rested her head on her arms, her face buried. Then with great effort she roused herself. "I've yet to thank ye, Callie, for saving her and bringing her to Mr. McRae and at such a terrible risk to yourself. Ye did us a service there, and I willna' forget it."

I waved my hand. It was little enough I'd done, taking the child to a rogue and trusting he would do right.

"I mean it, Callie. I owe something. I'll find a way to pay it."

"You owe me nothing," I insisted. "But I could use some help. Will you show me George Shakleton's office?" I explained how I wanted to search it. He may well have kept the indenture papers there, especially if Samuel Asher still owed him.

"I will." Mary stood and wiped her hands on her apron. "I've cleaned the place a time or two, so I know there aren't a lot of papers. But I can't tell what any of them might be. Ye ken I canna' read." She led the way through the kitchen to the hall, and pointed to the door straight across from the kitchen.

"That's the storeroom. He keeps it locked. I've never been in even to clean it." Mr. Shakleton's office was also on the first floor, the next door just beyond the storeroom. His office was not locked. Mary opened the door and followed me in.

It was a remarkably neat place for a man, just as the cabin on the boat had been, with quills lined up along one side of the desk next to a penknife for trimming them and a stoppered ink bottle in the corner. A chest stood against the wall next to the door. I rubbed my hands and pulled open the top drawer nearest me.

All the drawers had papers in them, most in files neatly labeled with such things as *Woolens, MacIntyre- Pendleton 1751* or *Pine lumber Asher-Oakum 1753*. I thumbed through the files quickly, and Mary tidied up behind me. I found a file that said *Bordeaux wine—McRae-Asher, 1753.* Davy's missing shipment, I mused, and pulled the file out to read. It didn't say much, just listing numbers of crates and arrival date. Mr. Shakleton's signature was scrawled across the bill of lading. I put the file back and kept looking.

I finished the last drawer without finding any file marked *Indentured servants from Edinburgh, 1754.* There was nothing of interest in his desk either. I reached for the door in the far corner of the room

"What's this? A closet?" I asked.

"I've never been in there." Mary peered over my shoulder. "A door to the storeroom perhaps?"

I tried the knob. It turned easily. The closet beyond was very dark, but I could tell at once it didn't lead to the storeroom. Shelves lined the wall to the left, but to the right a stairwell opened downward.

"I'll fetch a candle." Mary nodded at the papers stacked on the shelves. "Your paper could be there."

I took down the first bundle while she went to the kitchen. Before I could examine it, I heard voices in the front hallway. I pulled the door shut, and stood in the dark, hoping whatever the business was, it wouldn't involve this closet. Cautiously, I put my ear to the rough wood of the door.

George Shakleton's nasal whine was unmistakable. ". . . not thought to treat with you on this," he was saying. "As your brother is now in charge."

A second voice, too low and angry to hear clearly, interrupted him. "My <u>half</u> brother . . . claim less if I could. He . . . burn in Hell . . . no more than he deserves." The voice grew clearer, as if the speaker had moved toward the door behind which I hid and now stood only inches away on the other side. With a jolt, I realized the second speaker was Tom Asher. Involuntarily, I recoiled and missed his next words. Tom clearly hated his brother as much as he hated his father.

Mr. Shakleton spoke again. "The will undoubtedly shows Ethan the inheritor. Pity we haven't found the will, but it will be there, and if not, the law will divide it; a three way split, I should think, your father's three sons sharing equally."

"My father had only two sons," Tom barked, "as he well knew."

"What of the young brat? Sure I've seen your sister care for him often enough, but it was your mother who bore him, like it or not."

Tom's heavy boots clomped on the hollow wood floor, pacing back and forth, but he was shouting enough I could hear him anyway. "But not my father who sired him! That brat is more bastard than I, and he'll have no part in my father's inheritance, lest it come from his own father's share."

George Shakleton's reply was too soft to hear, but it must have angered Tom even more. A violent crash rattled the door on its hinges as Tom slammed Mr. Shakleton up against it. I cringed, fearing it would break.

George Shakleton kept talking, his whiny voice placating now. "My hands are tied in this matter. Surely you see that, as long as Ethan holds the titles."

"Ethan! It's time I dealt with him. I will be back!" His voice rumbled with anger. "And you will treat with me when I return!" The door slammed.

For a few minutes, I could hear George Shakleton opening drawers, clattering about, mumbling to himself. "What did old Asher know?" He slammed another drawer shut. "That idiot Tom doesn't have the whole of it, that much is clear." More rattling of papers hastily shoved together covered the next words. Then the tiny metallic click of a key in the lock made me freeze. I held my breath, praying he would not open this door. In the stillness, I heard Shakleton's next words as clearly as if he spoke directly to me instead of muttering them to himself. "Would Ethan have been idiotic enough to tell Bess as he lay on her pillow?" Shakleton's fist slammed against the door. "Damn that boy," he swore. "If I'm going to save his share, I've got to find that will before Tom does." I heard him stomp across the room and the door slam shut behind him.

Suddenly, I put it all together. I remembered the letter to George Shakleton I had seen on the ship to America. "Dear Father," it had started, but George Shakleton had no sons, or none he acknowledged openly. George Shakleton and Samuel Asher had been partners for three decades. Plenty of opportunity for Shakleton to take an interest in his partner's wife, Joan Asher. And Ethan on Bess Asher's pillow? Old Samuel Asher must have learned his eldest son and his youngest weren't his at all. What had he been writing the night of his death? His new will? A will that wrote both Ethan and the baby out of his inheritance and left only Tom as his heir? Mr. Shakleton wanted the will to destroy it, because he wanted his own son to inherit. Tom wanted the will to publish it. He would be the sole heir. Bastard though he was, born before Asher's marriage to Bess, he at least was Asher's true son, his only son.

With that thought, came another. I knew where the will was. Davy had it. I remembered the papers he had slipped into his shirt the night we fled. Everyone knew Davy and I had fled together. It would take no time at all for George or Tom to realize who had the will. If Tom Asher was preoccupied with killing Ethan, George Shakleton was after Davy. I had to warn him.

The room was silent. Shakleton was gone. Cautiously, I reached for the doorknob. It wasn't there. I could feel the planed and varnished wood of the door, but no knob, only a catch plate. Still silent, but growing more frantic by the minute, I felt every edge of the door. There was no latch or knob. I was trapped. The dark, which I had welcomed to hide me, now felt like it was closing in. It was all I could do not to scream.

"Callie?" An urgent whisper broke into my panic, and I leaned close to the crack at the door's edge.

"Mary, is that you?"

"Oh Callie." Relief flooded her voice. "I thought they'd killed ye, sure, what with all the shouting."

"Just open the door." I urged. "There's no knob on this side."

Mary took hold of the knob and pulled, but to no effect. "It's locked." She rattled the door as if to prove her words.

I remembered the crash against the door and the soft click. "Check the floor, Mary. Is there a key lying about?"

There was a pause, then, "Nae. None as I can see."

George Shakleton must have locked it and pocketed the key. But why lock a closet? The stairs must lead to some sort of a cellar. And cellars often had a second entrance, or exit in this case.

"Mary," I said urgently. "I've got to find a way out. Mr. Shakleton is after Davy. Tom Asher is set to murder Ethan, and we've got to stop them."

"His own brother?" Mary said incredulously. I could imagine her on the other side of the door, wringing her hands. "That's barbarous!"

No more barbarous than killing your father. "No. Not his brother and not Samuel Asher's son, either. Listen, Mary. I've got to go."

"What would ye have me do?" Mary's voice was steady now.

"Find help. Peg, if you can." I hesitated before adding, "Or Davy." Would he even try to save Ethan? Or would he flee, out to save his own skin? For that matter, what could Peg do? "Better yet, get a constable," I said grimly.

"But Callie," Mary protested through the door.

I didn't listen. There wasn't time. I had to find the way out, and soon, or it would not be old Sam Asher the family mourned.

CHAPTER 25

I started down the stairs, rough-cut stone, but even and well spaced. I moved at an agonizingly slow pace, keeping one hand on the rough stone and the other stretched out in front of me into the empty space. I felt each step with my toe before setting my weight on it. After about fifteen steps, the floor leveled out into a large, open area. I could feel a hint of breeze on one cheek and instinctively turned toward it. The area was open, but not empty. I stumbled into a stack of large wooden crates. The stack wobbled precariously. The top crate tumbled to the ground and cracked open. Some sort of glass bottles inside clinked against each other, muffled by straw packing. I stepped around the mess, only to find another stack flanking the first. I moved slowly, in spite of my impatience, feeling my way from one stack to anotherr.

In this way, I found a passageway leading out. It sloped down, but the floor was even, without steps. I remembered Davy talking about the wine and woolens he had unloaded and brought ashore. Tunnels, he'd said, leading into the cellars of various warehouses. A smuggler's tunnel. This could be one of those tunnels, and as such, it had to lead somewhere. I shuddered at the thought of feeling my way through a dark tunnel filled with spiders and rats, leading who knew where. But staying here, waiting, knowing what I knew now, was worse. If I stayed here, two lives, Ethan's and Davy's, were in danger.

With painstaking slowness, I felt my way forward. My heart raced with the urgency of finding Davy and Ethan, but at the same time I knew if there were more steps, I would never see them. I tried not to think about stumbling, breaking a leg, and lying helpless in the Stygian darkness.

The rough stone had rubbed my fingers raw by the time the darkness thinned and I thought I saw a faint crack of light ahead. I squinted, trying to decide if it was real, or only imagined. Real, I decided, after closing and opening my eyes several times to measure the difference. It had to be the end of the tunnel. But where was I?

I stumbled forward, and I bumped up against the rough, splintered wood of a solid door, surely the end of the tunnel. I sucked in my breath in relief and groped for a knob.

My fingers brushed heavy, metal hinges, then the thin crack between stone and wood. I found the knob and turned it. The catch didn't move. I rattled it and tried again. My relief evaporated as I realized this door, like the other, was locked. I felt the keyhole just below the knob. Whatever was in this tunnel Mr. Shakleton most desperately wanted to keep it hidden. I thought of those stacks of crates filling the room at the foot of the stairs. Then I shook my head. This was no time to think of hidden treasures. I had to get out! I could turn back. Perhaps Mary had found a key, or an ax to break the door down. But I couldn't face retracing my steps through that inky blackness.

"No!" I cried, kicking out. There was a hollow thunk, but the solid mass didn't even shake. I was trapped in the dark with a pair of murderers on the loose after both Davy and Ethan. I kicked again and again and finally, collapsed in a heap, leaning against the oak keeping me from my goal.

Then I heard sounds beyond the door, muffled by something thicker than the wood. Faintly, I heard men talking and glasses clinking. I didn't stop to think who those men might be. I screamed and renewed my pounding. Better by far to be caught, even by Mr. Shakleton, than to perish alone in this darkness.

The second time I paused there was a difference in the noise I heard. The casual, random sounds were gone, replaced by muffled scraping, shuffling, and short, urgent shouts. I yelled and pounded anew. The light in the cracks brightened, and the noises grew clearer.

Suddenly the door swung open and I, with my arm upraised to pound again, fell forward into the astonished arms of the man standing in front of me.

"Ma'amselle Beaton," he said, arms tightening to keep me upright. "Sacré bleu! What are you doing in there?"

André. For a moment, I sagged against him, relief outweighing all else. But only for a moment.

I straightened and pulled back. André was not alone. A half dozen men, mostly the crew of *Le Rossignol*, crowded the small storeroom into which I had stumbled, with crates and barrels scattered about, as if shoved aside in a hurry. Was that the scraping I had heard? I didn't take time to wonder. "We must hurry, André," I said. "Davy is in terrible danger."

André did not release his hold on my arms. "Easy, ma chérie," he said. "First things first. Where have you come from?" He peered around me at the doorway. It was flush with the stone wall of a rough cave, which appeared to have been turned into a storeroom, the boxes hiding the door. Certainly André seemed as surprised to see it as he was to see me. The other men were calling for torches, and one fellow with a lantern had already squeezed past me into the opening.

"Where have you come from?" André repeated.

"Mr. Shakleton's cellar," I answered, "but André . . ."

"Très bien," he said. Pulling me toward him, he planted a kiss on my cheek. "You have found it, ma chérie," he exclaimed. "To think it was here all the time, when we have been searching in the empty caves, north of the city." He kissed my other cheek exuberantly.

"The wine," I said, thinking of the crates I had passed. Davy's missing shipment.

"Oui." André smiled. "And the tunnel that salaud Shakleton has been using to steal our goods."

He looked so injured at that, I declined to point out the goods in question were smuggled in the first place. Instead I tried again to pull free of his grip. "André, forget the tunnel. We have to help Davy."

"Oh, non, ma chérie." He steered me now toward the door out of the storeroom. "Mon frère will not want us to forget the tunnel he has been looking for these three months and more." André towed me into the outer room, a groggery of the sort by the docks, set up in the caves along the shore of the Delaware River, empty now as all the men and the innkeeper had rushed into the storeroom to free me. The room was dark, lit by a pair of torches stuck in wall sconces. André pulled a chair out for me at the nearest table and pushed me into it. "Sit here un moment." Ever the gentleman, he grabbed a bottle of wine off the shelf behind the bar, knocked its top off, and splashed a good cupful into a mug. He set it before me, then turned to the storeroom.

"Wait!" I clutched at his shirt. "André, where's Davy? He's in terrible danger."

André took my hand in his, kissed it gently and curled it around the wine glass. "Do not worry about mon frère," he said, waving his hand. "The good capitaine has gone to fix his troubles."

"Gone? Where?"

André shrugged expressively. "On his own affairs. Do not worry," he repeated. "He can take care of himself."

"André," I insisted, jumping up, but I was pleading with his retreating back, as he rejoined the men in the storeroom and made ready to explore the tunnel.

"Drink your wine, girl." The voice was soft and melodious, with the rich r's and lush vowels of the Caribbean.

I whirled about. The groggery was not empty after all. Elise sat at a table in the shadows by the wall. "What are *you* doing here?"

Her eyes shone in the torchlight. "Having a drink before work," she said. "The wine is not so good, but strong." She raised her glass to me and drained it.

I took a step toward her. "Davy is in terrible trouble. We've got to help him."

Elise shook her head and laughed, her black curls bobbing about her face. "Fire in the barn, but horse stay put," she said enigmatically. "Who gots blinders now? Davy McRae is always in some sort of trouble. He's safe enough, I tell you."

"What do you mean? Do you know where he is?" I stepped closer to her, close enough to see the shine on the string of white pearls gracing her dark neck.

"Indeed I do." Again the chuckle. "He's in my bed, waiting for me."

I stopped short. Davy claimed Elise was André's fiancée. But she had her own cabin on his ship. Shared everything; was that it?

I took a swallow of wine. It was, as Elise said, quite strong and vinegary, and it burned going down. I set the glass on the table. So. Davy had no need of me. By now, Tom Asher could have murdered his brother. Without a glance back, I stepped out of the groggery. Elise was calling something after me, but I didn't want to listen.

Outside, I found myself facing the Delaware River. The fresh breeze was blowing inland. Docks and piers stretched out along the bank, and suddenly I knew where I was. Just there, I had rested with Leah before finding Davy. And that way lay Davy's ship at anchor. I started toward it, then stopped. If Davy was in Elise's bed, there was little point looking for him on board. In fact, there was little point in looking for him at all. I turned away from the river. From here, I knew my way to the Asher house. Perhaps I could at least warn Ethan. I hurried up the hill.

At the Asher house, I found Chloe wailing hysterically on the steps. I grabbed her by the shoulders and shook her. "Where's Tom? Ethan?" I demanded. "What's happened?"

Chloe was incoherent. She clung to me like she was drowning. "My baby," she cried, "My baby."

I slapped her, but she only cried the louder. Leaving her to her tears, I reached for the door. It was locked. From inside the kitchen I heard the sounds of fighting, a crash, and the clatter of pans. I snatched up the first rock that came to hand and heaved it through the window. The glass shattered, spilling tiny shards all over. Wrapping my apron around my hands, I scrambled through the small opening. Sharp splinters tore my chemise and scratched my arms.

The kitchen was a scene of chaos. Flour and onions were strewn across the floor among overturned pans and smashed crockery. Tom Asher lay motionless near the hearth, blood oozing from a gash on his head. Ethan Asher and his stepmother circled the table. Mistress Asher brandished a huge kitchen knife in an eerie replay of the scene a few months earlier with Samuel Asher. Except Ethan was not drunk. He wore the beguiling smile that won a lady's heart before she had time to think. So intent on each other were they that neither noticed me.

"Think, Bess," Ethan was saying in his soft, soothing voice. "You don't want to kill me. Old Asher is dead. We've nothing to stop us now. We could give our child his rightful name." He reached for the knife slowly, calmly.

Mistress Asher, her eyes wild, slashed at him and backed away. "You've killed my first boy," she said. "And brought me to murder. I'll not listen to you anymore,'"

"What? Tom?" Ethan circled slowly around the table, as Mistress Asher kept backing away. "He's not dead. He'll come to his senses in a bit and no harm done." He took a step toward her. "Be reasonable, Bess. Tom will be. He knows he's the bastard son of a dead man, conceived, if not born, before marriage. He has no claim to anything, but I'll see he doesn't starve."

Mistress Asher waved the knife, a huge thing, kept sharp for cleaving chickens. "He's no more bastard than you. At least his father acknowledged him!" she screamed shrilly. "What of George Shakleton? A father hiding all these years, cuckolding his own business partner."

Ethan's smile grew wider. "And that old fool never knew it. When did you tell him, Bess? Did you give him time to rewrite his will? Was it before you slipped the knife between his ribs?"

"You!" I gasped in surprise. "You killed your husband? It wasn't Tom or Ethan!"

Mistress Asher whirled, so startled by my sudden outburst that she lowered her guard. Ethan took advantage of her brief lapse and dove across the table, knocking her to the ground. In one deft motion, he grabbed the knife and turned it on her, driving it deep into her belly and twisting. Her scream ended in a gurgle.

CHAPTER 26

Before I could move Ethan was on his feet, advancing toward me, the bloody knife still in his hand. "Ah, 'Sally.'" His voice undulated with the smooth tone of a parlor conversation, not that of a man who has just killed. "For once, your timing is impeccable. In fact, your meddling is quite serendipitous."

"You can't kill me," I said, frantically searching for some reason why not.

"Oh?" He raised an eyebrow. "The wicked servant killed her master and returned to finish off the rest of the family. I don't think there will be much of an inquiry." He moved closer.

I backed away. What could I use for a weapon? There was a sack of onions on the table and a pan of bread. "Chloe's right outside." I challenged. "She'll tell the truth." I saw a poker by the hearth. Three more steps and I could reach it.

Ethan laughed, normally a pleasant sound, but ominous now. "Poor frightened Chloe? The dumpling? I think not," he said. "Chloe values our baby too much. She won't say a word."

"Your baby?" I stopped, startled. "You are the father of Chloe's baby?" I didn't need an answer. It was so obviously true. Ethan, with his smooth smile and easy grace, had been cuckolding the man he had called father and raping the girl he called sister. How could such vileness live behind such a charming face?

I took another step toward the hearth, but I was watching Ethan's face, not my feet. My foot came down on something soft. I had forgotten about Tom, lying senseless on the floor. I stumbled, fell to my knees, and crawled over Tom toward the poker.

Ethan lunged just as I snatched it. Before I could swing, the flat of the knife slammed down on my knuckles. I yelped in pain and dropped the poker. Ethan grabbed my wrist, pulled me to my feet, and twisted my arm up behind my back.

"There is one small matter left to settle," he said, "before I'm done with you." He was breathing a little harder than usual, but nothing else marked his efforts. "The will. My 'father' seemed bent on writing me out of it. I think it best for all concerned that no one knows exactly who is or isn't Samuel Asher's son. If that will comes to light, a good many people will be unpleasantly surprised. Where is it?"

"I don't know anything about it," I lied.

Ethan pushed up on my arm and pain shot up my shoulder. "I think you do. I think you found it the night his dear wife killed old Samuel and panicked before she could think to destroy it. Poor Bess, always stupid."

Ethan hustled me out of the kitchen, upstairs to the study. He yanked the cord from the draperies, then shoved me into the chair, the same one Samuel had died in. He twisted my arms behind me to tie my hands, lashing them to the chair. The cord bit painfully into my wrists and the back of the chair dug into my shoulder blades. Ethan licked his lips, then causally inserted the knife in the top of my bodice and slashed downward. I gasped as my bodice fell open, baring my breasts. Ethan lay the knife tip against one nipple. "What a pity to mar such beauty." he said softly. "Where is the will?"

A sudden commotion downstairs made him jump. The knife slipped, ever so slightly, and the razor sharp blade pressed against the skin. A thin red line of blood appeared against the pale skin of my breast.

Ethan swore. "It seems we will not have time to continue this discussion," he said. "But no matter. With both you and the will gone, there will be no trouble."

He picked up an oil lamp. It was nearly empty, but he splashed what there was on my skirts. "Tragic for you, 'Sally,' isn't it? But there's justice. We'll add arson to your crimes of murder. Makes one think twice about servants, doesn't it?" Ethan grabbed my chin, tilted my face up, and kissed me, brutally crushing my lips to his. The violence in his kiss belied his soft, persuasive voice. I trembled with the certain knowledge of just how much he could hurt me.

"Ah," he said, his hand still squeezing my chin. "I've wanted to do that since I saw you on the boat. Too bad we've no time for more." He turned to the desk and struck a spark onto a bit of char cloth.

The tumult from downstairs grew, and footsteps pounded on the stairs. The door to the study flew open and Davy stood there with a brace of pistols—one stuck in his belt and the other aimed at Ethan.

Ethan dropped the smoldering char cloth on the desk and whirled, grabbing me to hold the knife at my throat, the tip pricking the skin. "Mr. McRae, you are as much of a nuisance as the lady."

"Move away from her." Davy's right arm dangled in an odd manner by his side.

"I think not." Ethan spoke calmly. "I gather you care more about her life than I do."

"She's naught but a pawn in your game, man. Let her go. It's me ye have business with."

Ethan didn't answer. They stared at each other, unblinking. The papers under the char cloth crackled into flames, but neither man seemed to notice. A bit of glowing ash caught in a swirl of air and drifted onto the carpet. The carpet began smoldering red and black. If the embers reached my skirt, the oil would flare and burn. Beads of sweat slid between my breasts. As a small child I had been burned by the hearth fire when a spark caught on my petticoat and set it alight. Only Mam's quick thinking had saved me. She had dashed me to the ground and rolled me over, smothering the flames. Afterwards, Mam had dried my tears with her apron, while she hugged me to her, scolding all the while. Now, as I felt the heat move closer, I remembered the speed of those flames. A tongue of fire spurted up, reaching for my skirt.

It wasn't a decision; it was sheer panic. Better have my throat cut than be burned alive. I jerked my whole body sideways, away from Ethan and the knife and the fire. Ethan dropped the knife. The chair and I crashed to the floor, and the room seemed to explode. My head hit the floor as a pistol shot rang out. The chair broke, loosening the rope binding me to it. I twisted my wrists free and rolled away from the fire.

Davy's shot must have missed. The two men grappled with each other. The fire on the carpet flared brighter.

Ethan broke away from Davy and snatched up the knife. He made a wild stab at Davy's midriff. Davy leapt back, less nimbly than I had ever seen him, knocking over a second chair and scattering the burning papers from the desk. Flames caught the edge of the curtains. Ethan advanced on Davy, slashing wildly. The knife sliced across his leg, through pants and skin. Davy sucked in his breath.

Why didn't he fight as I had seen him before? His right arm seemed to hang useless. A dark-colored stain spread across his right shoulder. He had been wounded before this fight with Ethan. Ethan, larger, fresher, and bearing the only weapon, kept forcing Davy back. The curtains curled in flames. Smoke filled the room, making it harder to see. I crawled toward the door until my knee came down on something hard.

The second pistol. Davy must have dropped it. I snatched it up. Davy had grabbed up a piece of the broken chair and used it to parry Ethan's nasty jab with the knife. With his reach longer than Ethan's, Davy swung the chair leg like a club and beat at the outstretched knife.

Ethan stepped back and stumbled into me. Before I could think what to do, he grabbed my hair and hauled me up in a headlock, the knife once more at my throat. "Put it down," he said, his voice rasping from the smoke.

I couldn't break his iron grip, but my hands were free. And I held the forgotten pistol. Ethan's arm tightened on my neck, but his attention was all on Davy, who let the chair leg fall to the floor. I slowly tilted the pistol up, so it aimed straight at Ethan's belly, wrapped my finger around the trigger, and pulled.

The explosion knocked me back, out of Ethan's grasp. Pain shot through my wrist and I dropped the pistol. God, I've shot myself, I thought, as my head hit the door and I fell.

But the bullet hadn't hit me. Ethan had also fallen. He sat on the floor, his smile a trifle confused. He clutched his belly. Bright red blood poured out around his fingers. Slowly the color drained from his face and he slumped over.

I blinked, frozen. I've killed him, I thought. Not a deserter deep in the woods, but a man I knew. I began to shake.

Davy scrambled across the room and helped me to stand. "Not now, lass. Can ye walk?"

My tongue was too thick to move, so I nodded. Smoldering flames spit from hot spots on the carpet and reached toward the desk. Davy hauled me toward the stairs.

"The babies," I cried. I could hear the wailing of the two boys from their room.

Davy let go of me. "That way," he said, pushing me toward the stairs. He turned and ran toward the crying at the other end of the hall.

Smoke filled the hallway. I coughed, leaning against the wall for balance and trying desperately to breathe. Davy wanted me to flee, but he was wounded. He couldn't carry both babies with one arm. Still coughing, I plunged after him. Smoke blinded me. I stumbled toward the babies wailing in their cribs.

"Here," Davy said, his voice hoarse from the smoke. He shoved one of the boys at me. "Tie him on your back with the blanket and crawl," he wheezed. "There's more air near the floor." It took a few precious seconds to tie each boy in a sling, before we crawled toward the stairs. The roar of the fire grew monstrous as we scrambled down and burst out the front door.

Chloe still stood weeping ineffectively on the front steps. She took the crying babies from us, her sobs changing only in pitch as she realized they were safe. I fell to my hands and knees, gulping great lungfuls of air. It seemed I could never clear them of the smoke. With each rasping gulp came a spasm of pain.

Davy reached for me. "It's over."

I shook my head. "Tom," I choked. "I don't think he's dead."

"Where?" Davy asked, his own voice hoarse and scratchy.

"The kitchen." I led the way around to the back of the house.

We found the kitchen still mostly free of smoke. The fire roared above with a distant rumble, like a storm approaching. Lydia lay moaning over Mistress Asher. Tom still lay senseless on the floor.

Davy took hold of his wrist and dragged him toward the door.

"Come along," I told Lydia. "She's dead."

"She's the only mother I ever knew," Lydia said, her voice oddly detached, as if she floated far away.

"She's dead," I repeated. "The house is burning down. Come on now."

Lydia sat back and brushed her fingers across her mama's cheek. "My father's dead and my mother. I've no family left. Why shouldn't I die with them?"

"You've still got a brother and a sister," I said, "and they both need you now."

Lydia closed the wide staring blue eyes of the woman she had mocked and ignored and for all that, loved. "There is that, I suppose," she said and came away with me.

When I emerged from the house a second time, Mary fell on me, hugging me as if I were mortally wounded. She had not found a constable, but had roused the neighbors. A dozen men grabbed up the buckets and ladders each household kept for just such an emergency and formed a bucket brigade. Flames shot out the windows now. Davy left Tom lying on the walk with Lydia to care for him and hurried to join the workers.

"Callie, are ye hurt bad?" Mary dabbed my cheeks with her kerchief, looking for the wounds.

"I'm all right," I said. But I was a mess. My bodice was torn open. Soot mixed with blood covered my face, hands, and arms. Some of the blood was my own from the glass cuts and the knife, but more came from Mistress Asher and Ethan.

Then the realization of what I had done hit me with a force that took my breath away. I sank to the ground, trembling so hard I couldn't stop.

Mary took my bloody hands in hers and patted them. "Put your head down," she told me, "until the faintness passes." She wrapped her shawl around me.

They worked at the fire for a good hour, two lines of men sloshing bucket after bucket of water up one side and sending the empties back down the other. Then they gave up trying to save the house and concentrated the water on the buildings to either side. They took their long hooked poles to pull the structure down to save the neighboring houses. The house collapsed with a muffled boom, a cloud of ash and smoke exploding as the timber frame crashed in on itself. The bucket brigade continued for hours, pouring water on nearby houses, but eventually it was clear the fire was dying. Finally, blackened with smoke and grime, clapping each other on the back, they drifted off in pairs and bunches to find a tavern and wash the soot from their throats. What had been a home lay now in a sodden, dirty heap with tendrils of smoke curling here and there up to the sky.

Davy turned away from one of the last groups watching the mess in case of any lingering flare-ups and came over to me. We looked at each other without speaking. Then Davy put his good arm around me and held me tight.

I lay my cheek against the damp linen of his shirt, gray with smoke and smudged with blood. I felt the knot in my gut unwinding. I had so much I wanted to say, so much I couldn't untangle, but I could find words for only one question. "Aren't you supposed to be in Elise's bed?"

Davy tilted my chin up to look in my eyes, which were filling up with tears. "What are ye saying?"

"Elise said . . . she told me . . . well, I saw Elise at the groggery before coming here."

"And she told ye I was waiting for her?"

I nodded, my throat too choked up to speak.

Davy threw back his head and laughed. "Aye." He pulled me close. "I was in her bed."

I struggled to free myself, but he held me tight.

"Callie, I was in her bed for sure, but it's not what ye are thinking."

"Isn't there only one reason to wait in a whore's bed?"

"She put me there after bandaging my shoulder, George Shakleton having taken it into mind to try again to rid the world of me. Lucky thing, he's not so very good at his aim."

"Mr. Shakleton shot you and Elise bandaged you?"

"Aye."

"And you weren't waiting in her bed for . . . for anything else?"

Davy was shaking from laughter. "I don't know whether to scold ye for your silliness, or thank ye for the compliment."

"Why her bed?" I asked, still unwilling to believe what I heard.

"Ye would be happier if I was in the bed of a whore ye dinna' know than the one ye do? That doesn't make any sense, Callie."

I stiffened. Maybe it didn't, but I didn't care.

"Callie," he whispered, "Ye ken the groggery is a whorehouse, aye? The other beds, weel—they were in use." He tucked a stray wisp of hair back behind my ear and traced his finger along the side of my cheek. "Open your eyes, Callie, and look at me. Do ye not see that getting shot is no a verra good way to make a man amorous? But ye are the one, the only one, I want."

I opened my eyes and the truth of what he said was plain in the look he gave me. There was no laughter there now, only love.

"Oh, Davy." I closed my eyes again. The last lingering doubt melted away as his lips met mine.

CHAPTER 27

We stood arm in arm on the cobbled street until there was no doubt the fire had been completely extinguished. The constables had a few questions concerning who had come away safe and who had died, but they saved most of those for Tom. House fires were a fact of city life. One house and a couple of lives was a tragic loss to be sure, but nothing like what might have happened. As for the Asher family, their loss was much more personal. I looked at Lydia and Chloe, rocking back and forth together, the babies crushed between them, and I felt a twinge of sorrow. What would they do now?

By the time we left, twilight had given way to night. The moon shone on the river as Davy led the way to his ship. Mary came with us. Even with Shakleton on the run, she was afraid to go back to his house. Davy promised to smuggle her out to Godwin's Landing to see Leah. "It's too close to the city for ye to stay there," he warned as he helped her up the gangplank. "Shakleton will learn of this business and come after his property. Too many people have seen ye with me by now, and he'll find Godwin's Landing in time. Still, we'll find a way to keep ye and the bairn together. Maybe in Baltimore." He winked at me, and I smiled. He might never get to Baltimore, but he meant the promise nonetheless.

Mary's eyes shone with tears. She took Davy's hand and pressed it against her cheek. "Ye are a good man, Davy McRae, and don't let anyone tell ye different."

We settled ourselves in the salon. Hamish brought an ewer of clean water and knob of soap so we could wash away the grime. With Mary's help, I redressed Davy's wound as Elise's dressing had come loose in the struggle. It wasn't as bad as I thought. The musket ball had missed the bone entirely and gone straight through the muscle, leaving a jagged hole behind. But it looked clean and with any luck would heal nicely. Davy gritted his teeth as Mary held his arm and I poured alcohol over the shoulder wound and then wrapped it in clean strips of rag. I had nearly finished when the salon door flew open and André strode in.

"Where have ye been?" Davy said. "I sent a message."

André's face was serious, but one corner of his mouth kept twitching. "To be sure, I got the message, but while you have been out lollygagging, I've been working. Shall I show you?"

Mystified, Davy and the rest of us followed André to the hold of the ship. Two dozen crates lay stacked in rows, lashed to the bulkheads.

"The wine," Davy said, his eyes dancing in delight.

André and the crew had taken the stolen wine from the tunnel behind the groggery and loaded it while everyone else was busy at the fire. "No one to ask questions, eh?" André said.

"But how in the world did ye find where it was?" Davy asked. "We've been searching for weeks."

"For an answer to that, you have to thank Ma'amselle," he said with a wink at me. "She'll tell you there's a lot more where this came from. No telling who most of it belongs to now. You're a rich woman, Callie Beaton, once we have your share figured."

André told us that Shakleton had been cheating and cuckolding Samuel Asher for years. He couldn't pass up stealing from Davy when the opportunity arose and probably from just about everyone else he did business with. Shakleton had fled for now, but no one doubted he would be back. He had too much at stake to give it all up without a fight.

André handed the lantern to me and picked up a crowbar from the stack of tools next to the ladder. He cracked open one barrel and pulled out a dark, slender bottle. "What do you say, mes amis?" he said. "Shall we celebrate?"

We all slept late and were still at breakfast when Tom and Lydia came to talk to Davy. Lydia had washed her face and hands, but her clothes were still grimy with soot. Her eyes were heavy with sorrow; she seemed to have aged years overnight.

I took her hands. "I'm sorry for your loss," I said.

Lydia pulled away from me. "I mourn for Mama," she said, "but not Ethan. Brother or not, he killed my father and mother both."

"I thought Mistress Asher killed her husband."

"Mama's hand held the knife," she told me. She turned away, looking out the porthole, as if she could only look far enough, it would change what had happened. But of course, it couldn't. Lydia took a deep breath. "But 'twas Ethan's voice that guided that knife, with his whispers that Father was writing poor Tom out of the will or that he planned to put her and Jeb in the poorhouse. Ethan petted her and called her pretty, all the while lying to her about how Father was cheating her. Ethan drove her to it, to keep his own skin safe." Lydia faced me. "She didn't hate you, you know. No more than she hated Chloe. Only she knew you were young, and she never had any hold on Ethan. She was afraid she would lose everything." Lydia shook her head. "But she never had much of anything, did she?"

"No, I suppose not," I agreed softly.

Tom was clearly impatient with his sister. He pushed past her and stood squarely in front of Davy, still seated at the round table in the center of the salon. "I want the will," Tom said, without preamble.

Davy raised one eyebrow quizzically.

"No more games, McRae," Tom said. "I know you have it. Give it to me. It's mine now."

Davy rose slowly from the table and came to stand by me. He put one arm around my shoulders and faced Tom. "What do ye mean to do with your 'property'?"

Tom stared at me a full minute, a shadow of his crude leer measuring me and the man beside me. "What property?" he said at last. "Sally MacLaughlin died in the fire. Who you are is no concern of mine. In fact, I would be a great deal happier if I never see you again."

Davy pulled a rolled piece of foolscap from the top drawer in the chest behind him. "The will names ye heir," he said, handing it to Tom, "and guardian of both Jeb and Gideon. Your mam couldn't read, could she? She just listened to your brother, Ethan, and the lies he told her. Had she read it, she would have seen Samuel had learned of his first wife's unfaithfulness, and of Ethan's dalliances with his second wife. Samuel meant to cut Ethan, not ye, out of the will. If it's any comfort to ye, man, she killed him to protect your inheritance."

Tom tucked the will inside his shirt. "Would it comfort you?" he said dryly. He stuck out his hand. "I believe you had some arrangements with my Father. They'll be with me now."

Davy took his hand and shook it. "Aye, that they will."

Tom put his arm out for Lydia and led her away.

"Will ye work with him now?" Mary asked, "Won't ye find a new factor?"

Davy waved a hand. "It may take a bit of unraveling, but Tom Asher is up to the job. He will be a good deal easier to work with than the others."

"Tom Asher? Easier to work with?" I gaped at him. "The man is rude, coarse, and dishonest."

"Aye, he is all that." Davy agreed, unperturbed. "But he doesna want me dead, and I dare say that will make up for his faults."

"Davy McRae, you are a rogue, no doubt about it."

Davy took my hands in his. "Callie," he said seriously, "ye have found this cache, and by rights a share is yours. I said I would see a letter sent to your grandfather. But I'll do ye better. There's more than enough here to buy ye safe passage home."

I hadn't thought of home in a long time. Now I allowed myself to think of Mam and Elspeth, stitching quietly in the parlor, and of Grandfather, rumbly voice arguing with himself, if no one else obliged, and looking for a husband for me. Or maybe now for Elspeth. She would appreciate it more than I did, I knew. She had been quite impatient with my reluctance, complaining she would be an old maid before I so much as looked at a suitor.

Everyone was waiting for me to say something, Elise sat on André's lap, twirling a finger in his hair. Mary looked up, tears glittering on her cheeks.

In an instant, I felt quite cold. Going back to Scotland meant leaving my friends behind.

Davy was watching me, his eyes dark, the golden flecks as hidden as his feelings. My fingers tingled, and I itched to hold him, to pull him tight to me and never let go. No matter he was a rogue, a chancy fellow, with little to call his own and fewer prospects. Davy had not managed to keep me out of trouble, nor even particularly safe. But with every trouble I got myself into, he'd helped pull me through. In the end, didn't that matter more than property or position? The thought of leaving him left me trembling.

Mary patted my hand and smiled bravely at me. "Will ye carry a letter for me, Callie, and read it to me Mam?" Her voice caught, and she stopped, unable to hide the misery in her eyes. She would not let her envy touch our friendship, but it was there. Here she faced only service, her whole family stripped from her, her life a great emptiness.

I turned to Davy with a new idea. "Is there enough in my share to pay for two passages to Edinburgh?" I asked.

"Could be," he allowed. "What do ye have in mind?"

"With Mr. Shakleton on the run, there's naught to hold Mary to his house, is there? Couldn't we send her and Leah together back to Edinburgh?"

"Oh, Callie, what are you saying? Surely ye don't mean to stay behind?" Mary's voice was full of hope and anguish, but I ignored her.

"Davy," I said slowly. "I made a promise to Will Rawles. Here's a way I can keep it. Mary can carry a letter for me explaining to Mam. I'm sure it's a good deal quieter in the house without me to stir it up. They'll have worried of course…" I was blathering like an idiot. I took a deep breath and tried again. "Davy, what I'm trying to say is, did you mean what you said that night in the woods?"

Davy put his hands on my shoulders and turned me to face him, his eyes sparkling. "I've never meant anything more in my life. Callie Beaton, will ye marry me?"

"Yes."

Davy crushed me to him, kissing me hard enough to stop my chattering and take my breath away. It was all the answer I needed.

GLOSSARY

Eighteenth century America was a diverse place, with people from all over speaking many different languages. Here are a few terms to help in understanding some of the accents and dialects.

SCOTS

aboon: above
aye: yes

bairn, bairns: child, children

canna': can not

daft: crazy
dinna': do not, did not
dinna' fash: don't worry
dirk: dagger, knife

havena': have not

ma cushla: my darling or my dear

nae: no
no verra: not very
nuckelavee: a fearsome legendary creature of the sea, part horse, part human

sark: shirt
selkie: legendary creature- seal folk

verra: very

werena': were not
willna': will not
worritin': worrying

ye: you

FRENCH

certainement: certainly
le capitaine: the captain

enchanté: pleased (as in "pleased to meet you")

ma chérie: my dear
mal à la tête: headache
ma'amselle: miss (mademoiselle)
mon frère: my brother

n'est-ce pas: Isn't that so?
non: no

oui: yes

le rossignol: the nightingale

salaud: bastard or swine

très bien: very well, very good

EIGHTEENTH CENTURY SLANG

freight: passengers on a ship who paid for their passage by 'indenture', or exchanging a number of years of service to pay off the debt. Men and women might indenture themselves or their children. Criminals were sometimes punished with indenture. Many people were also snatched from the streets of London, Edinburgh or elsewhere and sold as indentured servants.

kirtle: skirt

roger: 18th century slang for intercourse

take a flourish: 18th century slang for intercourse
trous: trousers, pants